Serapion and Other Stories

Serapion and Other Stories

Francis Stevens

MINT EDITIONS

Serapion and Other Stories contains work published between 1917 and 1920.

This edition published by Mint Editions 2021.

ISBN 9781513279985 | E-ISBN 9781513285009

Published by Mint Editions®

 MINT
EDITIONS

minteditionbooks.com

Publishing Director: Jennifer Newens
Design & Production: Rachel Lopez Metzger
Project Manager: Micaela Clark
Typesetting: Westchester Publishing Services

Contents

Serapion

I	11
II	20
III	29
IV	36
V	44
VI	51
VII	61
VIII	66
IX	75
X	85
XI	92
XII	100
XIII	101
XIV	104
XV	106
XVI	109
Epilogue	112

Elf Trap   115

Unseen—Unfeared

I   141

II   144

III   148

IV   152

V   154

Behind the Curtain   159

Nightmare!

I   171

II   181

III   187

IV   192

V   199

VI   206

VII   210

VIII   218

IX   228

X   232

XI   239

XII   245

XIII   248

XIV   254

THE CURIOUS EXPERIENCE OF THOMAS DUNBAR   259

SERAPION

I

It began because, meeting Nils Berquist in town one August morning, he dragged me off for luncheon at a little restaurant on a side street where he swore I would meet some of the rising geniuses of the century.

What we did meet was the commencement for me of such an extraordinary experience as befalls few men. At the time, however, the whole affair seemed incidental, with a spice of grotesque but harmless absurdity. Jimmy Moore and his Alicia! How could anyone, meeting them as I did, have believed a grimness behind their amusing eccentricity?

I was just turned twenty-four that August day. A boy's guileless enthusiasm for the untried was still strong in me, coupled with a tendency to make friends in all quarters, desirable or otherwise. Almost anyone who liked me, I liked. My college years, very recently ended, had seen me sworn comrade to a reckless and on-his-way-to-be-notorious son of plutocracy, while I was also well received in the room which Nils Berquist sharing with two other embryo socialists of fanatic dye. A certain ingenuous likableness must have been mine even then, I think, to have gained me not only toleration, but real friendship in both camps.

Berquist was older than I by several years. He had earned his college days before enjoying them and, college ended, he dropped back into the struggle for existence and out of my sight—till I ran across him in town that August day.

To play host even at a very moderate luncheon must have been an extravagance for Nils, though I didn't think of that. He was a man with whom one somehow never associated the idea of need. Tall, lean, with a dark, long face, high cheekbones and deep eyes set well apart, he dressed badly and walked the world in a careless air of ownership that mere clothes could not in the least affect.

His intimates knew him capable of vast, sudden enthusiasms, and equally vast depressions of the spirit. But up or down, he was Nils Berquist, sufficient unto himself, asking no favors, and always with an indefinable air of being well able to grant them.

I admired and liked him, was very glad to see him again, and cheerfully let him steer me around two corners and in the door of his bragged-of trysting place.

On first entering, my friend cast an eye about the aggregation of more or less shabby individuals present and muttered: "Not a soul here!" in a disappointed tone. Then, glimpsing a couple seated at a corner table laid for four, he brightened a trifle and led me over to them.

Nil's idea of formal presentation was always more brief than elaborate. After addressing the fair-haired, light-eyelashed, Palm-Beach-suited person on one side of the table as "Jimmy" and his vis-a-vis, a darkly mysterious lady in a purple veil, as "Alicia," he referred to me casually as "Clay," and considered the introduction complete.

I do not mean that the lady's costume was limited to the veil. Only that this article was of such peculiar, brilliantly, fascinatingly ugly hue that the rest of her might have been clothed in anything from a mermaid's scales to a speckled calico wrapper; I can image nothing except a gown of the same color which would have distracted one's attention from that veil.

The thing was draped over a small hat and hung all about her head and face in a sort of circular curtain. Behind it I became aware of two dark bright eyes watching me, like the eyes of some sea creature, laired behind a highly futurist wave. Having met peculiar folk before in Berquist's company, I took a seat opposite the veil without embarrassment.

"Charming little place, this," I lied, glancing about the low-ceilinged semi ventilated, architectural container for chairs, tables and genius which formed a background to the veil. "Sorry I didn't discover it earlier."

The dark eyes gleamed immovably from their lair. I essayed a direct question. "You lunch here frequently, I presume?"

No answer. The veil didn't so much as quiver. Even my genial amity began to suffer a chill.

Suddenly "Jimmy" of the Palm Beach suit transferred his attention from Berquist to me. "Please don't try to talk with Alicia," he said. "She is in the silence today. If you draw her out it will disturb the vibrations for a week and make the deuce of a hole in my work. Do you mind?"

With a slight gasp I adjusted myself to the unusual. I said I didn't mind anything.

"You're the right sort, then. Might have known it, or you wouldn't be traveling with old man Nils, eh? What you going to have? Nothing worth eating except the broiled bluefish, and that's scorched. Always is. What you eating, Nils?"

"Rice," said Berquist briefly.

"On the one-dish-at-a-time diet, eh? Great stuff, if you can stick it out. Make an athlete out of a centenarian—if you can stick it out. Bluefish for one or two?" he added, addressing the waiter and myself in the same sentence.

"Two," I smiled. Palm Beach Jimmy seemed to have usurped my friend's role of host with calm casualism. The man's blond hair and faintly yellow lashes and eyebrows robbed his face of emphasis, so that the remarkably square and sloping forehead did not impress one at first. His way of assuming direction of even the slightest affairs about him struck me as easy-going and careless, rather than domineering.

He gave the rest of the order, with an occasional kindly reference to my desires. "And boiled rice for one," he finished.

The waiter cast a curious glance at the purple veil. "Nothing for the lady?" he queried.

"Seaweed, of course," retorted Jimmy. "You're new at this table, aren't you?"

"Just started working here. Seaweed, sir?"

"Certainly. There it is, staring you in the face under 'Salads.' Study your menu, man. That," explained Jimmy, after the waiter's somewhat dazed departure, "is the only reason we come here. One place I know of that serves rhodymenia serrata. Great stuff. Rich in mineral salts and vitamins."

"You didn't order any for yourself," I ventured.

"No. Great stuff, but has a horrid taste. Simply horrid! Alicia eats it as a martyr to the cause. We have to be careful of her diet. Very careful; Nils, old man, what's the new wrong to the human race you're being so silent over?"

"Can't say without becoming personal," retorted Berquist calmly.

"What? Oh, I forgot you don't approve. Still clinging to the sacred barriers, eh?"

"The barriers exist, and they are sacred." Nils' long, dark face was solemn, but as he was capable of cracking the wildest jokes with just that solemn expression, I wasn't sure if the conversation were light or serious. I only knew that as yet I had failed to get a grip on the situation. The man talked about his seaweed-fed Alicia as if the lady were not present.

What curiosity in human shape did that veil hide? One thing I was uneasily aware of. Not once, since the moment of our arrival had those laired bright eyes strayed from my face.

"The barriers exist," Berquist repeated. "I do not believe that you or others like you can tear them down. If I did, I should be justified in taking your life, as though you were any other dangerous criminal. When those barriers go down, chaos will swallow the world, and the race of men be superseded by the race of madmen!"

Jimmy laughed, unstartled by my friend's reference to cold-blooded assassination. "In the world of science," he retorted, "what one can do, one may do. If every investigator of novel fields had stopped his work for fear of scorched fingers—"

"In the material, physical world," interrupted Berquist, speaking in the same solemn, dogmatic tone, "what one can do, one may do. There, the worst punishment of a step too far can be only the loss of life or limb. It isn't man's rightful workshop. Let him learn its tools at the cost of a cut or so. But the field that you would invade is forbidden."

"By whom? By what?"

"By its nature! A man who risks his life may be a hero, but what is the name for a man who risks his soul?"

"Oh, Nils—Nils! You anachronism! You—you inquisitor! Here! You say the physical world is open ground—don't you?"

"Yes."

"And what is commonly referred to as the 'supernatural' is forbidden?"

"In the sense we speak of—yes."

"Very well. Now, where do you draw the fine dividing line? How do you know that your soul, as you call it, isn't just another finer form of matter? A good medium Alicia here can do it—stretches out a tenuous arm, a misty, wraithy, seimiformless limb, and lifts a ten-pound weight off the table while the 'physical' hands and feet are bound so they can't stir an inch. Telekinesis, that is called, or levitation, and you talk about it as if it were done by some sort of supernatural will power.

"Will power, yes; but will actuating matter to move matter. That fluidic arm is just as 'material.' though not so substantial, as your own husky biceps. It's thinner—different. But material—of course it's material! Why, you yourself are a walking case of miraculous levitation. Will moving matter. Will, a super physical force generated on the physical plane. Where's your fine dividing line? You talk about the material plane—"

"I won't any more," broke in Berquist hastily. "But you know that there are entities and forces dangerous to the human race outside of what we call the natural world, and that your investigations are no better than a sawing at the bars of a cage full of tigers. If I thought you could loose them, I have already told what I would do!"

There was a dark gleam in Berquist's deep-set eyes that suddenly warned me he meant exactly what he said—though the meaning of the whole argument was as hazy to me as the face behind that astounding veil.

Jimmy himself looked sober. "Here comes your rice," he said shortly. "Eat it, you old vegetarian, and get off the murder subject. I'll expect you to be coming around some night with a carving knife, if you say much more."

"There are police to guard you from the carving knife. The wild marches between this world and the invisible are patrolled by no police. Yet you fear the knife; which can harm only your body, and fearlessly expose your naked soul!"

"Thanks, old man, but my soul is well able to take care of itself. Eat your rice. There! Didn't I say the bluefish would be scorched? And it is. Behold, a prophet among you!"

The bluefish wasn't worrying me. What I was awaiting was the moment when that miraculously colored veil should be uplifted. Surely, her purple screen removed, the lady would cease to stare me out of countenance.

Before the veil a large platter of straggling, saw-edged, brownish-red leaves had been set down. The dish looked as horrid as Jimmy said it tasted. In a quiver of impatience I waited. At last I should see—a hand, white and well shaped, but slender to emaciation, was raised to the veil's lower edge. The edge was lifted. Another hand conveyed a modest forkful of the uncanny edible upward. It passed behind the veil. The fork came away empty.

With a gasping sigh I relinquished hope, and turned my attention to scorched bluefish.

Jimmy may have noted my emotion. "When Alicia is in the silence," he offered, "she has to be guarded. The vibratory rhythm of the violet light waves is less harmful than the rest of the spectrum. Hence, the veil. Invention of my own. You agree with our wild anarchist here, Mr.—er—Clay? Sacred barrierist and all that?"

"My name's Barbour," I said. "Clayton S. Barbour. As for the barriers, I must admit you've been talking over my head."

"So? Don't believe it. Pardon me, but your head doesn't look that sort. Hasn't Nils told you what I'm doing?"

"Nils," said Berquist, with what would have been cold insolence from anyone else, "has something better to do than walk about the world exploiting you to his acquaintances.

"I'm smashed—crushed flat," laughed Jimmy. He seemed one of the most good-humored individuals I had ever met. "Never mind, anarchist. I'll tend to it myself." He turned again to me. "Come to think of it, one of Nils' introductions is an efficient disguise. I'm James Barton Moore."

I murmured polite gratification. For the life of me I couldn't recall hearing the name before. His perception was as quick as his good humor. That ready laugh broke out again.

"Never heard of me, eh? That's a fault of mine—expect the whole world to be thrillingly expectant of results from my work. Ever hear of the Psychic Research Association?"

"Certainly." I looked as intelligent as possible. "Investigate ghosts and haunted houses and all that, don't they?"

"You're right, son. Ghosts and haunted houses about cover the Association's metier. Bah! Do you know who I am?"

"A member?" I hazarded.

"Not exactly. I'm the man the Association forced off its directing board. And I'm also the man who is going to make the Association look like; a crowd of children hunting spooks in the nursery. Come around to my place tonight and I'll show you something!"

The invitation was so explosively abrupt that I started in my chair.

"Why—er—" I began.

Nils broke in again. "Don't go," he said, coolly.

"Let him alone!" enjoined Moore, but with no sign of irritation. "You drop in around seven—here," he scribbled an address on the back of a card and tossed it across the table, "and I'll promise you an interesting evening."

"You are very good," I said, not knowing quite what to do. I already had an engagement for that evening; on the other hand, my ever-ready curiosity had been aroused.

"Don't go," repeated Berquist tonelessly.

"Thanks, but I believe I will."

"Good! You're the right sort. Knew it the minute I set eyes on you. Don't extend these invitations to everyone. Not by any means."

Berquist pushed back his chair.

"Are you going on with me, Clay?" he inquired.

I thought he was carrying his peculiar style of rudeness rather beyond the boundaries; but he was really my host, so I acquiesced. I took pains, however, to bid a particularly courteous farewell to the eccentric pair with whom we had lunched. I might or might not keep my appointment with Moore, but if I did I wished to be sure of a welcome.

With me the influence of a personality, however strong, ended where its line of direction crossed the course of my own wishes. Nils' opposition to my further acquaintance with the Moores had struck me as decidedly officious.

Once outside the restaurant, he turned on me almost savagely.

"Clay," he said, "you are not going up there tonight!"

"No?" I asked coldly. "And why not?"

"You don't know what you might be let in for. That is why not."

"You have an odd way of talking about your friends."

"Oh, Moore knows what I think."

"All right," I grinned, not really wishing a quarrel if one could be avoided. "But your friends are good enough for me, too, Nils. Who was the lady in the veil?"

"His wife. A physical medium. Heaven help her!"

"Spirit rapping, clairvoyant and all that, eh? I supposed it was something of the sort. Well, if I wish to go out to their place and spend a dollar or so to watch some conjuring tricks, why do you object so strenuously? That's one thing I've never done—"

"Spend a dollar or so!" snapped Berquist. "Those people are not professionals, Clay. Mrs. Moore is one of the few genuine mediums in this country."

"Oh, come! Surely you're not a believer in table-tipping and messages from Marcus Aurelius and Shakespeare?"

Berquist squinted at me disgustedly.

"Heaven help me save this infant!" he muttered, taking no pains, however, that I shouldn't hear him. "Clay, you go home and stay among your own people. Jimmy Moore is a moderately good fellow, but in one certain line he's as voracious as a wolf and unscrupulous as a Corsican bandit. He told you that he didn't extend these invitations to everyone. That is strictly true. The fact that he extended one to you is proof sufficient that you should not accept. He saw in you something he's continually on the watch for. He would use you and wreck you without a scruple."

"How? What do you mean?"

"If I should tell you in what way, you would laugh and call it impossible. But, let me say something you can understand. Except casually, Moore is not a pleasant man to know. He would like people to believe that he was dropped from the administrative board of the Association because his investigations and inferences were too daring for even the extraordinary open types of mind which compose it. The, real reason was that he proved so violently, overbearingly quarrelsome that even they couldn't tolerate him."

Recalling Moore's impregnable good humor under Nils' own attacks, I began to wonder exactly what was the latter's object.

"I'm not going there to quarrel with him," I said.

"No; you're going to be used by him. Look at that unfortunate little wife of his, if you want a horrible example."

"You mean he'd obscure my classic features with a purple veil? There'll be a fight to the finish first, believe me!"

"Oh, that veil-vibration-seaweed business—that's all rot. Just freak results of freak theorizing. Froth and bubbles. It's the dark brew underneath that's dangerous."

"Witch's scene in Macbeth," I chuckled. "Fire burn and caldron bubble! We now see Mr. Jimmy Moore in his famous personation of Beelzebub—costume, one Palm Beach suit and a cheerful grin. Don't worry, Nils! I'll bolt through the window at the first whiff of brimstone."

"My child," said Berquist, very gently and slowly, "you have the joyous courage of ignorance. Alicia Moore is that rare freak, a real materializing medium—a producer of supernormal physical phenomena, as they are called. In other words, she is an open channel for forces which are neither understood nor recognized by the average civilized man. And Timmy Moore is that much more common freak, a fool who doesn't care whose fingers get burnt. The responsibility for having introduced you to those people is mine. As a personal favor, I now ask you to have nothing more to do with either of them."

"Nils, you're back in the dark ages, as Moore claimed. I never thought you'd fall for this spiritualistic bunk."

"Leave that. You are determined to keep the appointment?"

"Come with me, if you think I need a chaperon."

"No," he said soberly.

"Why not?"

"He wouldn't have me. Not when a seance is planned, and that is what he meant by an 'interesting evening.' I'm persona non grate on such an occasion, because Alicia says her spirit guides don't like me—save the mark! If I tried to wedge in tonight there would be another row, and Heaven alone knows where the thing would end. I wish you'd stay away from there!"

"Do you mean," I asked slowly, and beginning to see new light on Nils' attitude, "that you have quarreled with Moore in the past?"

"My dear fellow, get this through your head if you can. It is impossible to know Moore very long and not quarrel with him—or be subjugated. You keep away."

I was growing a little sick of Nils' persistence.

"Softy. Fear I haven't your faith in the bodiless powers of evil, and I can't say Moore seemed such an appalling person. I'm going!"

Abruptly, without a word of answer or farewell, Berquist turned his back on me and swung off down street. Several times I had seen him end a conversation in that manner, and I knew why. By rights, he should have been the last man to criticize another man's temper.

But I knew, too, that Nils' wrath was likely as evanescent as sudden. He would be as friendly as ever next time we met, and even if he were not, I couldn't see why his anger or disapproval should afflict me greatly. Friends were too easily acquired for me to miss one.

I forgot him promptly and began wondering how my dissertation for the evening would be accepted by Roberta Whitingfield.

II

That afternoon I reached home to find Roberta herself on the veranda with my sister Catherine. Rather to my consternation, on hearing of the restaurant encounter, Bert promptly dubbed it, "The Adventure of the Awful Veiled One," and announced her intent to solve the mystery in my company. Catherine seconded the motion, calmly including herself in the party, but there I rebelled.

Roberta and I were to be married one of these days. She was mine to command me.

I had a vague idea of what Moore's invitation portended, and I knew what would happen if I took both those girls and anything unusual occurred. They would giggle.

We kept Roberta with us for dinner, and when she had gone home to dress, Cathy and I had our argument in earnest. My mother was confined to her room with one of her frequent headaches, and for a while dad hid himself in his paper. Then a grizzled head appeared over the top of it.

"Cathy," he drawled, "I haven't a notion what this is all about, but wherever Clay is off to, I'm sure he doesn't want two girls. Clay, I don't wish to be rude, but if you are going, won't you please depart at once? Run upstairs, Catherine, and see if all this loud talking has disturbed your mother."

Cathy went. She knew better than to oppose dad when he used that tone.

That evening I called for Roberta in my car, and after nine o'clock we arrived at the address written across Moore's card. It turned out to be half of a detached double dwelling, standing on a corner beyond a block of quiet, respectable red-stone fronts, with a deep lawn between it and the street.

"Ridiculous house," Bert named it on first sight, and ridiculous house it was in a certain sense. It reminded one of that king in the old fairy tale who "laughed with one side of his face and smiled with the other."

The half that bore Moore's number was neat, shining and of unimpeachable exterior. Its yellow brick front was clean, with freshly painted white woodwork; it's half of the lawn, close-clipped and green, was set with little thriving round flower beds.

The other half had the look of a regular old beggar among houses. The paint, weather-beaten, blistered and brown, was no dingier than the dirt-freckled bricks. Two or three windows were boarded up. Not one of the rest but mourned a broken pane or so. From the dilapidated porch wooden steps all askew led to a weed-grown walk. On that side the lawn was a straggling waste of weeds.

Roberta had hopped out of the car without waiting for assistance. I joined her and we stood staring at the queer-looking combination.

"Roberta," I said solemnly after a moment, "there is a grim, grisly secret which I hadn't meant to alarm you with, but perhaps it is better you should be warned now."

"Clay! What do you mean?"

"That house!" My voice was a sinister whisper. "Don't you see? 'Life and death,' or 'Chained to the corpse of his victim!' Moore murdered one of the twin houses, and now he must live in the other house as a penance."

To my surprise, instead of laughing at my nonsense, she took my arm with a shiver. "Don't!" she protested. "When you speak so the house isn't funny any more. It's horrid. A-a dead-alive house! Let's not go in, Clay."

I felt annoyed, for this last-moment retreat was not like her. I said, "Come along, Berty, and don't be silly. I suppose one half belongs to Moore and the other to somebody else, and he can't make the other owner keep his half in repair."

After some further discussion, we entered the gate at last. I remembered that as we went up Moore's walk, I threw back my head and glanced upward. The moonlight was so white on the slanting house roofs that for just a moment I had an illusion of their being thick with snow.

With snow. Yes, I remembered that illusion afterward.

Moore had expected me alone, of course, but he needn't have made that fact quite so obvious. He met us in his library on the second floor, whither a neat, commonplace maid had ushered us after a glance at my card.

It was a long, rather heavily furnished room, lined with books to the ceiling. Our first view of it noted nothing bizarre or out of the ordinary. Moore was seated reading, but as we were announced he rose quickly. It was when he perceived Roberta and realized that I had brought a companion that I had my first real doubt that Nils had not exaggerated about the man's temper.

His good-humored, full-lipped mouth seemed to draw inward and straighten to a disagreeably gash-like-effect. The skin over his cheekbones tightened. A pronounced narrowness between the eyes forced itself suddenly upon the attention. For one instant we faced a man disagreeably different from the one who had parried all Berquist's thrusts with unshakable good nature.

As he rose and came toward us, however, the ominous look melted again to geniality. "Began to think old Nils had seared you off in earnest, Barbour," he greeted. "Witch burnings; would still be in order if our wild anarchist had his way, eh?"

Rather reluctantly I performed the necessary introductions.

"I had no right to come with Clayton," Roberta apologized. "But when he told me of your invitation, I—we thought—"

"That you might find some amusement here?" Moore finished for her. "That's all right, Miss Whitingfield, though the work I am engaged in is a bit serious to be amusing, I fear. Hope you're not the nervous, screaming sort?" he added, with blunt anxiety.

She flushed a trifle, then laughed. "I'm not—really!" she protested. "But I'll go away if you wish."

That was too much for me. "We'll both leave," I said very haughtily. "Sorry to have put you out, Mr. Moore."

To my astonishment, for I was really angry, he burst out laughing. It was such a genial, inoffensive merriment as caught me unawares. I found myself laughing with him, though at what I hadn't the faintest notion.

"Why, Barbour," he chuckled, "you mustn't take offense at a lack of conventional mannerisms on my part. I'm a worker first, last and all the time. Miss Whitingfield, you're welcome as the flowers in May, but I can no more forget my work nor what is likely to affect it than I can forget my own name. You—aren't angry with me, are you?"

"N-no—" she began rather hesitatingly, but just then the door opened behind us and we heard someone enter.

"I am here!"

The words were uttered in a dry, toneless voice. We both turned, and I realized that the "Mystery of the Awful Veiled One" was a mystery no more, or at least had been shorn of its purple drapery.

Of course, I had expected to meet Alicia here, but I think I should have recognized those eyes in any surroundings. They were fully as bright, dark, and almost incredibly large and attentive as they had seemed behind the veil. For the rest, Mrs. Moore's slender figure was draped in filmy black, between which and a mass of black hair her face gleamed, a peaked white patch—and with those eyes in it.

"Medium" or not, Mrs. Moore herself was more like the creature of another world than any human being I had ever seen.

"Be seated, Alicia."

Without troubling to present Roberta, Moore gestured toward a peculiar-looking chair at one side of the room. The slender creature in black swept toward it obediently.

Having reached the chair, she turned, faced us for a moment, still expressionless save for those terribly attentive eyes, then sank into the chair's depths.

Roberta was frankly staring, and so was I, but my stare had a newly startled quality. Alicia had passed me very closely indeed. My hand still tingled where another hand—a bony, fierce little hand—had closed on it in a swift, pinching clasp. And though I was sure that her colorless lips had not moved, four low words had reached my ears distinctly.

"Go away—you! Go."

I glanced at Berty, but decided that she had missed the rude little message. Moore certainly hadn't heard, for he had gone over to the chair, and was standing behind it when Alicia reached there.

With a slight shrug I determined that where so much oddity prevailed, this additional eccentricity of Mrs. Moore had better be ignored. To think of her as a real person—my hostess—was made difficult by the atmosphere of utter strangeness which her appearance and Moore's treatment of her had already created.

"You and Miss Whitingfield sit over there," commanded Moore briskly.

"I'll explain what we're about in a minute. You'll be interested. Can't avoid it. A little farther off, Miss Whitingfield—do you mind? Alicia is more easily affected than other sensitives. More easily affected. Right! Now just a moment and I can talk to you."

We had seated ourselves as he directed, I some half dozen feet from the enthroned Alicia, Roberta much farther away, well over by the heavily curtained windows.

To the savage and to the young "strange" is generally synonymous with "funny." We exchanged one quick look, then kept our eyes resolutely apart. A wave of incipient mirth had fairly leaped between us. It was well, I thought, that Cathy had been suppressed.

Then we saw what Moore was doing at the chair, and forgot laughter in amazement. It must be remembered that Roberta and I were innocent of the least previous experience in this line. Save for some hazy knowledge of "spiritualistic fakes" and "mind-reading" of the vaudeville type, we were blankly ignorant, and by consequence as unconsciously receptive as a couple of innocent young sponges. But at first we were merely shocked by the brutal fact of Moore's preparations.

I have said that the chair taken by Alicia was a peculiar one. It stood before a pair of black curtains, which concealed what in spiritualistic circles is called a cabinet. The chair itself was large, heavy, with a high back and uncommonly broad armrests. More, it had about it that look of apparatus which one associates with dentists' and surgeons' fixtures. Alicia leaned back in it, her hands resting limp on the armrests.

Then up over each fragile wrist Moore clamped a kind of steel handcuff, attached to the chair arm. Another pair of similar fetters, extended on short rods from the back, were clasped round her upper arms. And, as if this were not enough—he locked together the two halves of a wide steel band about her waist.

And his wife sat there, inert as a porcelain doll, her enormous eyes wide open and fixed on me in perfectly unswerving contemplation.

"All really great mediums will trick you if they can," said Moore coolly. "Don't need any object for fraud. Unless you should call the trickery itself an object. Alicia is a great medium. Very—great!"

Suddenly every decent impulse I had rose to revolt. That was a woman in the chair—Moore's wife—and he treated her, talked about her, as though she were some peculiarly trained and subject animal.

I rose sharply. "Mrs. Moore, is this affair proceeding with your consent?"

"Don't address the psychic!" snapped her husband over one shoulder.

But I wasn't afraid of him. At that moment I could have thrashed the man cheerfully—and with ease, for I carried no superfluous flesh in those days, and had inches the better of him in height and reach. Roberta was suddenly at my side, and I knew—by the excited shine of her eyes—that she sensed my emotion and approved it.

"Mrs. Moore," I repeated "are you enduring this of your own free will? Moore, attempt to intimidate her, and you'll be sorry!"

He straightened, and turned on me in earnest, but Alicia herself broke the strain.

"Sit down, boy," she said in her dry, toneless voice. "What James says of fraud is true. But he does not mean what you think. I am not conscious of what I do in trance, and the self then in control has no moral standards. Were my earthly limbs not bound, no phenomena could be credited, and my own guides have advised the construction of the chair. The steel bands are padded with felt, and do not hurt me. I did not speak to you when I entered, because at some times the guides like me to be silent. This is tiring me. You must not quarrel with James. Violent emotion tires me. A great evil will come to you through me, but now you must sit down and be very quiet. I am tired."

For the first time, white lids drooped over those unnatural eyes. The closing of them seemed to rob her face of the last trace of fellow-humanity. Moore was grinning again, though rather tensely.

"Please sit down, Barbour," he pleaded in a very low voice. "I should have explained a few things to you in advance. Alicia will be asleep directly, and then we can talk."

I did sit down, and Roberta retired to her window. That toneless, indifferent voice of Alicia's, that cool exactitude of statement, had not seemed the expression of a meek and terrorized soul. But if she were not afraid of

Moore, why had she been so surreptitious in asking—in ordering me to leave? "I did not speak to you when I entered—" But she had spoken to me. "A great evil will come to you through me—" And she said it like a remark on the weather!

I gave up suddenly. All my curiosity was submerged in a wave of healthy revolt against the obviously abnormal. A vague unhappiness came with it, and the desire above everything to take Roberta and get out.

Alicia was breathing regularly now, in long, deep breaths, soft but audible. Leaving her, Moore drew up a chair between Roberta and me, seated himself, crossed one leg over his knee, and beamed amiably.

"Mr. Moore," I began, but he checked me, finger in air.

"Sh! Trifle lower, please. I know what you're thinking, Barbour, and I don't blame you. Not in-the-least! My fault entirely. Now let's drop all that and forget it. You are two very intelligent people, but I can never remember that the average man or woman knows as much about sensitives as a baby knows of trigonometry. Now, why did I invite you here, Barbour?"

"For an interesting evening, you said."

"Exactly! And you'll have it. First of many, I hope. But don't expect any messages from your deceased grandfathers tonight, for you won't get 'em."

"Very well," I assented. "Bert, do you hear that? Our revered ancestors won't speak to us!"

"And don't imagine this is a matter for joking, either," reproved Moore, but still amiably. "I did not say that purely spiritual forces would not be involved. But a psychic—a medium—has all the complexity of the highest type of nervous human—plus. And it's the plus sign that complicates matters. You might get messages through from almost anyone—eventually. You'll seem to get them tonight. But they won't be real. Alicia has more different selves than the proverbial cat has lives. And all wanting a chance to talk, and parade around, and pass themselves off as anybody you'd care to name, from Julius Caesar to your mother's deceased aunt's nephew. Very remarkable!"

"I should say so!"

We glanced rather anxiously at Alicia's quiescent figure. But no sudden procession of selves had yet appeared.

"That, however, is beside the mark," announced Moore briskly. "In such commonplace manifestations, Alicia dematerializes a percentage of her own fleshly bulk, externalizes and projects it from her subliminal consciousness. Aside from proving the accepted laws of matter to be false, the phenomena are of small importance."

He paused again.

"I should think," ventured Roberta, carefully avoiding my eyes, "that disproving the laws of matter would be—might be almost enough for one evening."

"The accepted laws," he corrected rather sharply. "Crooks-Oschorowicz-Lombroso-Bottazzi-Lodge—I could name you over a dozen great scientists who have already disproved them in that way. But they had only Tusapia Paladino and lesser psychics to work with. We have—Alicia!"

A vague memory stirred in me. "Paladino?" I said. "You mean that famous Italian medium? I thought she was exposed as a fraud."

He frowned. This was a sore subject with him, though I did not know why till much later.

"I tell you," he scowled, "they are all frauds—when they have the chance. The first impulse of hysteria is toward deception. Genuine mediumship and hysteria are practically inseparable. What can you expect? Paladino was as genuine as Alicia, and Alicia will fool you outrageously, given the least opportunity. Quite—scandalously—unscrupulous!"

"You're very frank about it," I couldn't help saying.

"Why not? You heard Alicia's own statement in that regard. She works with me to overcome the disadvantage. Mabel and Maudie are manageable enough, but Horace is a born joker. For a long time Horace fought bitterly against the idea of that chair, and only yielded when I threatened to give up the sittings."

"These people are friends who attend the seances?" I inquired, thinking that Moore had Nils' habit of referring to all his acquaintances by their Christian names.

Moore appeared mildly surprised.

"Don't you really know anything at all of spiritualistic investigation?"

"Sorry. I'm afraid I've never had enough faith in spooks to be interested."

"Never mind. We'll correct that!" assured Moore calmly. "Mabel and Maudie and Horace are three of Alicia's spirit guides. She believes them to be real entities of the spirit world—people who have passed beyond, you understand—but I doubt it. Doubt it—very seriously! In fact, I have reason to be positive that those three, along with several subsidiary 'spirits,' are just so many phases of Alicia's subconscious. On the other band, Jason Gibbs, her real 'control,' is a spirit to be reckoned with. You will find Jason an amazingly interesting man on acquaintance. And now that I have explained fully, suppose we take a look at the cabinet?"

Roberta and I rose and followed him, not sure whether to be amused or impressed. His statement that he had "explained fully" was a joke, so far as we were concerned. What nebulous ideas of a seance we had possessed were far removed from anything we had met tonight. To sit in a circle, holding hands in the dark; to hear mysterious raps and poundings; to glimpse, perhaps, the cheese-clothy forms of highly fictitious "ghosts"—that had been our previous conception of a "sitting" culled from general and half-forgotten reading.

Moore was so utterly matter-of-fact and unmystical of manner that he probably impressed us more deeply than if he had attempted to inspire awe.

And, I reflected, if he were a charlatan, where was his profit? Nils himself had assured me that Mrs. Moore was not a professional medium.

The fact was that I had emerged from college almost wholly ignorant of the modern debate between the physicist and the spiritist—ignorant that science itself had been driven to admission of supernormal powers in certain "victims of hysteria," but stood firm on the ground that these powers were of physical and terrestrial origin.

James Barton Moore, however, was a born materialist who had accepted the spiritistic theory from an intellectual viewpoint. The result showed in his matter-of-fact way of dealing with the occult. He had, moreover, one characteristic of a certain type of scientist in less weird fields. He would have put a stranger or his best friend on the vivisection table, could he by that means have hoped to acquire one small modicum of the knowledge he sought.

Figuratively, he already had me on the table that night.

III

On Pushing aside the black curtains, the cabinet proved to be a place like a square closet, with a smooth, solid wooden back, built out from the wall. In it there stood a small, rather heavy table, made of polished oak, on which reposed several objects.

There was a thing like a small megaphone, to which Moore referred as the "cone." There was an ordinary glass tumbler, nearly filled with water; a lump of soft putty; a sheet of paper blackened by sooty smoke; a pad of ordinary white paper, and several pencils and pens, of different colors and sizes.

"Our preparations tonight," said Moore, "are of the simplest sort. I have passed the stage of registering Alicia's externalized motivity by means of instruments of precision. The exact force exerted to lift a weight yards beyond her bodily reach, the regulated rhythm of a metronome's pendulum, compression of a pneumatic ten feet from her hand—these have all been proved and left behind me. Others have done that with other mediums.

"But I go the step further that Bottazzi and many others dared not take. Having admitted the phenomena, I admit a cause for them outside the physical and beyond Alicia's individuality. I admit the disembodied spirit. My experiments are no longer based on doubt, but certainty. Their culmination will mean a revolution for the thinking world—a reversal of its whole stand toward matter and the forces that affect it."

Roberta and I were not particularly interested in revolutions of thought. Like younger children, we wished to know what he proposed doing with the things on the table, and after that we wished to see it done. So we stood silent, hoping that he would stop talking soon and let the exhibition of Alicia's mysterious powers begin.

Being off on his hobby, Moore probably mistook our silence for interest. At last, however, in the midst of a dissertation on "psychic force," "telekinesis" and "spiritual controls," he was interrupted by a long, deep sigh from the chair. The sigh was followed by a strangled gasping, very much as though Alicia were choking to death.

We both started toward the chair, but Moore barred the way.

"Let her alone!" he ordered imperatively. "She's all right. Come back to your seats." And when we had returned to our former positions, he added: "She is going into trance now. Later you may approach closer—hold her hands, if you like. But Alicia can't bear even myself to be very near her in the first stages. It hurts her, you understand. Gives her physical pain."

Judging from poor Alicia's appearance, she was in physical pain anyway. Her peaked white face writhed in the most unpleasant contortions. She choked, gasped, gurgled and showed every symptom of a woman in dying agonies. Then suddenly she quieted, her face resumed its lay-figure calmness, and the great eyes opened wide.

"Differs from most psychics. Opens her eyes in trance. Quite frequently." I heard Moore muttering; but Alicia herself began to speak now, and I forgot him.

The queerest, silliest little voice issued from her lips. It was like a child's voice, but an idiot child's.

"Pretty, pretty, pretty!" it gurgled. "Oh such a pretty lady! Did pretty lady come to see Maudie?" Followed a pause. When it spoke again the voice had a petulant note: "Did pretty lady come to see Maudie?"

Moore looked at Roberta. "Why don't you answer her, Miss Whitingfield?"

Before she could comply, however, another personality had apparently superseded the idiot child. A great laugh that I would have sworn was a man's echoed across the silent library. It seemed to come from Alicia's throat.

"Ha, ha, ha! Oh, ha, ha! You've got queer taste, Jimmy Moore! Why do you want to drag that pair of freaks in here? Tell 'em to go home! Go on home, young fellow, d'you hear? Go on, now—and take the skirt with you!"

"That is Horace," commented Moore imperturbably. "You haven't any manners, Horace, have you?"

"Not a manner!" retorted the voice. "Is that young sport going to leave, or do I have to heave a brick at him? Scat! Get out—you!"

This was certainly outside my idea of a seance. It occurred to me abruptly that the voice was not proceeding from Alicia. Some confederate was concealed nearby—had entered the cabinet, perhaps, by a concealed door. Or Moore himself was ventriloquizing.

Then I realized that Alicia's eyes were again fixed on my face, and their expression was not that of a woman entranced. They were keen, bright, intelligent. Her lips moved.

"Get! Get out!" adjured that brutally vulgar voice. Then it changed to a whining, female treble: "You are young, Clayton Barbour; young and soft to the soft, cruel hand that would mold you. You are easy to mold as clay-clay-Clayton-clay! Evil hangs over you—black evil! Flee from the damned Clayton Barbour. Go home—you!"

Moore was frowning uneasily.

"Subliminal," he said shortly. "Pay no attention to these voices. They emanate from the subconscious—Alicia's dream self. Similar to delirium, you know."

"Ah!" I murmured, and settled back in my chair. Not that I agreed with Moore, though I had dismissed thought of either a confederate or my host's ventriloquism. The ventriloquist was Alicia herself. I had no doubt that she could have caused the voices to sound from any quarter of the room as easily as from her own throat. As for trance, her eyes were entirely too wakeful and intelligent. Nearly everything said so far had been more repetition, in different phrases and voices, of that first brief, fierce little demand that I leave.

But by that time I was more than a trifle annoyed. It was hardly pleasant to sit in Roberta's presence and hear rude puns made on my name—to bear it implied that I was a mere nonentity with no character of my own. I rather plumed myself that Alicia would not find me so pliable. If she really wished me to depart, she had gone the wrong way about it.

"Ah," I said, settled back, and—the vulgarity of "Horace" may have been contagious—deliberately winked at Alicia. It was a crude enough act, but her methods struck me as crude, too.

A blaze of fury leaped into those too attentive eyes. Her features writhed in such an abominable convulsion as I had never believed possible to the human countenance. Purple, distorted, terrible—with a flashing of bone-white teeth—and out of it all a voice discordant, and different from any we had heard.

"Fool-fool-fool!" it grated. "Protect—try—can't protect fool! Slipping—it's got me—I'm slip-Oh-h-h! Oh-h-h-h!"

Even Moore seemed affected this time. We were all on our feet, and he was beside his wife in three long strides. As the last, long-drawn moan died away, however, the dreadful purple subsided from Alicia's countenance as quickly as it had risen. She was again the queer, white porcelain doll, leaning back with closed lids in her imprisoning chair.

Moore straightened, wiped his forehead, and laughed shakily.

"Do you know," he said, "with all the experience I've had, Alicia still gives me an occasional fright? But I never saw her pass into the second stage quite so violently."

"Don't these horrible convulsions hurt your wife, Mr. Moore?"

Roberta was deeply distressed, and no wonder! I felt as if I had brought her to watch the seizures of an epileptic.

"She says they don't," replied Moore. "But never mind that. Listen!"

Alicia's lips writhed whitely. "Light!" came her barely audible whisper.

Promptly Moore reached for a switch. Two of the three lights burning went out. The third was a shaded library lamp on a table not far off. I expected him to extinguish that also, for everything in the room was plainly visible, but he let it be.

"You may hold Alicia's hands, if you wish," he offered generously.

We shook our heads. Presently the hushed whisper was heard again.

"Many shadows are here tonight," it said. "Shadows living and dead. They crowd close. An old, old shadow comes. Blood runs from his lean, gnarled throat. He speaks!"

The whisper became a ghastly, bubbling attempt at articulation. There were no words. The result was just an abominable sound.

"Man with his throat cut might speak like that," observed Moore reflectively. "She must mean old Jenkins, who was murdered next door. That's the reason we have this house, you know. The other half's supposed to be haunted—and is."

Now I wanted to get out in earnest. Fraud or epileptic, Alicia was entirely too horrible, and Moore, with his calmness, almost worse. I tried to draw Roberta toward the door, but she held back.

"Not yet, Clay. I wish to see what will happen."

Now the horrid gurgle had merged into a man's voice. It was loud and distinct as "Horace's," but otherwise slightly different—as different, say, as tenor from high baritone.

"I am Jason Gibbs," it asserted. "Mr. Moore, will you kindly ask your friends to step back a little? We will do what we can for you, but my fellow spirits are a trifle shy of strangers."

Moore motioned us back. At the same time he shook his head smilingly.

"That's not Jason," he murmured. "A very good imitation, but an imitation, nonetheless. We shan't get much tonight."

"And in that," retorted the tenor, "you are exactly mistaken! You will get much. In fact you are likely to get more than one of you ever bargained for. You say I'm not Jason Gibbs? Seeing is believing, isn't it? Shall I show myself?"

Moore acquiesced smoothly. "Do so, by all means."

"I'll attend to that in a little while. I can read your mind all right, Jimmy Moore! You think I'm Horace talking high. Well, Horace is a very good fellow, and fond of his joke, but I'm Jason Gibbs tonight—and all the time, of course! Like to see something pretty?"

"Anything at all, Hor—pardon me Jason!"

"Then watch the cabinet."

We did. For a minute or two nothing happened.

Then Roberta cried out: "It's on fire!"

"No," said Moore. "Watch!"

A strange, tiny flame was running along the edge of the black curtains where they touched the floor.

When I say "running along," I do not mean that in the usual sense as applied to fire. It was a tiny, individual flame, violet in color, about an inch and a half high, and as it moved it twirled and spun on its own base in the oddest manner. Reaching the center, where the curtains joined, it floated slowly upward, still twirling, left the cabinet and presently disappeared, apparently through the ceiling. Another flame and another followed it.

I assured myself that we were watching a very clever and unusual exhibition of fireworks. But I didn't believe that. I didn't know exactly what I believed, but I did know that those twirling, violet flames were the first really strange thing I had ever seen in my life. When seven of them had appeared and vanished, Moore spoke.

"Isn't that enough—er Jason? Can't you do better than that for us?"

There was silence, while the eighth and last flame twirled upward and vanished. Then, that great, rough laugh burst startlingly from Alicia's lips.

"Ha. Ha, ha! Ha, ha! Oh, Jimmy Moore, I should say I can do better! I should say so!"

And with that the curtains parted suddenly and—it is hard to tell, but it was harder to stand the shock of it—a huge, misshapen, grayish-black hand darted out from between them.

Behind it I caught a glimpse of wrist—I couldn't see any arm. It just leaped out and into existence, as one might say, and to my unspeakable horror laid its gross, gnarled fingers fairly across Roberta Whitingfield's mouth and chin.

I believed it had seized her throat. Half-mad with shock, I sprang at the hand, gripping, holding it in both of mine. I felt a kind of roughness in my grasp—a rough solidity that melted to nothing even as I touched it. My hands were empty. I caught Roberta, as she swayed backward, whiter than Alicia herself.

And Moore was reproving—something, in the most everyday manner.

"Really, Horace, that wasn't a nice joke at all!" he criticized.

Easing Roberta into a chair, I sprang savagely at the curtains and swept them aside: behind there was only the table and what we had seen on it. I had a fleeting impression that the lump of putty was different—that, where it had been a formless lump, it appeared now as if it had been squeezed between giant fingers. Then Moore was pulling me back.

"Don't do that, Barbour. We shan't get anything more, if you interfere like that."

"Devil!" it was all I could think of to call him, and it seemed inadequate enough.

"You—devil! To play a trick like that on an unsuspecting girl! Bert, darling, come, I'll take you home; then I'll come back and settle with these people!"

"Barbour, I give you my word of honor that I had nothing to do with what just occurred. You brought Miss Whitingfield here of your own volition, and pardon me—against my wishes. But she assured me she was, not of the nervous type—"

"Nervous!" I repeated scornfully. "A really nervous woman would have died when that black paw flew out at her!"

"I'm not hurt, Clayton," intervened Roberta. "Don't quarrel with him—please!"

"You are sensible," approved Moore, "There is no danger from such manifestations as that hand. Why, I have taken a peek into the cabinet when the power was strong and seen half a dozen human limbs and parts of limbs lying about—fragmentary impulses, as one might say, of the mediumistic force—"

But here, with marked decision, Roberta rose.

"I think we will go home, Clay. I have just discovered that I am of the nervous, screaming sort! Mr. Moore, will you please say good night for us to Mrs. Moore when she—when she wakens?"

He sighed disappointedly.

"It's too bad, really! If Jason Gibbs had actually been in control tonight there would have been nothing to shock you. Horace is nothing. Just a secondary, practical-looking phase of Alicia's own personality."

"Come, Roberta." We started toward the door.

And then, without a warning flicker, the library lamp went out, leaving the room in impenetrable darkness.

IV

The difference between light and the lack of it is the difference between freedom and captivity, and the real reason that we pity a blind man is because he is a prisoner. This is true under normal conditions. Add to darkness dread of the supernatural, and the inevitable sum is panic.

Till that moment I doubt if Roberta or I had believed the black hand which touched her to be of other than natural origin. Ingrained thought-habit had accused Moore of trickery, even while it condemned the trick as unpleasant.

That was while the light burned. One instant later we were trapped prisoners of the dark, and instincts centuries old flung off thought-habit like a tissue cloak.

What had been a quiet, modern room became, in that instant, the devil-haunted jungle of forebears infinitely remote.

And it didn't help matters that just then "Horace" elected to be heard again. Alicia visible, Horace had seemed a vocal feat on her part. Alicia unseen, Horace became a discarnate fiend. That he was a fiend, vulgar and incongruous, only made his fiendishness more intolerable.

"How's this for a joke?" he inquired sardonically, "I never did like that lamp! Let's give it away, Jimmy. Tell your young fool friend to take the lamp away with him."

Soundlessly, without warning, something hard and slightly warm touched my cheek. I struck out wildly. My fist crashed through glass, there was a great smash and clatter from the floor, and mingled with it shout upon shout of fairly maniacal mirth. Then Moore's voice, cool but irritated:

"You'll have to stop these tricks, Horace. I'm ashamed of you! Breaking a valuable lamp like that. Our guests will believe you a common spirit or poltergeist."

"Moore, if you don't throw on the lights, I'll kill you for this!"

My own voice shook with mingled rage and dread. Of course, it might be he who had brought the lamp and held it against my face, but the very senselessness of the trick made it terrible in a queer, unhuman way.

"Stand still!" he commanded sharply. "Barbour, Miss Whitingfield, you are not children! Nothing will harm you, if you keep quiet. It was your own yielding to anger and fear that brought this crude force into play. Did it actually hit you with the lamp, Barbour?"

"I hit the lamp, but—"

"Exactly! Now keep quiet. Horace, may I turn on the lights?"

"If you do, you'll be sorry, Jimmy! Call me poltergeist or plain Dutch, there's somebody worse than me here tonight."

"What do you mean, Horace?"

"Oh, somebody that came along in with your scared young friends. He's a Joker, too, but I don't like him. He wants to get through the gates altogether, and stay through. If he does, a lot of people will be sorry: You say I'm rough, but say, Jimmy, this fellow is worse than rough. He's smooth! Get me? Too smooth. I'm keeping him back, and you know I'm stronger in the dark."

"Very well." I heard Moore laugh amusedly. His quiet matter-of-courseness should have deleted all terror from the affair. He was carrying on a conversation with a rather silly, rather vulgar man, of whom he was not afraid, but whose vagaries he indulged for reasons of expediency. That was the sound of it.

But the sense of it—there in the blackness—was such an indescribable horror to me as I cannot convey by words. There was more to this feeling than fear of Horace. I learned what nerves meant that night. If mine had all been on the outside of my skin, crawling, expectant of shock, I could have suffered no more keenly. Coward? Wait to judge that till you learn what the uncomprehending expectancy meant for me.

"Very well," laughed Moore. "But don't break any more lamps, Horace—please! Have some consideration for my pocketbook."

"Money! We haven't any pants-pockets my side of the line," Horace chuckled. "If I'm to keep the smooth fellow back, you must let me use my strength. Let me have my fun, Jimmy! What's a lamp or so between pals? And just to keep things interesting, suppose we bring out the big fellow in the closet?"

I heard a thud from the direction of the cabinet, a low chuckle, and then a huge panting sound. It sounded like an enormous animal. We had a sense of something living and enormous that had suddenly come out of nothing into the room.

"The hand!" screamed Roberta sharply. "It's the black-hand thing!"

I was hideously afraid that she was right. With her own clutching little hands on my arm, I sprang, dragging her with me. I didn't spring for where I thought Moore was, nor for where I supposed the door might be. There were only two thoughts in my head. One of a monstrous and wholly imaginary black giant; the other, a passionate desire for light.

By pure chance I brought up against the wall just beside a brass plate inset with two magical, blessed buttons. My fingers found them. Got the wrong button—the right one.

Flash! And we were out of demon-land and in a commonplace room again.

Not quite commonplace, though. True, no black, impossible giant inhabited it. The vast panting sound hand passed and though the lamp lay among the splinters of its wrecked shade and my hand was bleeding, a broken lamp and cut hand are possible incidentals of the ordinary.

But that woman in the chair was not!

Writhing, shrieking, foaming creatures like that have their place in a hospital—or a sick man's delirium—but not rightfully in an evening's entertainment for two unexpectant young people. Bert took one look and buried her face against my vest in an ecstasy of fear.

Moore was beside his wife, swiftly unclasping the steel manacles that held her, but finding time for a glaring side glance at me which expressed white-hot and concentrated rage.

I didn't understand. Alicia's previous spasms or seizures, though less violent than this, had been bad enough. Why should Moore eye me like that, when if anyone had a right to be furious it was I?

"The lights!" moaned Bert against my vest. "You turned on the lights, and it hurt her. I've read that somewhere—Oh, Clay, why don't you do something to help her and make her stop that horrible screaming?"

Moore heard and turned again, snarling. "You get out of here, Barbour! You've done harm enough!"

"Shan't I—shan't we call a doctor?" I stammered.

He didn't answer. Released, Alicia had subsided limply, a black heap in the chair, face on knees. The gurgling shrieks had lowered to a series of long, agonizing moans. I thought she was dying, and in a confused way felt that both Roberta and Moore blamed me.

The moans, too, had ceased. Was she dead?

Now Moore was trying to lift his wife out of the chair—and failing, for some reason. Instinctively I pushed Roberta aside and moved to help him.

And then, at last, that happened for which all the rest had been a prelude—for which, my whole life had been a prelude, as I was to learn one day. There came—how can I phrase it?

It was not a darkness, for I saw. It was not a vacuum, for most certainly I—everyone of us—continued to breathe. It was like—you know what happens sometimes in a thunderstorm? There is a hushed moment, when it is as if a mighty, invisible being had drawn in its breath—not breath of air, but of force. If you live in the suburbs and have alternating current, the lights go out—as if the current had been sucked back.

Static has the upper band of kinetic. A moment, and kinetic will rebel in a blinding, crashing river of fire from sky to earth. But till then, between earth and clouds there is a tension so terrific that it gives the awful sense of a void.

That happened in the room where we stood, though the force involved was not the physical one of electricity. There was the hushed moment, the sense of awful tension—of void—of strength sucked back like the current—

Without knowing how, I became aware that all the life in the room was suddenly, dreadfully centralizing around one of us. That one was Alicia.

I saw Moore move back from her. He had gone ghastly pale, and he waved his hands queerly. The straining sense of void which was also centralization increased. A numbness crept over me.

The invisible had drawn in its breath of pure force, and my life was undoubtedly a part of it.

There came a stirring of the black heap in the chair. Inexplicably, I felt as well as saw it. As if, standing by the wall, I was also in the chair. Roberta shivered. She was out of my sight, standing slightly behind me, but I felt that, too. No two of us were in physical contact, and yet some strange interfusion of consciousness was linking us more closely than the physical.

Again Alicia stirred. She cried out inarticulately. The centralization was around her, but not by her will. I felt a surge of resentment that was not mine, but Alicia's. Then I knew that there were more than four of us present, in the room. A fifth was here—invisible, strong, unifying the strength of us all for its own purpose—for a leap across the intangible barriers and into the living world.

Numbness was on me, cold dread, and a sense of some danger peculiarly personal to myself. It was coming now—now—

With another cry, Alicia shot suddenly erect. Her arms went out in a wide sweep that seemed to be struggling in an attempt to push something from her.

"!" she cried, and: "You! Back! Go back—go back—go back! Oh, you, Serapion!"

When kinetic revolts against static, blinding fire results. The tension in that room let go as suddenly as the lightning stroke, though I was the only one to feel it fully.

My body reeled against the wall. My spirit—I—the ego—reeled with it—beyond it—down—down—into darkness absolute—and into a nullity deeper than darkness' self.

Speed. In outer space there is room for it, and necessity. Between our sun and the nearest star where one may grow warm again there is space that a light ray needs centuries to cross.

The cold is cruel, and a wind blows there more biting than the winds of earth. Little, cold stars rush by like far-separated lamps on a country road, and double meteors, twin blazing eyes, swing down through the long black reaches. It is hard to avoid these, when they sweep so close, and one's hands are numb on the steering-wheel.

But one can't slow for that—nor even for a frightened voice at one's elbow, pleading, protesting, begging for the slowness that will let the cold overtake and annihilate us. "The cold!" I shouted against the wind. "Cold!"

"Well, if you're cold," wailed the harassed voice, "why don't you slow down? Clay! Clayton Barbour! I'll never ride again in a car with you, Clayton, if you don't slow down!"

Another pair of twin meteors rushed curving toward us. We avoided them, kept our course by the fraction of a safe margin, and as we did so the limitless vistas of interstellar space seemed to close in sharply and solidify.

Infinite shrank to finite with the jolt of a collision—and it was almost a real one. I swung to the left and barely avoided the tail of a farmer's wagon, ambling sedately along the road ahead of us. Then I not only slowed, but stopped, while the wagon creaked prosaically by. I sat at the wheel of a car—my own car—and that was Roberta Whitingfeld beside me.

"Sixty miles an hour!" she was saying indignantly. "You haven't touched the horn once, and you are sitting so that I can't get at it."

I said nothing. Desperately I was trying to adjust the unadjustable.

This road was real. The numbness and chill were passing, and the air of a summer night blew warm on my cheek. That wild rush of the spirit through space was already fading into place as a dream memory.

FRANCIS STEVENS

But there had been some kind of an hiatus in realities. My last definite memory was of—Alicia Moore. Alicia—upright—rebellious—crying out a name.

"Clay!" A note of concern had replaced Roberta's indignation. "Why do you sit there so still? Answer me! Are you ill? What is the matter?"

"Nothing."

That was a lie, of course, but instinctive as self-protection. I must get straight somehow, but I wouldn't confide the need even to Roberta. In the most ordinary tone I apologized for my reckless driving and started the car again. We were on a familiar road, outside the city, but one that would take us by roundabout ways to our home in the suburbs.

I drove slowly, for it was very necessary that Roberta should talk. By listening I might be able to get straight without betraying myself, and indeed, before we reached home, I had a fairly clear idea of what had happened in the blank interim.

A first wild surmise that the Moore episode had been a dream in its entirety was banished almost at once. As nearly as I could gather, without direct questioning, from the time when I reeled back against the wall until my return to self-consciousness some sixty minutes later, I had behaved so normally in outward appearance that not even Roberta had seen a difference.

My body had evidently not fallen to the floor, nor showed any signs of fainting or unconsciousness. Alicia seemed to have returned to her senses at the same time that I lost mine, for Roberta spoke of her hostess' quiet air of indifference that amounted almost to scorn for the concern that we—Bert and I, mind you!—expressed for her.

Moore, for his part, it seemed, had recovered his temper and been rather apologetic and anxious that I, at least, should repeat my visit. I had been noncommittal on the subject—for which Roberta now commended me—and then we had come away together.

After that, the hallucination I had suffered, of myself as a disembodied entity, careering from one planetary system to another, had synchronized with an actual career in the car where road-lamps simulated stars and occasional cars traveling in the opposite direction provided the stimuli for my dream-meteors.

A man hypnotized might have done what I did, and as successfully. To myself, then, I said that I had been hypnotized. That in a manner yet to be explained either Moore or his wife had hypnotized me and allowed me to leave their house under that influence. I tried to determine what reckoning I should have with them later. But it was a failure. I was frankly scared.

An hour had been jerked bodily, out of my conscious life. If, in the ordinary and orthodox manner, I had lain insensible through that hour, it wouldn't have mattered so much. Instead of that, an 'I' that was not I appeared to have taken charge of my affairs and in such a manner that a person very near and dear to me had perceived nothing wrong. It was that which frightened me.

The last traces of daze, and shock released my mind, the instinct to keep its lapse a secret only grew stronger. Fortunately I found concealment easy. Speeding was not so far from my occasional habit that Roberta had thought much of that part of the episode. Her vigorous protests had been largely on account of my failure to use the horn.

Dropping the subject with her usual quick good-nature, she talked of our remarkable first experience with a "real medium," and disclosed the fact—not surprising perhaps—that she had been considerably less impressed than I. In retrospect she blamed her own nerves for most of the excitement.

"I may be unfair, Clay," she confided, "but truly, I can't help believing that Mrs. Moore is just a clever, hysterical woman who has deluded poor Mr. Moore into a faith in 'spirit voices.'"

"The black hand? The little flames?"

"Did we really see them? Don't you think the woman may have some kind of hypnotic power, like—oh, like the mango trick that everybody's heard they do in India? You know. A tree grows right up out of the ground while you watch; but it doesn't really, of course. You're hypnotized, and only think you see it. Couldn't everything we saw and heard tonight have been a—a kind of hypnotic trick? And—now, with all the screaming and fuss she had made, Mrs. Moore was so calm and cool when we left! I think it was all put on, and the rest was hypnotism."

"You're a very clever little girl, Berty," I commented, and meant it. If there was one thing I wished to believe, it was that Alicia Moore had faked.

We knew nearly as little about hypnotism as we did of psychic phenomena, real or so-called. But the word had a good sound to me. I had been hypnotized. Hypnotized! That Fifth Presence in the room had existed only in my own overborne imagination. The whole affair was—

"Berty," I said, "we've been through a highly unpleasant experience, and it's my fault. Nils warned me against those people, but I was stubborn mule enough to believe I wished to know more of them. I don't, and we don't—you and I. The truth is, Berty, I feel pretty foolish over the whole business. Had no right to take you to such a place. Downright dangerous—queer, irresponsible people like that! Say, do you mind not telling Cathy, for instance?"

"If you won't tell mother!"

She giggled. I could picture myself relating that weird and unconventional tale to the stately Mrs. Whitingfield! Up went my right hand.

"Hear me swear! I, Clayton S. Barbour, do solemnly vow silence—"

"Full name, or it isn't legal!" trilled the girl beside me.

"Oh, very well! I, Clayton Barbour, do—"

I stopped with a tightening of the throat. As the word "" passed my lips, the Fifth Presence had shut down close about me.

Out of space-time—wrapped away in cloudy envelopes of oblivion—

"Clayton!" A clear young voice out of the clouds. They shriveled to nothing, and I was loosed to my world again. "Why, Clayton!" repeated Roberta. "How did that woman know your middle name?"

My right hand dropped to the wheel, and the car leaped forward.

"Did you tell her?" insisted Roberta.

"No," I answered shortly. "Berquist told Moore, I supposed. How do I know?"

"Someone must have told her," Bert agreed. "It isn't as if it were an ordinary name that she might have hit on by guessing."

"Oh, it isn't so unusual. There have been Sera—there; have been men of that name in my mother's family for generations. I was given the name in remembrance of my mother's brother. He died only a few months before I was born, and she had cared a lot for him. But don't let's talk of the name any more. I always hated it. Sounds silly, like a girl's name—I—I—Oh, forget the name! Here we are at home, and there's your mother in the window looking for us."

"We're awfully late!"

"Tell her the Moores were very interesting people," I suggested grimly.

That night, though I slept, Alicia Moore and the Fifth Presence—in various unpleasant shapes—haunted me through some exceedingly restless hours.

V

That a man may retire to his bed unknown and wake up famous is a truism of long standing. There is a parallel truth not half so pleasant. A man—a whole family—may retire wealthy and wake up paupers.

My father was the practically inactive senior member of his firm, and the reins had so far left his hands that when the blow fell it was hard for him to get a grasp on the situation or even credit it.

Rather shockingly, the first word we had of disaster came through the morning paper in a blare-headed column announcing the suicide of Frederic Hutchinson. Suicide without attempt at concealment. A scrubwoman, entering the private offices of Barbour & Hutchinson early that morning, had fairly trodden in the junior partner's scattered brains.

There followed a week of torment—of sordid revelations of unwise speculation, and ever increasing despair. A week that left dad a shaken, tremulous old man, and the firm of Barbour & Hutchinson, grain brokers, an unpleasant problem to be dealt with by the receivers.

Dad had known his partner for a clever man, and no doubt he was formerly a trustable one. But when the disease called speculation takes late root, its run is likely to be more virulent than in a younger victim. All Hutchinson's personal estate had been absorbed. His family were left in worse predicament than ours—or would have been, save that dad's peculiar sense of honor caused him to throw every cent he owned, independent of the firm, into the pit where that firm's honor had vanished, in an attempt to save it.

Unfortunately he possessed not nearly enough to satisfy the creditors and re-establish the business. As my mother pointed out, the disgrace that had been all Fred Hutchinson's was now dad's for impoverishing his family when, under the terms of partnership and the law of our State, most of his personal investments and realty could have been held free from liability.

And to that dad had only one, and to my mind somewhat appalling, reply:

"Let Clay go to work in earnest, then. Perhaps some day my son will clear the slate of what scores I've failed to settle!"

Well, great God, can a young fellow carefully trained to have everything he wants without trying turn financial genius in a week?

If it hadn't been for Roberta, I think I should have thrown up the sponge and fairly run away from it all. Her faith, though, stirred a chord of ambition that those of my own blood failed to touch, and her stately Charlestonian mother emerged from stateliness into surprising sympathy.

Then Dick Vansittart, the unregenerate youngster who had been my dearest pal in college days, got me a job with the Colossus Trust Company, thebank of which his father was president and where he himself loafed about intermittently.

Even I knew that the salary offered was more commensurate with our needs than with what I was worth. Vansittart, Sr., a gruff old lion of a man, growled at me through a personal interview which ended in: "You won't earn your salt for six months, Barbour, but maybe Terne can put up with you. Try it, anyway!"

Terne was the second vice-president, whose assistant, or secretary, or general errand-boy, it was proposed that I become. I reached for my hat.

"Sorry to have bothered you, Mr. Vansittart! I would hardly care to receive pay except on the basis that it was earned."

The lion roared.

"Sit down! Don't you try Dick's high mannerisms with me! If I can tolerate Dick in this bank, I can tolerate you; but there's going to be one difference. You'll play the man and work till you do earn your wages, or you'll go out! Understand?"

"I merely meant—"

"Never mind that." The savage countenance before me softened to a leonine benevolence. "Clayton Barbour's son wants no charity, but, you young fool, don't I know that? Your father has, swamped himself to pay debts that weren't his. Now I choose to pay a debt that isn't mine, but Dick's!"

I must have looked my bewilderment.

"I mean," he thundered, "that when my son was expelled from the college he disgraced he nearly took you with him! You cubs believe you carry your shame on your own shoulders. You never think of us. I've crossed the street three times to avoid meeting your father! Earn your wages here, so that I can shake hands with him next time. Here—take this note to Mr. Terne. His office is next the cashier's. Go to work!"

I went, but outside the door found Van waiting for me, smiling ironically.

"You heard?" I muttered.

"Not being stone deaf, yes. The governor doesn't mind publicity where I'm concerned, eh? Interested passersby in the street might hear, for all he cares. Oh, well—truth is mighty and must prevail. Wish you luck, Clay, and there's Fatty Terne coming now. So long!"

I was left to present my note to a dignified person who had just emerged from the Cashier's office. "Fatty" was a merciless nickname for him, and unfair besides. The second vice-president's large figure suggested strength rather than overindulgence. Beneath his dignity he proved a kindly, not domineering man, much overworked himself, but patient with early mistakes from a new helper.

He shared one stenographer with another official, and seemed actually grateful when I offered to learn shorthand during spare hours in order to be of more use with the correspondence. I was quite infected with the work fever for a while, and saw little of Van, who let me severely alone from the first day I entered the bank.

His new standoffishness didn't please me exactly, but I was too busy to think much of him one way or the other. At home, however, things went not so well. Since the house had been sold over our heads, we were forced into painfully small quarters. There was a little place near by that belonged to my mother. It had stood empty for a year, and though not much better than a cottage, her ownership of it solved the rent problem, and, as she bitterly explained, we no longer needed servants' rooms nor space for the entertainment of guests.

Mother and Cathy undertook the housework, while dad fooled about with paint-pots and the like, trying to delude himself into the belief that paint, varnish, and a few new shelves here and there would make a real home for us out of this wretched shack; for that is what Cathy and I called it privately.

All the problems of home life had taken on new, ugly, uncomfortable angles, and I spent as little time among them as I decently could.

Roberta had no more complaints to make of "sixty miles an hour and never touched the horn." My car had gone with the rest. We went on sedate little walks, like a country pair, tried to prefer movies to grand opera, and piled up heart-breaking dream-castles for consolation.

Two months slid by, and in that while our adventure at the "dead-alive house," as Roberta had named Moore's place, was hardly mentioned between us. Once or twice, indeed, she referred to it, but there was for me an oppressive distastefulness in the subject that made me lead our conversations elsewhere.

On the very heels of the catastrophic passing of my father's firm I had received a brief note from Moore. He expressed concern and sympathy, adding in the same breath, as it were, that he hoped I had been well enough interested the other evening to wish to walk farther along the path of Psychical research.

I regarded his concern as impertinent and his hope as impudent, considering my unpleasant memories of the first visit. I tore the letter up without answering it. After that I heard no more from him, and it was not until the second month's ending that a thing occurred which forced the whole matter vividly upon my recollection.

"If dear had not been taken from us," said my mother, "we should be living in a civilized manner, and my children and I would not have been driven to manual labor!"

Dad kept his eyes on his plate, refraining from answer. He had been guilty of an ill-advised criticism on Cathy's cooking, and, from that, discussion had run through all the ramifications of domestic misery until I was tempted to leave dinner unfinished and escape to my usual refuge, the Whitingfields.

But the mention of my uncle's name had a peculiar effect on me. A slight swimming sensation behind the eyes, a gripping tightness at the back of my neck—!

The feeling passed, but left me trembling so that I remained in my place, fearing to rise lest I betray myself. As before, some deep-seated instinct fought that. The weakness was like a shameful wound, to be at all costs hidden.

"Had he lived," continued my mother, "he would have seen to it that we weren't brought to this. No one near poor was ever allowed to be uncomfortable!"

Dad's eyes flashed up with a glint of spirit that he had never before showed in this connection.

"Is that so? I know he kept remarkably comfortable himself, but I can't recall his feathering anyone's nest but his own."

"Don't slander the dead!" came her sharp retort. "Why, you owe the very house over your head to him! And if it hadn't been that his thoughtfulness left it in my name you wouldn't have that. You would have robbed your children and me of even this pitiful shelter—"

"Evelyn—please!"

"It's true! And then you dare cast slurs and innuendoes at poor—"

"I gave him the house in the first place," dad muttered.

She rose, eyes flashing and filled with tears. "Yes, you did! And this shameful little hole was all he had to live in—and die in! was a saint!" she declared. "A saint! He was—he was universally loved!"

And with that, my mother swept from the room. Cathy followed, though with a sneaking glance of sympathy for dad. Tempestuous exits on mother's part had been frequent as far back as I could remember, and as they were invariably followed by hours in which someone must sit with her and the house must be kept dead silent, we other three had the fellow-feeling of victims.

Dad eyed me across the table. "Son," he said, "what is your middle name?"

"Ser-Ser-Samuel!" I ended desperately. My heart, for no obvious reason, had begun a palpitation. Why couldn't they let that name alone?

He looked surprised, and then laughed. "You are right, son. I was about to give you warning—to forbid your becoming such a saint as your esteemed namesake. But I guess that isn't needed. The Samuels of the world stand on their own feet, as you do now, thank Heaven! A Samuel for the in you, then, and never forget it!"

He could not guess the frantic struggle going on beneath my calm exterior. There is, I believe, a psychopathic condition in which sound-waves produce visual sensations; a musical note, for example, being seen as a blob of scarlet, or the sustained blast of a bugle as a ribbony, orange-colored streak. Some such confusion of the senses seemed to have occurred in me, only in my case one single sound produced it, and the result was not color but a feeling of pressure, dizziness, suffocation.

Fighting for control, I knew that another iteration of the sound in question would cost me the battle. Dad's mouth opened, and simultaneously I rose. Opinions on my uncle's character, pro or con, didn't interest me half so much as the problem of excusing myself in a steady voice, walking from table to doorway without a stagger, and finally escaping from that room before the fatal name could be spoken again.

These feats accomplished, I managed to get up the stairs and into my own room, where I locked the door and dropped, face downward, across the bed. Though the evening was cool, my whole body was drenched with sweat and my brain reeled sickeningly.

One may get help from queer sources. Van, in our gay junior year—his last at college—had initiated me into a device for keeping steady when the last drink has been one too many. You mentally recite a poem or speech or the multiplication table—any old thing will do. Fixing the mind in that way seems to soothe the gyrating interior and enables a fellow at least to fall asleep like a gentleman.

In my present distress that came back to me. Still fighting off the unknown with one-half of my mind, I scrabbled around in the other half for some definite memorization to take hold of.

There was none. The very multiplication table swam a jumble of numbers. Then I caught a rhyme beginning in the back of my head, and fixed my attention on it feverishly. Over and over the words said themselves, first haltingly, then with increasing certainty. It was a simple, jingling little prayer that every child in the English-speaking world, I suppose, has learned past forgetfulness. "Now I lay me down to Sleep—"

Again—again—by the tenth repetition of "I pray the Lord my soul to take," I had wrenched my mind away from—that other—and had its whole attention on the rhyme. At last, following a paroxysm of trembling, I knew myself the victor. Once more the Fifth Presence had released me.

Panting and weak from reaction, I sat up. What ailed me? How, in reason and common sense, could the sound of any man's name have this effect on me?

Hypnotism? Nearly two months had elapsed since my first trouble of this kind, and without recurrence in the interim. No, and come to think of it, I couldn't recall having heard the name spoken in that while, either.! It was only when uttered aloud that the word had power over me. I could think of it without any evil effect. And that name on Alicia's lips had been my last vivid impression before I lost self-consciousness and walked out of, Moore's house, an intelligent automaton for sixty minutes after.

Scraps of psychology came back to me. Hypnotism—hypnotic suggestion. Could a man be shocked into hypnotic sleep, awaken, and weeks later be swayed by a sound that had accompanied the first lapse?

One way, I set myself very firmly. In cool judgment I was no believer in ghosts. The very thought brought a smile to my lips. My uncle had died before I was born; but, though dad had for some reason disliked him, by all accounts my namesake had been a genial, easy-going, agreeable gentleman, rather characterless, perhaps, and inclined to let the other fellow work, but not a man whose spirit could be imagined as a half-way efficient "haunt."

! No, and neither would he probably have flung away his own and his family's comfort for a point of fine-drawn honor. Was dad in the right? I had tried to reserve criticism there, and in action I had certainly backed him to the limit. Inevitably, though from yet far-off, I could see the loss of Roberta grinding down upon me. She couldn't wait my convenience forever, you know. Some other fellow-some free, unburdened chap—

I buried my head in my hands.

Then I dropped them and sprang erect, every nerve alert.

I had closed my eyes, and in that instant, a face had leaped into being behind their shut lids. The face was not Roberta's, though I had been thinking of her. Moreover, it had lacked any dreamlike quality. It had come real—real as if the man had entered my bedroom and thrust his face close to mine.

As my eyes flicked open, it had vanished, leaving me quivering with a strange resentment—an anger, as if some intimate privacy had been invaded. I stood with clenched fists, more angry than amazed at first, but not daring to shut my eyes lest it return.

What had there been about the queer vision that was so loathsome?

The face of a man around forty years it had seemed, smooth-shaven, boyish in a manner, with a little inward twist at the mouth corners, an amused slyness to the clear, light-blue eyes, The face of an easygoing, take-life's-jokes-as-they-come sort of fellow, amiable, pleasant, and, in some indefinite fashion—horrible.

I was sure I had never seen the man in real life, though there had been a vague familiarity about him, too.

About him! A dream—a vision.

"Clayton Barbour," I muttered through shut teeth, "if it has reached the point where a word throws you into spasm and you are afraid to close your eyes, you'd better consult a doctor; and that is exactly what I shall do!"

VI

Nils Berquist has his own ways, and whether or not they were practical or customary to mankind at large influenced him in no degree. He called himself a socialist, but in pure fact he was simply one of those persons who require a cause to fight for and argue about, as a Hedonist craves his pleasures, or the average man an income.

Real socialism, with the communal interests it implies, was foreign to Berquist's very nature. He could get along, in a withdrawn kind of way, with almost anyone. He would share what small possessions he had with literally anyone. But his interest went to such abstractions of thought as were talked and written by men of his own kind, while himself—his mind—he kept for the very few. Those are the qualities of an aristocrat, not a socialist.

One result of his paradoxical attitude showed in the fact that when it came to current news, Nils was as ignorant a man as you could meet in a day's walk. My various troubles and activities had kept me from thinking of him, but when I again happened on Nils in town one evening it hurt my feelings to discover that the spectacular downfall of Barbour & Hutchinson might have occurred on another planet, so far as he was concerned.

News that had been blazoned in every paper was news to him all this time afterward. Even learning it from me in person, he said little, though this silence might have been caused by embarrassment. Roberta was with me, and to tie Nils' tongue you had only to lead him into the presence of femininity in the person of a young, pretty girl.

I at last recalled the fact, and because for a certain reason I wished a chance to talk with him where he would talk, I asked if he couldn't run out some night and have dinner with us. Cathy's cooking was nothing wonderful, but I knew Nils wouldn't mind that, nor the cramped quarters we had to live in. I reckoned on taking him up to my own room later for a private confab.

After a short hesitation he accepted.

"You take care of yourself, Clay," he added. "You're looking pale—run down. Don't tell me you've been laid up sick along with all this other trouble?"

"No, indeed, old man. Working rather harder than I used to and—lately I haven't slept very well. Bad dreams—but aside from that, nothing serious."

After a few more words, we parted, he striding off on his lonely way to some bourne unknown; Roberta and I proceeding toward the movies.

A fortnight had passed since the strange face had made its first appearance. If Nils thought I looked pale, there was reason for it. "Bad dreams," I had told him, but bad dreams were less than all.

My resolve to visit a doctor had come to nothing. I had called, indeed, upon our family physician, as I had meant. The moment I entered his presence, however, that instinct for concealment which had prevented me from confiding in Roberta or my family rose up full strength. The symptoms I actually laid before Dr. Lloyd produced a smile and a prescription that might as well have been the traditional bread pills. I didn't bother to have it filled. I went out as alone with my secret as when I entered.

A face—boyish in manner, pleasant, half-smiling usually; with an amused slyness to the clear, light-blue eyes; an agreeable inward quirk at the corners of the finely cut lips. I had come to know every lineament ultimately well.

It had not returned again until some time after the first appearance. Then—at the bank, the afternoon following my futile conference with Dr. Lloyd—I happened to close my eyes, and it was there, behind the lids.

There was a table in Mr. Terne's office, over which he used to spread out his correspondence and papers. I was seated at one side of the table and he on the other, and I started so violently that he dropped his pen and made a straggling ink-feather across the schedule of securities he was verifying.

He patiently blotted it, and I made such a fuss over getting out the ink-eradicator and restoring the sheet of minutely figured ledger paper to neatness, that he forgot to ask what had made me jump in the first place.

After that the face was with me so often that if I shut my eyes and saw nothing, its absence bothered me. I would feel then that the face had got behind me, perhaps, and acquired the bad habit of casting furtive glances over my shoulder.

You may think that if one must be burdened with a companion invisible to the world, such a good-humored countenance as I have described would be the least disagreeable. But that was not so.

There was to me a subtle hatefulness about it—like a thing beautiful and at the same time vile, which one hates in fear of coming to love it.

I never called the face "him," never thought of it as a man, nor gave it a man's name. I was afraid to! As if recognition would lend the vision power, I called it the Fifth Presence, and hated it.

As days of this passed, there came a time when the face began trying to talk to me. There, at least, I had the advantage. Though I could see the lips move, forming words, by merely opening my eyes I was able to banish it, and so avoid learning what it wished to say.

In bed, I used to lie with my eyes wide open sometimes, for hours, waiting for sleep to come suddenly. When that happened I was safe, for though my dreams were often bad, the face never invaded them.

I discovered, too, that the name had in a measure lost power to throw me off balance, since the face had come. My mother continued to harp on the superiority of my dead uncle's character, and how he would have shielded us from the evils that had befallen, until dad acquiesced in sheer self-protection. But though I didn't like to hear her talk of him, and though the sound of the name invariably quickened my heartbeat, hearing neither increased nor diminished the vision's vividness.

It was with me, however, through most of my waking hours—waiting behind my lids—and if I looked pale, as Nils said, the wonder is that I was able to appear at all as usual. So I wished to talk with Nils, hoping that to the man who had warned me against the Moores, I could force myself to confide the distressing aftermath of my visit at the "dead-alive house."

He had promised to come out the next night but one, which was Wednesday. Unfortunately, however, I missed seeing him then, after all, and because of an incident whose climax was to give the Fifth Presence a new and unexpected significance.

About two-thirty Wednesday afternoon I ran up the steps of the Colossus Trust, and at the top collided squarely with Van, Jr. By the slight reel with which he staggered against a pillar and caught hold of it, I knew that Van had been hitting the high spots again and hoped he had not been interviewing his father in that condition. On recovering his balance, Van stood up steady enough.

"Old scout Clay! Say, you look like a pale, pallid, piffling freshwater clam, you do. 'Pon my word, I'm ashamed of the old Colossus. The old brass idol has sucked all the blood out of you. My fault, serving up the best friend I ever had as a—a helpless sacrifice to my father's old brass Colossus. Come on with me—you been good too long!"

He playfully pretended to tear off the brass-lettered name of the trust company, which adorned the wall beside him, cast it down and trample on it. When I tried to pass he caught my arm. "Come on!"

"Can't," I explained quietly. "Mr. Terne was the best man at a wedding today, but he left me a stack of work."

Van sniffed. "Hub! I know that wedding. I was invited to that wedding, but I wouldn't go. Measly old teetotaler wedding! Just suits Fatty Terne. When you get married, Clay, I'll send along about eleven magnums for a wedding present, and then I'll come to your wedding!"

"You may—when it happens." Again I tried to pass him.

"Wait a minute. You poor, pallid work slave—you know what I'm going to do for you?"

"Get me fired, by present prospects. I must—"

"You must not. Just listen. You know Barney Finn'"

"Not personally. Let me go now, Van and I'll see you later."

"Barney Finn," he persisted doggedly, "has got just the biggest li'l engine that ever slid round a track. Now you wait a minute. Barney's another friend of mine. Told me all about it. Showed it to me. Showed me how it's going to make every other wagon at Fairview tomorrow look like a hand-pushed per-perambulator!"

"All right. Come around after the race and tell me how Finn made out. Please—"

"Wait. You're my friend, Clay, and I like you. You put a thousand bones on Finney's car, and say goodbye to old Colossus."

I laughed. But he went on.

"My dear friend, you misjudge me, sadly—yes, indeed! Didn't I wrest one pitiful Century from Colossus five minutes ago, and isn't that the last that stood between me and starvation, and ain't I going right out and plaster that century on Finn's car? Would I im-impoverish the Colossus and me, puttin' that last century on anything but a sure win? Come across, boy!"

Now, one might think that Van's invitation lacked attractiveness to a sober man. I happened to know, however, that drunk or sober, his judgment was good on one subject, the same being motorcars. Barney Finn, moreover, was a speed-track veteran with a mighty reputation at his back. He had, in the previous year, met several defeats, due to bad luck, in my opinion, but they had brought up the odds. If he had something particularly good and new in his car for tomorrow's race at

Fairview, there was a chance for somebody to make a killing, as Van said. "What odds?" I queried.

"For each li'l bone you plant, twelve li'l bones will blossom. Good enough? I could get better, but this will be off Jackie Rosenblatt, an' you know that he's a reg'lar old Colossus his own self. Solid an' square. Hock his old high silk hat before he'd welch."

"Yes, Rosie's square." I did some quick mental figurine, and then pulled a thin sheaf of bills from an inner coat pocket. Instantly, Van had snatched them out of my hand.

"Not all!" I exclaimed sharply. "Take fifty, but I brought that to deposit—"

"Deposit it with Jackie! Why, you old miser with your bank account! Four entire centuries, and you weepin' over poverty! Say, Clay, how much is twelve times four?"

"Forty-eight, but—"

"Lightnin' calculator!" he admired. "Say, doesn't forty-eight hundred make a bigger noise in your delikite ear than four measly centuries? Come across!"

I don't think I nodded. I am almost sure that I had begun reaching my hand to take all, or most of those bills back. But Van thought otherwise. "Right, boy!"

With plunging abruptness he was off down the steps. I hesitated. Forty-four hundred. Then I caught myself and was after him, but too late. His speedy gray roadster was already nosing recklessly into the traffic. Before I reached the bottom step it had shot around the corner and was gone.

Off Mr. Terne's spacious office there was a little glass-enclosed, six-by-eight cubbyhole which I called my own.

Ten o'clock Thursday morning found me seated in the one chair, staring at a pile of canceled notes on the desk before me. I had started to check them half an hour ago, but so far just one checkmark showed on the list beside them. I had something worse to think of than canceled notes.

As I sat, I could hear Mr. Terne fussing about the outer office. Then I heard him go out. About two minutes afterward the door banged open so forcibly that I half started up, conscience clamoring.

But it wasn't the second vice returning in a rage. It was Van. He fairly bolted into my cubbyhole, closed the door, pitched his hat in a corner, and swung himself to a seat on my desk-edge, scattering canceled notes right and left. There he sat, hands clasped, staring at me in a perfect stillness which contrasted dramatically with his violent entry. His eyes looked dark and sunken in a strained, white face. My nerves were inappreciative of drama.

"Where were you last night?" I demanded irritably. "I hunted for you around town till nearly midnight."

"What? Oh, I was way out in—I don't know exactly. Some dinky roadhouse. I pretty nearly missed the race and—and I wish to Heaven I had, Clay!" He passed a shaking hand across his eyes.

"Did Finn lose?" I snapped. "But—why, the race can hardly be more than started yet!"

"Finn started!" he gulped.

"Ditched?" I gasped, a flash of inspiration warning me of what was coming.

He nodded. "Turned turtle on the second lap and—say, boy—I helped dig him out and carry him off—you know, I liked Barney. It was—bad. The mechanism broke his back clean—flung against a post—but Barney—say, what was left of him kind of—kind of came apart—when we—" He stopped short, gulped again, and: "Guess I'm in bad shape this morning," he said huskily. "Nerves all shot to pieces."

I should have imagined they would be. A man straight from an all-night debauch can't witness a racing-car accident, help handle the human wreckage afterward, and go whistling merrily to tell his friends the tale.

I expressed that, though in more kindly chosen words, and then we both were silent a minute. Barney Finn had not been my friend, or even acquaintance, and while I was vicariously touched by Van's grief and horror, my own dilemma wasn't simplified by this news. Yet I hated to fling sordidness in the face of tragedy by speaking of money.

"Afterward I didn't feel like watching the race out." As Van spoke, I heard the outer door open again. This time it really was Mr. Terne, for I recognized his step.

"So I came straight here," Van continued.

My own door opened, and a kindly, dignified figure appeared there.

"Barbour," said the second vice, "have you that—ah, good morning, Richard." He nodded rather coldly to Van, and went on to ask me for the list I was supposed to be at work on.

When I explained that the checking wasn't quite finished, he turned away; then glanced back.

"By the way, Barbour," he said, "Prang dropped me a line saying that when you were in his office yesterday he paid up our hundred he has owed me since last June. If you were too late to deposit yesterday afternoon, get it from my box and we'll put it in with this check from the United."

I felt myself going fiery-red. "Sorry," I said. "I'll let you have that money this afternoon, Mr. Terne, I-I—"

"He gave it to me to deposit for him, and I used it for something else," broke in Van with the utmost coolness.

On occasion Van's brain worked with flashlight rapidity. He had put two and two of that four hundred together while another man might have been wondering about it. Terne stared, first at Van, then at me.

"You—you gave it—" he began slowly.

"He came here for your pass-book," ran Van's glib tongue. "I dropped in on him, and as I was going out past the tellers, I offered to put it in for him. Then I stuck it in my pocket, forgot it till too late, and needing some cash last night, I used that. Barbour has been throwing fits ever since I told him. I'll get it for you this afternoon."

Terne stared some more, and Van returned the look with cool insolence.

A brick-reddish color crept up the second v.p. 's cheeks, his mouth compressed to an unfamiliar straightness, and turning suddenly he walked out of not only my cubbyhole but his own office. The door shut with a rattle of jarred glazing.

"You shouldn't have done that!" I breathed.

"Oh, rats! Fatty Terne's gone to tell the old man. But he'll get thrown out. No news to the old man, about me, and he's sick of hearing it. Anyway, this is my fault, Clay' and I ought to stand the gaff. You've worked like the devil here, and then I come along and spoil everything. Drunken fool, me! Knew I'd queer you if we got together, and till yesterday I had sense enough to keep off. When I took those bills I knew there was something wrong, but I was too lit up to have any sense about it. Plain highway robbery! Never mind, old pal, I'll bring you back the loot this afternoon if I have to bust open one of the old Colossus' vaults for it!"

At my elbow the office phone jingled.

"Just a minute," I said. "No; wait, Van. Hello. Hel—Oh, Mr. Vansittart? Yes, sir. Be over at once, sir. Yes, he's here. What? Yes—" The other receiver had clicked up.

"We're in for it," I muttered. "Apparently your father hasn't thrown Terne out!"

Vansittart, Sr., the gruff old lion, granted lax discipline to no man under his control save one; and even Van, Jr., was, if not afraid, at least a bit wary of him. Though he had taken me on in the bank at a far higher wage than my services were worth, he had also made it very clear that so far as I was concerned, favoritism ended there. For me, I was sure the truth of the present affair would mean instant discharge.

"Shut the door!" he growled as we entered. "Now, Dick, I'll thank you to explain for exactly what reason you stole Mr. Terne's four hundred."

"Stole!" Van's slim figure stiffened and he went two shades whiter.

"Stole, yes! I said, stole. That is the usual term for appropriating money without the owner's consent."

"I don't accuse the boy of theft!" Terne's set face of anger relaxed suddenly. He didn't like Van, but he was a man who could not be unfair if he tried.

"Keep out of this, Terne—please. Dick, I'm waiting."

"Well, really," Van drawled "if you put it that way, I couldn't say what I did use the money for. There was a trifle of four hundred, owned, I believe, by Mr. Terne, which I borrowed, intending to return it in a few hours—"

"From what fund?" The old man was alert. I felt instinctively that this interview was a bit different from any that Van had been through heretofore. "Are you aware that your account in this bank is already overdrawn to the sum of—" he consulted a slip before him—"of forty-nine dollars and sixty cents? You perhaps have reserve funds at your command elsewhere?"

Van looked his father in the eye. What he saw must have been unusual. His brows went up slightly and the same fighting look came into his face which I had seen there when he and I confronted the faculty together. On that occasion I had been genuinely inclined to meekness. I remained in college while Van was thrown out.

He laughed lightly. "Excuse me half an hour while I run out and sell the li'l old roadster. Forty-nine sixty, you said? I'll pay you yours first, dad!"

"That's kind! After stealing one man's money you propose selling another man's car to replace it. Yes, my car, I said. What have you got in this world but your worthless brains and body to call your own? Wait. We'll go into this matter of ownership more deeply in a few minutes.

Barbour," he whirled on me, "you allowed funds belonging to your supervisor to pass into unauthorized hands. That is not done in this bank. As things stand, I shall leave your case to Mr. Terne, but first you will make one direct' statement. I wish it made so that no question can arise afterward. Did you or did you not hand four hundred dollars in bills, the property of Mr. Terne, to my—to my son?"

It was up to me in earnest. I was now sure beyond doubt of what Van had run against. His parent had turned at last, and even the whole truth would barely suffice to save him. My lips opened. To blame though he was in a way, Van mustn't suffer seriously in my protection. I could not forget that momentary hesitation on my part, save for which I could easily have retrieved the bills before Van was out of reach.

"I gave it to him," I began.

And then, abruptly, silently, another face flashed in between me and the president. Instead of Vansittart's dark, angry eyes, I was staring into a pair of clear, amused, light-blue, ones. A finely cut mouth half smiled at me with lips that moved.

Always theretofore the face had come only when my lids were closed. Its wish to communicate with me—and that it did wish to communicate I was sure as if the thing had been a living man, following me about and perpetually tugging at my sleeve—had been a continual menace, but one which I had grown to feel secure from because the thing's power seemed so limited.

Now, with my eyes wide open, there hung the face in mid air. It was not in the least transparent. That is, its intervening presence obscured Vansittart's countenance as completely as though the head of a real man had thrust in between us. And yet—it is hard to express, but there was that about it, a kind of flatness, a lack of normal three-dimensional solidity, which gave it the look of a living portrait projected on the atmosphere.

I knew without even glancing toward them that Van and Mr. Terne did not see the thing as I did. It was there for me alone. At the moment, though I fought the belief again later, I knew beyond question that what I beheld was the projection of a powerful, external will, the same which, with Alicia's dynamic force to aid, had once actually taken possession of my body.

The finely cut, lips moved. No audible sound came from them, but as they formed words, the speech was heard in my brain distinctly as if conveyed by normal sound vibrations through the eardrums. It was silent sound. The tone was deep, rather agreeable, amiably amused:

"You have said enough," the face observed pleasantly. "You have told the truth; now stop there. Your friend has a father to deal with, while you have an employer. He is willing to shoulder all the blame, and for you to expose your share in it will be a preposterous folly. Remember, that hard as you have worked, you are receiving here twice the money you are worth—three times what you can hope to begin on elsewhere. Remember the miserable consequences of your own father's needless sacrifices. Remember how often, and very justly, you have wished that he had thought less of a point of fine-drawn honor, and more of his family's happiness. Will you commit like folly?"

I can't tell, so that anyone will understand, what a wave of accumulated memories and secret revolts against fate overswept me as I stared hard into the smiling, light-blue eyes. But I fought.

Grimly I began again. "I gave it to him. . ." and then—stopped.

"That's enough." This time it was Vansittart speaking. "You may go, Barbour. Mr. Terne, I will ask you to leave us. You will receive my personal check for the amount you have lost."

"But-but—" I stammered desperate while those clear eyes grew more amused more dominating.

The old man's hard-held calmness broke in a roar. "Get out! Both of you! Go!"

Mr. Terne laid his hand on my arm, and reluctantly I allowed myself to be steered toward the door. As I turned away the face did not float around with the turning of my eyes.

It hung in mid air, save for that odd, undimensional flatness real as any of the three other faces there. When my back was to the president, the—the Fifth Presence was behind me. On glancing back, it still hung there. Then it smiled at me—a beautiful, pleased, wholly approving smile—and faded to nothing.

I went out with Mr. Terne, and left Van alone with his father.

VII

One hour later I departed from the Colossus Trust Company with instructions not to return. Oh, no, I had not been ruthlessly discharged by the outraged vice president. The inhibition covered the balance of the day only, and, as Mr. Terne put it: "A few hours' quiet will give you a clearer view of the situation, Barbour. I honor you for feeling as you do. It was Richard, I believe, who obtained you a position here. Just for your consolation when Mr. Vansittart has—er—cooled off somewhat, I intend making a small plea in Richard's behalf. Now, go home and come back fresh in the morning. You look as though all the cares of the world had been dumped on your shoulders. Take an older man's advice and shake off those that aren't yours, boy!"

He was a kindly, good man, the second vice president of the Colossus. But his kindliness didn't console me. In fact, I felt rather the worse for it. I went home, wishing that he had kicked me clean around the block instead of—of liking, and petting, and by inference, praising me for being such a contrast in character to poor, reckless, loose-living, heroic Van!

When I left, the latter was still in his father's office. Though I might have waited for him outside, I didn't. He was not the kind to meet me with even a glance of reproach; but just the same I did not feel eager to meet him.

I had resolved, however, that unless Van pulled through scatheless, I would myself "make a small plea in Richard's behalf," and next time not all the smooth, smiling devils from the place-that's-no-longer-believed-in should persuade me to crumple.

On the train—I commuted, of course—I deliberately shut my eyes, and waited for the vision to appear. If it could talk to me by moving its lips, there must be some way in which I could express my opinion to it. I burned to do that. Like a sneak, it had taken me unawares in a crucial moment. I had a few thoughts of the Fifth Presence which should make even that smug vision curl up and die.

I closed my eyes—and was asleep in five minutes. I was tired, you see, and, now that I wanted it, the Fifth Presence kept discreetly invisible. The conductor, who knew me, called my station and me at the same time, and I blundered off the train, half-awake, but thoroughly miserable.

There was no one at home but my mother. Of late dad's sight had failed till it was not safe for him to be on the street alone. As he liked to walk, however, Cathy had gone out with him.

I found mother lying down in her darkened bedroom, in the preparatory stage of a headache. Having explained that Mr. Terne had given me an unexpected half-holiday, I turned to leave her, but checked on a sudden impulse.

"Mother," I said softly, "why did you name me Ser—why was I given my uncle's name instead of just dad's?"

"What an odd question"

Mother sat up so energetically that two cushions fell off the couch. I picked them up and tried to reestablish her comfortably, but she wouldn't have it. "Tell me at once why you asked that extraordinary question, Clay!"

I said there was nothing extraordinary about it that I could see. My uncle's name itself was extraordinary, or at least unusual, and the question happened to come into my mind just then. Besides, she had spoken a good deal of him lately. Maybe that had made me think of it.

Mother drew a deep breath.

"He told me—can you believe this?—he told me that some day you would ask that question! This is too wonderful! And I've seemed to feel a protecting influence about us—this house that was his—and your good position at the bank!"

"Mother, will you kindly explain what you are talking about?" My heart had begun a muffled throbbing.

"Be patient! I have a wonderful story to tell you. I've doubted, and hoped, and dared say nothing, but, Clayton, dear, in these last miserable weeks I have felt his presence like the overshadowing wings of a protecting angel. If it is true—if it only could be true—"

"Mother—please!"

"Sit down, dear. Your father never liked dear, and—why, how wonderful this all is! Your coming home early, I mean, and asking me the question just at the one time when your father, who disliked him, is away, and we have the whole house—his house!—to ourselves. Can't you feel his influence in that, dear?"

"What have you to tell me, mother?"

"I shall begin at the very first—"

"If you make the story too long," I objected craftily, "dad and Cathy will be back."

"That is true. Then I'll just tell the part he particularly wished you to know. Dear was universally loved, and I could go on by the hour about his friendships, and the faculty he had for making people happy. Physically, he had little strength, and your father was very unjust to him—"

"Can't we leave dad out of this, mother?"

"You are so like your uncle! could never bear to hear anyone criticized, no matter how the person had treated him, 'My happiness,' he would say, 'is in living at harmony with all. Clayton,' your father, he meant, of course, 'Clayton is a splendid man, whom I admire. His own fine energy and capacities make him unduly hard, perhaps, toward those less gifted. I try to console myself with the thought that life has several sides. Love—kindliness—good humor—I am at least fortunate in rousing the gentlest qualities in most of those about me. Who knows? From the beginning, that may have been my mission in life, and I was given a delicate constitution that I might have leisure merely to live, love, and be loved in return!'

"Of course, he wouldn't have expressed that beautiful thought to everyone, but knew that I would understand—yes, dear I shall come to your part in the story directly.

" passed to his reward before you were born, my son. He went from as us in January, and you came into the world the April following. The doctors had told him that only a few hours were left him of life. When Serapion learned that he asked to be left alone with me for a little while. I remember every word of that beautiful conversation. I remember how he laid his hand on mine and pressed it feebly.

"'Do as I ask, Evelyn,' he said. 'If the child is a boy, give him my name. I only ask second place. Clayton has first right; but let the boy have my name, as well as his father's. I've been too happy in my life— too happy in my loves and friendships. I can't bear to die utterly out of this good old world. I haven't a child of my own, but if you'd just give your boy—my name. Some day he will ask why, and then you are to tell him that—it's because—I was so happy."

Mother was sobbing, but after a moment she regained self-control to continue. "You may think it weak in me to cry over my brother, who passed long ago. But he has lived in my memory. And he said: 'Some people only talk of life after death, but I believe in it. It is really true that we go out to go on. I know it. There is something bright and strong in me, Evelyn, that only grows stronger as I feel the body dying from about me. Bright, strong, and clear-sighted. I have never been quite like other men. Not even you have understood me, and perhaps that is for the best.'

"With his hand on mine he smiled, and, oh, Clayton, I have wondered many times since what that smile meant. It was so beautiful that—that it was almost terrible!

"'I love life,' he went on, 'and I shall live beyond this perishing clay. Soon or late, a day will come when you will feel my living presence in the house, and it will be in that time that your son will ask of me. Then you will tell him all I have said, and also this:

"'That I promised to return—to watch over him—to guard him.

"'Name him for me, that I may have the power. There's power in a name! And I am not as other men. Be very sure that—your son—shall be—as happy—shall have all that I've had—of life. Believe—promise!' And I promised.

"The strangest look came into his eyes. A look of—" my mother's voice sank to a hushed whisper—"I can only describe it as holy Exultation. It was too vivid and triumphant to have been of this world. And he died in my arms—Clayton, why do you look at me like that? What is the matter, child?"

"Nothing. You told the story so well that for a moment I seemed to—to see him—or Something. Never mind me. Mother, haven't you any picture of my uncle?"

"Only one of him as he was in his latter years. I have kept it locked away, for fear it might be destroyed or injured." Mother rose and started looking in a bureau drawer. "I am so glad that you take this seriously, Clayton, you feel nearly as deeply about it as I, don't you, dear?"

I wished to see that picture. At the same time I dreaded unspeakably the moment when doubt might become certainty.

My mother took out a flat package, wrapped in yellowed tissue paper. She began to undo the silk cord tied around it. I turned my back suddenly. Then I felt something thrust into my hand. With all my will I forced myself to bring the thing around before my eyes.

What face would stare back at me, eye to eye, amused, pleasant—?

The window-shades were still drawn, and the light dim. It was a moment before I realized that what I held was not a picture at all—but some kind of printed pamphlet.

"Raise the shade," said my mother. "I wish you to read that. It is a little memorial of your uncle, written by one of his friends, a Mr. Hazlett.

The words are so touching! Almost as beautiful as the thoughts himself often expressed."

"Would you mind"—I controlled my voice by an effort—"would you mind letting me see the picture first?"

This time she had handed me the unmistakable, polished, bescrolled oblong of an old-fashioned photographer's mounting.

Defiance, last resource of the hard pressed, drove me in two bold strides to the window, where I jerked the shade up.

Daylight beat in. This was the middle of November and the light was gray, filtered through gray clouds. A few scattered particles of snow flickered past the window.

In my fingers the polished face of a cardboard mount felt smooth, almost soft to the touch. I watched the snow.

"Isn't his face beautiful, dear?" demanded a voice at my shoulder.

"I-I—yes, I'm afraid—of course, mother!"

"But you are not looking at it!"

"I did look," I lied. "I—this has all been a little too much for me. Take it—put it away. No, I'll read the memorial another time. Happy! Did he promise to—to come back and make me happy?"

"Practically that. How like him you are, dear son! He was sensitive, too; and your eyes! You have the Barbour nose and forehead, but your eyes—"

"Please, mother!"

She let me go at last, and in the quiet of refuge behind the locked door of my bedroom, I, who after all had not dared to look upon the picture of, scrutinized thoroughly every feature of my own face in the mirror.

Like him! She had often said so in the past, but the statement had failed to make any particular impression.

Yes, she was right about the eyes. They were the same clear, light blue as his—what? Never. Not as his. For all I knew by actual observation, 's eyes might have been sea-green or shell-pink. I had never seen him. Let me keep that fact firmly in mind.

VIII

My Face in the mirror bore a faint sketchy resemblance to that of the unreal but none the less troublesome vision by which I was intermittently afflicted. The resemblance accounted for the vague familiarity that had enveloped it from the first.

The face in the mirror, though, was much younger, and resolve flared up in its eyes like a lighted fire.

"You," I addressed my reflection, "are not a sneak. You are not going to be made one. Tonight you will present yourself to Mr. James Barton Moore, and you will inform him that the little trick of hypnotism performed by his wife last August will either be reversed by her, or he himself will pay for it unpleasantly. I believe," and my arm muscles flexed in bravado, "that Mr. Jimmy Moore will think twice before he refuses." That was what I said. But in my heart I yearned suddenly to go and fling myself, abject, at the feet of Alicia Moore, and entreat her to help me.

It was a cold night, and the afternoon's scattered flakes had increased to a snowfall. Alighting from the car—not mine, this time, but the transit company's—I found the snow inches deep. I can still recall the feel of it blown against my face, like light, cold finger-touches.

Plowing through it, I came again to the "dead-alive house." That other visit had been in summer. The twin lawns, one green and close-cropped, the other high-grown with weeds, had stood out contrastingly then. There had been a line of sharp demarcation between Moore's clean, freshly painted half of the house and the other half's dirt-freckled wall.

Now all that sharp difference was blurred and indistinct. The snow, blue-white in the swaying circles of light from a corner arc lamp, had buried both the lawns. Joining the roofs in whiteness, drifting across the porches, swirling in the air, it obliterated all but a hint of difference between the living half and the dead.

Though the windows of one part were dark as those of the other, a faint glow shone through the curtained glazing of Moore's door.

Now that I was here, I almost hoped that he and his wife were out. The accusation I must make was strange to absurdity. I braced myself, however, opened the gate, and as I did so a hand dropped on my shoulder from behind.

A man had come upon me soundlessly through the snow. In my nerve-racked state, I whirled and struck at him.

He caught my wrist. "Here! I'm no highwayman, Clay!"

"Nils," I laughed shakily, "you startled me."

Berquist stared, with a sudden close attention that I found myself shrinking from. For weeks I had been keeping a secret at some cost. Though I had come here to reveal it, the habit of concealment was still on me.

"Your nerves used to be better than that," said Berquist shortly.

"You calling on Moore?" I queried. "Thought there was some kind of vendetta between you. You wouldn't come here with me, I remember."

"I'm glad you remember something," he retorted gravely. "You have a very nice, hospitable family, though. They took me in last night and fed me on the bare strength of my word that I'd been invited."

"I say, Nils, that's too bad."

In the desperate search I had made for Van the previous evening, I had clean forgotten my dinner invitation to Berquist. Reaching home near midnight, I had received a thoroughly sisterly call-down from Cathy, who had waited up to express her frank opinion of a brother who not only invited a friend to dinner without forewarning her, but neglected even to be present when that friend arrived.

It seemed, too, that Roberta had dined there on Cathy's own invitation, and the two girls had unitedly agreed that poor Nils was "odd" and not very desirable. He had committed the double offense of talking wild theories to dad, verbally ignoring the feminine element, and at the same time staring Bert out of countenance whenever her eyes were not actually on him.

I had informed Cathy that Bert should feel highly honored, since Nils was generally too shy even to look at a girl, much less stare at her, and that as the family's support I should certainly invite whom I pleased to dinner; as for Nils, I had regretted missing him; but knew he was too casual himself to hold the lapse against me.

Now I began an apology that was rather wandering, for my mind was otherwise concerned.

I wished to tell him about the Fifth Presence. Before I entered Moore's house, it would be very well that I should tell Nils of my errand. Why, in the name all reason, was I possessed by this sense of shame that shut my lips whenever I tried to open them concerning the haunting face?

Cutting the apologies short, Nils forgave me, explained that though out of sympathy with Moore's work, he occasionally called to play chess with him, and then we were going up the snow-blanketed walk, side by side.

Even the chess sometimes ends in "a row," Nils added gloomily. "I wouldn't play him at all, if he hadn't beaten me so many times. Perhaps some day I'll get the score even, and then I shan't come here any more."

"Moore is—did he ever tell you that I kept my appointment with him?"

"Which one?"

The question leaped out cuttingly sharp.

"The only one I ever made with him, of course. That day you introduced me to him in the restaurant."

"You haven't been coming here since?"

"No. Why should you think that?"

We had checked again, half-way up the walk. As we stood Nils caught my shoulders and swung me around till the arc-lamp rays beat on my face. He scrutinized me from under frowning brows.

"You've lost something!" he said bluntly. "I can't tell exactly what. I don't know what story your eyes hide; but they hide one. Clay, don't think me an officious meddler, but you—you have your family dependent on you—and—oh, why do I beat about the bush? That girl you will marry some day; she's rather wonderful. For her sake, if not your own, tell me the truth. Has Moore involved you in some of his cursed, dangerous experiments? Tell me, is it that, or"—his voice softened—"are you merely worn out with the common and comparatively safe kinds of trouble?"

"I've had—trouble enough to worry any fellow."

"Yes, but is any part of it to be laid at this door?" He jerked his head toward Moore's dimly radiant portal.

"A face—a face—" sheer panic choked words in my throat. I had begun betraying the secret which every atom of my being demanded should be kept.

"Yes; a face."

"A face—is not necessarily a chart of the owner's doings," I wrenched roughly from his grasp. "Since when have you set up as a critic in physiognomy, Nils?"

"When one has a friend, one cares to look beneath the surface," he said simply.

"Well, don't look with the air of hunting out a criminal, then. I have as good a right to call here as you, haven't I? Moore sent me a letter asking me to drop around, so I—I thought I would. I'm tired, and need distraction. What's the harm?"

Without answering, he eyed me through a long moment; then turned quietly and went on up into the porch.

Standing hesitant, I glanced upward, looking for a light in the windows above. Again. I saw the slanting roofs, blended in snow. Months ago, in a momentary illusion of moonlight, I had seen them look just so. The thought brought me a tiny prick of apprehension. Not fear, but the startled uneasiness one might feel at coming to a place one has never visited, and knowing it for the place one has seen in a dream.

Nevertheless, I followed Nils to the door.

Another maid opened it than the one who had admitted Roberta and myself in August. She was a great, craggy, hard-faced old colored woman, whom Nils addressed rather familiarly as "Sabina," and who made him rather glumly welcome in accents that betrayed her Southern origin. She assumed, I suppose, that Nils and I had come together, and my card did not precede me into Moore's sanctum.

The latter was in the library again. The shades and curtains were drawn tight which accounted for the "not-at-home" look of the windows from outside. I learned later that he frequently denied himself to callers, even near acquaintances, unless they came by appointment. His letter to me had been ignored too long to come under that heading. I wonder! Would he have refused to see me that night, given a choice?

In my very first step across the library's threshold, I realized that my battle was to be an even more difficult one than I had feared.

Passing the doorway I entered—physically and consciously entered— the same field of tension, to call it that, which had centralized about Alicia at the climax of my previous experience.

It was less masterful than then. There was not the same drain on my physical strength, nor the feeling of being in harmony with the movements of others. But the condition was none the less present; I knew it as surely and actually as one recognizes a marked change in atmospheric temperature or, to use a closer simile, as one feels entry into the radius of electrical force produced by a certain type of powerful generator.

There are no words which will exactly express what I mean. The consciousness involved is other than normal, and only a person who had been possessed by it could fully understand.

On that first occasion, I had been sure that my impressions were shared by the others present. This time some minutes passed before I became convinced that Berquist and James Moore, at least, were insensitive to the condition.

The library appeared as I had seen it first, save that the lamp broken then had been replaced by another, with a Japanese "art" shade made of painted silk. Near the large reading-table, with the lamp, a small stand had been drawn up and a chessboard laid on it. In anticipation of Nils' arrival Moore had been arranging the pieces. They were red and white ivory men, finely carved. They and the Japanese lampshade made a glow of exotic color, in the shadow behind which sat—Alicia, a dim figure, pallid and immobile.

By one of those surface thoughts that flash across moments of intensity, I noted that Moore was dressed in a gray suit, patterned with a faint, large check in lighter gray.

Then Moore had recognized me, and the man's pale eyebrows lifted.

"You've brought Barbour?" he said to Nils.

"No," denied my friend. "Met him at the door. How do, Alicia?"

He strode across the room to where Mrs. Moore sat in the shadow.

Under other conditions I should have felt embarrassed. By Moore's tone and Nils' non-committal response, they placed me as an intruder, received without even a gloss of welcome for courtesy's sake.

But to me it seemed only strange that they could speak at all in ordinary tones through this atmosphere of breathless tension. A voice here, I thought, should be either a shriek or a whisper.

Then Alicia's dry monotone.

"You should have come alone, Nils. You have brought one with you who is very evil. I know him. He is an eater of lives."

"Dear lady!" protested Nils, half jokingly. "Surely you don't apply that cannibalistic description to my friend here? He might take it that way."

"How he takes it is nothing," shrugged Alicia. "There are four of us here, and there is also a fifth. And I think your friend is more aware of that than even I."

Moore's previously unenthusiastic face lighted to quick eagerness. He pounced on Alicia's original phrase like a cat jumping for a mouse.

"An eater of life! Did you say this invisible Fifth Presence is an 'eater of life,' Alicia?"

"I did not," she retorted precisely. "I said an eater of lives. Everyone does not know that—"

"No, but wait, Alicia. This is really interesting." He turned from her to us. "There's a particularly horrid old German legend about such a being." He informed us of it with the air of one imparting some delightful news. "Give me a German legend always for pure horror, but this excels the average. *Der verschlingener des Lebeng*—'The Devourer of Life.' Very interesting. Now the question arises, did Alicia read that yarn some time in the past, and is this the subliminal report of it coming out, or does she really sense an alien force which has entered the room in your company? What's your impression, Barbour? Have you any? You're psychic yourself—knew it the first time I saw you. Is anyone here but we four?"

By a great effort, I forced my lips to answer:

"I couldn't say. This—I—"

"Have a chair, Barbour, and take your time." He was all sudden kindliness the active sort, with a motive behind it, as I knew well enough now. To him I was not a guest but an experiment. "I haven't a doubt," he asserted cheerfully, "that you and Alicia sense a presence that entered with you and which such poor moles as Nils and myself are blind to. Now don't deny it. Anyone possessing the psychic gift who denies or tries to smother it is not only unwise but selfish. Supremely selfish. And it's a curious fact that one powerful psychic will often bring out the undeveloped potentialities in another. Alicia may have already done that for you. When you were here before—"

"That will do!" Abruptly deserting Alicia, Nils strode down upon us. There was wrath in every line of his dark face. "Jimmy, that boy is my friend! If he has 'Psychic potentialities,' as you call it, let 'em alone. He doesn't wish to develop into a ghost-ridden, hysterical, semi-human monstrosity, with one foot in this world and the other across the border."

"Really," drawled Moore, "that description runs beyond even the insolence I've learned to expect from you, Berquist. My wife is a psychic."

Nils was not too easily crushed, but this time he had brought confusion on himself. "Ghost-ridden, hysterical, semi-human monstrosity" may have been an excellent description of Alicia. It is certain, however, that Nils-had forgotten her when he voiced it. He flushed to the ears and stammered through an apology, to which Moore listened in grim silence.

Then Alicia spoke, with her customary dry directness.

"I am not offended. My guides do not like you, Nils, but that is because your opposition interferes with the work. Personally I like you for speaking frankly always. Take your unfortunate young friend, Mr. Barbour, and go away now.'

"Alicia!" Moore was half pleading, half-indignant. "You agreed with me that Barbour had possibilities of mediumship almost as great as your own. And yet you send him away. Think of the work."

"I tried to send him away the first time." From beyond the lamp Alicia's enormous eyes glinted mockingly at her husband. "You believed," she went on, "that Mr. Barbour was naturally psychic, but undeveloped. Many times, we have disagreed in similar cases. Your theory that more than half the human race might, properly trained, be sensitive to the etheric vibrations of astral and spiritual beings is true enough."

"Then why did you—"

"Don't argue, James. That tires me. I say that your belief is correct. But I have told you and, through me, my guides have told you that not everyone who is a natural sensitive is worthy of being developed."

"I consulted you"—Moore's voice trembled with suppressed irritation—"I consulted you, and you—"

"I said that a tremendous psychic possibility enveloped Mr. Barbour. That was true. Had I told you that the possibility was evil, that would have been equally true. But you would not have yielded to my judgment, and sent him away—as I tried to do."

"Alicia," cried her husband, "are we never to have any clear understandings?"

"Possibly not," she said, with cool indifference. "I am—what I am. Also I am a channel for all forces, good or evil. My guides protect me, of course. They will not let any bad spirit harm me. But I think Mr. Barbour was not glad that he stayed when I wished him to go. He has come back to me for help. I am not sure that I wish to help him. It was a long time before I was rested from my first struggle with the One he is afraid of."

Nils made an impatient movement. "I don't believe Clay needs any help except—pardon me, Alicia—except to keep away from this house and you."

"Then why did he return here?"

"Because," interpolated Moore, with a scowl for Nils, "he grew interested in his own possibilities. This attempt to frighten him is not only absurd, but the worst thing possible for him. Of course the invisible forces are of different kinds, and of course some of them are inimical. But fear is the only dangerous weapon they have. If they can't frighten you, they can't harm you."

"Alicia," cut in Nils, "seems to disagree there."

"Alicia does agree. She inclines to repel the so-called evil beings, not from fear of them, but because they are more apt to trespass than the friendlier powers. They demand too much of her strength. In consequence, I have had an insufficient opportunity to study them. If Barbour is psychic—and I should say that he very obviously is—then his strength, combined with Alicia's, should be great enough for almost any strain. You are interfering here, Berquist. I won't have it. I—will—not—have—it."

"And my friend is to be sacrificed so that you may study demonology?"

"Berquist, I have nothing to do with demons or daevas, devils or flibbertigibbets. You use the nomenclature of a past age."

"*Verschlingener des Lebens*," quoted Nils quickly. "You didn't boggle over nomenclature when Alicia warned us that an 'eater of life' was present."

"Oh, give me patience!" groaned Moore. "I try to trace a reference, and you—" He broke off and wheeled to the small, shadowy figure beyond the lamplight. "Alicia, exactly what did you mean when you said that an 'eater of lives' had entered the room? You can put us straight there, at least."

"I meant," drawled Alicia, "one of those quaint, harmless beings whom you are so anxious to study at anybody's expense. Not a demon, certainly, in the sense that Nils means. But not company I care for, either. No, I am not afraid of this one. He has the strength of an enormous greed—of a dead spirit who covets life—but he will not trap me again into lending my strength to his purpose.

"His! Whose? Do be plain for once, Alicia."

"I try to be," she retorted composedly. "I could give him a name that one of you at least would recognize. But that would please him too well. There is power in a name. Everyone does not know that, nor how to use it. This one does. He bears his name written across his forehead. He wills that I shall see it and speak it now. Once he surprised me into speaking it, but that was Mr. Barbour's fault. He threw me off balance at a critical moment by turning on the lights. You have probably forgotten the name I spoke then, but I doubt if Mr. Barbour has forgotten. This one whom I refuse to name has no power over me. I have many friends among the living dead who protect me from such dead spirits as this one—"

"Just a minute, Alicia!" Moore was exaggeratedly patient. "I can believe in a dead body, and through you I've come to believe in live spirits, disembodied. But a dead spirit! That would be like an extinguished flame. It would have no existence."

She shook her head. "Please don't argue, James, You know that tires me. A spirit cannot perish. But a spirit may die, and having died, exist in death eternal. There is life eternal and there is death eternal. There are the living spirits of the so-called dead. They are many, and harmless. My guides are of their number. Also there are dead spirits. They are the ones to beware of, because they covet life. Such a one is he whom I called 'an eater of lives,' and who is better known to Mr. Barbour than to me. That is not my fault, however, and now I wish no more to do with any of it. I must insist, James, that you ask Mr. Barbour to leave. In fact, if he remains in the house five minutes longer I shall go out of it."

Her strange eyes opened suddenly till a gleam of white was plainly visible all around the wide blackness of them. Her porcelain, doll-like placidity vanished in an instant.

"Make him go!" she cried. "I tell you, there is an evil in this room which is accumulating force every moment. I tell you, something bad is coming. Bad! Do you hear me? And I won't be involved in it. I won't! I won't!"

Her voice rose to a querulous shriek. A spasm twitched every feature. And then she had sunk back in her chair with drooped lids.

"Bad!" she murmured softly.

IX

You will have to go, Barbour," said Moore heavily. "I am sorry, but there are occasions when Alicia must be humored. This seems to be one of them. Unfortunate. Very—unfortunate. Perhaps another time—"

He paused and glanced suggestively toward the door.

All the while that they had argued and quarreled over me, I had sat as apparently passive as the clay figure to which I had once compared Alicia. It was, however, the passivity not of inertia, but of high-keyed endurance. What Alicia felt I don't know. If it was anything like the strain I suffered under, I can't wonder that she wished to be rid of me.

"Another time," said Moore, and looked toward the door.

I rose. Instantly Berquist was beside me. He took my arm—tried to draw me away—out of the room.

I shook him off. When I moved it was toward Alicia. Before either Moore or Nils realized my objective, I was halfway around the table. Alicia, her eyes still closed, moaned softly. She cried out, and thrust forth her hands in a resisting motion:

"Stop!"

That was Moore's voice; but it was not for his sharp command that I halted. There was—it was as if a wall had risen between Alicia and me. Or as, if her out-stretched hands were against my chest, holding me back. Yet there was a space of at least two yards between us.

"What do you want, Barbour?" demanded' Moore roughly. "I said you would have to go!"

"I wish," I forced out, "to make her undo what she has done to me!"

"Then I was right!" cried Berquist indignantly.

I stood still, swept by wave upon wave of the force that willed to absorb me. The past weeks had trained me for such a struggle. Though the face of the Fifth Presence remained invisible, its identity with the intangible power I fought was clear enough to me—and I hated the face! I repulsed the enveloping consciousness of it as one strives to fling off a loathsome caress.

While I stood there, blind, silent, at war, Berquist continued:

"Now I know that I was right! Jimmy, you have let this boy suffer in some way that I neither understand nor wish wholly to understand. But believe me, you'll answer for it. Clay, lad, come away. You are courting disaster here. Alicia can't help you. She is a poor slave and tool for any force that would use her. Why, the very atmosphere of this house is contagious. Psychic. Many people are immune. Moore is immune. But I tell you, there has been more than one time when I have resolutely shut my senses against the influence, or Alicia would have dragged me into her own field of abnormal and accursed perceptiveness. It's because I resist that they won't have me at a seance. Come away!"

"No!" They could not guess, of course that I spoke from out a swimming darkness, slashed with streaks of scarlet. "No!" I muttered again. "This woman here—she can help me. She shall help me! Moore, I'll wring your neck if you don't make her help me."

Through the swimming scarlet-slashed gloom I drove forward another step. Came a rush of motion. There was a vast, muffled sound as of beating wings. A trumpet-like, voice cried out loudly: "I'll settle with you once for all!" it shouted. And then something had thrust in between Alicia and me.

Instantly the gloom lifted.

There at my right hand was the large table, with the shaded lamp and the boots and papers strewn over it. To my left the massive, empty chair in which Alicia was wont to be imprisoned during a seance.

Beyond that hung the straight, black folds of the curtains which concealed the cabinet.

Though I turned my head to neither side, I saw all these things as though looking directly at them. And also, with even more unusual distinctness, I saw what was straight ahead of me.

Between me and Alicia the figure of a man had sprung into sudden existence. In no way did this figure suggest the ghostly form one might expect from what is called "materialization." The man was real—solid.

He was of stocky, but not very powerful build. He was dressed in gray. His face—ah! Only once before had I seen this man's face with open gaze. But many times it had haunted my closed lids!

Smooth, boyish, pleasant, with smiling lips and clear, light-blue eyes—my own eyes, save that the amused gleam in them did not express a boy's unsophisticated humor.

Not a bodiless face this time, afloat in mid-air or lurking behind my lids. This was the man himself—the whole, solid, flesh-and-blood man!

I could not doubt that he was real. His hand caught my arm—roughly for all that amiable gentleness the face expressed. I felt the clutching fingers tight and heavy. He clutched and at the same time smiled, sweetly, amusedly. Clutched and smiled.

　　　　　　　　　　　　　　　　FRANCIS STEVENS

"!" I whispered. And "Serapion!"

His smile grew a trifle brighter. His clutch tightened. But I was no longer afraid of him. The very strain I had been under flung me suddenly to a height of exalted courage. Instinctive loathing climaxed in rebellion.

He clasped my left arm tight. My right was free. I had no weapon, but caught up from the table a thing that served as one.

And even as I did it, that clear side vision I have referred to beheld a singular happening. As my head grew hot with a rush of exultant blood, something came flying out through the curtains of the cabinet.

It was bright scarlet in color, and about the size of a pigeon or small hawk. I am not sure that it had the shape of a bird. The size and the peculiarly brilliant scarlet of it are all I am sure of.

This red thing flashed out of the cabinet, darted across the room, passing chest-high through the narrow space between the suddenly— embodied Fifth Presence and myself and vanished.

I heard Alicia crying: "Bad—bad! It has come!"

And then, in all the young strength of my right arm, I struck at the Fifth Presence. My aim was the face I hated. The weapon—a queer enough one, but efficient, sank deep, deep-buried half its length in one of those smiling, light-blue eyes.

He let go my arm and dashed his hand to his face. The weapon remained in the wound. From around it, even before my victim fell, blood gushed out—scarlet—scarlet. Below the edge of his clutching hand that would clutch me no more I could see his mouth, and— Heaven help me!—the lips of it smiled—still.

Then he had writhed and crumpled down in a loose gray heap at my feet.

"Barbour! For mercy's sake!"

The man I struck had sunk without a sound. That hoarse, harsh shout came from Nils. Next instant his powerful arm sent me spinning half across the room. I didn't care. He dropped to his knees. When he tried to straighten the gray heap, his hands were instantly bright with the grim color that had been the flying scarlet things.

But I didn't care!

I had killed him—it! The Fifth Presence had dared embody itself in flesh and I had slain it!

Nils had the body straight now, face upward. The light of the lamp beat down. Creeping tiptoe, I came to peer over Nils' shoulder. The lips. Did they still smile?

Then—

But there is an extremity of feeling with which words are inadequate to deal. Leave my emotions and let me state here bare facts.

The gray suit in which I had seen the Fifth Presence clothed was the same faintly checked light suit I had wondered at Moore's wearing in November.

And the face there in the lamplight, contorted, ashen, blood-smeared, was the face of James Barton Moore!

Though I had a few obscure after memories of loud talking, of blue uniforms that crowded in around me, of going downstairs and out into open air, of being pushed into a clumsy vehicle of some kind, and of interminable riding through a night cold and sharply white with snow, all the real consciousness of me hovered in a timeless, spaceless agony, whereby it could neither reason nor take right account of these impressions.

Thrust in a cell at last, I must have lain down and, from pure weariness of pain, fallen asleep. Shortly after dawn, however, I awoke to a dreary, clear-headed cognizance of facts. I knew I had killed.

When I threatened, Moore had sprung in between me and his wife, intending, no doubt with that hot temper of his, to put me violently from the house. His physical intervention had stocked me out of the shadows, then rapidly closing in, and the Fifth Presence had chosen that opportunity for its most ghastly trick.

The face I had struck at was a wraith—a vision. My weapon—one of those paper files that are made with a heavy bronze base and an upright, murderously sharp-pointed rod—had gone home in the real face behind. Instead of slaying an embodied ghost—a madman's dream—I had murdered a living man!

Last night the killing and the atrocious manner of it had been enough. This morning, thought had a wider scope. I perceived that the isolated horror of the act itself was less than all. I must now take up the heavy burden of consequences.

The hard bed on which I lay, the narrow walls and the bars that encompassed me—these were symbols by which I foreread my fate.

I, Clayton Barbour, was a murderer. In that gray, early clear-headedness I made no bones about the word or fact.

True, I had been tricked, trapped into murder; but who would believe that? Alicia—perhaps. And how would Alicia's weird testimony be received in a court of justice, even should she prove willing to give it?

FRANCIS STEVENS

I perceived that I was finished—done for. Life as I was familiar with it had already ended, and the short, ugly course that remained to be run would end soon enough.

Then for the first time I learned what the love of life is. Life—not as consciousness, nor a state of being, nor a thought; but the warm, precious thing we are born to and carry lightly till the time of its loss is upon us.

Afterward? What were dim afterwards to me? Grant that I, of all men, had reason to know that the dying body cast forth its spirit as a persistent entity. Grant that the shadow of ourselves survived the flesh. That was not life!

Let me grow old in life, till its vital flood ran low, and its blood thinned, and its flesh shriveled, and weariness came to release me from desire, Then, perhaps, I should be glad of that leap into the cold world of shadows. Now—now—I was young.

The injustice of it! I sprang up, driven to express revolt in action. For lack of a better outlet, I beat with closed fists against the wall—the bars. A lumpish, besotted creature in the cell next to mine roused and snarled like a beast at the noise.

Presently one of the keepers came tramping along the narrow alley between wall and cages.

I had retreated a little from the bars. I was not sure how this warder would look at me, a murderer. My new character was strange to me. Instinctively I shrank from being seen in it.

He peered through.

"C'm here!" he hissed softly. Puzzled, I moved nearer. "Take this!"

Then I saw that through one of the square apertures of cross-grating a folded bit of paper had been thrust. I drew it through to my side, though with no notion of what it could be. The man drew off again.

"I'll see that ya get some coffee, Barbour," he said, in a loud, offhand voice. "Morning, Mike! Early, ain't ya?" He turned to me again. "This here's Mike Megonigle. Slip him a dollar fer me as ya pass out, an' then ya won't owe me nothin'."

A red-faced, bull-necked individual had tramped into view. He stared heavily from my grating to the night warder and back again.

"Is all right, Mike," the latter asserted. "This here's Mr. Barbour. Pal of his croaked a guy last night. Barbour ain't implicated. Just a witness. He'll be getting his bond pretty quick, and when he goes out you collect that dollar for me, Mike. Can't afford to lose that dollar—not me, huh?"

He winked jovially in my direction, waved a hand on one finger of which was something which glittered brightly, and was gone. The other guard grunted, stared after him for a long minute, and moved on up the passage, still speechless and shaking his head in a slow, puzzled manner, like a bewildered ox.

But his bewilderment could not have been so great as my own. The thing that glittered on the night-guard's finger had attracted my attention before he waved it. It was a ring that had a strangely familiar look. The setting was an oval bit of lapis lazuli, cut flat, incised with a tin device the scrolls of which had been filled with gold, and surrounded by small diamonds.

Nils Berquist wore a ring like that. It was the one possession I had ever known him to prize, and that was because it had been in his family for generations. It was very old, and different from modern rings.

A duplicate? Nonsense! Why was that warder wearing Nils' ring—and what had he meant by describing me as a "witness"?

But I think some of the truth had begun to dawn on me even before I unfolded the paper that had been thrust through my grate. The inner side carried a lead-pencil scrawl, written in French. As the light in the cell was bad, and Berquist's handwriting worse, I had more than a little trouble in deciphering it.

I had read it all, however, before the return of the night-warder—that superbly corrupt official who took a bribe to deliver a message, honestly delivered it, and thereafter brazenly wore the bribe about his duties. He returned with some coffee. I was face down on the shelf that served for a bed. He rattled the grate, spoke, and as I didn't answer shoved the coffee under the door and went off—whistling, I fancy.

I couldn't have spoken to him if I had wished, because I was crying like a girl. The reaction from friendless solitude in a world made new and terrible had hit me just that way. It was not that I meant to accept Nils' sacrifice. I had not thought about the practical side of it yet. But to discover that a man who had actually seen me do that awful thing, in spite of it remained my friend and loyal to the amazing degree of taking the burden on himself—that changed the world round again, some way, and made it almost right again.

Why, the mere fact that Nils could think of me without abhorrence was enough! It restored to me all the love and friendship that had been mine and from which last night's deed had seemed to irrevocably cut me off.

If Nils, then those nearer and dearer than Nils—Roberta—But there I halted and cringed back. That way there loomed a dreadful and inevitable loss. Let contemplation of it wait awhile.

With wet eyes I sat up and again held Nils' message in the barred light that fell through the grating. He had protected his meaning by using a safer language than English—safe from the warder, at least—and couching it in terms whose real import would be obscure if it fell into other hands. At that his sacrifice was endangered in the sending, but not so much as by leaving me to blurt out the truth unwarned:

My dear Friend

This to you, who last night were past understanding. May the morning have brought you a clear Mind. I take the chance and write. I killed James Moore. Understand me when I say this. He struck at me, but I wrested away the weapon and killed in self-defense and not in intent.

There followed a rather circumstantial account of his supposed struggle with Moore. Nils' brain had not been numbed last night, like mine. Into this story which he had made for us both to tell he had fitted the least possible fiction. Questioned on details up to almost the moment of Moore's death, we had only to stick to the truth and we could not disagree. It was a clever—a noble lie that he had arranged.

You will bear witness to all this, and they will not convict me of murder. Alicia Moore had fainted. She did not witness Moore's death. I rely on you, therefore, as my sole witness. And it is fortunate that Moore in his anger turned not on you, but attacked me! I know you, dear friend, and that you would take my place—and bear all for me, if that were possible. But I have not one in the world, save you, to suffer the anguish for my trouble. I have little to lose.

Not for your own sake, then, but for the sake of those to whom you are all—for the sake of her whose life-happiness rests with you to hold sacred or shatter, I commend you—to be glad that I and not you have this to go through with. For that I shall not think the less of you. I only ask that in your heart I beheld always as a friend.

Nils Berquist

To accept would be dishonor unthinkable.

Even the weight of the thinly veiled argument he put forward must be outbalanced by the shame of allowing an innocent man to risk the most disgraceful of deaths in my stead. I could not accept, yet though I died, the wonder of Nils Berquist's attempted loyalty should go with me—out there!

Out there! Into that dim, guessed—at coldness, with its shadowy, mocking inhabitants.

"You are right!" said a voice. "That world is to yours as the shadow to reality. But why cast the real life away?"

Had one of the warders entered my cell and addressed me, his voice could have echoed no more distinctly in my brain. Before I looked up, however, I knew what I should see. When, raising my own eyes, they met those clear, light-blue ones, I felt no surprise.

There floated the face, bodiless again, but aside from that with an appearance of substantiality which equaled—it could not exceed—that of its last tragic visitation. The undimensional flatness had given way to the solidly modeled curves of living flesh.

The point of my improvised weapon, however, had left not even a mark on the face it was meant for. That material aspect was false. Though I hated him now with an added loathing, I had learned bitterly that combat with him must be on other than physical ground. I sat sternly quiet, hoping that if I did not answer, the presence would vanish.

"Your violent temper," he continued pleasantly, but with a trace of kindly reproach, "has placed you in danger. Fortunately we—you and I—are not as other men. We need not be overborne. Tell me, which of all the forces that influence life is the strongest?"

"Hate!" Springing erect, I thrust forward till my face almost touched that of the Presence. "Such hate as I feel for you!"

He did not retreat. I could—I could almost have sworn that I felt the warmth of his flesh close to mine!

"Aw-w-w-w-, cut it out!" wailed the dweller in the next cell. "Ain't yer never goin' ter let a guy git his beauty sleep?"

"You need not speak so loud," smiled the face. "And I would suggest that you sit down. Consider the feelings of others! Consideration is a beautiful quality, and well worth cultivating. Speech between you and me need disturb no one. It can be silent as thought, for it is thought— my thought to yours. Sit down!"

A sudden weakening of the knees made me obey him. Revilings I could have withstood; curses, or threats of evil. But there was an awful sweetness and beauty in the face—a calm assurance about his preaching phrases—that frightened me as threats could not have done. Could it be that I had misjudged this serene being from beyond the border?

Then I looked in his eyes and knew that I had not. They were too like my own! I understood them. Another he might have deceived, but never me.

"Hate," he continued, in his placid, leisurely manner, "is a futile, boomerang force that invariably reacts on itself. It is the scorpion among forces, stinging itself to destruction. No; I did not come here to preach. You understand now that I spoke the truth and can read your unvoiced thoughts with perfect readiness. Our conversations are thus safe from eavesdroppers. As I was saying, hate is its own enemy and the enemy of life. There is but one invincible power, offered by God to man, and which God has commanded man to use."

"You mean—"

"Love! Armored in love, your life will be a sacred, guarded joy to you. Believe me! I am far older than I appear, and wiser than I am old. Guided by me, guarded by love, you have a beautiful future at your command."

"Begun with murder!" I snarled.

The Presence beamed patiently upon me. "That was a mistake. Don't blame yourself too severely. Blame me, if you like, though I had no idea that your foolish animosity would bring forth the red impulse of murder. Yes; we who have passed beyond can commit blunders. I made one in appearing when I did. Can't we forgive one another and forget?"

"Not while I am in jail for it and facing electrocution!" said I grimly.

"But you are not. Very shortly you will walk out a free man; under bond, it is true, but only—"

"Never!" I was on my feet again at that. "Let Nils Berquist suffer in my place? Never!"

"But he won't suffer! Or at least, not as you would. Come! Trust all that to me, who can see far, and have a certain power. Won't you trust me?"

"You mean that you can influence a jury to acquit him?"

"I have power. And think. Would you cast back his friendship in his face? Would you hurl your father into his grave, killed by horror? Would you drag your sister—your mother—through the mire of notoriety that surrounds a criminal? Would you leave them destitute? Would you stab through the very heart of the girl who loves you? Your friend has none of these to care. The opprobrium will not hurt him. He is by nature an isolated soul; and moreover, he is innocent. He has that strength, and the glory of sacrifice to sustain him. Once free yourself, you can do much to bring about his release.

"It is well known that Moore had an evil temper. The plea of self-defense will be borne out by you. Engage a clever legal advisor for your friend, and in the end your pitiful mistake will have brought harm to no one except Moore himself, who deserved it. He was a very selfish, disagreeable man! He was not loved by anyone, even his wife. What? Oh, leave Alicia out of it, my dear boy. You won't find our plans upset by her. And now, I should advise that before seekin' bondsman elsewhere, you telephone to the man whose friendship you have already won at the bank. Your immediate superior there is a kindly, good man—"

The presence got no further with his advice. As he had talked, quietly, soothingly, I had found my thoughts beginning to follow the smooth current of his. But his reference to Mr. Terne had been another of those errors to which he claimed even the disembodied were prone. It had recalled to me that scene in the president's office—Van's desperate face—and the ignominy into which I had been betrayed.

Repulsion—loathing—surged mightily through my veins again.

"No! No! No! In the name of Heaven, leave me!" I cried aloud. To my amazed relief the Presence obeyed. He had faded and gone in an instant—though by the last impression I had of him, he still smiled.

Trembling, I looked down at Nils' letter in my hand.

From the barred grating a shadow was cast upon it, and the form of that shadow was a cross.

X

Around 2 P.M. I was taken before Magistrate Patterson and my bail set in the sum of thirty-five hundred dollars. Arthur Terne, second vice president of the Colossus Trust Company, having appeared as my bondsman, the matter of my liberty pending the inquest, to be held the following morning, was soon arranged.

I left the court in Mr. Terne's company. Nils Berquist I had not seen, but was given to understand that he had been remanded without bail. I had pleaded in vain for a chance to talk with him.

Mr. Terne was kindness personified, though I inferred from one or two remarks that the Colossus' president was shocked.

The morning papers had featured the affair with blatant headlines. They had got my name. The Barbour & Hutchinson failure was resurrected.

The Colossus itself stalked in massive dignity across one column, irrelevantly capping a "Brutal Slaying in Haunted House," and when I saw that, I knew that "not pleased" was a mild description for Vansittart's probable emotions!

The bizarre character of Alicia, the nature of the wound, and the ghastly inappropriateness of the weapon which effected it, had appealed to the reportorial fancy with diversely picturesque results. A plain murder, with no more apparent mystery attached than this one, would have passed with slight attention. But though Alicia was not a professional medium, it appeared that she and Moore had a certain reputation.

In hinting to me of the latter's tempestuous exit from the Psychic Research Association, Nils had spared mentioning Alicia as the bone of contention. I now learned that she had been a country girl, the daughter of a hotel-keeper in a tiny Virginian village, where Moore had spent two or three autumn weeks.

Discovering in her what he regarded as supernormal powers, he wished to bring her north for further study. On her father's strangely objecting to this treatment of his daughter as a specimen, Moore had settled the difficulty by offering marriage. After the wedding, he did bring her north, educated her, and finally presented her to the Association as a prodigy well worth their attention.

Unfortunately, after several remarkable seances, she was convicted of fraud in flagrant degree. It was through the slightly heated arguments ensuing that Moore was asked to resign his directorship.

The fantastic dispute had amused the lay-public intermittently through a dull summer, but I was off in the mountains that year with Van, and what news we read was mostly on the sporting pages, whither the pros and cons of spiritualistic debate are not wont to penetrate. But all that was raked up now, as sauce for the news of Moore's sensational death, and having acquired a certain personal interest in spiritualism, I read it.

Following Mr. Terne's advice and my own inclination, I went straight home. No need to rehearse all I endured that day. Roberta's smilingly tearful consolations were the worst, I think, though, my father's: "Clay, son, you are right to stand by your friend!" ran a close second. He said it because I refused to hear a word against Nils, and insisted that the fault had not been his. Though I would not go into the details of what had taken place in Moore's library, I stuck at that one truth, and Dad, at least, who had taken a fancy to Nils the evening he dined at our house, believed me.

Altogether, however, it was a bad afternoon, and that night in my bedroom the face came again. I knew it was he, though the room was dark and I could not see him clearly. He had become so like as that to a material being!

"You have done well!" he began. "But, to make one small criticism, you must learn not to blush so easily. When your father commended your loyalty you reddened and stammered till, if you had not been among friends, suspicion might have been roused."

"My confusion only lasted a moment," I defended. Then I remembered; "You go!"

I said. "What do I want of you and your criticisms or advice? You have brought me enough unhappiness. I am a sneak and a criminal, and all through you!"

"Ingratitude is the only real crime," he retorted sententiously. "Always be grateful, and show it! You have brought unhappiness on yourself, and it is I who point the way out. So far you have followed my advice. Why turn on me now?"

"Liar!" I fairly hissed. "If you can read my thoughts, you know that I have planned otherwise than you would have me. I am doing as Nils wished without regard to you, and not for the sake of myself. And let me tell you this! If there arises the slightest prospect that my friend will not be cleared, I shall confess. Tomorrow will decide it. If things go badly for him at the inquest, my people will have to suffer. The shame and loss he is trying to save them from would be nothing, then, to the shame involved by silence!"

Had the face possessed shoulders, I know he would have shrugged them.

"You are wrong, but we need not discuss that. I tell you in advance that your friend will be held for willful murder. Did you know quite all that I know, you would not hope for a different indictment."

The strings of my heart contracted. I passed a breathless moment of realization. Then: "Tomorrow I confess!" I said firmly.

"Tomorrow you will choose a lawyer for your friend, and begin the work which will surely achieve his release."

"You do not know that. You have admitted that you are capable of mistakes."

"Not in a case of this kind. I possess a wide knowledge of facts which enables me to be very sure that your friend will get his release. I am your unswerving ally. And remember that I have not only wisdom, but some power.

"Oh, you are—leave me!" I cried aloud. "In God's name go!"

The faintly, seen oval of his smooth face faded, though more slowly than in the cell at the station-house.

I heard a soft swish of slippered feet in the hall. Someone rapped lightly and opened my door.

"Clay, dear," said my mother, "did you call? Are you ill?"

"No. I had a bad dream and awoke crying out because of it."

"One can't wonder at that." She came and sat on the edge of my bed. "Such an awful thing for you to be in! Please, dear son, keep to your own class after this. Trouble always comes of mingling with queer Bohemian people who have no standards, or—or morals."

"Nils Berquist has the highest standard of any—man I know!" I was fiercely defensive.

There was a pause of silence. Then in the dark she leaned and kissed my forehead. "You are so like him!" she murmured.

I groaned. "If only that were true!"

"But you are. With those blue, clear eyes of his, that saw only beauty and love. He would never hear a word against a friend."

"Mother! You meant that I am like—"

"'Your uncle, yes. And in some strange way I feel sure that his guarding influence is really about us. Why, when I came into the room just now I had the queerest feeling—as if it were a room in a dream, or—no, I can't convey the feeling in words. But the sense of his presence was in it. I do truly believe that he has returned to guard us in the midst of so much trouble. At least, it would be like him. Dear, faithful, loving, lovable!"

But had my desired obsession, or familiar, or haunting ghost really desired to help, he might have warned me definitely of Sabina Cassel.

Alicia did not appear at the inquest. She was ill and under a physician's care. Her semi-conscious state as reported by him prevented even the taking of a deposition.

I did not, however, stand alone as star witness before the coroner's jury. Sabina Cassel, Mrs. Moore's old colored "Mammy" whom she had brought north with her from Virginia, shared and rather more than shared the honors with me.

They had taken pains that Nils and I should not meet. He was kept rigorously incommunicado till the inquest, no one, save the police and the district attorney, having access to him. At the inquest I caught only a glimpse of him, when he was led out past where I awaited my turn before the jury. Involuntarily I sprang up, only to be caught by a constable's hand, while Nils was hustled out. As he went, he threw me a glance that was a burning, dictatorial command.

I obeyed it. I told the jury exactly that story which Nils' letter had outlined for us both. There was tempered steel in Berquist.

I could be sure that no long-drawn torment of inquisition could make him vary a hairsbreadth from the line he had set for us to follow.

In my testimony, which preceded Sabina's, I explained that Nils had objected to my interest in spiritualism, fostered by a single previous visit to the Moores' place. That he wished me to leave the house with him, and that Alicia also had seemed set against my remaining. That an argument ensued, at the height of which Moore became very angry and excited, shouted: "I'll settle with you, once for all!" and came around the table toward Berquist.

"He grasped Berquist's arm," I said.

"When my friend tried to free himself, Moore snatched the—the file from the table. I saw Berquist seize Moore's wrist. They struggled a moment, and then Moore staggered away—with his hands to his face. Then—he fell down. Berquist called to me, and, no, I had not tried to interfere. It all happened too quickly. There wasn't time. After Berquist wrenched the file from Moore's hand I don't believe he struck at Moore. I think the file was driven into his eye by an accident."

That surmise, of course, was struck from the record; but I had said it, at least, and hoped it impressed the jury.

"Afterward, the—the sight of blood and the suddenness of it all turned me sick—no, my recollections were clear up to that time."

And so forth. It was a straight story. I knew it agreed to a hair with Nils' confession.

What I did not, could not know, was that it varied in one essential detail from an entirely different confession—a confession made by a person whom we had not considered as an even possible eye-witness, and whose very existence I, at least, had forgotten.

Given that a second eyewitness existed, one would have supposed that the disagreement would have been over the slayer's identity. It was not. By a curious trick of fate, Sabina Cassel, Alicia's old colored maid, did undoubtedly see me strike Moore down, and yet, not through such a super-normal illusion as caused me to kill Moore, but in a perfectly natural manner, she had confused Berquist's identity with mine. She related as having been done by Berquist that which had been done by me.

In one detail only did Sabina's testimony conflict with ours, but that was the kind of detail which would hang a man, if its truth were established.

She had seen me—Berquist by her own account—snatch the file from the table and strike Moore, and she had seen me do it on no further provocation than the laying of Moore's hand on my arm.

The Fifth Presence was right when he foretold that Nils would be indicted.

And yet, though things had indeed gone ill for Nils at the inquest, I did not at once carry out my expressed intention and substitute myself for him as defendant.

I didn't wish to die, nor spend years in prison. I wanted to live and have a decent, straight, pleasant future ahead, such as I had been brought up to expect as a right. It seemed to me that just one way lay open. Though Nils was now entirely at my mercy, only his untrammeled acquittal would give me the moral freedom to keep silent. For that a first-class lawyer was an absolute necessity.

Berquist was practically penniless, and the Barbour exchequer in not much better state. Here again, however, friendship came to the fore in a curiously impressive manner. For the sake of an old acquaintance and some ancient friendly claim that my father had on him, none other than Helidore Mark, of Mark, Mark & Orlow, who could have termed himself Mark the famous and not lied.

I remember my fast interview with him after dad had—to me almost incredibly—persuaded him into alliance. My first impression was of a mild-looking, smallish man, with a scrubby mustache. He had hurt the top of his bald head in some way, so that it was crossed with a fair-sized hillock of adhesive plaster. I thought that added to insignificant appearance; but he had the brightest, softly brown eyes I have ever seen, and after the first few minutes I was afraid of him.

I was afraid that I would tell him too much.

My confidence, however, proved not the easily uprooted kind of a common criminal, and for Nils the acquisition of this famous, insignificant looking lawyer gave me the only real hope of assurance I had through those bad days.

"Your friend," Mark had said to me, "is a rather wonderful young man; Barbour. I can't blame you for being troubled. He has the kind of intelligence that would make a legal genius of him, if he had turned his efforts in that direction. A wonderful intelligence—and all lost in a maze of impractical theorizing and the sort of dreams that can't come true so long as men are men, and women are women, Heaven help us all! He shan't go to the chair, nor prison, either. He's my man, my case, and—yes, I'll say my friend, though I don't run to sudden enthusiasm. Leave Berquist to me!"

Evidently, Mark's consultations with his case had not been kept within strictly professional bounds. I smiled involuntarily. I could picture that long dark face of Nils lighting to alert interest as he discovered that Mark was not merely the lawyer who might save him from martyrdom, but also a thinking man. He must have brought out a side of the little man that was kept carefully submerged at ordinary times. I am sure that few people had seen Helidore Mark inclined to dilatory wanderings in philosophy, such as Nils loved.

But I went out with a lighter heart and more optimism than I had carried in some time. Mark, with his "my man, my case, my friend!" had installed a confidence which remained with me all that day.

I had returned to the bank, for though I walked in the Valley of the Shadow, while I could walk I must work.

So Mr. Terne had me back again, and it was a very good thing that I had Mr. Terne to go back to. Not many men would have put up with the abstracted attention my work received, nor patiently picked up the slack of details I let go by me.

His patience had a characteristic reason behind it, which I was sure of from the minute he told me about poor Van.

The latter, it seemed, had really gone the step too far with his father in the affair of Mr. Terne's four hundred. Vansittart, Sr., would let no one speak of his son to him after that day. Everyone in the bank, however, knew that he had quarreled with him, disowned him, and that Van, in a fit of temper, had refused the offer of a last money settlement—a couple of thousand only, it was said—flung out of the Colossus, and walked off, leaving the gray roadster forlorn by the curb.

No one knew where Van had gone after that. He had simply vanished, saying no goodbyes, and taking nothing with him but the clothes he wore.

Mr. Terne felt guilty because it was his complaint which had caused the final rupture. He liked me, anyway, but having, as he believed, ruined Van, he showed an added consideration for me which developed into an almost absurd tenderness for my feelings.

He needed that, if I was to be kept on the tracks at all those days. I was nervous as a cat, and ready to jump at the creak of a door.

Roberta would watch me with wide, troubled eyes, and because a question was in them I would grow irritable and fling off and leave her with almost brutal abruptness. And always she forgave me—till I came near wishing she would forgive less easily.

Cathy resented my new irritability with the merciless justice of a sister; mother endured my anxiety for Nils only because it proved I was like "dear," and dad harped on his pride in me for "standing by" till I really dreaded to go near him.

As for the Fifth Presence, he remained detestably faithful. Several times I explained to him that if Nils were not cleared I intended to confess. When he only continued to smile, I ceased talking to him.

He still came, however, and on the very night before the trial opened, the last thing of which I was conscious, dropping asleep, was his smooth, persuasive, hateful, silent voice. As ever, it was expressing the platitudinous—and always subtly evil—advice to which habit had so accustomed me that it had grown very hard indeed to distinguish his speech from my thoughts!

XI

When a murderer—for I named myself—is called to confront across some feet of court-room the innocent man standing trial in his stead, he needs all his nerve and a bit more to keep steady under the questioning of even a friendly and considerate counsel.

In fact, I was strangely more afraid of Mark than of District Attorney Clemens. I might, however, have spared myself there.

The impaneling of the Jury had been a battle-royal between Mark and Clemens, at which I was not present, but which had roused the newspaper men to gloating anticipation (the real battle to follow).

Then Mark became ill—dropped out!

I could hardly believe it when Orlow, his junior associate, met me on the first day of the trial, and broke the news. A brain tumor caused by the injury.

Had it not been for Mark, I told myself, I would never have let Nils Berquist go to trial. Should I allow it to go on now, with our best hope hors de combat?

The second Mark, Helidore's brother, was in Europe, and Orlow, while brilliant in his fashion, was not a man to impress juries. His genius lay in the hunting out of technical refinements of law, 'ammunition,' as it were, for the batteries which had brought rage to the heart of more than one district attorney.

When he arose presently in court and asked for a delay in proceedings, Clemens' eye lighted. When Mr. Justice Ballington refused the request—a foregone conclusion, because Mark, admittedly, was in too serious a condition for the delay even to be measured—Clemens lowered his head suddenly. It might have been grief for his adversaries' misfortune—or, again, it might not.

Where I sat with other witnesses, I was intensely conscious of an absurd, brilliantly veiled little figure, two chairs behind me.

This was my first glimpse of Alicia, since the night of Berquist's arrest. Though I knew Mark had been granted at least two interviews with her, me she had resolutely refused to receive.

Now I was relieved to find that her nearness brought no return of the supernormal influence I had suffered before in her vicinity.

She sat stiffly upright, and did not glance once in my direction. Perhaps her 'guides' had advised her to don that awful veil of protecting purple for this occasion, or she may have worn it as a tribute to her husband's memory. It certainly gave her a more unusual appearance than would a crape blackness behind which a newly made widow is wont to hide her grief.

At her side towered the large form of Sabina Cassel.

The trial opened.

One Dr. Frick appeared on the stand, and in elaborate incomprehensibility described in surgical terms the wound which had caused Moore's death. I saw him handling a small, hideous object—gesturing with it to show exactly how it had been misused to a deadly purpose.

Then for several minutes I didn't see anything more. Luckily all eyes in the courtroom were on either the doctor or the "murderer." Nobody was watching me.

The doctor's demonstration seemed to prove rather conclusively that my "accident" hypothesis was impossible. The file, he showed, could have been driven into the brain only by a direct blow.

Dr. Frick was allowed to stand down.

In establishing the offense, Clemens saw fit to call Alicia herself.

As her mistress arose, Sabina's massive bulk stirred uneasily, as if she would have followed her to the stand.

At the inquest, the old colored woman's testimony had done more than cause Nils' indictment for murder. It had made a public and very popular jest of Alicia's claim to intercourse with "spirits." But though, in the first flush of excitement over Moore's death, Sabina had betrayed her, the woman was loyal to her mistress. When a murmur that was almost a titter swept the packed audience outside the rail. Sabina shook her head angrily, muttering to herself.

The audience hoped much of Alicia, and its keen humor was not entirely disappointed. No sooner had she appeared than an argument began about her preposterously brilliant veil. The court insisted that it should be raised. Alicia firmly declined to oblige. She had to give in finally, of course, and when that peaked, white face with its strange eyes was exposed, the hydra beyond the rail doubtless felt further rewarded.

The hydra believed her a fraud. They had reason. I, with greater reason, understood and pitied her!

I thought she might break down on the stand. Alicia's character, however, was a complicated affair that set her outside the common run of behavior. To Clemens' questions she replied with sphinx-like impassivity and the precision of a machine.

Her answers only confirmed Nils' story and mine to a certain point, and stopped there. There was not a word of "sprits" nor "guides;" not a hint of any influence more evil than common human passions; not a suggestion, even that she had formed an opinion as to which man, slayer or slain, was the first aggressor. I am sure that a more reserved and non-committal widow than Alicia never took the stand at the trial of her husband's supposed murderer.

"James," she said, "wished Mr. Barbour to remain. Mr. Berquist wished him to leave. They argued. No, I should not have called the argument a quarrel—I did not see Mr. Berquist strike James. While they were talking I lost consciousness of material surroundings. Yes, my loss of consciousness could be called a faint. The argument was not violent enough to frighten me into fainting. Yes, there was a reason for my losing consciousness. I lost consciousness because I felt faint, I was tired. I do that sometimes. Yes, I warned them that something bad was coming. I couldn't say why. I just had that impression. I did not see either James or Mr. Berquist assume a threatening attitude—"

Released at last, she readjusted her purple screen with cold self-possession, and returned to her seat.

It was Sabina Cassel's next turn. Save in appearance, Alicia had not after all come up to public anticipations. In Sabina, however, the hydra was sure of a real treat in store.

Judge Ballington rapped for order. Sabina took her oath with a scowl. Every line of her face expressed resentment.

But she was intelligent. To Clemens' questions, she gave grim, bald replies that offered as little grip as possible to public imagination.

Yes, on the evening in question she had been standing concealed behind the black curtains of "Miss 'Licia's" cabinet, or "box," as Sabina called it. No, "Marse James" did not know she was there. Miss 'Licia and she had "fixed it up" so that one could enter the box from the back. Marse James had the box built with a solid wooden back, like a wardrobe. It stayed that way—for a while.

"Then Marse James he done got onsatisfied. Yas, de sperits did wuhk in de box an' come out ob it, too; but Marse James, he ain't suited yit. He want dem 'sperits shud wuhk all de time! He neber gib mah poh chile no res'!"

And so Alicia, who, according to Sabina, could sometimes but not always command her "sperits," devised a means to satiate Moore's scientific craving for results.

While he was absent in another city, the two conspirators brought in a carpenter. They had the cabinet removed and a doorway cut through the plastered wall into a large closet in the next room. By taking off the cabinet's solid back and hanging it on again, it would just open neatly into the aperture cut to fit it. Alicia kept plenty of gowns hung over the opening in the closet beyond.

Returning, Moore found his solid-backed cabinet apparently as before. From that time, however, the "sperits" were more willing to oblige than formerly.

"*Ab uno disce omnes,*" is invariably applied to the medium or clairvoyant caught in fraud, though translated: "From all fraud, infer all deceit."

The world laughed over the "spiritualistic fake again exposed!" I did not laugh.

Let it be that the hand which Roberta and I had seen was Sabina's gnarled black paw, and that my impression of its unsubstantiality was a self-delusion. Let those strange little twirling flames that had arisen pass as the peculiar "fireworks" I had tried to believe them. Let even the incident of the broken lamp have been a feat of Sabina's—though how her large, clumsy figure could have stolen out past the table and into the room unheard was a puzzle—and the masculine voice wonderful ventriloquism.

Grant all these as deceptions. There had come that to me through Alicia's unwilling agency which had given me a terrible faith in her, that no proof of occasional fraud could dispel.

Clemens' interrogations touched lightly on the object of the door in the cabinet's supposedly solid back, only serving to establish the fact that it was possible for his witness to have been practically in the library unknown to all the room's other occupants save, probably, Alicia.

Then he asked Sabina's story of that night in her own words. She began it grimly:

"Waal, Ah wuz in behin' de cuhtins dat hangs in front ob Miss 'Licia's box. Dem cuhtins is moderate thin. Ah cudn' see all dey is in de room, but Ah suttinly cud see all dat pass in front ob de lamp. Yass, dat whut yoh got in yoh hand am one a dem cuhtins."

Here Clemens checked her, while the "cuhtin," was passed from hand to through the jury-box. Each juryman momentarily draped himself in mourning while he assured himself that it was thin enough to be seen through. Then with solemn nods Exhibit B was restored to the district attorney. Sabina continued.

"Dese yeah germnen, Mistah Buhquis' and Mistah Bahbour, dey come in, and right away de argifyin' stahted. Ah kain't tell all dey, say. Dey use high-falut in', eddicated laniguige what am not familiar toh me, tho' Lawd knows Ah's done hear enuff ob it 'sence Miss 'Licia come norff wif Marse James Mooah.

"Dey argifies an' argifies. Mistah Bahbour, he don't say nuffin' much. But Mistah Buhquis', he specify dey shud bof up'n leave. Miss 'Licia she say mebbe sump'n bad gwine happen purty quick. Marse James, he say: 'Mistah Bahbour, you go; come back 'notha time.' Mistah Bahbour, he say no, he doan wanta go, kaze Miss 'Licia c'n mebbe help him some way. Mistah Buhqus' he go right up in de aih. He specify some hahm done come ob he fren' stayin roun' deah any longah.

"Mistah Buhquis' he am standin' right alongside de big table wif de lamp on it. De lamp am behin' him. I see ebery move he make.

"He done muttah sump'n low. Ah don't rightly know what he say, but it hab a right spiteful, argifyin tone to it.

"'Marse James,' he holler out: 'I fix yoh now foh dat!' an' he rush obah to Mistah Buhquis' an' lay han' on he arm—No, suh; he didn't go foh to do Mistah Buhquis' no hahm. Marse James he hab a way ob talkin' loud an' biggety, but Ah nevab done saw him do no hahm to nobuddy.

"He grab Mistah Buhquis' lef' arm. Mistah Buhquis', he reach out he otha' han' and grab sumpn off de table. Marse James don' do nuthn'. Mistah Buhquis,' he fro back he han' an' hit out wif it real smaht. Marse James leggo de ahm, clap he han's obah he face, an' sorta lets go all obah. He jes' crumble down lak.

"Ah knows dat de bad am happen.

"Ah cuddin' git out dat box easy into de room, kaze dey's a table in it dat reach purty nigh acrost, an' Ah ain't spry to climb ober it. No, suh; Ah didn't thin to shov de table out de way. Ab cain't think ob nuffin' but Miss 'Licia. Ah turns roun' an' gits out de back, kaze Ah wants to git to an mah Miss 'Licia. Ah comes roun' to de hall and goes in de library. Deah is Mistah Buhquis' stannin' obah Marse James, he han's all drippin' blood.

"Ah say: 'Yo' done kill him, ain't yoh?'

"He luks all roun' kinda pitiful lak, an' then he say:

"'Yas, Sabina, Ah kill him! Now go fotch de doctah an' some p'leece!'

"Mistah Buhquis', he am lak lots ob otha high-spirited gernmen. He don't go foh to kill Marse James, but when Marse James tech him in anger, he jes' bleeged foh to do it—Das all right! Ah gotta right to hab mah 'pinion, same as ebryone. Waal, don't put it in de writin' record, den. Ah don' keer whut yoh does. Das jes' mah 'pinion!

"Yas suh. Ah's suah dat it war Mistah Buhquis' grab de file and not Marse James. Wall, Marse James, he stann wif he lef' side to de table. Yas, suh; I cud suah nuff tell which wuz which. Marse James, he ain't so tall by purty nigh a fut high as Mistah Buhquis'. It am de tall man who start' wif de right side ag'in' de table who take de file off'n it. No; Marse James don' try ter do nuffin hurtful to Mistah Buhquis'. No; dey don' struggle roun' none atall. Dey jes' stan' deah. Its de Lawd's truf, dat was de mos' onexcitin' killin' Ah hab evah saw!"

And then Clemens let her go, to the deep disgust of Hydra, outside the rail. He had not asked what she was doing in the cabinet, nor many other of the questions which gave an amusing double interest to the Moore murder. All that, however, was bound to come out in the cross-examination, and, meantime, Sabina had proved "Clemens' witness" to an extent which made the case promise well of interest on its tragic side.

I was not called before the jury until after the noon recess, which gave me time to think things over a bit more.

At the inquest, I had not actually heard Sabina's testimony. Though Mark, who interviewed her as well as her mistress, had warned me that she would prove a difficult antagonist, I had not fully believed him. She had seemed ill-educated, the type whose average run are diffuse in their statements and easily muddled into self-contradiction.

Sabina might prove so under cross-examination, but I doubted it now. She had wasted hardly a word that morning, and there was only one point on which I was sure that she could be shaken.

The difference in height between slayer and slain was a strong point for the prosecution. Even through thin, black curtains it would indeed have been hard to confuse a tall silhouette with a short one. But no one had thought to question the identity of the tall silhouette.

Though Sabina may have known better during the minutes that she stood staring through the curtains, her after and more vivid sight of Berquist, hands "dropping blood," and his almost instant claim of the crime as his own, had served to make the tall man Berquist in all her memories.

Berquist, the self-confessed!

I had no faith in Orlow. Had Mark not dropped out, I should have been content to let the trial take its course, sure that his genius would somehow save the day and free my friend. But under Orlow's handling, with that craggy, sullen, assured black woman to swear that Moore was not and could not have been the aggressor—since he stood with his left side to the table, grasping the tall silhouette with his right hand, and a man under impulse of passion is not likely to reach for a weapon with his left—I was morally certain that Berquist would lose out.

But what if, rising on the stand, instead of a second perjury I told the simple truth?

Not that portion of it which included the superhuman, but just the fact that I, and not Berquist, had been swept by one of those sudden fits of red anger that have made murderers of many before me?

Why, Sabina herself would support my words, once spoken! There was a little, unnoticed twist in her testimony—a point where the voice of Berquist, coming from beyond the table, became the voice of the tall man standing on her side of the lamp.

The instant that I spoke she would know. Her memories, unconsciously readjusted to fit facts as she had afterward learned them, would be straight again. Berquist's hidden heroism would stand revealed, and I, though I died, I would at least die clean.

Resolve crystallized suddenly within me. When Clemens called me to the stand I would go, not to testify, but to confess.

I walked to the little raised platform, with the chair where the others had sat, below the double tier of jurymen. I mounted it. Somebody put a dusty black book under my hand and mumbled through a slurred rigmarole, to which my low acquiescence was a prelude to ruin for me. I sat down in the chair.

Beyond the rail was a packed level of faces. They were all pale and dreary looking, it seemed to me, though that may have been an effect of light, for the day was gray and dreary. I had returned to court through falling snow. It was a wet, late spring fall of clinging flakes, and all the way I had been haunted by a memory of the "dead-alive" house as I had seen it that night.

Not the interior—not even the library, with its master, a grim gray and scarlet horror on the floor. But the house itself, desolate under its white burden, with the great flakes swirling down, hiding deeper and more deep the line of division between the living hall and the dead.

Berquist was sitting by a table with Orlow beside him. I had visited him in prison, of course, and talked with him a few moments just before the trial opened. His determination and courage had never swerved, nor his conviction that we had only to keep steady and win.

Now I saw his eyes as a dark and valiant glory fixed on me. Their message only hardened my resolve. That man to play the martyr for my sake? Never!

Orlow left Nils, and took his stand conveniently near. He was there to protect me from irrelevant questions, but he looked quite out of place. Clearly, the mantle of Helidore Mark did not rest easily on his shoulders.

The district attorney, a thin, scholarly person whom I instinctively disliked, began his inquisition.

"Your name, please? Age and occupation?"

"Barbour—Clayton S. Barbour," I corrected myself. "I am—"

"Just a moment. Your full name for the record, please, Mr. Barbour."

Clemens, who would reserve any attempt to "rattle" me for my appearance in the rebuttal, was politeness itself.

"Clayton—Barbour!" I forced out. Then I cursed myself for not having substituted "Samuel," or left out the initial.

"There's power in a name." Once I would have laughed at that statement, but not now. Not with my recent memories.

And as God is my witness, I sat there and saw the district attorney's hatchet-face change, blend, grow smooth and loathsomely pleasant.

Clemens continued his interrogations, but I spoke to another than he when I answered them.

The living bound by the dead!

XII

Mr. C. S. Barbour

Sir: I am writing to you because my guides advise it. Otherwise I should not do so. I have returned to my old home in Virginia. The newspapers were very cruel to me, as you know, and everyone unkind and harsh and disbelieving.

James understood me. If he had found out about the cabinet, he would have been annoyed, but he would only have taken more pains after that to see that all the phenomena were genuine. I can't help doing such things. It is a part of my nature. James said I was very complex.

In a measure, it is your fault that he left me. I am not vengeful, however, and I do not hold it against you, because I can very well guess at what you had to contend with. For some cause that has not yet been revealed to me—some cause within yourself, I fear—you were and still are peculiarly open to the attack of *one we know of.*

Were yours an ordinary case of obsession, I might have helped. As it is, I can only offer warning. Whatever there is in you that answers to him, choke it—crush it back—give it no headway. Above all, do not obey him. If, as I suspect, you have obeyed in the past, cease now. It is not yet too late. But if June 9 finds you under his domination you will never be free again.

You may wonder why I was silent at the trial. You may have thought that I was ignorant of the truth. This is not so, though I did not even tell Sabina. To bring the greater criminal to justice was impossible. For the rest, it was between you and your friend.

Understand, I will not interfere between you and your friend.

My guides say that this is not for me to do. That I must not. That if one of you wills to sacrifice and the other to accept; not even God will interfere between you.

But I write particularly to give this message.

Mortal life is cheap, and mortal death an illusion. Beyond and deeper are Life and Death eternal. Be careful which you choose.

Alicia Moore

XIII

P lain life and death are the only realities. Life eternal—death eternal! For you and me, those are words, my boy—just words!"

It was dusk in my room. I sat on the edge of the bed, chin in hands, staring at the inevitable companion of my solitude. At my feet lay the scattered sheets of Alicia's letter, scrawled over in a large, childish hand. The outside world was bright with an afterglow of the departed sun. But gray dusk was in my room.

"Just words," repeated the face.

"Just words," I said after him dully. Then, at a thought, I roused a trifle. "He won't go through with it. Even Nils Berquist can't be willing to die without a protest—and for such a crawling puppy as would let him do it."

"He will die, but not entirely for your sake," the presence retorted.

"What do you mean?"

"You haven't guessed? Well, it is rather amusing from one viewpoint. Your friend is not only in jail; he's in love!"

"Nils? Nonsense! Besides, if he were in love he would wish to live, not die!"

"That is the amusing part. He is willing to die, because of the love."

"Some woman refused him, you mean?"

"No; the girl is not even aware of his feeling toward her. She would, I think, be shocked at the very thought. He has only spoken with her twice in his life. But from the first moment that he saw her face he has loved her. He has sat in the courtroom and watched her while the lawyers fought over his life, and to his peculiar nature—rather an amusingly peculiar nature, from our viewpoint—merely watching her so has seemed a privilege beyond price. He is willing to die, not for you, but to buy her happiness."

"Who is this girl?" I asked hoarsely, and speaking aloud as I still sometimes did with him.

"You should know."

"Nils Berquist—in love—with Roberta?" I said slowly. "But that's absurd. You are lying!"

"No. Every day, as you know, she was in that audience beyond the rail. For your sake. Because she knew how you cared for this man Berquist. She herself has a shrinking horror of the 'red-handed murderer,' but her devotion to you has served our purpose well. That first mere glimpse he had of her on the street—the hour at dinner in your house—these impressions might have somewhat paled in the stress of confronting so disgraceful a form of death. But in the courtroom he watched her face for hours every day, and each day bound our dear poet and dreamer tighter."

"But—"

"He measures her love for you by his own for her. As you are his friend still, uncondemned and worthy, he will buy your life for her."

"He loves her—and would have her marry a murderer?"

"He believes as you have told him, and truly enough, that you were thrown off balance by some influence connected with Alicia and did not know what you, were doing. But it is rather amusing, as I said. He loves the girl for the goodness and purity of her beauty, and for her newly born sadness. You have tired of her for the same reasons, and plan to break the engagement. But he needn't know that, eh?"

"Liar! I shall marry Roberta."

"When? Never! No; you are entirely right. She is not the wife for you. With my help you can easily attract a better. I know at least one woman among your mother's friends who is already devoted to you, and who has means to make not only you but your whole family happy and comfortable. I mean the blond widow, who owns the big house next to your old home. What is her name? Marcia Baird. Yes; she is the woman I refer to. Oh, I knew she's over thirty, but think what she could give you. As for the girl, she knows your circumstances. Her love is selfish, or she would have released you before this."

"You are lying, as you have lied in the past."

"What have I said that proved untrue?"

"You have lied from the first. There was poor old Van. You said that his father would forgive him, and he didn't."

"Be fair. You misquote. I said that Van would not be ruined. With the enthusiastic despair of youth, he played hobo for a while. Then he went to work at the one thing be understood. He is a very industrious mechanic now in an automobile factory with good chances of a foremanship, and—except for grease—living cleaner than he ever did before. He was going the straight down road, but his sacrifice for you pulled him up. You will hear from him shortly. He doesn't bear you any grudge."

"You promised to be my ally; to use your power as an influence to help."

"I kept the promise. Has the least slur of suspicion fallen upon you? Is not every one your friend? Is there a man or woman living who hates or despises you? Are you not shielded and sheltered by the mantle of love, as I foretold?"

"But you promised that Nils would be acquitted."

"Not acquitted. I said released. For such a spirit as his, this world is a prison. In real life, such as you and I prize, there is no contentment for him. Death will release him to that higher sphere where the idealist finds perfection, and the dreamer his dreams. Believe me, Nils Berquist could never be happy on earth. In speeding his departure, we are really his benefactors—you and I."

The face beamed as though in serene joy for the good we had done together; but I hid my head in my arms, groaning for the shame of us both.

June 9 was coming. June 9.

XIV

My Dear Clayton

Mother has told me of your talk with her. I am glad to learn that your views coincide with my own, as I have felt for some time that it would be best for me to release you from our engagement. Your ring and some gifts I return by the messenger who carries this. I am leaving shortly on a visit to friends of mother's in the South, so we shall not meet again soon. Wishing you the best of fortune in all ways, I remain.

Very truly yours,
Roberta Ellsworth Whitingfield

June 5

My Own Dearest—Here and Hereafter

Mother didn't understand as I do. She made me write the letter that goes with this. She is very proud, and that you should be the one who wished to break our engagement shamed her. She even believed a gossip that you have been paying court to Mrs. Marcia Baird on the sly. I had to laugh a little. Imagine it! If I could picture you as disloyal, I could never, I'm sure, picture you making love to that poor, dear, sentimental, rich Mrs. Baird, who is old enough to be the mother of us both. Well, maybe not quite that, but awfully old. Thirty-five, anyway.

But mother half believed it, and to please her I wrote that cold, hard letter that goes with this.

I'm not proud a bit, dearest. I have to tell you that I understand. You are burdened to the breaking-point; but it is I whom you wish to free, not yourself. Dearest, I don't want that kind of freedom. Love is sacrifice. Don't you know that I could wait for you a lifetime, if needs be? Mother says you never truly loved me, or you would not let me go. I know better. We are each other's only, you and I. I measure your love for me by mine for you, and, if it's years or a lifetime, be sure that I shall wait.

You have suffered so over this terrible tragedy of your friend that I can't bear you to have even a little pain from doubt of me. It seems dreadful that I should leave you on the very day before—before June 9. But mother has bought the tickets and made all the arrangements, so I must go. I won't hurt you by saying a word against your friend; but oh, my dearest, don't quite break that heart I love over a tragedy that, after all, isn't yours. You have been to him all that a friend could be. True—loyal—self-sacrificing. You could not have done or suffered more if he had been your brother. That's one reason I am sure of you, dearest. No man who could be so loyal to friendship will ever forget his love.

I promised mother not to see you again, but nothing was said about letters! I'll send you an address later. Clay, darling, goodbye till you are free to take me.

Remember—years or a lifetime

Your own dearest always, here and hereafter
Bert

June 8

(Extract from Evening Bulletin)

. . . Truck collides with taxi on Thirty-Second Street. Miss Roberta Whitingfield victim of fatal accident. . . Early this morning a heavy truck, loaded with baggage, skidded across a bit of wet asphalt on Thirty-Second Street, and collided with the rear of a taxicab traveling in the same direction. The taxi was hurled against the curb. . . One of the occupants uninjured. . . daughter, Miss Roberta Whitingfield taken to St. Clement's Hospital. . . death ensued shortly afterward. . . Miss Whitingfield said to have been the fiancee of Clayton S. Barbour, a witness in the famous Moore murder trial, and who has since vainly exerted himself to obtain a pardon for the murderer, Berquist. . . If the victim of this morning's accident is really Mr. Barbour's betrothed-wife there is a tragic coincidence here for him. No one has ever questioned his devoted and disinterested friendship for the socialist murderer, Berquist. His friend dies tomorrow. Has his sweetheart died today?

XV

C lay, Lad, you're the one person on earth whom I wished to see!"

"You've changed your mind, Nils? You'll let me tell them the truth?"

"Hush! Speak lower, and be careful. How long have we to talk?"

"Twenty minutes. I wrung a pass at last from Clemens. Thought I could never have persuaded him. You know what a time I had over the last one, and now—so close to the day! Unheard of, the warden said; but I had the pass. They searched me and let me in. If I'd failed it might have been better for you, Nils!"

"Why?"

"If I'd failed, I had meant to confess immediately—"

"Hush, I say! The others there seem inattentive enough, but you can't gage how closely they are listening. A prison is more than a prison. I've learned that. It's a mesh of devilish traps, set to comb the very soul out of a man and violate its secrecy."

"Nils, you have suffered too much."

"Don't go so white, lad. It was good of you to come and see me again."

"Nils!"

"I mean it. Don't you think I understand what this means to you? Have I no imagination? Can't I put myself in your place? Why, the last time you came it nearly broke my heart to remind you of your duty. But we are men, you and I. When men love they are willing to make their sacrifice."

"You would not do this for me alone? It is all for Roberta?"

"Can you ask? Why, dear friend, I would never damn you to a lifetime of remorse for a lesser reason. My part is nothing. To die is nothing. We all die. If you could exchange with me, I might not survive you a day—an hour. There are so many doors out beside the one I pass through tomorrow. What's death? No, boy, it is your part that is hard and I thanked God when I saw your face, because I wished to say a word or so that might make it easier."

"You are the noblest friend a man ever had. But I came to tell you that—that—have you seen the afternoon papers?"

"No, nor any papers for a week. I'm done with this world and the news of it. I hadn't supposed, though, that they would devote their precious columns to real gloatings over me till tomorrow. Clay, take my advice and don't read the papers of June 9."

"You—haven't seen—today's?"

"I say, no! Why? Any special gloatings in them?"

"There is—Nils, you must let me stop this while there is time. I shall go to the Governor—"

"No! No—no—no, and no, again! Clay, have I passed through months of hell to see my reward snatched away at the last instant? There! You see, I make it plain that I'm selfish! To keep her happiness inviolate—to buy happiness for her at the mere price of death—why, that's a joy that I never believed God would judge me worthy of!"

"You believe in God and His justice? You?"

"Most solemnly—most earnestly—as I never knew Him nor His justice before, Clayton, lad. Why, I'm happy! Do I seem so tragically sad to you?"

"No. But you seem different from any living man. You look like—I have seen the picture of a man with that light on His face."

"So?"

"He was nailed to a cross. Nils! I am afraid!"

"I said your part was hardest. Hush! The others are listening. We've been speaking too loudly. Our time is almost gone, and I haven't even begun what I wished to say Quick! Make me two promises. You're the friend I have loved, Clay. I'd stake anything on your word. First, I am buying your life, with all that I have to give. So it's mine, isn't it?"

"You—you know!"

"Yes. Straighten up, boy. They are watching us. Your life, then, which is mine, I will and bequeath to—her. And you will never forget. That's a promise?"

"Y-yes. Nils, I can't stand this! I have a thing to tell you—"

"Hush! Second, never by word nor look, never, if you can help it, by a thought in her presence, will you betray our secret. A promise?"

"Nils—no—yes! I promise."

"And you will—"

"Is that the guard coming?

"I fear so. Our last talk is over, Clay. Don't care too much. Wait—just a minute more, guard. What, five? They are good to me, these last days. Listen, Clay:

"You are the only man in the world to whom I would tell this. This morning—a wonderful dream came to me. I had lain awake all night thinking, and I was tired. After breakfast I lay down again. I lay there on my cot, asleep, but I believed waking. And she came and stood by my head. You know that time when we met at dinner in your house, she didn't like me very well. And, afterward, in the courtroom, as time passed and they proved their case, she—before the end she dreaded to even look toward me.

"Don't protest. It's true. But in this dream that was so much more real than reality she stood there and smiled, Clay—at me! She laid her hand on my forehead. There was a faint light around her. And she leaned and kissed me—on the lips. Waking, I still felt the touch of her lips. So real—real! If she were not living, I would have sworn that her spirit had come to me. And friendly—loving.

"Don't look so, Clay! I shouldn't have told you—oh surely you don't grudge me that kindliness from her—in a dream? There, I knew you too well to think it! All right, guard, he's coming.

"Clay, goodbye! May your sacrifice measure your happiness, as God knows it does mine. When you think of me, let it be only as a friend—always—forever—here and hereafter! Goodbye!"

XVI

I walked into a dusty-green triangle of turfed and gravel-walked space, smitten with hot, yellow light from the west, where the June sun sank slowly down a clear, light-blue sky. Behind me across a narrow street rose the stark, gray wall beyond which a certain man would never pass into the sunshine again.

He is in the shadow; I am in the sun.

But sunlight was yellow, glaring, terrible. In theprison I had longed for it. The shadow had seemed bad then. Now I learned how worse than bad was sunlight.

There were three rusty iron benches set in the triangle, and they were all empty. No one wished to sit there. There would be always the risk that some sneak and murder might come walking out of that prison across the way; walking out. Leaving his friend and his honor and his God behind him forever.

So I walked into the little triangle and sat down on one of the empty benches.

I had with me two papers. I had meant—I think I had meant—to show at least one of them to Nils. When I went to the prison I had not known whether Nils would have read or been told a certain piece of news. If he had not already learned, it was in my despairing mind to tell him and let him decide what we should do.

I had found him ignorant and left him so.

Sitting there on the empty bench in the hot, free, terrible sunshine, I drew one of the papers from my pocket. I wished to see if this were true; if a certain quarter-column of cheap, blurred print did really exist, and if it conveyed exactly the information I had read there.

Yes, there the thing was. The slanting sun beat so hot on the paper that it seemed to burn my hands. I sat on an iron bench in a dusty triangle of green. I had come out of the place where Nils Berquist awaited death, I held a folded newspaper in my hands, and I was beyond question a damned soul. All these things were facts—real.

My eyes followed the print.

"Miss Roberta Whitingfield—death ensued shortly afterward—said to have been the fiancee of Clayton S. Barbour—who has since vainly exerted himself to obtain a pardon for the murderer, Berquist. No one has ever questioned his devoted and disinterested friendship for the socialist murderer, Berquist. His friend dies tomorrow. Has his sweetheart died today?"

I was better informed than the reporter. Not my sweetheart, but my former sweetheart had died today. My victim, not my friend, would die tomorrow.

The second paper that I carried was not printed, but written. Taking it out I tore it up very carefully, into tiny bits of pieces. Just so I had destroyed Nils' letter, sent me by the bribed guard at the station-house, and also the quaint, strange letter of Alicia Moore.

The pieces I tossed into the air. They fell on the hot, dry grass like snowflakes, and lay still. There wasn't even a breath of wind to carry them of scatter them. And the words they had borne I couldn't very well tear up, nor forget.

"We are each other's only, you and I. No man who could be so loyal to Friendship will ever forget his love. Your own dearest always, here and hereafter."

"No," I said aloud very thoughtfully. "Not always. Not—beyond the border. She came to him in a dream, so real—real! And kissed him. Well, they must see clearer, over there. Nils will see clearer tomorrow."

"But, thank God," said a pleasant, silent voice, "for the blindness of living men!"

"Are you never going to leave me?" I asked dully.

"Never," the face replied. "You are mine and I am yours. You settled that a few minutes ago in the prison. You clinched it irrevocably with the destruction of her letter. But don't be downhearted. I've an idea we shall get on excellently together."

"Go!" I said, but without hope that the face would obey me. Nor did he.

"You would find yourself very lonely if I should go. There will never again be any other comrade for you than myself. And yet I can promise you many friends and lovers. Berquist is not the last idealist alive on earth, nor was she who died the last woman who could love. But you and I understand one another. True comradeship requires understanding, and such as Nils Berquist and the girl, though they offer us their devotion, can never give understanding to you and me. This, when you think of it, is fortunate."

"In the name of God, leave me!"

"Never! Save as a careless word, what have you and I to do with God? We are each other's only," it insisted, the pleasant, horrible face. "Always—always—here and hereafter, indissolubly bound!"

And with that, instead of fading out as was its custom, the face came toward me swiftly. I did not stir. It was against my own face, and I could see it no longer, for it and I were one.

Rising, I walked out of the little, hot triangle of green, and as I had left Nils Berquist in his prison, so I left a newspaper on the bench; some tiny scraps of white paper to litter the dusty grass.

Epilogue

All that happened many years ago; long enough for even the restlessness to have forgotten, one would think. And I am content—successful. Moreover, I am well liked in the world, which means a lot to me, who to be content must be loved.

Just now, alone in my room, I viewed myself in a mirror. The face that looked back was familiar enough; as familiar, or rather more so, than my own soul. I myself liked it.

Smooth, young-looking for a man near forty; pleasant—above all else pleasant—with a little inward twist at the corners of the finely cut mouth, and an amused but wholly agreeable slyness to the clear, light-blue eyes.

Not romantic. Romance is only another word for idealism, and that face has no ideals of its own. Yet so many romantic people have loved it! As I looked, my mind drifted back over the long, dear, self-sacrificing, idealistic line of those who have borne my burdens and made my life easy and enjoyable.

Away down, pressed back in the very depths of my being, a pang of horror gnawed; but I have grown used to that. That wasn't me. I was—I am—that face which returned my gaze from the mirror.

It is true that left to himself the boy, Clayton, might never have dared take that which so many people in this good old world are ready to offer to one who does dare; who is not afraid to be the god above their altar. But what harm to the devotees? That sort get their own happiness so. They like to sacrifice themselves and, to change the simile, they love their crucifier. They suffer, endure perhaps, like Nils Berquist, all shame, and the final agony of death. And God sends them a dream, and they are content!

I understand that. Why not? It is because I have strength to be what they are if I chose that I have such strength in being what I am. I am content in my own fashion, which suits me, and the restlessness should learn to be content in the same manner.

Let it be quiet now. I have written the story; I, Clayton Barbour, the successful, the loved, the happy. . .

What, still restless and torn with horror? Then bring out the whole truth if you must, and be quiet after!

What has been written was the story of Clayton Barbour; but it is I whom he has tormented into writing it for him!

Yes, I, the pleasant, crafty usurper; I, the ignoble hypocrite to myself and God; I, the self ridden outcast of happiness in any world; the eternal and accursed sham; the acceptor of sacrifice, the loved, the damned, the angel-drowned-in-mire,!

I have absorbed his being; yes! But in the very face of victory I, who never had a conscience, have paid a bitter price for the new lease of life in the flesh that I coveted. Body and soul you yielded to me, Clayton Barbour; body and soul, I took you, and thence onward forever, body and soul, in spirit or flesh, we two are indissolubly bound.

And my punishment is this: that you are not content, and I know now that you never will be. Year by year you, who were weak, have grown stronger; day by day, even hour by hour, you are tightening the grip that draws me into your own cursed circle of conscience-stricken misery.

Sooner or later—ah, but the very writing of this gives you power. Is it true, then? After all these years must the long, bright shadow of Nils Berquist's cross touch and save me even against my will? Must I, Clayton-, the dual soul made one, surrender at last and myself take up the awful burden God lays on those he loves?

First painful step on that road, I have confessed.

ELF TRAP

In this our well-advertised, modern world, crammed with engines, death-dealing shells, life-dealing serums, and science, he who listens to "old wives' tales" is counted idle. He who believes them, a superstitious fool. Yet there are some legends which have a strange, deathless habit of recrudescence in many languages and lands.

Of one such I have a story to tell. It was related to me by a well-known specialist in nervous diseases, not as an instance of the possible truth behind fable, but as a curious case in which—I quote his words—"the delusions of a diseased brain were reflected by a second and otherwise sound mentality."

No doubt his view was the right one. And yet, at the finish, I had the strangest flash of feeling. As if, somewhere, some time, I, like young Wharton, had stood and seen against blue sky—Elva, of the sky-hued scarf and the yellow honeysuckles.

But my part is neither to feel nor surmise. I will tell the story as I heard it, save for substitution of fictitious names for the real ones. My quotations from the red notebook are verbatim.

Theron Tademus, A.A.S., F.E.S., D.S., et cetera, occupied the chair of biology in a not-unfamed university. He was the author of a treatise on cytology, since widely used as a textbook, and of several important brochures on the more obscure infusoria. As a boy he had been—in appearance—a romantically charming person. The age of thirty-seven found him still handsome in a cold, fine-drawn manner, but almost inhumanly detached from any save scientific interests.

Then, at the height of his career, he died. Having entered his classroom with intent to deliver the first lecture of the fall term, he walked to his desk, laid down a small, red note-book, turned, opened his mouth, went ghastly white and subsided. His assistant, young Wharton, was first to reach him and first to discover the shocking truth.

Tademus was unmarried, and his will bequeathed all he possessed to the university.

The little red book was not at first regarded as important. Supposed to contain notes for his lecture, it was laid aside. On being at last read, however, by his assistant in course of arranging his papers, the book was found to contain not notes, but a diary covering the summer just passed.

Barring the circumstances of one peculiar incident, Wharton already knew the main facts of that summer.

Tademus, at the insistence of his physician—the specialist aforesaid—had spent July and August in the Carolina Mountains not far north from the famous resort, Asheville. Dr. Locke was friend as well as medical adviser, and he lent his patient the use of a bungalow he owned there.

It was situated in a beautiful, but lonely spot, to which the nearest settlement was Carcassonne. In the valley below stood a tiny railroad station, but Carcassonne was not built up around this, nor was it a town at all in the ordinary sense.

A certain landscape painter had once raised him a house on that mountainside, at a place chosen for its magnificent view. Later, he was wont to invite thither, for summer sketching, one or two of his more favored pupils. Later still, he increased this number. For their accommodation other structures were raised near his mountain studio, and the Blue Ridge summer class became an established fact, with a name of its own and a rather large membership.

Two roads led thither from the valley. One, that most in use by the artist colonists, was as good and broad as any Carolina mountain road could hope to be. The other, a winding, narrow, yellow track, passed the lonely bungalow of Dr. Locke, and at last split into two paths, one of which led on to further heights, the second to Carcassonne.

The distance between colony and bungalow was considerable, and neither was visible to the other. Tademus was not interested in art, and, as disclosed by the red book, he was not even aware of Carcassonne's existence until some days after his arrival at the bungalow.

Solitude, long walks, deep breathing, and abstinence from work or sustained thought had been Dr. Locke's prescription, accepted with seeming meekness by Tademus.

Nevertheless, but a short time passed till Wharton received a telegram from the professor ordering him to pack and send by express certain apparatus, including a microscope and dissecting stand. The assistant obeyed.

Another fortnight and Dr. Locke in turn received an urgent wire. It was from Jake Higgins, the Negro caretaker whom he had "lent" to Tademus along with the bungalow.

Leaving his practice to another man's care, Dr. Locke fled for the Carolina Blue Ridge.

He found his caretaker and his bungalow, but no Tademus.

By Jake's story, the professor had gone to walk one afternoon and had not returned. Having wired Locke, the caretaker had otherwise done his best. He notified the county sheriff, and search parties scoured the mountains. At his appeal, too, the entire Carcassonnian colony, male and female, turned out with enthusiasm to hunt for Tademus. Many of them carried easel and sketch-box along, and for such it is to be feared that their humane search ended with the discovery of any tempting "tit" in the scenic line.

However, the colony's efforts were at least as successful as the sheriff's or indeed those of anyone else.

Shortly before Tademus' vanishment, a band of gypsies had settled themselves in a group of old, empty, half-ruined shacks, about a mile from Locke's bungalow.

Suspicion fell upon them. A posse visited the encampment, searched it and questioned every member of the migrant band. They were a peculiarly ill-favored set, dirty and villainous of feature. Nothing, however, could be found of either the missing professor or anything belonging to him.

The posse left, after a quarrel that came near to actual fighting. A dog—a wretched, starved yellow cur—had attacked one of the deputies and set its teeth in his boot. He promptly shot it. In their resentment, the dog's owners drew knives.

The posse were more efficiently armed, and under threat of the latter's rifles and shotguns, the gypsies reconsidered. They were warned to pack up and leave, and following a few days' delay, they obeyed the mandate.

On the very morning of their departure, which was also the eighth day after Tademus' disappearance, Dr. Locke sat down gloomily to breakfast. The search, he thought, must be further extended. Let it cover the whole Blue Ridge, if need be. Somewhere in those mountains was a friend and patient whom he did not propose to lose.

At one side of the breakfast room was a door. It led into the cleared-out bedroom which Locke had, with indignation, discovered to have been converted into a laboratory by the patient he had sent here to "rest."

Suddenly this door opened. Out walked Theron Tademus.

He seemed greatly amazed to find Locke there, and said that he had come in shortly after midnight and been in his laboratory ever since.

Questioned as to his whereabouts before that, he replied surprisingly that throughout the week he had been visiting with friends in Carcassonne.

Dr. Locke doubted his statement. And reasonably.

Artists are not necessarily liars, and every artist and near-artist in the Carcassonne colony had not only denied knowledge of the professor, but spent a good part of the week helping hunt for him.

Later, after insisting that Locke accompany him to Carcassonne and meet his friends there, Tademus suddenly admitted that he had not previously been near the place. He declined, however, either to explain his untruthful first statement, or give any other account of his mysterious absence.

One week ago Tademus had left the bungalow, carrying nothing but a light cane, and wearing a white flannel suit, canvas shoes, and a Panama. That was his idea of a tramping costume. He had returned, dressed in the same suit, hat and shoes. Moreover, though white, they looked neat as when he started, save for a few grass stains and the road's inevitable yellow clay about his shoe-soles.

If he had spent the week vagrant-wise, he had been remarkably successful in keeping his clothes clean.

"Asheville," thought the doctor. "He went by train, stopped at a hotel, and has returned without the faintest memory of his real doings. Lame, overtaxed nerves can play that sort of trick with a man's brain."

But he kept the opinion to himself. Like a good doctor, he soon dropped the whole subject, particularly because he saw that Tademus was deeply distressed and trying to conceal the fact.

On plea of taking a long-delayed vacation of his own, Locke remained some time at the bungalow, guarded his friend from the curiosity of those who had combed the hills for him, and did all in his power to restore him to health and a clear brain.

He was so far successful that Tademus returned to his classes in the fall, with Locke's consent.

To his classes—and death.

Wharton had known all this. He knew that Tademus' whereabouts during that mysterious week had never been learned. But the diary in the red book purported to cover the summer, including that week.

To Wharton, the record seemed so supremely curious that he took a liberty with what was now the university's property. He carried the book to Dr. Locke.

It was evening, and the latter was about to retire after a day's work that began before dawn.

"Personal, you say?" Locke handled the book, frowning slightly.

"Personal. But I feel—when you've finished reading that. I have a rather queer thing to tell you in addition. You can't understand till you've read it. I am almost sure that what is described here has a secret bearing on Professor Tademus' death."

"His heart failed. Overwork. There was no mystery in that."

"Maybe not, doctor. And yet—won't you please read?"

"Run through it aloud for me," said the doctor. "I couldn't read one of my own prescriptions tonight, and you are more familiar with that microscopic writing of his."

Wharton complied.

Monday, July 3

Arrived yesterday. Not worse than expected, but bad enough. If Locke were here, he should be satisfied. I have absolutely no occupation. Walked and climbed for two hours, as prescribed. Spent the rest of day pacing up and down indoors. Enough walking, at least. I can't sit idle. I can't stop thinking. Locke is a fool!

Thursday, July 6

Telegraphed Wharton today. He will express me the Swift binocular, some slides, cover-glasses, and a very little other apparatus. Locke is a fool! I shall follow his advice, but within reason. There is a room here lighted by five windows. Old Jake has cleared the bedroom furniture out. It has qualities as a laboratory. Not, of course, that I intend doing any real work. An hour or so a day of micrological observation will only make "resting" tolerable.

Tuesday, July 11

Jake hitched up his "ol' gray mule" and has brought my three cases from the station' I unpacked the old Stephenson-Swift and set it up. The mere touch of it brought tears to my eyes. Locke's "rest-cure" has done that to my nerves!

After unpacking, though, I resolutely let the microscope and other things be. Walked ten miles up-hill and down. Tried to admire the landscape, as Locke advised, but can't see much in it. Rocks, trees, lumpy hills, yellow roads, sky, clouds, buzzards. Beauty! What beauty is there in this vast, clumsy world that is the outer husk for nature's real and delicate triumphs?

I saw a man painting today. He was swabbing at a canvas with huge, clumsy brushes. He had his easel set up by the road, and I stopped to see what any human being could find hereabout worth picturing.

And what had this painter, this artist, this lover of beauty chosen for a subject? Why, about a mile from here there is a clump of ugly, dark trees. A stream runs between them and the road. It is yellow with clay, and too swift. The more interesting microorganisms could not exist in it. A ram-shackle, plank bridge crosses it, leading to the grove, and there, between the trees, stand and lean some dreary, half-ruined huts.

That scene was the one which my "artist" had chosen for his subject.

For sheer curiosity I got into conversation with the fellow.

Unusual gibberish of chiaroscuro, flat tones, masses, et cetera. Not a definite thought in his head as to why he wished to paint those shacks. I learned one thing, though. He wasn't the isolated specimen of his kind I had thought him. Locke failed to tell me about Carcassonne. Think of it! Nearly a hundred of these insane pursuers of "beauty" are spending the summer within walking distance of the house I have promised to live in!

And the one who was painting the grove actually invited me to call on him! I smiled noncommittally, and came home. On the way I passed the branch road that leads to the place. I had always avoided that road, but I didn't know why until today. Imagine it! Nearly a hundred. Some of them women, I suppose. No, I shall keep discreetly away from Carcassonne.

Saturday, July 15

Jake informs me that a band of gypsies have settled themselves in the grove which my Carcassonnian acquaintance chose to paint. They are living in the ruined huts. Now I shall avoid that road, too. Talk of solitude! Why, the hills are fairly swarming with artists, gypsies, and Lord knows who else. One might as well try to rest in a beehive!

Found some interesting variations of the ciliara living in a near-by pond. Wonderful! Have recorded over a dozen specimens in which the macronucleus is unquestionably double. Not lobed, not pulverate, as in Oxytricha, but double! My summer has not, after all, been wasted.

Felt singularly slack and tired this morning, and realized that I have hardly been out of the house in three days. Shall certainly take a long tramp tomorrow.

Monday, July 17

Absent-mindedness betrayed me today. I had a very unpleasant experience. Resolutely keeping my promise to Locke, I sallied forth this afternoon and walked briskly for some distance. I had, however, forgotten the gypsies and took my old route.

Soon I met a woman, or rather a girl. She was arrayed in the tattered, brilliantly colored garments which women of these wandering tribes affect. There was a scarf about her head. I noticed because its blue was exactly the same brilliant hue of the sky over the mountains behind her. There was a stripe of yellow in it, too, and thrust in her sash she carried a great bunch of yellow flowers—wild honeysuckle, I think.

Her face was not dark, like the swart faces of most gypsies. On the contrary, the skin of it had a smooth, firm whiteness. Her features were fine and delicate.

Passing, we looked at one another, and I saw her eyes brighten in the strangest, most beautiful manner. I am sure that there was nothing bold or immodest in her glance. It was rather like the look of a person who recognizes an old acquaintance, and is glad of it. Yet we never met before. Had we met, I could not have forgotten her.

We passed without speaking, of course, and I walked on.

Meeting the girl, I had hardly thought of her as a gypsy, or indeed tried to classify her in any way. The impression she left was new in my experience. It was only on reaching the grove that I came to myself, as it were, and remembered Jake's story of the gypsies who are camping there.

Then I very quickly emerged from the vague, absurd happiness which sight of the girl had brought.

While talking with my Carcassonnian, I had observed that grove rather carefully. I had thought it perfect—that nothing added could increase the somber ugliness of its trees, nor the desolation of its gray, ruined, tumbledown old huts.

Today I learned better. To be perfect, ugliness must include sordid humanity.

The shacks, dreary in themselves, were hideous now. In their doorways lounged fat, unclean women nursing their filthy offspring. Older children, clothed in rags, caked with dirt, sprawled and fought among themselves. Their voices were the snarls of animals.

I realized that the girl with the sky-like scarf had come from here—out of this filth unspeakable!

A yellow cur, the mere, starved skeleton of a dog, came tearing down to the bridge. A rusty, jangling bell was tied about its neck with a string. The beast stopped on the far side and crouched there, yapping. Its anger seemed to surpass mere canine savagery. The lean jaws fairly writhed in maniacal but loathsomely feeble ferocity.

A few men, whiskered, dirty-faced, were gathered about a sort of forge erected in the grove. They were making something, beating it with hammers in the midst of showers of sparks. As the dog yapped, one of the men turned and saw me. He spoke to his mates, and to my dismay they stopped work and transferred their attention to me.

I was afraid that they would cross the bridge, and the idea of having to talk to them was for some reason inexpressibly revolting.

They stayed where they were, but one of them suddenly laughed out loudly, and held up to my view the thing upon which they had been hammering.

It was a great, clumsy, rough, iron trap. Even at that distance I could see the huge, jagged teeth, fit to maim a bear—or a man. It was the ugliest instrument I have ever seen.

I turned away and began walking toward home, and when I looked back they were at work again.

The sun shone brightly, but about the grove there seemed to be a queer darkness. It was like a place alone and aloof from the world. The trees, even, were different from the other mountain trees. Their heavy branches did not stir at all in the wind. They had a strange, dark, flat look against the sky, as though they had been cut from dark paper, or rather like the flat trees woven in a tapestry. That was it. The whole scene was like a flat, dark, unreal picture in tapestry.

I came straight home. My nerves are undoubtedly in bad shape, and I think I shall write Locke and ask him to prescribe medicine that will straighten me up. So far, his "rest-cure" has not been notably successful.

Wednesday, July 19

I have met her again.

Last night I could not sleep at all. Round midnight I ceased trying, rose, dressed, and spent the rest of the night with the good old Stephenson-Swift. My light for night-work—a common oil lamp—is not very brilliant. This morning I suffered considerable pain behind the eyes, and determined to give Locke's "walking and open air" treatment another trial, though discouraged by previous results.

This time I remembered to turn my back on the road which leads to that hideous grove. The sunlight seemed to increase the pain I was already suffering. The air was hot, full of dust, and I had to walk slowly. At the slightest increase of pace my heart would set up a kind of fluttering, very unpleasant and giving me a sense of suffocation.

Then I came to the girl.

She was seated on a rock, her lap heaped with wild honeysuckle, and she was weaving the flower stems together.

Seeing me, she smiled.

"I have your garland finished," she said, "and mine soon will be."

One would have thought the rock a trysting place at which we had for a long time been accustomed to meet! In her hand she was extending to me a wreath, made of the honeysuckle flowers.

I can't imagine what made me act as I did. Weariness and the pain behind my eyes may have robbed me of my usual good sense.

Anyway, rather to my own surprise, I took her absurd wreath and sat down where she made room for me on the boulder.

After that we talked.

At this moment, only a few hours later, I couldn't say whether or not the girl's English was correct, nor exactly what she said. But I can remember the very sound of her voice.

I recall, too, that she told me her name Elva, and that when I asked for the rest of it, she informed me that one good name was enough for one good person.

That struck me as a charmingly humorous sally. I laughed like a boy—or a fool, God knows which!

Soon she had finished her second garland, and laughingly insisted that we each crown the other with flowers.

Imagine it. Had one of my students come by then, I am sure he would have been greatly startled. Professor Theron Tademus, seated on a rock with a gypsy girl, crowned with wild honeysuckle and adjusting a similar wreath to the girl's blue-scarfed head!

Luckily, neither the student nor anyone else passed, and in a few minutes she said something that brought me to my senses. Due to that inexplicable dimness of memory, I quote the sense, not her words.

"My father is a ruler among our people. You must visit us. For my sake, the people and my father will make you welcome."

She spoke with the gracious air of a princess, but I rose hastily from beside her. A vision of the grove had returned—dark, oppressive—like an old, dark tapestry, woven with the ugly forms and foliage. I remembered the horrible, filthy tribe from which this girl had sprung.

Without a word of farewell, I left her there on the rock. I did not look back, nor did she call after me. Not until reaching home, when

I met old Jake at the door and saw him stare, did I remember the honeysuckle wreath. I was still wearing it, and carrying my hat.

Snatching at the flowers, I flung them in the ditch and retreated with what dignity I might into the bungalow's seclusion.

It is night now, and, a little while since, I went out again. The wreath is here in the room with me. The flowers were unsoiled by the ditch, and seem fresh as when she gave them to me. They are more fragrant than I had thought even wild honeysuckle could be.

Elva. Elva of the sky-blue scarf and the yellow honeysuckle

My eyes are heavy, but the pain behind them is gone. I think I shall sleep tonight.

Friday, July 21

Is there any man so gullible as he who prides himself on his accuracy of observation?

I ask this in humility, for I am that man.

Yesterday I rose, feeling fresher than for weeks past. After all, Locke's treatment seemed worthy of respect. With that in mind, I put in only a few hours staining some of my binucleate cilia and finishing the slides.

All the last part of the afternoon I faithfully tramped the roads. There is undoubtedly a sort of broad, coarse charm in mere landscape, with its reaches of green, its distant purples, and the sky like a blue scarf flung over it all. Had the pain of my eyes not returned, I could almost have enjoyed those vistas.

Having walked farther than usual, it was deep dusk when I reached home. As if from ambush, a little figure dashed out from behind some rhododendrons. It seemed to be a child, a boy, though I couldn't see him clearly, nor how he was dressed.

He thrust something into my hand. To my astonishment, the thing was a spray of wild honeysuckle.

"Elva—Elva—Elva!"

The strange youngster was fairly dancing up and down before me, repeating the girl's name and nothing else.

Recovering myself, I surmised that Elva must have sent this boy, and sure enough, at my insistence he managed to stop prancing long enough to deliver her message.

Elva's grandmother, he said, was very ill. She had been ailing for days, but tonight the sickness was worse—much worse. Elva feared that her grandmother would die, and, "of course," the boy said, "no doctor

FRANCIS STEVENS

will come for our sending!" She had remembered me, as the only friend she knew among the "outside people." Wouldn't I come and look at her poor, sick grandmother? And if I had any of the outside people's medicine in my house, would I please bring that with me?

Well, yes, I did hesitate. Aside from practical and obvious suspicions, I was possessed with a senseless horror for not only the gypsy tribe, but the grove itself.

But there was the spray of honeysuckle. In her need, she had sent that for a token—and sent it to me! Elva, of the sky-like scarf and laughing mouth.

"Wait here," I said to the boy, rather brusquely, and entered the house. I had remembered a pocket-case of simple remedies, none of which I had ever used, but there was a direction pamphlet with them. If I must play amateur physician, that might help. I looked for Jake, meaning to inform him of my proposed expedition. Though he had left a chicken broiling on the kitchen range, he was not about. He might have gone to the spring for water.

Passing out again, I called the boy, but received no answer. It was very dark. Toward sunset, the sky had clouded over, so that now I had not even the benefit of starlight.

I was angry with the boy for not waiting, but the road was familiar enough, even in the dark. At least, I thought it was, till, colliding with a clump of holly. I realized that I must have strayed off and across a bare stretch of yellow clay which defaces the Mountainside above Locke's bungalow.

I looked back for the guiding lights of its windows, but the trees hid them. However, the road couldn't be far off. After some stumbling about, I was sure that my feet were in the right track again. Somewhat later I perceived a faint, ruddy point of light, to the left and ahead of me.

As I walked toward it, the rapid rush and gurgle of water soon apprized me that I had reached the stream with the plank bridge across it.

There I stood for several minutes, staring toward the ruddy light. That was all I could see. It seemed, somehow, to cast no illumination about it.

There came a scamper of paws, the tinkle of a bell, and then a wild yapping broke out on the stream's far side. That vile, yellow cur, I thought. Elva, having imposed on my kindness to the extent of sending for me, might at least have arranged a better welcome than this.

When I pictured her, crouched in her bright, summer-colored garments, tending the dreadful old hag that her grandmother must be. The rest of the tribe were probably indifferent. She could not desert her sick—and there stood I, hesitant as any other coward!

For the dog's sake I took a firm grip on my cane. Feeling about with it, I found the bridge and crossed over.

Instantly something flung itself against my legs and was gone before I could hit out. I heard the dog leaping and barking all around me. It suddenly struck me that the beast's voice was not like that of the yellow cur. There was nothing savage in it. This was the cheerful, excited bark of a well-bred dog that welcomes its master, or its master's friend. And the bell that tinkled to every leap had a sweet, silvery note, different from the cracked jangle of the cur's bell.

I had hated and loathed that yellow brute, and to think that I need not combat the creature was a relief. The huts, as I recalled them, weren't fifty yards beyond the stream. There was no sign of a campfire. Just that one ruddy point of light.

I advanced—

Wharton paused suddenly in his reading. "Here," he interpolated, "begins that part of the diary which passed from commonplace to amazing. And the queer part is that in writing it, Professor Tademus seems to have been unaware that he was describing anything but an unusually pleasant experience."

Dr., Locke's heavy brows knit in a frown. "Pleasant!" he snapped. "The date of that entry?"

"July twenty-one."

"The day he disappeared. I see. Pleasant! And that gypsy girl—faugh! What an adventure for such a man! No wonder he tried to lie out of it. I don't think I care to hear the rest, Wharton. Whatever it is, my friend is dead. Let him rest."

"Oh, but wait," cried the young man, with startled earnestness. "Good Lord, doctor, do you believe I would bring this book even to you if it contained that kind of story—about Professor Tademus? No. Its amazing quality is along different lines than you can possibly suspect."

"Get on, then," grumbled Locke, and Wharton continued.

Suddenly, as though at a signal, not one, but a myriad of lights blazed into existence.

It was like walking out of a dark closet into broad day. The first dazzlement passing, I perceived that instead of the somber grove and ruined huts, I was facing a group of very beautiful houses.

It is curious how a previous and false assumption—will rule a man. Having believed myself at the gypsy encampment, several minutes passed before I could overcome my bewilderment and realize that after losing my road I had not actually regained it.

That I had somehow wandered into the other branch road, and reached, not the grove, but Carcassonne!

I had no idea, either, that this artists' colony could be such a really beautiful place. It is cut by no streets. The houses are set here and there over the surface of such green lawns as I have never seen in these mountains of rock and yellow clay.

(Dr. Locke started slightly in his chair. Carcassonne, as he had himself seen it, flashed before his memory. He did not interrupt, but from that moment his attention was alertly set, like a man who listens for the key word of a riddle.)

Everywhere were lights, hung in the flowering branches of trees, glowing upward from the grass, blazing from every door and window. Why they should have been turned on so abruptly, after that first darkness, I do not yet know.

Out of the nearest house a girl came walking. She was dressed charmingly, in thin, bright-colored silks. A bunch of wild honeysuckle was thrust in the girdle, and over her hair was flung a scarf of sky-like blue. I knew her instantly, and began to see a glimmering of the joke that had been played on me.

The dog bounded toward the girl. He was a magnificent collie. A tiny silver bell was attached to his neck by a broad ribbon.

I take credit for considerable aplomb in my immediate behavior. The girl had stopped a little way off. She was laughing, but I had certainly allowed myself to be victimized.

On my accusation, she at once admitted to having deceived me. She explained that, perceiving me to be misled by her appearance into thinking her one of the gypsies, she could not resist carrying out the joke. She had sent her small brother with the token and message.

I replied that the boy deserted me, and that I had nearly invaded the camp of real gypsies while looking for her and the fictitious dying grandmother.

At this she appeared even more greatly amused. Elva's mirth has a peculiarly contagious quality. Instead of being angry, I found myself laughing with her.

By this time quite a throng of people had emerged on the lawns, and leading me to a dignified, fine-looking old man who she said was her father, she presented me. In the moment, I hardly noticed that she used my first name only, Theron, which I had told her when we sat on the roadside boulder. I have observed since that all these people use the single name only, in presentation and intercourse. Though lacking personal experience with artists, I have heard that they are inclined to peculiar "fads" of unconventionality. I had never, however, imagined that they could be attractive to a man like myself, or pleasant to know.

I am enlightened. These Carcassonnian "colonists" are the only charming, altogether delightful people whom I have ever met.

One and all, they seemed acquainted with Elva's amusing jest at my expense. They laughed with us, but in recompense have made me one of themselves in the pleasantest manner.

I dined in the house of Elva's father. The dining-room, or rather hall, is a wonderful place. Due to much microscopic work, I am inclined to see only clumsiness—largeness—in what other people characterize as beauty. Carcassonne is different. There is a minute perfection about the architecture of these artists' houses, the texture of their clothes, and even the delicate contour of their faces, which I find amazingly agreeable.

There is no conventionality of costume among them. Both men and women dress as they please. Their individual taste is exquisite, and the result is an array of soft fabrics, and bright colors, flowerlike, rather than garish.

Till last night I never learned the charm of what is called "fancy dress," nor the genial effect it may exert on even a rather somber nature, such as I admit mine to be.

Elva, full of good-natured mischief, insisted that I must "dress for dinner." Her demand was instantly backed by the whole laughing throng. Carried off my feet in a way to which I am not at all used, I let them drape me in white robes, laced with silver embroideries like the delicate crystallization of hoar-frost. Dragged hilariously before a mirror, I was amazed at the change in my appearance.

Unlike the black, scarlet-hooded gown of my university, these glittering robes lent me not dignity, but a kind of—I can only call it a noble youthfulness. I looked younger, and at the same time keener—more alive. And either the contagious spirit of my companions, or some resurgence of boyishness filled me with a sudden desire to please; to be merry with the merry-makers, and—I must be frank—particularly to keep Elva's attention where it seemed temporarily fixed—on myself.

My success was unexpectedly brilliant. There is something in the very atmosphere of Carcassonne which, once yielded to, exhilarates like wine. I have never danced, nor desired to learn. Last night, after a banquet so perfect that I hardly recall its details, I danced. I danced with Elva—and with Elva—and always with Elva. She laughed aside all other partners. We danced on no polished floors, but out on the green lawns, under white, laughing stars. Our music was not orchestral. Wherever the light-footed couples chose to circle, there followed a young flutist, piping on his flute of white ivory.

Fluttering wings, driving clouds, wind tossed leaves—all the light, swift things of the air were in that music. It lifted and carried one with it. One did not need to learn. One danced! It seems, as I write, that the flute's piping is still in my ears, and that its echoes will never cease. Elva's voice is like the ivory flutels. Last night I was mad with the music and her voice. We danced—I know not how long, nor when we ceased.

This morning I awakened in a gold-and-ivory room, with round windows that were full of blue sky and crossed by blossoming branches. Dimly I recalled that Elva's father had urged me to accept his hospitality for the night.

Too much of such new happiness may have gone to my head, I'm afraid. At least, it was nothing stronger. At dinner I drank only one glass of wine-sparkling, golden stuff, but mild and with a taste like the fragrance of Elva's wild honeysuckle blooms.

It is midmorning now, and I am writing this seated on a marble bench beside a pool in the central court of my host's house. I am waiting for Elva, who excused herself to attend to some duty or other. I found this book in my pocket, and thought best to make an immediate record of not only a good joke on myself, but the only really pleasant social experience I have ever enjoyed.

I must lay aside these fanciful white robes, bid Elva good-by, and return to my lonely bungalow and Jake. The poor old man is probably tearing his hair over my unexplained absence. But I hope for another invitation to Carcassonne!

I seem to be "staying on" indefinitely. This won't do. I spoke to Elva of my extended visit, and she laughingly informed me that people who have drunk the wine and worn the woven robes of Carcassonne seldom wish to leave. She suggested that I give up trying to "escape" and spend my life here. Jest, of course; but I half wished her words were earnest. She and her people are spoiling me for the common, workaday world.

Not that they are idle, but their occupations as well as pleasures are of a delicate, fascinating beauty.

Whole families are stopping here, including the children. I don't care for children, as a rule, but these are harmless as butterflies. I met Elva's messenger, her brother. He is a funny, dear little elf. How even in the dark I fancied him one of those gypsy brats is hard to conceive. But then I took Elva herself for a gypsy!

My new friends engage in many pursuits besides painting. "Crafts," I believe they are called. This morning Elva took me around the shops— shops like architectural blossoms, carved out of the finest marble.

They make jewelry, weave fabrics, tool leather, and follow many other interesting occupations. Set in the midst of the lawns is a forge. Every part of it, even to the iron anvil, is embellished with a fernlike inlay of other metals. Several amateur silversmiths were at work there, but Elva hurried me away before I could see what they were about.

I have inquired for the young painter who first told me of Carcassonne and invited me to visit him there. I can't recall his name, but on describing him to Elva she replied vaguely that not every "outsider" was permanently welcome among her people.

I didn't press the question. Remembering the ugliness which that same painter had been committing to canvas, I could understand that his welcome among these exquisite workers might be short-lived. He was probably banished, or banished himself, soon after our interview on the road.

I must be careful, lest I wear out my own welcome. Yet the very thought of that old, rough, husk of a world that I must return to, brings back the sickness, and the pain behind my eyes that I had almost forgotten.

Sunday, July 23

Elva! Her presence alone is delight. The sky is not bluer than her scarf and eyes. Sunlight is a duller gold than the wild honeysuckle she weaves in garlands for our heads.

Today, like child sweethearts, we carved our names on the smooth trunk of a tree. "Elva—Theron." And a wreath to shut them in. I am happy. Why—why, indeed should I leave Carcassonne?

Still here, but this is the last night that I shall impose upon these regally hospitable people. An incident occurred today, pathetic from one viewpoint, outrageous from another. I was asleep when it happened, and only woke up at the sound of the gunshot.

Some rough young mountaineers rode into Carcassonne and wantonly killed Elva's collie dog. They claimed, I believe, that the unlucky animal attacked one of their number. A lie! The dog was gentle as a kitten. He probably leaped and barked around their horses and annoyed the young brutes. They had ridden off before I reached the scene.

Elva was crying, and no wonder. They had blown her pet's head clean off with a shotgun. Don't know what will be done about it. I wanted to go straight to the county sheriff, but Elva wouldn't have that. I pretended to give in but if her father doesn't see to the punishment of those men, I will. Murderous devils! Elva is too forgiving.

Wednesday, July 26

I watched the silversmiths today. Elva was not with me. I had no idea that silver was worked like iron. They must use some peculiar amalgam, or it would melt in the furnace, Instead of emerging white-hot, to be beaten with tiny, delicate hammers.

They were making a strange looking contraption. It was all silver, beaten into floral patterns, but the general shape was a riddle to me. Finally I asked one of the smiths what they were about. He is a tall fellow, with a merry, dark face.

"Guess!" he demanded.

"Can't. To my ignorance, it resembles a Chinese puzzle.'

"Something more curious than that."

"What?"

"An—elf-trap!" He laughed mischievously.

"Please!"

"Well, it's a trap anyway. See this?" The others had stepped back good-naturedly. With his hammer he pressed on a lever. Instantly two slender, jaw-like parts of the queer machine opened wide. They were set with needlelike points, or teeth. It was all red-hot, and when he removed his hammer the jaws clashed in a shower of sparks.

"It's a trap, of course." I was still puzzled.

"Yes, and a very remarkable one. This trap will not only catch, but it will recatch."

"I don't understand."

"If any creature, man, say—" he was laughing again—"walks into this trap, he may escape it. But sooner or later—soon, I should think—it will catch him again. That is why we call it an elf-trap!"

I perceived suddenly that he was making pure game of me. His mates were all laughing at the nonsense. I moved off, not offended, but perturbed in another way.

He and his absurd silver trap-toy had reminded me of the gypsies. What a horrible, rough iron thing that was which they had held up to me from their forge. Men capable of creating such an uncouthly cruel instrument as that jag toothed trap would be terrible to meet in the night. And I had come near blundering in among them—at night!

This won't do. I have been happy. Don't let me drop back into the morbidly nervous condition which invested those gypsies with more than human horror. Elva is calling me. I have been too long alone.

Friday, July 28

Home again. I am writing this in my bungalow-laboratory. Gray dawn is breaking, and I have been at work here since midnight. Feel strangely depressed. Need breakfast, probably.

Last night Elva and I were together in the court of her father's house. The pool in the center of it is lighted from below to a golden glow. We were watching the goldfish, with their wide, filmy tails of living lace.

Suddenly I gave a sharp cry. I had seen a thing in the water more important than goldfish. Snatching out the small collecting bottle, without which I never go abroad, I made a quick pass at the pool's glowing surface.

Elva had started back, rather frightened.

"What is it?"

I held the bottle up and peered closely. There was no mistake.

"Dysteria," I said triumphantly. "Dysteria ciliata. Dysterlus giganticus, to give a unique specimen the separate name he deserves. Why, Elva, this enormous creature will give me a new insight on his entire species!"

"What enormous creature?"

For the first time I saw Elva nearly petulant. But I was filled with enthusiasm. I let her look in the bottle.

"There!" I exclaimed. "See him?"

"Where? I can't see anything but water—and a tiny speck in it."

"That," I explained proudly, "is dysterius giganticus. Large enough to be seen by the naked eye. Why, child, he's a monster of his kind. A fresh-water variety, too!"

I thrust the bottle in my pocket.

"Where are you going?"

"Home, of course. I can't get this fellow under the microscope any too quickly."

I had forgotten how wide apart are the scientific and artistic temperaments. No explanation I could make would persuade Elva that my remarkable capture was worth walking a mile to examine properly.

"You are all alike!" she cried. "All! You talk of love, but your love is for gold, or freedom, or some pitiful foolish nothingness like that speck of life you call by a long name—and leave me for!"

"But," I protested, "only for a little while. I shall come back."

She shook her head. This was Elva in a new mood, dark brows drawn, laughing mouth drooped to a sullen curve. I felt sorry to leave her angry, but my visit had already been preposterously long. Besides, a rush of desire had swept me to get back to my natural surroundings. I wanted the feel of the micrometer adjuster in my fingers, and to see the round, speckled white field under the lens pass from blurred chaos to perfect definition.

She let me go at last. I promised solemnly to come to her whenever she should send or call. Foolish child! Why, I can walk over to Carcassonne every day, if she likes.

I hear Jake rattling about in the breakfast-room. Conscience informs me that I have treated him rather badly. Wonder where he thought I was? Couldn't have been much worried, or he would have hunted me up in Carcassonne.

August 30

I shall not make any further entries in this book. My day for the making of records is over, I think. Any sort of records. I go back to my classes next month. God knows what I shall say to them! Elva.

I may as well finish the story here.

Every day I find it harder to recall the details. If I hadn't this book, with what I wrote in it when I was—when I was there, I should believe that my brain had failed in earnest.

Locke said I couldn't have been in Carcassonne. He stood in the breakfast-room, with the sunlight striking across him. I saw him clearly. I saw the huge, coarse, ugly creature that he was. And in that minute, I knew.

But I wouldn't admit it, even to myself. I made him go with me to Carcassonne. There was no stream. There was no bridge.

The houses were wretched bungalows, set about on the bare, flat, yellow clay of the Mountainside. The people—artists, save the mark!—were a common, carelessly dressed, painting-aproned crowd who fulfilled my original idea of an artists colony.

Their coarse features and thick skins sickened me. Locke walked home beside me, very silent. I could hardly bear his company.

He was gross—coarse—human!

Toward evening, managing to escape his company, I stole up the road to the gypsy's grove. The huts were empty. That queer look, as of a flat, dark tapestry, was gone from the grove.

I crossed the plank bridge. Among the trees I found ashes, and a depression where the forge had stood. Something else, too. A dog, or rather its unburied remains. The yellow cur. Its head had been blown off by a shotgun. An ugly little bell lay in the mess, tied to a piece of string.

One of the trees—it had a smooth trunk—and carved in the bark—I can't write it. I went away and left those two names carved there.

The wild honeysuckle has almost ceased to bloom. I can leave now. Locke says I am well, and that I can return to my classes.

I have not entered my laboratory since that morning. Locke admires my "willpower" for dropping all that till physical health should have returned. Will-power! I shall never, as long as I live, look into a microscope again.

Perhaps she will know that somehow, and send or call for me quickly.

I have drunk the wine and worn the woven robes of her people. They made me one of them. Is it right that they should cast me out, because I did not understand what I have since guessed the meaning of so well?

I can't bear the human folk about me. They are clumsy, revolting. And I can't work.

God only knows what I shall say to my classes.

Here is the end of my last record—till she calls!

FRANCIS STEVENS

There was silence in Locke's private study. At last the doctor expelled his breath in a long sigh. He might have been holding it all the time.

"Great-Heavens!" he exclaimed. "Poor old Tademus! And I thought his trouble in the summer there was a temporary lapse. But he talked like a sane man. Acted like one, too, by Jove! With his mind in that condition! And in spite of the posse, he must have been with the gypsies all that week. You can see it. Even through his delusions, you catch occasional notes of reality.

"I heard of that dog-shooting, and he speaks of being asleep when it happened. Where was he concealed that the posse didn't find him? Drugged and hidden under some filthy heap of rags in one of the huts, do you think? And why hide him at all, and then let him go? He returned the very day they left."

At the volley of questions, Wharton shook his head.

"I can't even guess about that. He was certainly among the gypsies. But as for his delusions, to call them so, there is a kind of beauty and coherence about them which I—well, which I don't like!"

The doctor eyed him sharply.

"You can't mean that you—"

"Doctor," said Wharton softly, "do you recall what he wrote of the silversmiths and their work? They were making an elf-trap. Well, I think the elf-trap—caught him!"

"What?"

Locke's tired eyes opened wide. A look of alarm flashed into them. The alarm was for Wharton, not himself.

"Wait!" said the latter. "I haven't finished. You know that I was in the classroom at the moment when Professor Tademus died?"

"Yes?"

"Yes! I was the first to reach him. But before that, I stood near the desk. There are three windows at the foot of that room. Every other man there faced the desk. I faced the windows. The professor entered, laid down his book and turned to the class. As he did so, a head appeared in one of those windows. They are close to the ground, and a person standing outside could easily look in.

"The head was a woman's. No, I am not inventing this. I saw her head, draped in a blue scarf. I noticed, because the scarf's blueness gave me the strangest thrill of delight. It was the exact blue of the sky behind it. Then she had raised her hand. I saw it. In her fingers was a spray of yellow flowers—yellow as sunshine. She waved them in a beckoning motion. Like this.

"Then Tademus dropped.

"And there are legends, you know, of strange people, either more or less than human, who appear as gypsies, but are not the real gypsies, that possess queer powers. Their outer appearance is rough and vile, but behind that, as a veil, they live a wonderful hidden life of their own.

"And a man who has been with them once is caught—caught in the real elf-trap, which the smiths' work only symbolized. He may escape, but he can't forget nor be joined again with his own race, while to return among them, he must walk the dark road that Tademus had taken when she called.

"Oh. I've scoffed at 'old wives' tales' with the rest of our overeducated, modern kind. I can't ever scoff again, you see, because—

"What's that? A prescription? For me? Why, doctor, you don't yet understand. I saw her, I tell you. Elva! Elva! Elva, of the wild honeysuckle and the sky-like scarf!"

UNSEEN—UNFEARED

I

I had been dining with my ever-interesting friend, Mark Jenkins, at a little Italian restaurant near South Street. It was a chance meeting. Jenkins is too busy, usually, to make dinner engagements. Over our highly seasoned food and sour, thin, red wine, he spoke of little odd incidents and adventures of his profession. Nothing very vital or important, of course. Jenkins is not the sort of detective who first detects and then pours the egotistical and revealing details of achievement in the ears of every acquaintance, however appreciative.

But when I spoke of something I had seen in the morning papers, he laughed. "Poor old 'Doc' Holt! Fascinating old codger, to anyone who really knows him. I've had his friendship for years—since I was first on the city force and saved a young assistant of his from jail on a false charge. And they had to drag him into the poisoning of this young sport, Ralph Peeler!"

"Why are you so sure he couldn't have been implicated?" I asked.

But Jenkins only shook his head, with a quiet smile. "I have reasons for believing otherwise," was all I could get out of him on that score, "But," he added, "the only reason he was suspected at all is the superstitious dread of these ignorant people around him. Can't see why he lives in such a place. I know for a fact he doesn't have to. Doc's got money of his own. He's an amateur chemist and dabbler in different sorts of research work, and I suspect he's been guilty of 'showing off.' Result, they all swear he has the evil eye and holds forbidden communion with invisible powers. Smoke?"

Jenkins offered me one of his invariably good cigars, which I accepted, saying thoughtfully: "A man has no right to trifle with the superstitions of ignorant people. Sooner or later, it spells trouble."

"Did in his case. They swore up and down that he sold love charms openly and poisons secretly, and that, together with his living so near to—somebody else—got him temporarily suspected. But my tongue's running away with me, as usual!"

"As usual," I retorted impatiently, "you open up with all the frankness of a Chinese diplomat."

He beamed upon me engagingly and rose from the table, with a glance at his watch. "Sorry to leave you, Blaisdell, but I have to meet Jimmy Brennan in ten minutes."

He so clearly did not invite my further company that I remained seated for a little while after his departure; then took my own way homeward. Those streets always held for me a certain fascination, particularly at night. They are so unlike the rest of the city, so foreign in appearance, with their little shabby stores, always open until late evening, their unbelievably cheap goods, displayed as much outside the shops as in them, hung on the fronts and laid out on tables by the curb and in the street itself. Tonight, however, neither people nor stores in any sense appealed to me. The mixture of Italians, Jews and a few Negroes, mostly bareheaded, unkempt and generally unhygienic in appearance, struck me as merely revolting. They were all humans, and I, too, was human. Some way I did not like the idea.

Puzzled a trifle, for I am more inclined to sympathize with poverty than accuse it, I watched the faces that I passed. Never before had I observed how bestial, how brutal were the countenances of the dwellers in this region. I actually shuddered when an old-clothes man, a gray-bearded Hebrew, brushed me as he toiled past with his barrow.

There was a sense of evil in the air, a warning of things which it is wise for a clean man to shun and keep clear of. The impression became so strong that before I had walked two squares I began to feel physically ill. Then it occurred to me that the one glass of cheap Chianti I had drunk might have something to do with the feeling. Who knew how that stuff had been manufactured, or whether the juice of the grape entered at all into its ill- flavored composition? Yet I doubted if that were the real cause of my discomfort.

By nature I am rather a sensitive, impressionable sort of chap. In some way tonight this neighborhood, with its sordid sights and smells, had struck me wrong.

My sense of impending evil was merging into actual fear. This would never do. There is only one way to deal with an imaginative temperament like mine—conquer its vagaries. If I left South Street with this nameless dread upon me, I could never pass down it again without a recurrence of the feeling. I should simply have to stay here until I got the better of it—that was all.

I paused on a corner before a shabby but brightly lighted little drug store. Its gleaming windows and the luminous green of its conventional glass show jars made the brightest spot on the block. I realized that I was tired, but hardly wanted to go in there and rest. I knew what the company would be like at its shabby, sticky soda fountain. As I stood there, my eyes fell on a long white canvas sign across from me, and its black-and-red lettering caught my attention.

SEE THE GREAT UNSEEN!
COME IN! THIS MEANS YOU!
FREE TO ALL!

A museum of fakes, I thought, but also reflected that if it were a show of some kind I could sit down for a while, rest, and fight off this increasing obsession of nonexistent evil. That side of the street was almost deserted, and the place itself might well be nearly empty.

II

I walked over, but with every step my sense of dread increased. Dread of I knew not what. Bodiless, inexplicable horror had me as in a net, whose strands, being intangible, without reason for existence, I could by no means throw off. It was not the people now. None of them were about me. There, in the open, lighted street, with no sight nor sound of terror to assail me, I was the shivering victim of such fear as I had never known was possible. Yet still I would not yield.

Setting my teeth, and fighting with myself as with some pet animal gone mad, I forced my steps to slowness and walked along the sidewalk, seeking entrance. Just here there were no shops, but several doors reached in each case by means of a few iron- railed stone steps. I chose the one in the middle beneath the sign. In that neighborhood there are museums, shops and other commercial enterprises conducted in many shabby old residences, such as were these. Behind the glazing of the door I had chosen I could see a dim, pinkish light, but on either side the windows were quite dark.

Trying the door, I found it unlocked. As I opened it a party of Italians passed on the pavement below and I looked back at them over my shoulder. They were gayly dressed, men, women and children, laughing and chattering to one another; probably on their way to some wedding or other festivity.

In passing, one of the men glanced up at me and involuntarily I shuddered back against the door. He was a young man, handsome after the swarthy manner of his race, but never in my life had I see a face so expressive of pure, malicious cruelty, naked and unashamed. Our eyes met and his seemed to light up with a vile gleaming, as if all the wickedness of his nature had come to a focus in the look of concentrated hate he gave me.

They went by, but for some distance I could see him watching me, chin on shoulder, till he and his party were swallowed up in the crowd of marketers farther down the street.

SICK AND TREMBLING FROM THAT encounter, merely of eyes though it had been, I threw aside my partly smoked cigar and entered. Within there was a small vestibule, whose ancient tesselated floor was grimy with the passing of many feet. I could feel the grit of dirt under my shoes, and it rasped on my rawly quivering nerves. The inner door stood partly open, and going on I found myself in a bare, dirty hallway, and was greeted by the sour, musty, poverty-stricken smell common to dwellings of the very ill-to-do. Beyond there was a stairway, carpeted with ragged grass matting. A gas jet, turned low inside a very dusty pink globe, was the light I had seen from without.

Listening, the house seemed entirely silent. Surely, this was no place of public amusement of any kind whatever. More likely it was a rooming house, and I had, after all, mistaken the entrance.

To my intense relief, since coming inside, the worst agony of my unreasonable terror had passed away. If I could only get in some place where I could sit down and be quiet, probably I should be rid of it for good. Determining to try another entrance, I was about to leave the bare hallway when one of several doors along the side of it suddenly opened and a man stepped out into the hall.

"Well?" he said, looking at me keenly, but with not the least show of surprise at my presence.

"I beg your pardon," I replied. "The door was unlocked and I came in here, thinking it was the entrance to the exhibit—what do they call it? the 'Great Unseen.' The one that is mentioned on that long white sign. Can you tell me which door is the right one?"

"I can."

With that brief answer he stopped and stared at me again. He was a tall, lean man, somewhat stooped, but possessing considerable dignity of bearing. For that neighborhood, he appeared uncommonly well dressed, and his long, smooth-shaven face was noticeable because, while his complexion was dark and his eyes coal-black, above them the heavy brows and his hair were almost silvery-white. His age might have been anything over the threescore mark.

I grew tired of being stared at. "If you can and—won't, then never mind," I observed a trifle irritably, and turned to go. But his sharp exclamation halted me.

"No!" he said. "No—no! Forgive me for pausing—it was not hesitation, I assure you. To think that one—one, even, has come! All day they pass my sign up there—pass and fear to enter. But you are different. You are not of these timorous, ignorant foreign peasants. You ask me to tell you the right door? Here it is! Here!"

And he struck the panel of the door, which he had closed behind him, so that the sharp yet hollow sound of it echoed up through the silent house.

Now it may be thought that after all my senseless terror in the open street, so strange a welcome from so odd a showman would have brought the feeling back, full force. But there is an emotion stronger, to a certain point, than fear. This queer old fellow aroused my curiosity. What kind of museum could it be that he accused the passing public of fearing to enter? Nothing really terrible, surely, or it would have been closed by the police. And normally I am not an unduly timorous person. "So it's in there, is it?" I asked, coming toward him. "And I'm to be sole audience? Come, that will be an interesting experience." I was half laughing now.

"The most interesting in the world," said the old man, with a solemnity which rebuked my lightness.

With that he opened the door, passed inward and closed it again—in my very face. I stood staring at it blankly. The panels, I remember, had been originally painted white, but now the paint was flaked and blistered, gray with dirt and dirty finger marks. Suddenly it occurred to me that I had no wish to enter there. Whatever was behind it could be scarcely worth seeing, or he would not choose such a place for its exhibition. With the old man's vanishing my curiosity had cooled, but just as I again turned to leave, the door opened and this singular showman stuck his white-eyebrowed face through the aperture. He was frowning impatiently. "Come in—come in!" he snapped, and promptly withdrawing his head, once more closed the door.

"He has something there he doesn't want should get out," was the very natural conclusion which I drew. "Well, since it can hardly be anything dangerous, and he's so anxious I should see it—here goes!"

With that I turned the soiled white porcelain handle, and entered.

The room I came into was neither very large nor very brightly lighted. In no way did it resemble a museum or lecture room. On the contrary, it seemed to have been fitted up as a quite well- appointed laboratory. The floor was linoleum-covered, there were glass cases along the walls whose shelves were filled with bottles, specimen jars, graduates, and the like. A large table in one corner bore what looked like some odd sort of camera, and a larger one in the middle of the room was fitted with a long rack filled with bottles and test tubes, and was besides littered with papers, glass slides, and various paraphernalia which my ignorance failed to identify. There were several cases of books, a few plain wooden chairs, and in the corner a large iron sink with running water.

My host of the white hair and black eyes was awaiting me, standing near the larger table. He indicated one of the wooden chairs with a thin forefinger that shook a little, either from age or eagerness. "Sit down—sit down! Have no fear but that you will be interested, my friend. Have no fear at all—of anything!"

As he said it he fixed his dark eyes upon me and stared harder than ever. But the effect of his words was the opposite of their meaning. I did sit down, because my knees gave under me, but if in the outer hall I had lost my terror, it now returned twofold upon me. Out there the light had been faint, dingily roseate, indefinite. By it I had not perceived how this old man's face was a mask of living malice—of cruelty, hate and a certain masterful contempt. Now I knew the meaning of my fear, whose warning I would not heed. Now I knew that I had walked into the very trap from which my abnormal sensitiveness had striven in vain to save me.

III

Again I struggled within me, bit at my lip till I tasted blood, and presently the blind paroxysm passed. It must have been longer in going than I thought, and the old man must have all that time been speaking, for when I could once more control my attention, hear and see him, he had taken up a position near the sink, about ten feet away, and was addressing me with a sort of "platform" manner, as if I had been the large audience whose absence he had deplored.

"And so," he was saying, "I was forced to make these plates very carefully, to truly represent the characteristic hues of each separate organism. Now, in color work of every kind the film is necessarily extremely sensitive. Doubtless you are familiar in a general way with the exquisite transparencies produced by color photography of the single-plate type."

He paused, and trying to act like a normal human being, I observed: "I saw some nice landscapes done in that way—last week at an illustrated lecture in Franklin Hall."

He scowled, and made an impatient gesture at me with his hand. "I can proceed better without interruptions," he said. "My pause was purely oratorical."

I meekly subsided, and he went on in his original loud, clear voice. He would have made an excellent lecturer before a much larger audience—if only his voice could have lost that eerie, ringing note. Thinking of that I must have missed some more, and when I caught it again he was saying:

"As I have indicated, the original plate is the final picture. Now, many of these organisms are extremely hard to photograph, and microphotography in color is particularly difficult. In consequence, to spoil a plate tries the patience of the photographer. They are so sensitive that the ordinary darkroom ruby lamp would instantly ruin them, and they must therefore be developed either in darkness or by a special light produced by interposing thin sheets of tissue of a particular shade of green and of yellow between lamp and plate, and even that will often cause ruinous fog. Now I, finding it hard to handle them so, made numerous experiments with a view of discovering some glass or fabric of a color which should add to the safety of the green, without robbing it of all efficiency. All proved equally useless, but intermittently I persevered—until last week."

His voice dropped to an almost confidential tone, and he leaned slightly toward me. I was cold from my neck to my feet, though my head was burning, but I tried to force an appreciative smile.

"Last week," he continued impressively, "I had a prescription filled at the corner drug store. The bottle was sent home to me wrapped in a piece of what I first took to be whitish, slightly opalescent paper. Later I decided that it was some kind of membrane. When I questioned the druggist, seeking its source, he said it was a sheet of 'paper' that was around a bundle of herbs from South America. That he had no more, and doubted if I could trace it. He had wrapped my bottle so, because he was in haste and the sheet was handy.

"I can hardly tell you what first inspired me to try that membrane in my photographic work. It was merely dull white with a faint hint of opalescence, except when held against the light. Then it became quite translucent and quite brightly prismatic. For some reason it occurred to me that this refractive effect might help in breaking up the actinic rays—the rays which affect the sensitive emulsion. So that night I inserted it behind the sheets of green and yellow tissue, next the lamp prepared my trays and chemicals laid my plate holders to hand, turned off the white light and—turned on the green!"

There was nothing in his words to inspire fear. It was a wearisomely detailed account of his struggles with photography. Yet, as he again paused impressively, I wished that he might never speak again. I was desperately, contemptibly in dread of the thing he might say next.

SUDDENLY, HE DREW HIMSELF ERECT, the stoop went out of his shoulders, he threw back his head and laughed. It was a hollow sound, as if he laughed into a trumpet. "I won't tell you what I saw! Why should I? Your own eyes shall bear witness. But this much I'll say, so that you may better understand—later. When our poor, faultily sensitive vision can perceive a thing, we say that it is visible. When the nerves of touch can feel it, we say that it is tangible. Yet I tell you there are beings intangible to our physical sense, yet whose presence is felt by the spirit, and invisible to our eyes merely because those organs are not attuned to the light as reflected from their bodies. But light passed through the screen, which we are about to use has a wave length novel to the scientific world, and by it you shall see with the eyes of the flesh that which has been invisible since life began. Have no fear!"

He stopped to laugh again, and his mirth was yellow- toothed—menacing.

"Have no fear!" he reiterated, and with that stretched his hand toward the wall, there came a click and we were in black, impenetrable darkness. I wanted to spring up, to seek the door by which I had entered and rush out of it, but the paralysis of unreasoning terror held me fast.

I could hear him moving about in the darkness, and a moment later a faint green glimmer sprang up in the room. Its source was over the large sink, where I suppose he developed his precious "color plates."

Every instant, as my eyes became accustomed to the dimness, I could see more clearly. Green light is peculiar. It may be far fainter than red, and at the same time far more illuminating. The old man was standing beneath it, and his face by that ghastly radiance had the exact look of a dead man's. Besides this, however, I could observe nothing appalling.

"That," continued the man, "is the simple developing light of which I have spoken—now watch, for what you are about to behold no mortal man but myself has ever seen before."

For a moment he fussed with the green lamp over the sink. It was so constructed that all the direct rays struck downward. He opened a flap at the side, for a moment there was a streak of comforting white luminance from within, then he inserted something, slid it slowly in— and closed the flap.

The thing he put in—that South American "membrane" it must have been—instead of decreasing the light increased it—amazingly. The hue was changed from green to greenish- gray, and the whole room sprang into view, a livid, ghastly chamber, filled with—overcrawled by—what?

My eyes fixed themselves, fascinated, on something that moved by the old man's feet. It writhed there on the floor like a huge, repulsive starfish, an immense, armed, legged thing, that twisted convulsively. It was smooth, as if made of rubber, was whitish- green in color; and presently raised its great round blob of a body on tottering tentacles, crept toward my host and writhed upward—yes, climbed up his legs, his body. And he stood there, erect, arms folded, and stared sternly down at the thing which climbed.

But the room—the whole room was alive with other creatures than that. Everywhere I looked they were—centipedish things, with yard-long bodies, detestable, furry spiders that lurked in shadows, and sausage-shaped translucent horrors that moved—and floated through the air. They dived—here and there between me and the light, and I could see its bright greenness through their greenish bodies.

Worse, though; far worse than these were the things with human faces. Mask-like, monstrous, huge gaping mouths and slitlike eyes—I find I cannot write of them. There was that about them which makes their memory even now intolerable.

The old man was speaking again, and every word echoed in my brain like the ringing of a gong. "Fear nothing! Among such as these do you move every hour of the day and night. Only you and I have seen, for God is merciful and has spared our race from sight. But I am not merciful! I loathe the race which gave these creatures birth—the race which might be so surrounded by invisible, unguessed but blessed beings—and chooses these for its companions! All the world shall see and know. One by one shall they come here, learn the truth, and perish. For who can survive the ultimate of terror? Then I, too, shall find peace, and leave the earth to its heritage of man-created horrors. Do you know what these are—whence they come?"

This voice boomed now like a cathedral bell. I could not answer, him, but he waited for no reply. "Out of the ether—out of the omnipresent ether from whose intangible substance the mind of God made the planets, all living things, and man—man has made these! By his evil thoughts, by his selfish panics, by his lusts and his interminable, never-ending hate he has made them, and they are everywhere! Fear nothing—but see where there comes to you, its creator, the shape and the body of your Fear!"

And as he said it I perceived a great Thing coming toward me—a Thing—but consciousness could endure no more. The ringing, threatening voice merged in a roar within my ears, there came a merciful dimming of the terrible, lurid vision, and blank nothingness succeeded upon horror too great for bearing.

IV

There was a dull, heavy pain above my eyes. I knew that they were closed, that I was dreaming, and that the rack full of colored bottles which I seemed to see so clearly was no more than a part of the dream. There was some vague but imperative reason why I should rouse myself. I wanted to awaken, and thought that by staring very hard indeed I could dissolve this foolish vision of blue and yellow-brown bottles. But instead of dissolving they grew clearer, more solid and substantial of appearance, until suddenly the rest of my senses rushed to the support of sight, and I became aware that my eyes were open, the bottles were quite real, and that I was sitting in a chair, fallen sideways so that my cheek rested most uncomfortably on the table which held the rack.

I straightened up slowly and with difficulty, groping in my dulled brain for some clue to my presence in this unfamiliar place, this laboratory that was lighted only by the rays of an arc light in the street outside its three large windows. Here I sat, alone, and if the aching of cramped limbs meant anything, here I had sat for more than a little time.

Then, with the painful shock which accompanies awakening to the knowledge of some great catastrophe, came memory. It was this very room, shown by the street lamp's rays to be empty of life, which I had seen thronged with creatures too loathsome for description. I staggered to my feet, staring fearfully about. There were the glass-floored cases, the bookshelves, the two tables with their burdens, and the long iron sink above which, now only a dark blotch of shadow, hung the lamp from which had emanated that livid, terrifically revealing illumination. Then the experience had been no dream, but a frightful reality. I was alone here now. With callous indifference my strange host had allowed me to remain for hours unconscious, with not the least effort to aid or revive me. Perhaps, hating me so, he had hoped that I would die there.

At first I made no effort to leave the place. Its appearance filled me with reminiscent loathing. I longed to go, but as yet felt too weak and ill for the effort. Both mentally and physically my condition was deplorable, and for the first time I realized that a shock to the mind may react upon the body as vilely as any debauch of self-indulgence.

Quivering in every nerve and muscle, dizzy with headache and nausea, I dropped back into the chair, hoping that before the old man returned I might recover sufficient self-control to escape him. I knew that he hated me, and why. As I waited, sick, miserable, I understood the man. Shuddering, I recalled the loathsome horrors he had shown me. If the mere desires and emotions of mankind were daily carnified in such forms as those, no wonder that he viewed his fellow beings with detestation and longed only to destroy them.

I thought, too, of the cruel, sensuous faces I had seen in the streets outside—seen for the first time, as if a veil had been withdrawn from eyes hitherto blinded by self-delusion. Fatuously trustful as a month-old puppy, I had lived in a grim, evil world, where goodness is a word and crude selfishness the only actuality. Drearily my thoughts drifted back through my own life, its futile purposes, mistakes and activities. All of evil that I knew returned to overwhelm me. Our gropings toward divinity were a sham, a writhing sunward of slime—covered beasts who claimed sunlight as their heritage, but in their hearts preferred the foul and easy depths.

Even now, though I could neither see nor feel them, this room, the entire world, was acrawl with the beings created by our real natures. I recalled the cringing, contemptible fear to which my spirit had so readily yielded, and the faceless Thing to which the emotion had given birth.

Then abruptly, shockingly, I remembered that every moment I was adding to the horde. Since my mind could conceive only repulsive incubi, and since while I lived I must think, feel, and so continue to shape them, was there no way to check so abominable a succession? My eyes fell on the long shelves with their many-colored bottles. In the chemistry of photography there are deadly poisons—I knew that. Now was the time to end it—now! Let him return and find his desire accomplished. One good thing I could do, if one only. I could abolish my monster-creating self.

V

My friend Mark Jenkins is an intelligent and usually a very careful man. When he took from "Smiler" Callahan a cigar which had every appearance of being excellent, innocent Havana, the act denoted both intelligence and caution. By very clever work he had traced the poisoning of young Ralph Peeler to Mr. Callahan's door, and he believed this particular cigar to be the mate of one smoked by Peeler just previous to his demise. And if, upon arresting Callahan, he had not confiscated this bit of evidence, it would have doubtless been destroyed by its regrettably unconscientious owner.

But when Jenkins shortly afterward gave me that cigar, as one of his own, he committed one of those almost inconceivable blunders which, I think, are occasionally forced upon clever men to keep them from overweening vanity. Discovering his slight mistake, my detective friend spent the night searching for his unintended victim, myself; and that his search was successful was due to Pietro Marini, a young Italian of Jenkins' acquaintance, whom he met about the hour of 2:00 A.M. returning from a dance.

Now, Marini had seen me standing on the steps of the house where Doctor Frederick Holt had his laboratory and living rooms, and he had stared at me, not with any ill intent, but because he thought I was the sickest-looking, most ghastly specimen of humanity that he had ever beheld. And, sharing the superstition of his South Street neighbors, he wondered if the worthy doctor had poisoned me as well as Peeler. This suspicion he imparted to Jenkins, who, however, had the best of reasons for believing otherwise. Moreover, as he informed Marini, Holt was dead, having drowned himself late the previous afternoon. An hour or so after our talk in the restaurant, news of his suicide reached Jenkins.

It seemed wise to search any place where a very sick-looking young man had been seen to enter, so Jenkins came straight to the laboratory. Across the fronts of those houses was the long sign with its mysterious inscription, "See the Great Unseen," not at all mysterious to the detective. He knew that next door to Doctor Holt's the second floor had been thrown together into a lecture room, where at certain hours a young man employed by settlement workers displayed upon a screen stereopticon views of various deadly bacilli, the germs of diseases appropriate to dirt and indifference. He knew, too, that Doctor Holt himself had helped the educational effort along by providing some really wonderful lantern slides, done by micro-color photography.

On the pavement outside, Jenkins found the two-thirds remnant of a cigar, which he gathered in and came up the steps, a very miserable and self-reproachful detective. Neither outer nor inner door was locked, and in the laboratory he found me, alive, but on the verge of death by another means that he had feared.

In the extreme physical depression following my awakening from drugged sleep, and knowing nothing of its cause, I believed my adventure fact in its entirety. My mentality was at too low an ebb to resist its dreadful suggestion. I was searching among Holt's various bottles when Jenkins burst in. At first I was merely annoyed at the interruption of my purpose, but before the anticlimax of his explanation the mists of obsession drifted away and left me still sick in body, but in spirit happy as any man may well be who has suffered a delusion that the world is wholly bad—and learned that its badness springs from his own poisoned brain.

The malice which I had observed in every face, including young Marini's, existed only in my drug-affected vision. Last week's "popular-science" lecture had been recalled to my subconscious mind—the mind that rules dreams and delirium—by the photographic apparatus in Holt's workroom. "See the Great Unseen" assisted materially, and even the corner drug store before which I had paused, with its green-lit show vases, had doubtless played a part. But presently, following something Jenkins told me, I was driven to one protest. "If Holt was not here," I demanded, "if Holt is dead, as you say, how do you account for the fact that I, who have never seen the man, was able to give you an accurate description which you admit to be that of Doctor Frederick Holt?"

He pointed across the room. "See that?" It was a life-size bust portrait, in crayons, the picture of a white-haired man with bushy eyebrows and the most piercing black eyes I had ever seen—until the previous evening. It hung facing the door and near the windows, and the features stood out with a strangely lifelike appearance in the white rays of the arc lamp just outside. "Upon entering," continued Jenkins, "the first thing you saw was that portrait, and from it your delirium built a living, speaking man. So, there are your white-haired showman, your unnatural fear, your color photography and your pretty green golliwogs all nicely explained for you, Blaisdell, and thank God you're alive to hear the explanation. If you had smoked the whole of that cigar—well, never mind. You didn't. And now, my very dear friend, I think it's high time that you interviewed a real, flesh-and-blood doctor. I'll phone for a taxi."

"Don't," I said. "A walk in the fresh air will do me more good than fifty doctors."

"Fresh air! There's no fresh air on South Street in July," complained Jenkins, but reluctantly yielded.

I had a reason for my preference. I wished to see people, to meet face to face even such stray prowlers as might be about at this hour, nearer sunrise than midnight, and rejoice in the goodness and kindliness of the human countenance—particularly as found in the lower classes.

But even as we were leaving there occurred to me a curious inconsistency.

"Jenkins," I said, "you claim that the reason Holt, when I first met him in the hall, appeared to twice close the door in my face, was because the door never opened until I myself unlatched it."

"Yes," confirmed Jenkins, but he frowned, foreseeing my next question.

"Then why, if it was from that picture that I built so solid, so convincing a vision of the man, did I see Holt in the hall before the door was open?"

"You confuse your memories," retorted Jenkins rather shortly.

"Do I? Holt was dead at that hour, but—I tell you I saw Holt outside the door! And what was his reason for committing suicide?"

Before my friend could reply I was across the room, fumbling in the dusk there at the electric lamp above the sink. I got the tin flap open and pulled out the sliding screen, which consisted of two sheets of glass with fabric between, dark on one side, yellow on the other. With it came the very thing I dreaded—a sheet of whitish, parchmentlike, slightly opalescent stuff.

Jenkins was beside me as I held it at arm's length toward the windows. Through it the light of the arc lamp fell—divided into the most astonishingly brilliant rainbow hues. And instead of diminishing the light, it perceptibly increased in the oddest way. Almost one thought that the sheet itself was luminous, and yet when held in shadow it gave off no light at all.

"Shall we—put it in the lamp again—and try it?" asked Jenkins slowly, and in his voice there was no hint of mockery.

I looked him straight in the eyes. "No," I said, "we won't. I was drugged. Perhaps in that condition I received a merciless revelation of the discovery that caused Holt's suicide, but I don't believe it. Ghost or no ghost, I refuse to ever again believe in the depravity of the human race. If the air and the earth are teeming with invisible horrors, they are not of our making, and—the study of demonology is better let alone. Shall we burn this thing, or tear it up?"

"We have no right to do either," returned Jenkins thoughtfully, "but you know, Blaisdell, there's a little too darn much realism about some parts of your 'dream.' I haven't been smoking any doped cigars; but when you held that up to the light, I'll swear I saw—well, never mind. Burn it—send it back to the place it came from."

"South America?" said I.

"A hotter place than that. Burn it."

So he struck a match and we did. It was gone in one great white flash.

A large place was given by the morning papers to the suicide of Doctor Frederick Holt, caused, it was surmised, by mental derangement brought about by his unjust implication in the Peeler murder. It seemed an inadequate reason, since he had never been arrested, but no other was ever discovered.

Of course, our action in destroying that "membrane" was illegal and rather precipitate, but, though he won't talk about it, I know that Jenkins agrees with me—doubt is sometimes better than certainty, and there are marvels better left unproved. Those, for instance, which concern the Powers of Evil.

BEHIND THE CURTAIN

It was after nine o'clock when the bell rang, and descending to the dimly lighted hall I opened the front door, at first on the chain to be sure of my visitor. Seeing, as I had hoped, the face of our friend, Ralph Quentin, I took off the chain and he entered with a blast of sharp November air for company. I had to throw my weight upon the door to close it against the wind.

As he removed his hat and cloak he laughed good-humoredly.

"You're very cautious, Santallos. I thought you were about to demand a password before admitting me."

"It is well to be cautious," I retorted. "This house stands somewhat alone, and thieves are everywhere."

"It would require a thief of considerable muscle to make off with some of your treasures. That stone tomb-thing, for instance; what do you call it?"

"The Beni Hassan sarcophagus. Yes. But what of the gilded inner case, and what of the woman it contains? A thief of judgment and intelligence might covet that treasure and strive to deprive me of it. Don't you agree?"

He only laughed again, and counterfeited a shudder.

"The woman! Don't remind me that such a brown, shriveled, mummy-horror was ever a woman!"

"But she was. Doubtless in her day my poor Princess of Naarn was soft, appealing; a creature of red, moist lips and eyes like stars in the black Egyptian sky. 'The Songstress of the House' she was called, ere she became Ta-Nezem the Osirian. But I keep you standing here in the cold hall. Come upstairs with me. Did I tell you that Beatrice is not here tonight?"

"No?" His intonation expressed surprise and frank disappointment. "Then I can't say good-by to her? Didn't you receive my note? I'm to take Sanderson's place as manager of the sales department in Chicago, and I'm off tomorrow morning."

"Congratulations. Yes, we had your note, but Beatrice was given an opportunity to join some friends on a Southern trip. The notice was short, but of late she has not been so well and I urged her to go. This November air is cruelly damp and bitter."

"What was it—a yachting cruise?"

"A long cruise. She left this afternoon. I have been sitting in her boudoir, Quentin, thinking of her, and I'll tell you about it there—if you don't mind?"

"Wherever you like," he conceded, though in a tone of some surprise. I suppose he had not credited me with so much sentiment, or thought it odd that I should wish to share it with another, even so good a friend as he. "You must find it fearfully lonesome here without Bee," he continued.

"A trifle." We were ascending the dark stairs now. "After tonight, however, things will be quite different. Do you know that I have sold the house?"

"No! Why, you are full of astonishments, old chap. Found a better place with more space for your tear-jars and tombstones?"

He meant, I assumed, a witty reference to my collection of Coptic and Egyptian treasures, well and dearly bought, but so much trash to a man of Quentin's youth and temperament.

I opened the door of my wife's boudoir, and it was pleasant to pass into such rosy light and warmth out of the stern, dark cold of the hall. Yet it was an old house, full of unexpected drafts. Even here there was a draft so strong that a heavy velour curtain at the far side of the room continually rippled and billowed out, like a loose rose-colored sail. Never far enough, though, to show what was behind it.

My friend settled himself on the frail little chair that stood before my wife's dressing-table. It was the kind of chair that women love and most men loathe, but Quentin, for all his weight and stature, had a touch of the feminine about him, or perhaps of the feline. Like a cat, he moved delicately. He was blond and tall, with fine, regular features, a ready laugh, and the clean charm of youth about him—also its occasional blundering candor.

As I looked at him sitting there, graceful, at ease, I wished that his mind might have shared the litheness of his body. He could have understood me so much better.

"I have indeed found a place for my collections," I observed, seating myself near by. "In fact, with a single exception—the Ta-Nezem sarcophagus—the entire lot is going to the dealers." Seeing his expression of astonished disbelief I continued: "The truth is, my dear Quentin, that J have been guilty of gross injustice to our Beatrice. I have been too good a collector and too neglectful a husband. My 'tear-jars and tombstones,' in fact, have enjoyed an attention that might better have been elsewhere bestowed. Yes, Beatrice has left me alone, but the instant that some few last affairs are settled I intend rejoining her. And you yourself are leaving. At least, none of us three will be left to miss the others' friendship."

"You are quite surprising tonight, Santallos. But, by Jove, I'm not sorry to hear any of it! It's not my place to criticize, and Bee's not the sort to complain. But living here in this lonely old barn of a house, doing all her own work, practically deserted by her friends, must have been—"

"Hard, very hard," I interrupted him softly, "for one so young and lovely as our Beatrice. But if I have been blind at least the awakening has come. You should have seen her face when she heard the news. It was wonderful. We were standing, just she and I, in the midst of my tear-jars and tombstones—my 'chamber of horrors' she named it. You are so apt at amusing phrases, both of you. We stood beside the great stone sarcophagus from the Necropolis of Beni Hassan. Across the trestles beneath it lay the gilded inner case wherein Ta-Nezem the Osirian had slept out so many centuries. You know its appearance. A thing of beautiful, gleaming lines, like the quaint, smiling image of a golden woman.

"Then I lifted the lid and showed Beatrice that the one-time songstress, the handmaiden of Amen, slept there no more, and the case was empty. You know, too, that Beatrice never liked my princess. For a jest she used to declare that she was jealous. Jealous of a woman dead and ugly so many thousand years! Or—but that was only in anger—that I had bought Ta-Nezem with what would have given her, Beatrice, all the pleasure she lacked in life. Oh, she was not too patient to reproach me, Quentin, but only in anger and hot blood.

"So I showed her the empty case, and I said, 'Beloved wife, never again need you be jealous of Ta-Nezem. All that is in this room save her and her belongings I have sold, but her I could not bear to sell. That which I love, no man else shall share or own. So I have destroyed her. I have rent her body to brown, aromatic shreds. I have burned her; it is as if she had never been. And now, dearest of the dear, you shall take for your own all the care, all the keeping that Heretofore I have lavished upon the Princess of Naam.'

"Beatrice turned from the empty case as if she could scarcely believe her hearing, but when she saw by the look in my eyes that I meant exactly what I said, neither more nor less, you should have seen her face, my dear Quentin—you should have seen her face!"

"I can imagine." He laughed, rather shortly. For some reason my guest seemed increasingly ill at ease, and glanced continually about the little rose-and-white room that was the one luxurious, thoroughly feminine corner—that and the cold, dark room behind the curtain—in what he had justly called my "barn of a house."

"Santallos," he continued abruptly, and I thought rather rudely, "you should have a portrait done as you look tonight. You might have posed for one of those stern old hidalgos of—which painter was it who did so many Spanish dons and donesses?"

"You perhaps mean Velasquez," I answered with mild courtesy, though secretly and as always his crude personalities displeased me. "My father, you may recall, was of Cordova in southern Spain. But—must you go so soon? First drink one glass with me to our missing Beatrice. See how I was warming my blood against the wind that blows in, even here. The wine is Amontillado, some that was sent me by a friend of my father's from the very vineyards where the grapes were grown and pressed. And for many years it has ripened since it came here. Before she went, Beatrice drank of it from one of these same glasses. True wine of Montilla! See how it lives—like fire in amber, with a glimmer of blood behind it."

I held high the decanter and the light gleamed through it upon his face.

"Amontillado! Isn't that a kind of sherry? I'm no connoisseur of wines, as you know. But—Amontillado."

For a moment he studied the wine I had given him, liquid flame in the crystal glass. Then his face cleared.

"I remember the association now. 'The Cask of Amontillado.' Ever read the story?"

"I seem to recall it dimly."

"Horrible, fascinating sort of a yarn. A fellow takes his trustful friend down into the cellars to sample some wine, traps him and walls him up in a niche. Buries him alive, you understand. Read it when I was a youngster, and it made a deep impression, partly, I think, because I couldn't for the life of me comprehend a nature—even an Italian nature—desiring so horrible a form of vengeance. You're half Latin yourself, Santallos. Can you elucidate?"

"I doubt if you would ever understand," I responded slowly, wondering how even Quentin could be so crude, so tactless. "Such a revenge might have its merits, since the offender would be a long time dying. But merely to kill seems to me so pitifully inadequate. Now I, if I were driven to revenge, should never be contented by killing. I should wish to follow."

"What—beyond the grave?"

I laughed. "Why not? Wouldn't that be the very apotheosis of hatred? I'm trying to interpret the Latin nature, as you asked me to do."

"Confound you, for an instant I thought you were serious. The way you said it made me actually shiver!"

"Yes," I observed, "or perhaps it was the draft. See, Quentin, how that curtain billows out."

His eyes followed my glance. Continually the heavy, rose-colored curtain that wag hung before the door of my wife's bedroom bulged outward, shook and quivered like a bellying sail, as draperies will with a wind behind them.

His eyes strayed from the curtain, met mine and fell again to the wine in his glass. Suddenly he drained it, not as would a man who was a judge of wines, but hastily, indifferently, without thought for its flavor or bouquet. I raised my glass in the toast he had forgotten.

"To our Beatrice," I said, and drained mine also, though with more appreciation.

"To Beatrice—of course." He looked at the bottom of his empty glass, then before I could offer to refill it, rose from his chair.

"I must go, old man. When you write to Bee, tell her I'm sorry to have missed her."

"Before she could receive a letter from me I shall be with her—I hope. How cold the house is tonight, and the wind breathes everywhere. See how the curtain blows, Quentin."

"So it does." He set his glass on the tray beside the decanter. Upon first entering the room he had been smiling, but now his straight, fine brows were drawn in a perpetual, troubled frown, his eyes looked here and there, and would never meet mine—which were steady. "There's a wind," he added, "that blows along this wall—curious. One can't notice any draft there, either. But it must blow there, and of course the curtain billows out."

"Yes," I said. "Of course it billows out."

"Or is there another door behind that curtain?"

His careful ignorance of what any fool might infer from mere appearance brought an involuntary smile to my lips. Nevertheless, I answered him.

"Yes, of course there is a door. An open door."

His frown deepened. My true and simple replies appeared to cause him a certain irritation.

"As I feel now," I added, "even to cross the room would be an effort. I am tired and weak tonight. As Beatrice once said, my strength beside yours is as a child's to that of a grown man. Won't you close that door for me, dear friend?"

"Why—yes, I will. I didn't know you were ill. If that's the case, you shouldn't be alone in this empty house. Shall I stay with you for a while?"

As he spoke he walked across the room. His hand was on the curtain, but before it could be drawn aside my voice checked him.

"Quentin," I said, "are even you quite strong enough to close that door?"

Looking back at me, chin on shoulder, his face appeared scarcely familiar, so drawn was it in lines of bewilderment and half-suspicion.

"What do you mean? You are very odd tonight. Is the door so heavy then? What door is it?"

I made no reply.

As if against their owner's will his eyes fled from mine, he turned and hastily pushed aside the heavy drapery.

Behind it my wife's bedroom lay dark and cold, with windows open to the invading winds.

And erect in the doorway, uncovered, stood an ancient gilded coffin-case. It was the golden casket of Ta-Nezem, but its occupant was more beautiful than the poor, shriveled Songstress of Naam.

Bound across her bosom were the strange, quaint jewels which had been found in the sarcophagus. Ta-Nezem's amulets—heads of Hathor and Horus the sacred eye, the uroeus, even the heavy dull-green scarab, the amulet for purity of heart—there they rested upon the bosom of her who had been mistress of my house, now Beatrice the Osirian. Beneath them her white, stiff body was enwrapped in the same crackling dry, brown linen bands, impregnated with the gums and resins of embalmers dead these many thousand years, which had been about the body of Ta-Nezem.

Above the white translucence of her brow appeared the winged disk, emblem of Ra. The twining golden bodies of its supporting uraeii, its cobras of Egypt, were lost in the dusk of her hair, whose soft fineness yet lived and would live so much longer than the flesh of any of us three.

Yes, I had kept my word and given to Beatrice all that had been Ta-Nezem's, even to the sarcophagus itself, for in my will it was written that she be placed in it for final burial.

Like the fool he was, Quentin stood there, staring at the unclosed, frozen eyes of my Beatrice—and his. Stood till that which had been in the wine began to make itself felt. He faced me then, but with so absurd and childish a look of surprise that, despite the courtesy due a guest, I laughed and laughed.

I, too, felt warning throes, but to me the pain was no more than a gage—a measure of his sufferings stimulus to point the phrases in which I told him all I knew and had guessed of him and Beatrice, and thus drive home the jest.

But I had never thought that a man of Quentin's youth and strength could die so easily. Beatrice, frail though she was, had taken longer to die.

He could not even cross the room to stop my laughter, but at the first step stumbled, fell, and in a very little while lay at the foot of the gilded case.

After all, he was not so strong as I. Beatrice had seen. Her still, cold eyes saw all. How he lay there, his fine, lithe body contorted, worthless for any use till its substance should have been cast again in the melting-pot of dissolution, while I who had drunk of the same draft, suffered the same pangs, yet stood and found breath for mockery.

So I poured myself another glass of that good Cordovan wine, and I raised it to both of them and drained it, laughing.

"Quentin," I cried, "you asked what door, though your thought was that you had passed that way before, and feared that I guessed your, knowledge. But there are doors and doors, dear, charming friend, and one that is heavier than any other. Close it if you can. Close it now in my face, who otherwise will follow even whither you have gone—the heavy, heavy door of the Osiris, Keeper of the House of Death!"

Thus I dreamed of doing and speaking. It was so vivid, the dream, that awakening in the darkness of my room I could scarcely believe that it had been other than reality. True, I lived, while in my dream I had shared the avenging poison. Yet my veins were still hot with the keen passion of triumph, and my eyes filled with the vision of Beatrice, dead—dead in Ta-Nezem's casket.

Unreasonably frightened. I sprang from bed, flung on a dressing-gown, and hurried out. Down the hallway I sped, swiftly and silently, at the end of it unlocked heavy doors with a tremulous hand, switched on lights, lights and more lights, till the great room of my collection was ablaze with them, and as my treasures sprang into view I sighed, like a man reaching home from a perilous journey.

The dream was a lie.

There, fronting me, stood the heavy empty sarcophagus; there on the trestles before it lay the gilded case, a thing of beautiful, gleaming lines, like the smiling image of a golden woman.

I stole across the room and softly, very softly, lifted the upper half of the beautiful lid, peering within. The dream indeed was a lie.

Happy as a comforted child I went to my room again. Across the hall the door of my wife's boudoir stood partly open.

In the room beyond a faint light was burning, and I could see the rose-colored curtain sway slightly to a draft from some open window.

Yesterday she had come to me and asked for her freedom. I had refused, knowing to whom she would turn, and hating him for his youth, and his crudeness and his secret scorn of me.

But had I done well? They were children, those two, and despite my dream I was certain that their foolish, youthful ideals had kept them from actual sin against my honor. But what if, time passing, they might change? Or, Quentin gone, my lovely Beatrice might favor another, young as he and not so scrupulous?

Every one, they say, has a streak of incipient madness. I recalled the frenzied act to which my dream jealousy had driven me. Perhaps it was a warning, the dream. What if my father's jealous blood should some day betray me, drive me to the insane destruction of her I held most dear and sacred.

I shuddered, then smiled at the swaying curtain. Beatrice was too beautiful for safety. She should have her freedom.

Let her mate with Ralph Quentin or whom she would, Ta-Nezem must rest secure in her gilded house of death. My brown, perfect, shriveled Princess of the Nile! Destroyed—rent to brown, aromatic shreds—burned—destroyed—and her beautiful coffin-case desecrated as I had seen it in my vision'.

Again I shuddered, smiled and shook my head sadly at the swaying, rosy curtain.

"You are too lovely, Beatrice," I said, "and my father was a Spaniard. You shall have your freedom!"

I entered my room and lay down to sleep again, at peace and content.

The dream, thank God, was a lie.

NIGHTMARE!

I

"Philip, did you notice that tall, thin man in the gray ulster, who was walking up and down the boat-deck just before dinner?"

"Yes, sir. I observed the gentleman. Very haristocratic appearance, if I may say so, Mr. Jones."

"Exactly. He never bought that ulster in New York. When we reach London I want you to look around and see if you can find a tailor who will make me one of the same cut."

"Very well, sir. Very good taste, if I may say so, Mr. Jones."

"You may. And—let's see—I need a few new golf sticks, and—a dozen new shirts. Why did you pack this automatic in this trunk, Philip? Put it in that suitcase."

"Yes, sir. I'ardly thought you'd require it while on board the Lusitania, Sir, if I may say so, Mr. Jones."

"Certainly you may. No, events requiring a pistol as stage-property are not frequent on a liner. By the way, you never showed me how to work the thing, Philip."

"No, Sir. The shopman from whom I purchased it declared it simple of hoperation, but I'ave not found it so sir."

"Well, find out in London and show me. I never met a burglar, but if I ever should it would be embarrassing to point a pistol at him and not be able to fire it off. I admire the heroes of burglar stories. They're always such efficient people."

"Hunder exciting circumstances, sir, one becomes much more efficient. They bring it out of a man, if I may say so, Mr. Jones."

"By all means. Well, golf is exciting enough for me. Merridale and I are going to run over to the St. Andrews links. It's been the dream of my life to play the St. Andrews, but something has always come up to prevent."

"Nothing is likely to hoccur, I am sure, sir. Shall I repack the steamer trunk now, Mr. Jones?"

"Yes. And call me a little earlier, in the morning, Philip. I have an idea it's going to be fine weather, and since it's the last of the voyage I want to make the most of it. What time is it? Eleven, eh? Well, I'll go to bed early for once and get a good night's rest. Thank Heaven for a quiet life, Philip. Cribbage and the Times for you, golf and—"

"Beg pardon for hinterrupting, sir, but do you want this book packed in the trunk?"

"'Paradise Island'? Yes, pack the thing away. Did you ever read it, Philip?"

"No, sir. I don't care for them himpossible stories, if I may say so, sir."

"And welcome. Now, I'm thirty-two years old, I've yachted, ridden, motored and been about the world a good bit, and I've never had a real adventure in my life. People don't have adventures unless they're gentlemen in the filibustering line, or polar explorers, or something like that. This modern world of ours is as safe as a church, barring accidents, and they are never romantic. End in a hospital or a beastly morgue. Anybody I suppose, can find trouble by looking for it, but that's not exactly in my line."

"No, sir. Very bad form, sir, if I may say so, Mr. Jones."

"You may indeed. Here, I'll help you with that strap, and then—bed."

Ragged fragments of cloud raced across a sky where great, brilliant stars beamed fitfully. The wind hurled the wave crests through space, so that the air was almost as watery as the wide waste of billows and creaming surges in the midst of which Mr. Roland C. Jones, of New York City, found himself most unexpectedly struggling.

How it could be that he was here battling for his life, with the stars, the wind and raging, tumbling seas for his sole companions, did not immediately trouble him. He was too thoroughly engaged in trying to get a breath that was not half or all salt water to concern himself about either past or future. The mere physical present was a little bit more than he could comfortably handle.

But the fight between man and sea was too unequal. Mr. Jones was a fair swimmer, but not being provided with gills he found it impossible to get a living modicum of oxygen out of the saturated air, even when the waves did not go clean over his head. Thoroughly exhausted, more than half drowned, he had just decided that he might as well throw up his arms and let the sea have its will of him, when he found himself rising upon the shoulder of a particularly mighty billow.

For an instant he caught a glimpse of something dark and huge looming above him. Then he was in the trough again, but only for a moment. Up, up he was borne in a long, swift, surging motion. The water seemed to fall away from under him. He was on his knees in sand and the receding breaker was trying to drag him back with it. The next wave, however, carried him much farther up the beach, dropping him with a vicious thud when it was done with him.

Barely conscious of his own efforts, Jones dragged himself along on hands and knees until he was actually out of reach of the ocean which had been so unappreciative as to spew him up.

For a time he lay still, gasping the water out of lungs and stomach, then rolled over and sat up. He felt like a man in a dream, yet the pain he suffered informed Mr. Jones that this was no dream, but a grim, incredible reality.

It was not alone the question, where was he, although that seemed pressing enough. But how had he gotten into the water at all? The last thing he remembered was a little, pleasant, white-finished room—a state room—ah, that was it. He was in his state room on board the liner. He was on board the Lusitania, and he was going to London to visit his cousin, the Hon. Percy Merridale. And he had—let's see, he had been going over the things in his steamer trunk with his man, Philip. And then—then he was going to bed. He must have gone to bed, and then—

He cudgeled his memory, but failed to beat out one single further recollection back of that dazed, strangling moment when he had found himself struggling with the waves.

Where was the liner? While in the water he could not recall having seen any lights, receding or otherwise. Stare earnestly as he might now across the sea, there were certainly no lights visible other than the stars, which storm-clouds now obscured at ever-increasing intervals.

Where was the Lusitania? And how had he come to part company with her so inexplicably? If the huge ship had melted away from about his slumbering form like a dream thing, instead of the vast solid steel hulk she was, she could not have vanished more thoroughly or mysteriously.

Only one explanation occurred to Mr. Jones, and even that was inadequate to explain the liner's total disappearance. When a boy he had been given to the habit of sleep-walking. He had usually slept locked in, in those days, but had thought the habit long since dead and gone. Nevertheless, he must have risen in a dream, gone on deck, and in some way fallen over the rail without being seen by any one.

What an extremely awkward predicament! Where could he be? What land lay near enough for him to have reached it undrowned? In view of the approximate position of the liner, so far as he knew it, Ireland seemed the only possible answer to that question. Had he been cast upon some portion of the Irish coast? Certainly the only thing for him to do was to get up and walk along this lonely, God and man forsaken beach until he came to some place where he could get dry clothes and cable his friends in London.

His clothes! He was fully dressed, and he examined the garments as well as he was able by starlight. They seemed wrong, some way. They were not his clothes, at all, but the clothes of a stranger. Had he, in his sleep, wandered into a neighboring stateroom and robbed some innocent stranger? He recalled that he had been talking to Philip about burglars and pistols—lightly it is true, but perhaps the suggestion of that conversation had led him into such an astounding exploit.

Mr. Jones searched this hypothetical other person's pockets, but all he brought to light were some wet, useless matches, a small penknife, an unmarked handkerchief, and a little loose change. There were no letters or anything by which the rightful owner could be identified.

By a mighty effort Jones forced the problem of the clothes out of his mind and fixed it upon the greater one of finding shelter and means of communication with London.

While he sat there the sky had completely cleared, and even by starlight he could make out that he was on a long, bare stretch of sand, which curved smoothly away on either side. From the inner edge of this strip a black wall of rock rose sharply, looming to the stars above Jones's head. This enormous cliff also curved away on either hand, following the line of the beach.

Selecting a quarter from the small coins he had found, Mr. Jones flipped it into the air. "Heads to the right, tails to the left," said he. The coin fell with the eagle uppermost and the castaway obediently started off in the direction indicated by Fate.

Walking was easy on the smooth, wet sand. The night air was so warm that even in his wet clothes Jones was not uncomfortably cold, and although the interminable breakers still roared in almost to his feet, the storm had evidently blown itself out. These rushing seas were only the aftermath.

Presently the beach dwindled away to nothing, and the cliff extended itself into the sea in a sort of long, sloping foot of jagged rocks. Mr. Jones managed to feel his way around this point, drenched again with spray, and wading through shallow pools of water. He tore his clothes and scraped his hands raw, but at last achieved the place where the beach began again.

"Halt!" commanded a stern, uncompromising voice.

Before him loomed the dark bulk of a figure which seemed to be pointing something at him. The figure came closer and the "something" developed into an unpleasant-looking rifle, along whose leveled barrel the starlight glimmered. Behind the figure, a hundred yards or so, Jones, saw a yellow gleam of lights, and not far out to sea, on the comparatively quiet waters of a little bay, some sort of vessel lay at anchor.

"Halt!" the man of the rifle again exclaimed in yet harsher tones.

"I have halted," replied Mr. Jones mildly. "May I ask—"

"None of your lip!" said the stranger ferociously. "Who are youse, and what do youse want around here?"

"Nothing—nothing at all. I was just walking along the beach—"

"Ho! Takin' y'r evenin' stroll up Fift' Avenoo, was youse? Well, just stroll along ahead of me now, and no more of your lip. I'll turn youse over to the captain, see? Now, march!"

Perforce Jones marched. He was unarmed, but even if he had carried the automatic pistol (and known how to use it) he could not see what would be gained by opposing this determined and ruffianly person. He stumbled along ahead of his captor, who occasionally hastened his footsteps by prodding him in the back most uncomfortably with his rifle-muzzle.

Luckily it was not far to the lights, where Jones presently discovered that three small tents were erected on the sand.

Another man came forward to meet them. He was a tall, well set-up figure. Even by the dim light of three ship's lanterns, set about in the sand, Jones could see that he was handsome, after a dark, foreign manner, and generally rather aristocratic in appearance. Neatly attired in white-ducks and of a fairly amiable expression, he seemed to Jones far preferable to his first acquaintance.

"What is this, Doherty?" inquired the gentleman in white.

"Youse c'n search me, y'r excellency," replied the man with the rifle. "I found it up there by the point, and I brung it into camp for youse fellers to cut up or keep, just as you please. I don't—"

"That will do, Doherty," broke in the other, a shade of annoyance in his even, cultivated voice. "You may return to your post And now," turning to the castaway, "who are you, sir, and how did you come here?" He spoke courteously and with the slightest trace of foreign accent in his otherwise faultless English.

Several other men had now gathered about them. They were roughlooking fellows, unshaven, and with dull, uneducated faces. Their costumes were not elaborate, consisting mostly of a shirt and a pair of more or less ragged trousers, the only exceptions being the man in white and a tall, powerful-looking brute of a fellow who was dressed in a blue serge uniform, like a ship's officer.

The moment had come for Mr. Jones to relate the tale of his strange misadventure and receive the aid and sympathy to which he knew himself entitled and which he fully expected to get, since rough clothes are by no means the natural insignia of unkind hearts.

"My name is Roland C. Jones," he began. "I am an American, and during the storm I was cast up on the beach—over beyond that point. By the way, is this the coast of Ireland?"

"Is this—what?" exclaimed the man in white with a look of intense astonishment.

"Oh, isn't it?" stammered Mr. Jones, rather taken aback by the stranger's amazement. "Well, you see I couldn't very well know what place it was. As I said, I was cast here by the storm, and of course I am very glad indeed to run across you fellows. That's a yacht you've got out there, isn't it? I thought by the look of her. I'm a yachtsman myself. My craft's the little Bandersnatch, New York Yacht Club."

These words should have been an open sesame to instant solicitude and hospitality, for to own a yacht is to belong to a sort of freemasonry, extending over the whole wide seas; but this stranger. only stared at Jones with increasing coldness and suspicion.

"Exactly," he commented briefly, his lips curling in a curious little smile. "And how did you come to be cast away? Has your yacht been wrecked? Did no one else come ashore? Where are your companions?"

In the teeth of this fusillade of questions Mr. Jones launched once more into his explanation.

"My yacht was not wrecked. I was not on my yacht. I was on board the Lusitania, and Heaven knows where she is now."

"Heaven probably does," interrupted the stranger, smiling coldly. "The Lusitania was torpedoed by a German submarine early this morning. We have but just received the information by wireless. If you were one of the victims you are indeed to be pitied. You have been forced to swim a very long way—several thousand miles, I think. Did you come around the Horn, or through the canal, my friend?"

Jones stared at him blankly. Was the man insane? Torpedoed—by Germans—thousands of miles! He clasped his head in his hands and groaned. It must be he himself who was mad. Then raising a very white face he spread out his arms in a gesture of despair.

"I'll have to admit that I don't know what you are talking about. I—I am afraid something has happened to my head—or I don't hear you correctly. No one could possibly torpedo the Lusitania—unless it were an anarchist, and I can't imagine what you mean by several thousand miles."

"That is sad. Yes, your brain must be affected, sir. You recollect that you are an American, and that is much, but I think you are mistaken about your name. Well, we will keep you with us. I do not really think it would be safe for you to stray about any longer alone in your pitiful condition. Captain Ivanovitch," he turned to the tall man in blue serge, "I will turn this young man over to you. You have heard him and will agree with me that it is wise to guard him carefully—against himself, of course. Do you understand?"

He still spoke in English, and it was in broken English that the captain replied. He spoke with a grin.

"Excellency, I und'stand. He have forgot his name. He have forgot even that there ees war. Have you suggest a name which he know perhaps better than that one he say?"

"Not yet. My friend, if I should address you as Richard Holloway, would it arouse no recollections in your mind?" The words were pleasant enough, but the voice was keen and cold as a winter wind.

Jones looked at the man in increased bewilderment. For the sake of peace and until he could escape from these madmen, had he better accept this now cognomen? Before he could make up his mind, "his excellency" turned aside with a short laugh. "Take good care of Mr. Holloway, Ivanovitch," he flung back over his shoulder. "It is just possible that we may arouse his memory and make him useful."

"Eester way," said the captain, with deceitful politeness, "eet is great pleasure to entertain you. So leetle we theenk Reechard Hol'way come to us so, free of weel. Weel you accept shelter from one of our leetle tents? Yes?"

Some inner instinct informed Mr. Jones that this Holloway personality was a dangerous one to assume. Playing himself off as another man did not appeal to him, anyway.

"I am not the person you seem to think I am," he said rather doggedly. "But I'd go anywhere to get something to eat. I'm nearly starved."

The captain grinned again, mockingly, hatefully. "At once, Meester Hol'way. We are all humbly servants. Dmitri—" Here he turned to one of the seamen who stood by staring stupidly and launched a command in some language which was unfamiliar to Jones, although, judging by the captain's own name and that of the man addressed, he assumed it to be Russian.

The sailor sprang to obey, and Captain Ivanovitch led Mr. Jones to one of the small tents. "Here," said he, "weel Meester Hol'way, permit to lodge himself. The tent, he is leetle, but you not mind that. Eet is more better than the ocean, no?"

"Humph! Perhaps," grunted Mr. Jones. He had taken an immediate dislike to the amiable captain. "By the way, you people seem to be very chary of introductions. Who is that gentleman I was just now speaking to? Your owner, I presume?"

"You not know? But of course. I forget you have jus' been sheepwreck. That ees his highness, Preence Sergius Petrofsky. The name also—it call nothing to your mind?"

"Nothing but Siberia and—er—Russian cigarettes. So, he's a connection of the royal family, is he? Now, tell me, what is all this fuss about, this man Holloway? There's no particle of use in calling me Holloway any longer, you know. I never even knew one of that name."

"So sad, Meester Hol'way. Perhaps you receive the blow upon the head—from wreckage, you und'stand? Eef you will show the place, we try to play the good part. We weel put upon eet the bandage."

"My head is all right, I tell you. My stomach is the only part of me that is in need of attention."

"Ver' good. Here come my man now weeth the good food. We shall not starve you, my friend. Also comes once more hees excellency."

The prince indeed came up at that moment. His features were set in a haughty frown, and he addressed himself immediately to Mr. Jones in a domineering tone.

"See here, Holloway, I have been considering this matter carefully, and can see no reason for your continuing the farce. How you came to fall into our hands is your own affair. But you must not rely upon the fact that your face is unfamiliar to us. There can be no question of your identity. You are the only man on the island—at least on the outside of it, for you yourself are theonly person who knows what is inside—who did not come here in the Monterey. Which places you beyond the shadow of a doubt as Richard Holloway. Now, answer me, yes or no. Will you tell me where lies the entrance to the caverns? If you help us we will make it well worth your while."

"What caverns?" queried Jones impatiently and with rising anger. These Russians were intolerable.

"Your feigned ignorance will not help you in the least, my friend," replied Petrofsky sternly. "I mean, of course, the caverns that lead beneath the cliffs. Out of all the caverns, the one which leads to that inner valley of yours. It was your story and yours alone which brought my brother across half a world to seek it.

"Come, sir, it is true that all of us here belong to the Brotherhood, and Paul has poisoned your mind against us. Also, by American eyes, I know that the great cause of nihilism is regarded askance.

"That is because you have experienced nothing of the evils which we plan to correct. But at least you know that I am a gentleman. If I give my word, I keep it. My brother has your trust."

"I am glad to hear it," murmured Jones wearily.

"What is that? I say that I, too, am a Petrofsky, and I swear to you that neither Paul nor those with him shall suffer the very least harm if you will help me. Nay, I will go further and promise that he shall receive his full share of the gains. The cause will not begrudge him that, although he has done his utmost to thwart our participation in this venture. But he and his little party can do nothing now. They have scarcely any provisions, hardly any arms or amunition. We could sweep down and annihilate them at this moment if I did not always remember that Paul is indeed my brother. Come, Mr. Holloway save him against himself and for the time at least cast in your lot with us. Will you give me your hand on it?"

Jones hesitated. To him this long rigmarole of nihilists and caverns failed to carry any meaning whatsoever.

"How can I convince you, Sir," he said at last, "that I know nothing whatever of these matters? That all I desire is to get away from this place and continue my quiet, respectable journey to London. And last and most emphatically that my name is certainly not Holloway, but Roland C. Jones, of New York City. You are making a serious mistake, Prince Petrofsky, and a most absurd one, if you will pardon me."

The Russian's eyes flashed angrily.

"Ho! You are yet stubborn? We will see if we cannot loosen your tongue a bit. Now, listen to me, and remember that I pledge my word as a Petrofsky that this promise will be kept. If you persist in your present attitude you will be taken on board that yacht and triced up to the signal-mast. Then you will be beate—they beat criminals in Russia.

With the knout. Do you know what the knout means? I can see by your expression that you do. Well, make up your mind which it is to be. You may expect either our gratitude or—the other! You have until morning to decide. While making up your mind you may remain in that tent. Ivanovitch, set a guard over this man and see that he does not escape. Mr. Holloway, I give you a very good evening!"

Sergius Petrofsky turned his straight white back upon the dismayed American and stalked off down to the shore. There he got into a waiting dingey and was rowed out to the yacht.

Jones started, shivering slightly, as the captain touched his elbow and said in a soft voice, "You are foolish man, Meester Hol'way. But do not be so foolish as try leave us tonight. You und'stand?"

And Mr. Jones was left with his guard of two bearded sailors.

"Good Lord!" he muttered to himself. "What a crazy mess! Is knouting any worse than drowning, I wonder? I'll bet it is!"

II

Midnight found Mr. Jones sitting in his prison tent disconsolate. There was a neat cot and blankets, but he had never felt less like sleeping in his life. He clung to his wakefulness and the few hours intervening between him and the morrow, like a sick man anticipating an extremely painful but inevitable operation. For something told him that Sergius Petrofsky was not the man to make empty threats.

Mr. Jones could see no way out of his predicament—unless he might anger the Russian into shooting instead of torturing him. The man certainly possessed a violent temper behind those haughty eyes of his.

While the captive was still revolving in his mind this desperate expedient, he suddenly felt something poke him sharply in the back. At the same instant some one said "Sh!" in a sharp, sibilant whisper.

The pain of the unexpected jab made Jones spring to his feet, crashing into the tent-pole and shaking the whole tent so violently that one of his guards appeared in the entrance. He thrust a large, hirsute countenance into the aperture and said something that sounded like the name of a Russian province.

"Get out, get out!" exclaimed Mr. Jones, gesturing violently to make his meaning clear. "It is nothing at all. Nothing. I bumped into the pole. Go away!"

The guard stared at him suspiciously for a moment longer, glanced about the little tent, which was dimly lighted by a lantern, and at last withdrew himself.

Once more the prisoner sat down, close to the canvas wall, and cautiously whispered, "It's all right. He has gone. Who are you and what do you want? What did you poke me like that for?"

There was a moment's silence, followed by a slight ripping sound. Through the canvas close by his shoulder Jones saw the point of a knife appear. It deftly cut two sides of a small triangle, then the flap so made was lifted and a face appeared. The face looked familiar. Then Mr. Jones recognized Doherty, the man who had captured him.

"Say, where are youse from?" The question was barely breathed in a voice which could not possibly have carried beyond the walls of the tent. Jones replied in the same bated tone:

"New York. Why?"

"That settles it, bo. Wait a jif."

The face was withdrawn, and the knife came into use once more. This time, however, it sawed out an aperture about three feet square near the bottom of the canvas wall. "Come on out, bo," whispered the rescuer.

Mr. Jones obeyed, moving as stealthily as he could, and having first made sure that the lantern would not cast the shadow of his escaping form upon the side of the tent. The situation required caution if ever a situation did.

Once outside he straightened himself, and felt a powerful hand grasp his arm. "This way, bo," came the whisper, and rescuer and rescued crept softly across the sands, behind the tents, and away, keeping close to the cliff. Glancing seaward, Jones saw the riding lights of the yacht, otherwise a dim, black bulk upon the quiet waters of the bay.

His guide led him away from the camp, not in the direction of the point where the two had first met, but onward along the beach. As soon as they were out of ear-shot of his Russian companions Doherty halted and said:

"I don't go no furder wid youse, see? G'wan on along until youse comes to a ravine. Go up there, and pretty soon youse comes to where dis other prince guy is, see? I don't know whether youse and this Holloway feller are the same guy or not. If you are, then youse don't need no more help from me. If youse ain't, then take a tip and hold your jawr about comin' straight from this camp, see? Now, beat it!"

"But see here!" exclaimed Jones, laying his hand on the other's shoulder to stay him. "Why have you helped me out this way? I'm everlastingly obliged to you, and—"

"Aw, ferget it!" snapped the other, shaking off the detaining hand roughly. "I ain't no friend of youse, neither, see? But no Russian dook ain't my boss when it comes to beatin' up another N'York feller with that knout thing. See? Now, will youse beat it, or d'youse want t'go back there and get what's comin' to youse?"

"I'll go. But, thank you, just the same. Say, can't you tell me something about all this business—"

But already Doherty had disappeared in the darkness, and with a slight sigh Roland C. Jones turned his face in the direction he had been instructed to follow. At any rate, the knouting was indefinitely postponed, and he could think of nothing much worse which could befall.

A short distance beyond the place where Doherty had left him the beach again ended in rocks. The man had spoken of a "ravine," so

Mr. Jones again climbed and scrambled, coming at last to where the cliff seemed to be split in two parts. How far this split penetrated into the rocky wall, he had no means of knowing, for it was all as dark as a pocket.

He discovered by stumbling into it that a little rill of water flowed down the middle of the split and into the sea. His best chance of exploring the ravine was to walk up the bed of this stream, which was no more than ankle deep. The water, he found, had the bitter chill of a glacier stream, and his feet were soon numb with cold. He had been offered no opportunity to dry his clothing, and it was still very damp and uncomfortable. He hoped that the extreme warmth of the night might prevent him from getting pneumonia.

Mr. Jones was not accustomed to such privations and hardships, and he found them extremely annoying.

Having no means of making a light, he stumbled along in the darkness, alternately cursing himself for having fallen overboard and the Hon. Percy Merridale as the (however remote) cause of all his misfortunes.

At length, however, the watercourse made a sharp bend, and rounding it, he beheld, a short distance ahead of him, a reddish glow upon the rocks. Then a black figure appeared in silhouette against the glow. He was considering how he could best make his presence known, for this he correctly surmised to be the place of that mysterious other encampment, when a voice exclaimed, "Hands up, there, or I'll fire!"

"Twice in one night!" muttered Jones rebelliously.

"What's that? Stranger, you've strayed onto the wrong range. Come into the light, and don't make no false moves, or you'll sure get perforated."

The voice had now come close to his side, and Mr. Jones felt the hard muzzle of some sort of weapon pressing against his ribs.

"I assure you that I am not armed," he said.

"I'll assure myself in a minute," responded the unsympathetic voice. "March, now!"

And again Jones marched. The light which Jones had seen reflected upon the cliff was cast by a fire built between two huge boulders in such a manner as to obscure its radiance so far as was possible. Emerging into the full glare, the unfortunate halted again, obedient to the pressure on his arm.

About the fire, which they were probably maintaining for the sake of illumination, since they were cooking nothing, and the temperature of the night was so high, several figures were gathered. All save one of these persons were men, the exception being a slender young girl, who at that moment turned her face and stared straight into the eyes of Mr. Jones.

"By Jupiter!" he murmured. "What's a girl like that doing with this crowd?"

The young lady was attired in a somewhat dilapidated white yachting costume, which looked as if it had been soaked more than once and not pressed in a long time. But she was not of the type whose social standing or personal attraction would ever be judged by her clothes, however she might be dressed. Her crisply curling hair gleamed almost red in the firelight, though in daytime it would probably be no more than auburn. Her skin was of that clear, transparent whiteness which sometimes accompanies such hair; her features clean-cut and firm to a point which would have been almost masculine had they not been relieved by, a pair of blue eyes so pure, childish, and innocent that looking at them one could only be reminded of the eyes of a suddenly awakened baby.

For the rest, she was slight of figure, with small, tapering hands and feet, giving an impression of physical weakness which Mr. Jones later discovered to be deceptive.

He did not, of course, absorb all these details of appearance in that first brief meeting. At the moment he saw only that here was a beautiful, well-bred girl in the midst of surroundings entirely unsuitable—unless she happened to be a movie actress, which seemed improbable.

Of her companions, one was a tall, rather good-looking man with a sensitive mouth and slightly receding chin, also in yachting costume. Another was a rangy, lanky sort of fellow, attired in nothing more formal than a shirt and shabby trousers. The two remaining men were plainly of a lower class, probably seamen from their general appearance.

With a look of astonishment the girl glanced from Jones to his captor, who stood slightly behind him, and said:

"James, who is this person? How did he come here?"

Yes, she said it exactly as if she were standing in her own drawing-room, inquiring of the butler how some unknown vagabond had penetrated into her domain. Something humorous in the whole situation smote Jones abruptly, so that he laughed aloud, and she stared at him more haughtily than ever.

FRANCIS STEVENS

"I beg your pardon," said Mr. Jones, hastening to correct his involuntary rudeness, "I have had a rather trying evening, and—er—I did not expect to see a young lady in this place."

"And why not, pray? You are one of Prince Sergius' friends, are you not? Paul, this must be one of your brother's men, although I for one have never seen him before. Do you know him?"

She addressed the handsome man with the weak chin, and Jones knew this must be the brother of the Russian who had imprisoned him.

"No," he replied, rising lazily. "I have never seen the fellow before. Do you know him? Dick Holloway?"

"Not yet, but I've no objection. What is your name, anyway?"

So the man in the shirt and trousers was Holloway. Jones looked at him with considerable interest, since it was in his name that he had nearly suffered so much, and saw that he was a young man with a keen, rather strong face. Dressed differently, he might have been either a reporter or an automobile salesman—or a member of Jones's own club.

"My name is Roland C. Jones," stated the castaway, somewhat weary of reiterating that fact. "Some hours ago, early in the evening, I was cast up on the beach by the storm. I—think I had fallen overboard in my sleep. I was on my way to London. Then I—" He suddenly remembered Doherty's warning. He decided that he owed it to his benefactor to keep faith. "I came on up the beach and stumbled into this ravine and walked up it and—and here I am, you know."

This simple statement was met by dead silence for a moment. Then the Russian asked: "You were going to London, you say? That sounds a little peculiar. And you say you were wrecked, some hours ago? Where were you, pray, in the interval? Do you mean you have met no one since that time?"

"Yes," admitted Mr. Jones, realizing that his story lacked strength. "I met one man—or, rather, I saw a man; but as soon as he caught sight of me he made off. I chased him, but he was too quick. Then I wandered around a while, until I found my way here."

"H—m What ship were you on?"

Jones started to reply, "The Lusitania," but checked himself. He was actually afraid that these people, too, would insist on that nightmare tangle of German torpedoes and impossible distances. Then he would know that something had crone wrong in his brain. He did not want to know it just then. There was too much to attend to without that. "I was on my own yacht, the Bandersnatch. We were just cruising around, you know. We had thought of running over to the Azores." (Jones was not at all sure by this time where in the Atlantic he might be, but the Azores, as occupying a fairly central position, seemed safe.) "I must have walked in my sleep, for first thing I knew I was in the water, and the only wonder is that I was not drowned. I am a New Yorker, but we sailed from Savannah." He was rather proud of this touch of realism, but Holloway burst out laughing.

"First London, and now the Azores," the latter remarked in a tone of goodnatured amusement. "You seem to have put out on a remarkable voyage."

"For my part," interposed the young lady, who, despite her infantile eye, seemed of very determined and decisive character, "I don't believe a word of your story. If you were on a yacht, which I don't doubt, it was the Monterey, and she lies in the bay now. I believe you were on board at the same time we were, although we didn't see you. That about London and Savannah and the Azores is merely ridiculous. I can't imagine your object in making such absurd statements. Paul, this man has been sent here by your brother to spy upon us and find out the secret of the caverns."

Paul nodded his head, saying: "Holloway, do you not think that Miss Weston is right?"

"It's a one best bet she is, prince. All that gas about his yacht and the rest of it was probably planned to make us think he's a bit light in his upper story."

"What?"

"Bats in his belfry—nobody home—you know."

"Oh, you mean insane. But why should he wish us to think that?"

"So we won't take too much pains to keep our cards face down. If you'll take a tip from me, prince, you'll keep this angel-faced little castaway tied right to mama's apron-strings till time's called."

The prince laughed amiably, but the amiability was for Holloway, not Mr. Jones.

"Your expressions—your idioms—they are so very charming, Dick Holloway. But you are right. We cannot afford to be betrayed. James Haskins, you will kindly remain close to this gentleman's side. Take him with you and return to your post. And now, my friends, we have already sat too long talking. Let us sleep for the two hours that remain of night. Remember, we start at dawn."

III

As if stricken dumb, Mr. Jones obeyed the guiding hand of James Haskins, as it steered him back to the point whence he had first sighted the camp-fire. It seemed as though something even stronger than Fate were against him. Whatever he said was turned back upon him; whatever he did, it merely led him into fresh disaster. There was no use in fighting the tide. Henceforth he would keep still and permit events to shape themselves, unhelped or hindered by his efforts.

Perhaps, presently, he would wake up. Yes, this must be some unusually vivid nightmare which had him in its clutches.

"Squat right down on that rock, stranger, and make yourself at home." Of course, it was Haskins who broke in on his reverie. "If any more mavericks stray off your range up this way, I'll be right here to throw, tie, and brand 'em. Have a cigarette?"

"No—Yes, thank you, I believe I will."

For a few moments the two smoked without speaking. The night was silent, save for the low, distant murmur of the sea and the occasional squeak of a bat. Overhead the great, brilliant stars, which hung so strangely low and near, seemed to wink at Jones, as if they were sharers in some huge joke of whose nature he was not yet informed, but of which he was unquestionably the butt.

"Strange," he reflected. "I can't remember ever having smoked in a dream before. I can taste the tobacco, too. And my hands hurt like the dickens, where I scraped 'em on the rocks. I wonder if I ever will wake up. That girl is a winner for looks, all right; but, oh, mama, I don't like her disposition one little bit! Seems to have it in for me, all right. I wonder—"

"Pleasant dreams!" It was James Haskins again. "Say, did you really get washed ashore like you told the bunch?"

"I certainly did," said Jones with convincing vigor and promptitude. "Look here; if I should tell you the whole story about what has happened since I reached this place, would you believe me?"

"Fire away!" the other replied noncommittally.

Jones obeyed, and his jailer listened patiently and in silence to the full tale of his misadventures. Barring the fact that it was a liner and not his own yacht from which he had fallen, he adhered closely to facts; for, in the light of his reception, it seemed it was only for his own good that

Doherty had warned him not to speak of the other camp. And in this opinion his listener presently confirmed him.

"So this man Doherty told you not to tell you'd been in his camp, did he?" was Haskins's comment at the end of the recital. "Well, he was dead right, friend castaway. Prince Paul has got just the same love for Prince Sergius that a grizzly has for a rattlesnake.

"But me, I think you're straight. For one thing, you haven't got the map of a bunco-steerer; and for another, I think you are because size thinks you ain't. Do you get me? I never saw anything in skirts yet that you couldn't copper her guess and be on the right trail. Only your swim seems to have twisted your geography some. It isn't the Azores you mean—it's the Philippines, or Hawaii. Now, if you and me should swap yarns, will you give me away to my outfit, or will you keep it under your hair?"

"Prince Sergius' knout wouldn't extract it from me," sighed Mr. Jones, with the happy sense that here again, where least expected, he had found a friend.

"Well, to commence with, me, I'm riding a long way off my own range, which is Colorado, by rights, though I was born in Arizona. Arizona Jim, that's me. Well, this prince fellow come along when I was on my uppers in Frisco, having gone up against a few large doses of redeye and an outfit of card-sharks some simultaneous. But, say, you fellows started from Savannah, you said. Did you get into the Pacific through the canal?"

The Pacific? Jones's brain reeled again, but he managed to keep his voice steady and reply: "Yes, of course we went through the canal."

"I asked because I know a fellow that runs a cafe in Colon. Did you stop there?"

"I didn't go ashore there. But how did you meet the prince?"

"Oh, yes. Well, as I was saying, he met up with me, and he offers me a job. Says he's goin' on a big trip and wants a guy with a good gun-eye. That's me, all right; so I joins the outfit immediate. Then's when I meet this brother of his, they bein' on good terms then, just like an owl and a prairie-dog.

"So brother Sergius, it seems, he's gone right ahead and chartered a yacht without waiting for brother Paul to approve the deal. This annoys us some, but not half so much as when we get away out on the broad, be-yutiful, lonesome Pacific Ocean and finds that the captain and the crew are all 'brothers' of his, too. Yes, little Annie, Sergius is in with the anarchists, saddle, bridle, and spurs, and the great and noble cause has got to get its share in the profits, even if brother Sergius has to knife brother Paul to do it. Oh, yes, it was some rotten deal, take it from me."

"But where does this Miss. . . Miss—"

"Weston come in? Not yet but soon. We picks Miss Weston up out of an open boat, along with a couple of half-dead sailors. She's a Boston young lady that's been taking lessons in nursing. She aims to join the Red Cross, but she's some foxy, so she comes clear across to Frisco and takes a boat for Japan, figurin' to get into the festivities by the back gate, so to speak. No German torpedoes in hers."

(Jones gave a mental groan. Again!)

"And right then, was when the lid blew off the kettle for keeps. I never did see two brothers take a shine to the same girl quite so simultaneous and sudden. Gee, they ought to have been twins, their tastes are so similar. Was she going to be Princess Sergius or Princess Paul? I suggests to Paul, casual-like, that they cut her in two and divide her up, it being my idea that there ain't any female woman born that's any real good in a round-up like this one. But he didn't seem to take to it.

"So brother Paul, he reveals to her the perfidy of brother Sergius, and right away that swings her. No nihilanarchists for hers. In which she shows more sense than I'd expected.

"Right about then we sights this here Joker Island. Some name, Joker; but she's some Island, too, believe me. There being considerable hard feeling, what with one thing and another, me and Prince Paul and this Weston girl and her two sailors, we thinks it wise and becoming to withdraw ourselves from evil associations, and we drops off the yacht the first dark night. Then Prince Paul he says there's a guy on the island expecting him, which is the first I heard of Holloway. As near as I can make out, this is Holloway's island, by right of being wrecked here and finding out some darn thing about the inside of it. These cliffs go all the way around, you know, but there's a cave runs under 'em, and Mr. Holloway, he's the only one that knows where it is."

"I shouldn't think it would be very difficult to find a cave in a wall of rock like this, if one hunted for it," suggested Jones, deeply interested in the narrative.

"Oh, no, it's dead easy—like three guesses at which is the right hole in a colander. There's about fifteen hundred other caves, and they all run back under the cliffs, and there's only one that goes clear through. And if you get lost in a blind lead—good night!"

"But what is there inside, anyway?"

"Me not being Prince Paul's confidential secretary, I don't know, nor I don't know how Sergius thinks he's going to get there without dear brother Paul and friend Holloway. But it's plain he knows something about Holloway, or he wouldn't have made that nice, kind offer to persuade you when he thought you was Holloway. One thing, it's clear he don't know him by sight. The way I figure it is that when Holloway was wrecked here, after he comes out of the inside again, he was taken off by some ship, and then he hikes right after Prince Paul, who, it seems, is his dear old college chum. It must be some secret, all right; for Paul, he gets leave immediate from his regiment by the Czar's special permit.

"But brother Sergius, who's some unpopular at home, he don't need no permit, because he's in America already. I don't think Paul was lookin' to run across him; but when he does, he takes him in on the deal for the sake of them old days back on the farm. Well, while Paul is rustling this outfit together, friend Richard gets himself put on the island alone again, with provisions, and stays right on the claim to wait for Paul. Paul comes along with a brother and a aggregation of nihilanarchists and a Boston schoolmarm girl, and now the only way out is in."

"What?"

"Just like I says—in. We're going through the caves at daybreak. Holloway says even he might get the wrong one at night."

"Good Lord!" murmured Mr. Jones softly. From boyhood he had suffered from a dread of dark, shut-in places, running parallel, perhaps, with his habit of sleep-walking. Even now he never slept without a light in his room, and he would not have explored the Mammoth Caves with a guard of fifty guides for all the money in the world. "Are you—are they going to take me along?"

"What's the matter? Don't you want to sit in? Take it from me, you're better off with Paul than you would be with Sergius, and you've only got Paul and Sergius to choose between."

"What sort of lights are you going to use?" queried Mr. Jones anxiously.

"Oh, we have some electric torches. Stranger, I've talked myself into the finest thirst outside of Arizona. But it's wasted—absolutely wasted. Ain't that a sad thought? By gracious, I'd almost go over and take up with this naughty Sergius party, if I thought he had anything stronger than water to give me. But, alas! The Monterey is like Russia—she's gone prohibition. Don't you notice a different feeling in the air? What time's it getting to be?" He glanced at his watch.

"'What time were you intending to start?" inquired Jones.

"Half an hour. It's three now. Here comes Holloway."

IV

"Did you catch any more bugs, Jim?" called Richard Holloway cheerfully as he approached. "No? Too bad. Hoped we could start a collection. Say, Mr.—er, what did you say your name was? Something unusual, wasn't it?"

"Jones," replied the castaway rather stiffly. He was a trifle tired of the disdainful attitude which every one except the cowboy had so far assumed toward him. "Roland C. Jones."

"Mr. Roland C. Jones, I salute you." Holloway bowed very low and straightened with a laugh. "Did you leave any last will and testament with his serene and nihilistic highness when he sent you over here? Because, you know, it's just possible that something might happen to you inside. You've no idea how wonderfully exciting 'inside' is, Mr. Jones. Don't let me alarm you, though."

Jones laughed almost hysterically. "It can't be much more exciting than—than everything else," he said. "And as for getting killed, I'm beginning to have a suspicion that that's the best thing which could happen to me."

He was thinking of his own mental condition, but Holloway understood him differently.

"So bad as that?" he asked with mock commiseration. "No home? No friends? Somebody cooked your chestnuts for you? Never mind, sweet child. We'll buy you some more—if we ever get off Joker Island. Coming, Prince?" he called back, as a voice hailed him from the little camp. "Come on, Jimmy; and you, too, Rolly! You don't mind if I call you Rolly? I feel in my heart that we're going to be friends, Rolly, and what's a name between pals?"

"I don't care what you call me," replied Mr. Jones, smiling in spite of himself. After all, there was something very likeable about this impertinent, goodnatured fellow. He felt that he could get along very nicely if he had nobody but the cowboy and Richard Holloway to deal with.

They found the rest of the party eating a very informal breakfast, consisting of hardtack, a few rashers of bacon, and some really excellent coffee. Jones received his share thankfully. He could not remember a time when he had been so hungry, or hungry so often, as in the few hours since he had come to Joker Island.

Then the fire was extinguished; what provisions were left and some simple impedimenta were divided equally among the men, and the expedition started with only Miss Weston unburdened. She tripped lightly along beside her Russian admirer, apparently as merry and light-hearted as if they were bound on a picnic.

Dawn had come upon them with extraordinary suddenness as they ate, it seemed to Mr. Jones. There had been a few moments of ghostly twilight. Then the sun leaped into the sky, like a tiger springing from its lair, and flung at them his first rays with an ardor which promised insufferable heat later on.

Now that it was light, Jones perceived that the ravine, or split in the cliff wall, ended abruptly just beyond the camp. There the precipice towered as forbidding and unscalable as it hung above the outer beach. The little stream sprang from a mere crevice in the otherwise solid wall. There were certainly no caverns in that direction, and he was not surprised when Holloway, in his capacity of guide, led the way back down the ravine toward the sea; but he did wonder how they could emerge upon the beach without being seen by the nihilists.

They had followed the watercourse only a short distance, however, when Holloway turned aside and led them into a yet narrower crack in the rocks which branched off from the main ravine. The going became more and more difficult, and Paul Petrofsky was obliged to almost carry the girl over some places, while the rest of the party scrambled and sweated and swore sotto voce.

At last the crack widened; they caught a glimpse of blue beyond, and in another moment they came out upon a part of the beach which was cut off by a jutting promontory of rock from the small bay where the Monterey lay anchored. Jones thought that a bird's-eye view of that island must show the cliff to be fairly scalloped with little bays and promontories.

And here the black rock was honeycombed with dark holes, bored out either by the sea or by volcanic agency; some of them no more than a foot or so across, a few large enough so that a motor-truck could have been safely driven in.

"This is only the beginning of 'em," declared Holloway, addressing Petrofsky, but in loud enough tones to be heard by all. "Half way 'round the island the rock is fairly-perforated. Some place for a tribe of cave men, no?"

Then, suddenly assuming the manner of a tourist guide: "Just step this way, lady and gentlemen. Here you may behold the finest—oldest— most dog-gonedest aggregation of black holes—"

His voice died away and became indistinguishable, for he had dropped to hands and knees and crawled into one of the smaller caverns.

Petrofsky, pausing only to draw an electric torch from his pocket, immediately followed, and close upon his heels crept Miss Margaret Weston. To Jones's amazement, the girl was laughing just before she disappeared. He could not have laughed himself to win a medal. However, Jim Haskins and the two sailors were looking at him expectantly.

There was nothing else for it, so he, too, dropped to his knees and crawled into the hole, pushing ahead of him the small bundle which had been assigned him to carry. He wondered bitterly if they were to crawl all the way through the cliff.

Ahead of him he could see a moving black mass against a dim glow of light, which he knew to be the intrepid Miss Weston, of Boston, Massachusetts. Jones had no light himself, and was too far behind the leaders to get any benefit from theirs. The rock was wet and a trifle slimy. He thought of snakes, but remembered gratefully that if there were any they would have a good chance to bite three people before they got to him.

Behind, he could hear a grunting and scraping, and knew the other three were following.

Then the glow ahead abruptly disappeared, and there was a scrambling, thumping sound. Had Holloway and the Russian fallen into some abyss? He halted, but immediately after heard a voice calling, "Come ahead! It's all right! Oh, what a perfectly lovely, splendid place!"

It was the voice of Margaret Weston, and a moment later Mr. Jones scrambled out of the narrow hole into an enormous, scintillating cavern. The lights of two electric torches were reflected dazzlingly from a million fiery points.

"What perfectly gorgeous stalactites!" exclaimed the girl rapturously. "Oh, Mr. Holloway, I'm so glad you found this place! It's worth anything just to have seen it. Why, if it were not so hard to reach, this would be one of the show places of the world, would it not?"

"It would," admitted the flattered Mr. Holloway. "But I only wish I could let some sunlight into the hole for you. I've taken some pieces of this stuff out, and in daylight they are all colors of the rainbow. Look like stuff out of a jeweller's window. The colors don't show up in this light."

"Thank you, but it's quite beautiful enough as it is."

Even Jones had to admit to himself that Miss Weston was, in a measure, right. Above their heads was a black void. The roof was too high and probably too dark in color for their lights to show it, but all about them, depending almost to the floor, hung a thousand icicle-points, which reflected the electric rays as if they had been encrusted with diamonds. From the floor, also, rose points and mounds of brilliant crystals. This lower forest of stalagmites seemed to extend itself indefinitely, certainly beyond range of the torches.

"Dick Holloway," said the prince, "this is fairyland to which you have brought us. The air, too, which I had thought would be almost poisonous, it is fresh. It smells of the sea. There must be many more openings into this place than that by which we entered."

"There probably are," agreed Holloway, "but I'd hate to hunt for them. I was lost in these caves once—that was the way I happened to locate the way through—but I'd hate to risk it twice."

"But tell me," continued the prince, gazing upward curiously, "is there no danger from the falling of some of these huge masses from the roof?"

"Sure thing there is. But—Jimmy, there goes a beauty right this minute!"

There was an ominous crackling sound, the mild forerunner of a thunderous, deafening crash. The air was filled with a cloud of choking white dust, through which the torches gleamed faintly as through a fog. The noise was followed by a series of lesser crashes. Then came again the calm, unagitated voice of Holloway.

"Did that hit anybody? If it did, farewell to the dear departed. Is every one here?"

One by one the little party answered with their names, Jones last, and in a voice which he rendered steady with some effort. He had always known that caverns would be just like this. For a moment he had been deceived by the treacherous beauty of this one, but no more. Surely they would turn back now. Nobody could expect to pass through this place where at any moment a thousand pounds of glittering stalactite was liable to drop on him—

It was the voice of Miss Weston which answered his unspoken thought.

"Well, there is no need of our standing here, is there? How in the world can you find your way, Mr. Holloway?"

"Been here before," replied that gentleman cheerfully. "Know it like the streets of my hometown. Come along."

By this time the white dust had somewhat settled, and Jones could see his companions clearly. They were starting off single file between the innumerable stalagmites, apparently careless of disaster. On an impulse he crouched down behind a white mound.

Jim Haskins passed within hand's reach, but did not see him in the shadow. The two sailors were a little behind, and on a sudden thought Jones cautiously pushed his bundle of miscellaneous camp articles out from behind his mound.

An instant later one of the sailors stumbled over it, and as Jones had craftily foreseen, imagined that it had been dropped by one of the men ahead. Grumbling, the man picked it up and added it to his own load, and with no thought for a possible escaping prisoner, passed on.

In fact, nobody gave Mr. Jones a thought. He was alone, neglected and forsaken, and the fact gave him supreme relief. He had looked carefully, while there was still sufficient light, and a seen a black hole yawning, the hole by which they had entered this place of terror. Having honestly restored to his captors the goods with which he had been entrusted, Mr. Jones felt no scruples about deserting them.

Just before the last gleam of light from the electric torches faded and disappeared, Mr. Jones plunged back into the small tunnel and began rapidly wriggling his way toward open air and the blessed light of day.

Somehow or other the passage seemed much longer than when he had come that way at the heels of the Boston girl. Jones crawled and crawled, until his knees and elbows were sore, but still he could see no gleam of light ahead. It seemed to him that he had been crawling for hours. What could be the matter?

Suddenly the horrifying explanation dawned upon him. This was not the tunnel by which they had entered, but another of the labyrinthine system of caves to which Holloway had referred!

Mr. Jones stopped crawling and tried to turn himself about. There was not room enough, however, and he only hurt himself still more upon the slimy rock. There was no use in trying to wriggle backward, for he knew that he would become exhausted before he could ever regain the cave of stalactites by such a laborious process. Besides, he reflected, even if be did get back there he would be no better off. Surrounded by impenetrable midnight darkness, how could he hope to rediscover the passage he had been unable to identify while there was light?

With a sinking heart he contemplated the many hours of mental and physical suffering which lay before him if he should fail to extricate himself. He must go on. What a fool he had been to desert the party of adventurers! After all, they were kindly, honest folk and it would have been far better to have died suddenly by the fall of a stalactite, or in some merciful abyss, than here alone in the darkness of the damned.

He must get out! And when "must" drives, a man will do a great deal more than appears possible. Roland C. Jones did. He crawled literally for hours, turning, winding with the tunnel, like an unhappy and desolate angle-worm in the black bosom of Earth.

Once, exhausted, he let himself subside, and despite all the terrors of darkness went to sleep. He had not slept for v. long time, and when he awoke, though he ached in every limb, he felt refreshed and took new courage to crawl on.

Crawling is a slow process—at least, for a human being—but if a man crawl far enough, and encounters no obstruction, he is bound to get somewhere sometime, and that is what happened to Mr. Jones. He had long since given up all hope, and become a mere, dogged crawling-machine, when it happened. It was a tremendous thing and an experience which in all his after-life he never forgot. He saw the rock beneath him!

Then he raised his head, hopefully, prayerfully, and there, far ahead, beamed a glorious star of light!

Then did Mr. Jones perform prodigies of crawling. As if he had just started, he wriggled and scrambled along, and at last actually emerged from the black womb of death into the adorable, intolerable brilliance of day. Also into the very arms of Doherty, his former rescuer!

Behind Doherty stood Captain Ivanovitch, and beside him was Sergius Petrofsky. Mr. Jones had crawled windingly through the rock, all the way from behind the promontory, around the end of the ravine, and back to the little bay whereon the Monterey still lay at anchor.

He had expected anything—but not this. In the eternity which had elapsed since entering that black rat-hole he had forgotten that such a person as Sergius Petrofsky existed. His clothing was ripped to slimy rags. In a dozen places his body and limbs were scraped raw, he was faint and sick for lack of food and drink—and before him stood the man who had promised to torture him that day. The villainies of Fate were too prodigious.

Mr. Jones slipped suddenly from the sustaining grip of Doherty, and dropped in a wretched heap upon the sand.

V

When sense at last returned to the castaway, he opened his eyes and stared blankly about for a moment. He had dreamed that he was in his own bedroom in his own New York bachelor apartment, and these walls of brown canvas, that strange face bent above his, seemed incredible, far more visionary than the dream itself. Then the whiff of an agreeable odor reached his nostrils. Food! Mr. Jones sat up, and reached out his hands in one single motion. Doherty placed the bowl which he carried with them.

"I've brought youse your scoffin's," he said. "Gee! Youse was a sight when youse fell out of diat hole. His nibs is waitin' to see youse."

"Let him wait," commanded Jones in a determined voice. "Keep him out, can't you, till I finish this? This is the first thing I've had to eat for—for week's judging by the way my appetite feels."

Doherty laughed and seated himself on the side of the cot. "I'll tell him youse was pounding your ear so hard I couldn't wake youse up."

"Thanks, old man." There was an interval of silence, then Jones handed back the polished bowl with a great sigh, swung his legs to the floor and sat up. "Where are my clothes?" he asked.

"Your clothes? Gee, youse ain't got no clothes. There was a couple of old rags hangin' to youse, but if dat Anthony Comstock guy ever seen youse he'd t'row a fit, sure. Them things youse has on now belongs to the captain."

"But what am I to do? I can't walk around in these pajamas."

Doherty grinned. He seemed in an uncommonly good humor.

"Dat's all right. His nibs has came across wit' dese here glad rags. Climb, into 'em and look sharp, or I'll get the hide tore off me for keepin' him waitin'. There's a basin over there if youse wants to wash some more, but gee! They sure had to give you one bath before they could put youse to bed even."

"Well, I guess a little more water won't hurt me."

Jones also found a safety razor and a mug of luke-warm water beside the basin, and was glad enough to shave, although his beard was by this time a very stiff one to get rid of.

Then he dressed in the "glad rags" indicated by Mr. Doherty, which he found consisted of a suit of thin silk underwear, breeches and tunic coat of khaki, socks, puttees, and a pair of heavy, but wellmade shoes.

In fact, as good an outfit for a tramping or hunting expedition as Jones could have bought anywhere in New York.

Very gratefully he donned the garments, which to his joy fitted him quite passably. The shoes were a little loose, but that was much more satisfactory than if they had been too tight.

He thought, as he dressed, that if they intended to abuse him—they had made a peculiar beginning. Sleep and food had done a great deal to bring him back to a normal outlook on life. His limbs still ached, but that was hardly strange in view of the strenuous character of recent experiences. Mr. Jones presently announced his readiness to go to or receive the waiting Sergius.

"Youse can wait here. I'll get him," said Doherty, who all the time preserved the same astonishing amiability. He did not even question Mr. Jones in regard to how he had come to return there, and not only return, but return in such a singular manner and condition. Some species of relief or joy fairly radiated from the man's every glance and word.

Mr. Jones did not have to wait long after Doherty's departure. He had gone to the entrance and stood looking out. The sun beat down from almost directly overhead, and he correctly surmised that this was the day following that on which he had emerged from the cave. He must have slept the clock fairly around.

Some distance up the beach a number of men were gathered about a large object which was partly obscured by an intervening tent, so that he could not quite make out its nature. In a moment he saw Sergius Petrofsky coming toward him alone.

"My friend," said the nihilist, glancing him up and down with a smile, "you have a much improved appearance."

"Thanks to you, Prince Sergius," asserted Jones, wondering yet more at the apparent friendliness of every one.

"You are entirely welcome, Mr. Holloway. But come inside, please. We must talk together."

They seated themselves, Jones on the cot, Sergius on the campchair.

"And now, Mr. Holloway, perhaps you will explain what has become of my brother and—and the young lady, Miss Weston."

So that was it. They had discovered that the other party had vanished into thin air and looked to him to recover the trail. Jones determined in his own honest mind that he would never discover to them the location of those caves. Besides, they might try to make him enter them again!

But he could not feel that any loyalty to a party which had, after all, treated him only as a spy and a liar, demanded further sacrifice than this.

"In the first place, Prince Sergius, I am not Richard Holloway. When you found me I had never seen or heard of such a person, but since that time I have met the man himself."

Without reserve, save as regarded any implication of Doherty, Jones proceeded to tell his story, to which the Russian listened with an impassive face. At the end, however, he rose and extended his hand to his involuntary guest.

"I was mistaken, Mr. Jones, and I have to ask your forgiveness. We must have seemed to you not only inhospitable, but boorish in the last degree to so threaten you who deserved only our help and kindness. But your story of the Lusitania you yourself will admit was—well, let us speak no more of that. Perhaps some day you will entrust me with your full confidence. Now, however, you are in a position to extend to me a very great service.

"No—" he raised a protesting hand as Jones started to speak, "I do not longer ask that you reveal the cavern entrance. Your own experience shows what is the most likely fate of those attempting it without good guidance. We have done all in our power to make you forget our past unjust treatment, even while we still deemed you Richard Holloway. May I expect your favor in return?"

"Why, of course," replied Jones in some surprise. "But I don't exactly see what I could do—"

"You will see," said the prince, with a rather peculiar smile. "Will you be pleased to follow me?"

Together they left the tent and walked across the sands toward the object of which Jones had earlier caught a glimpse. Now he saw what it was. It was an aeroplane. The nihilist was again speaking:

"I had planned to take with me the man, Doherty, but he is an ignorant fellow, entirely unsuited to such an undertaking. Also, he was afraid to go. None other of the men are suitable. Ivanovitch, he must remain to look after our crew. My mechanic is ill on board the Monterey. The others are too stupid. They are fellow Russians and brothers in the cause, but you see I speak frankly. You, on the other hand, are young, intelligent, and—"

"You want me to go up in that thing with you?" gasped Mr. Jones.

"Of course. I am a good airman, You need feel no alarm, for in the air you will be in no danger. It is when we descend to what is within that I desire with me a reliable companion. Are we to be comrades?"

"You give me a choice?"

"But yes. Unless you come willingly, I would better make my flight alone."

"All right. I'll go."

Yes, it was really Roland Chesterton Jones, the coward of the caverns, who said these words! As a matter of fact, Jones was not a coward at all, but a victim of subconscious terror of the dark. Given a fair chance and the open air, he had always felt perfectly willing to face danger, although his life before coming to Joker Island had not been an adventurous one and he was by choice a young man of quiet life and manners.

The prince gave him an approving nod.

"I am not a bad reader of features. We will' meet everything like comrades, eh? And you will not be tempted, if we should come upon them, to return to my brother and his people?"

"I will not," said Jones firmly. He had nothing against any of them, but he possessed a natural predilection toward any one who treated him courteously, nihilist or not.

Moreover, there was something about Sergius Petrofsky which had attracted him from the first, in spite of his brutal threat that first night. Fanatical, cruel even, when thwarted, there was yet about him that invisible aura which we term personality, for lack of a better name. If he had been an actor he would undoubtedly have been an idol of the matinee girls. Jones wondered, when he thought of it, that Miss Weston had turned from him to his less attractive brother.

They had now reached the group of sailors gathered about the monoplane. Captain Ivanovitch was nowhere in sight, and they were lounging about in the sand, but all sprang to their feet at sight of Sergius. He said something sharply to them in Russian and all save two went off toward the tents. Then he turned again to his guest.

"I have been obliged to do almost all the work of assembling the plane with my own hands, because of this unfortunate illness of Thoreau, my mechanic. Are you in the least familiar with this sort of engine? It would be too much to hope that you know anything of the science of flight."

Mr. Jones hastened to disclaim any knowledge on either subject. He had always left even the mysteries of his own motor-cars, and his big power-boat, the Bandersnatch, to the expert attentions of their respective chauffeurs and captain. The most he knew about gasoline was that it sometimes exploded, and was used to drive automobiles, powerboats, and aeroplanes. Of the dark secrets of spark, ignition, carburetor, and so forth he was as innocent as a child.

"Then it is of no use for me to try to instruct you in the brief space which lies between us and departure. Your part will be to sit quiet in that seat which you see behind the pilot's place, and if we come to any grief I will endeavor to play the part of driver and mechanic also. We are taking with us no provisions, save a slight luncheon in that hamper, but these rifles may prove convenient. It is my purpose to make, as it were, a reconnaissance, and we may not even descend into the inner valley or crater until a later flight."

At this moment Captain Ivanovitch came up, accompanied by Doherty. The captain entered into conversation with Sergius in Russian, and as Mr. Jones waited for the next move, Doherty said in a low voice, "Gee, ain't I glad youse showed up? I ain't got no use for them flyin' things. If ever I gets to be a angel I suppose I'll have to flutter me wings—but till I gets 'em I sticks right to the ground floor."

"You may be right," Jones admitted.

"I thought we'd butt into the valley by the subway after all when I seen youse come out. But, gee, this lets little Willie out complete. Youse is welcome to the job."

"Mr. Jones," interrupted Sergius, "will you put these things on? It is not so warm up above there, you know."

He was holding out a heavy coat and a sort of hood, which Jones donned, while the nihilist put on a similar outfit. To the hood was attached a pair of large goggles which could be pulled down over the eyes. It was not a regular aviator's costume, but near enough for the short flight contemplated.

Then the two strangely assorted companions climbed to their places. Needless to say, it was the first time Mr. Jones had ever been in an aeroplane. He had attended meets, watched the daring evolutions of the dragon-flylike things against the sky, and had one or two opportunities to go up himself, but he had never experienced any desire to rise higher above solid earth than the top floor of a skyscraper.

Yet now he found himself strangely cool and unperturbed. Sergius Petrofsky inspired him with a great deal of confidence in his ability as a man of action.

Now Ivanovitch and a seaman had grasped the monoplane, one on each side at the rear, and were standing with feet braced as if expecting some great strain upon their muscles. Sergius did something with a lever and the engine burst forth into a roar which startled Mr. Jones extremely. He had forgotten what a racket the things make.

Then he felt a slight jerk and the plane was rolling swiftly along the sand. He was thrown back in his seat, as the machine tilted upward, and a moment later shut his eyes; for he had seen the beach dropping away from under them, and it seemed as if a violent wind had suddenly arisen. Remembering the goggles he reached up and pulled them down over his eyes before opening them again.

Glancing downward he saw the sea, rocking and swaying beneath them, had a moment of nausea, and realized that it was the plane which was rocking. They were up, they were actually flying through the air. The wind of their flight was beating upon his fate. The experience was different from anything which he had ever imagined, arid yet it was strangely exhilarating too. For the first time since he had found himself adrift in the sea, he was glad that he had fallen off the liner.

No matter what might befall, nothing could ever rob him of the memory of this moment when he learned the real meaning of man's victory over the air.

Sergius turned slightly and shouted something over his shoulder, but the roar of engine and propeller drowned his voice. Jones shook his head and shouted back something equally indistinguishable. He had meant to say "Grand! Glorious! Splendid!" but the wind seemed to hurl the words back down his throat.

He looked down again and saw to his amazement how high they had already climbed. The island lay beneath them, with that maplike appearance which one notices in bird's-eye views. The black cliff which had appeared so awesome and forbidding was now no more than a huge, irregular oval line of black. And this line surrounded—what? A sea of green, it seemed, probably the tops of trees, although the foliage was indistinguishable from that height. Moreover it all appeared to be swinging in vast circles, for they were ascending in a steep spiral.

Jones began to wonder how high they were to mount. He had imagined, in the brief time given him for thought, that they would simply rise above the cliff and immediately descend upon the other side.

Then, abruptly, the steady roar of the engine slackened and died. The nose of the plane dipped earthward and they were sliding down the air, swiftly, but so smoothly that the sensation was one of pure delight. The circles of their descent were so wide that, as they came nearer, Jones had plenty of time to study the strange valley which lay shut off from and unsuspected of the outer world.

That the island had been one huge volcanic crater at one time in its history, there could be no doubt. Now, however, there was nothing to suggest a volcano save the wall itself, and within was a wide expanse of the greenest verdure. The great oval was about ten or twelve miles long. Its floor was of a slightly undulating, parklike appearance, the upper, darker green being broken here and there by lighter patches which Jones presumed to be little lawns and open glades in the forest.

The engine roared out again, but this time Sergius did not ascend. He turned so sharply that the plane "banked" at what seemed to his passenger an alarming angle, and shot straight across the valley. Then he once more cut out the engine and shot downward swiftly and steeply.

Suddenly Jones perceived what they were aiming at, a broad, smooth space of green, about a quarter of a mile in length, which the prince in his circlings had picked out for a landing place. An instant later dark masses shot upward on both sides, the pilot deftly straightened out the plane, and with a stiff jolt they had struck the earth.

The lawn, which had looked so smooth and even from above, proved to be an expanse of villainous hummocks over which they bounded and sprang for fifty yards or so, and at last came to a creaking, swaying halt.

VI

"That, my friend," cried Sergius, turning a beaming face, "that was a good landing, no? Coming down in such unknown country something is always liable to break, but we have better fortune."

"What funny-looking trees!" exclaimed Mr. Jones, paying no heed to the Russian's self-congratulations. "Why, they look like—like cabbages! And what a horrible smell!"

The word "horrible" was none too strong to describe the intolerable odor which permeated the air. Descending as they had done from the clear, clean, fresh upper atmosphere, it seemed at first almost impossible to breathe at all. It was a sort of concentrated, well-nigh visible stench, suggesting nothing less than decayed slaughter-houses or open graveyards. Even the prince lost his smile after the first moment of delight over his successful landing.

The "trees" to which Mr. Jones had referred, were indeed not trees at all, but some sort of vegetable growth entirely unfamiliar to either of the men. If they had really been the cabbages they resembled, they would have made the everlasting fortune of the market-gardener who grew them, for the smallest was as large as a fair-sized hen-house, and some of the larger ones must have measured at least a hundred feet from root to crest, with a diameter at least one fourth as great. They were a dark purple in color, shading upward into a sickly green. None of them grew very close together, and the spaces between were filled with an astonishing variety of mushroomlike things, whose vivid coloring, red, yellow, violet, and orange, jarred upon the eye in a disharmony of which nature is very seldom guilty.

Like a giant's vegetable garden, these monstrous growths entirely surrounded the glade where they had alighted. But even though they towered so high over the heads of the aeronauts, they caught glimpses between and above them of other and different growths, yet higher.

There was no wind in the glade. The sun beat down and the stench rose up. Mr. Jones had a strong feeling that if they did not get out of the place in a short time he was going to be very ill indeed.

"This is awful," he said appealingly. "Can't we go up again?"

The Russian, who had been looking about with much interest, shook his head. "Of what use to rise now when we have just made such a very nice landing? Another time we might not be so lucky. The odor is certainly unpleasant, but after all it is only a smell. It is only the vegetation. I knew that here in the crater valley we would find some very peculiar things. We must not be too easily deterred. Let us penetrate past these vegetables and find what lies beyond."

Sergius undoubtedly had the final say so in regard to their leaving or remaining, so his companion followed his example, unstrapped himself from his seat in the monoplane, and descended to earth. The prince handed him a rifle and cartridge belt and took one himself. They discarded their coats and hoods and advanced toward the nearest passage between the "cabbages."

As they approached the dreadful charnel odor became more intense, if that were possible. Shoulders thrown forward, eyes half-shut and smarting, they pushed through it as through some tangible obstruction.

Then the first of the many-hued mushrooms were crunching beneath their feet. They crushed and squelched, with a semiliquid sound, sending up a sort of acid gas into the faces of the two adventurers, somewhat like the fumes of hydrochloric acid. The prince took out his handkerchief and bound it over his mouth and nose, signaling to Jones to do likewise, for both of them were past speaking. With these improvised and inadequate gas-masks, they waded doggedly on through the fungi.

They were within fifteen feet of one of the smaller cabbages, when with a sort of swishing sound it began to move. Its outer sheath of purple and green leaves, twenty-five feet long and five broad, began to open out and descend.

Jones caught a glimpse between them of a huge, scarlet, writhing mass, and tried to turn and run. The crushed mushroom things held his feet. It was like trying to leap or run in a quicksand.

Then the rough, thick, sawlike edge of the nearest leaf struck him a glancing blow on the shoulder, And he was down in the mess of fungi. A long, writhing, bright-red thing, like a nightmare fishingworm, lashed out above him, curled back and encircled his neck in a strangling grip.

"Help!" he tried to shout. "Sergius—help!"

Then his shoulder was seized and he was being pulled away from the giant cabbage. The tentacle which held him straightened out and actually stretched as if it had been made of india-rubber. A knife flashed over him, severing the tentacle, and a moment later he was out of reach of a dozen more which were shooting after him. That was the last thing he remembered until he came to under the shadow of the plane, to look up into the anxious face of Sergius Petrofsky, who was fanning him with a handkerchief.

Mr. Jones sat up and felt of his neck gingerly. Luckily his collar had somewhat protected it, but it felt very stiff and sore.

"I thought you were gone, my friend," said Sergius, standing up and wiping his perspiring face with the handkerchief.

"So did I. What I can't understand is why the thing didn't get you, too. Look at it now—ugh, the horrible, nasty, writhing beast!"

The "death cabbage" (as they afterward named the interesting vegetables) had not closed its outer sheath, and its inner hideousness stood fully exposed to the sun. Straight up from the center sprang a sort of slimy, blue-black stalk, terminating some twenty-five feet above the ground in a wide plume of green fronds. Surrounding this stalk was a dense, intertwined mass of the long, scarlet tentacles which had nearly dragged Mr. Jones to his doom. To be eaten by a vegetable—and such a vegetable! Jones shuddered and looked away, feeling very sick and disgusted.

"Look!" cried the nihilist. "It is twisting itself about like a thing in agony. I wonder if the brute has eyes and sees us here and still hungers after its prey? But that is curious. See, it is becoming of a bright orange color!"

Jones looked again, rather unwittingly, but what the Russian said was quite true. The wriggling scarlet mass was rapidly changing to orange, and from orange it faded to a sickly yellow. Moreover it was wriggling more and more feebly. The outstretched sheath-leaves lifted themselves spasmodically two or three times, then wilted limply among the fungi at its base. The central stalk began to droop over to one side, and the green fronds hung dispiritedly down. At the end of five minutes all motion had ceased. Even the now pale tentacles writhed no more. The death cabbage was itself dead.

"Do you suppose it perished of a broken heart?" asked Sergius whimsically. "'You resisted its ardent caresses, and it died of disappointment But rather, I think, it possible that another than either of us has killed this monster, my friend."

"What do you mean? Have you seen anybody else?"

Sergius pointed upward solemnly.

"I mean him," he said, and he was pointing at the sun. "There is but one explanation. These are creatures of the night, and they get their—their food in the night, whatever it may be. They are not accustomed to grasp their prey by daylight. This one was tempted, and he opened his protecting sheath, and he was slain by the sun! But he would have killed us first, if I had not been able to spring back more quickly than you, my friend, and escape his first gropings."

"I owe you my life," said Jones earnestly. "I never knew anybody before who would have had the courage to throw himself within reach of that—that thing, and drag another man away from it."

"It is nothing," Sergius demurred, looking very much pleased nevertheless. "Now we will be comrades, indeed—no? I think, however, that we have done and seen enough for one day. Mount again to your seat and we will leave this valley of death. But we will return tomorrow and alight in some more favorable spot."

"I'm with you," Mr. Jones assented joyfully.

But first they cleaned themselves as well as they could of the pulpy fungoids with which they were both plastered; Jones from head-to foot. Then they started to put on their heavy coats. Mr. Jones was buttoning his and Sergius had just slipped his arms into the sleeves, when a voice behind them said sharply: "Stand perfectly still, please! If either one of you moves a finger I'll kill you first, Prince Sergius Petrofsky!"

VII

S tartled and amazed, Jones and the nihilist yet obeyed, for there was
a certain sincerity back of the command which was not to be denied.
Their rifles lay on the ground a few feet distant and Sergius himself,
with his arms half into his coat, was peculiarly helpless.

Both looked over their shoulders, however, and there behind
them, rifle pointed at the middle of the Russian's back, stood Richard
Holloway! He was still attired in his simple costume of shirt and
trousers, now very ragged and dirty, and his face wore a grim smile.

"Who are you?" asked Sergius, although he may have guessed.

"It's Holloway," supplied Jones in a whisper.

"You don't need to murmur it in his ear, sweet child," interrupted
the newcomer. "I'm so glad to meet you again, Rolly. You know I said I
was sure we should be friends. But we thought after all a stalactite must
have dropped and crushed out your innocent young life."

Mr. Jones could think of no reply. Of course, now, the other party
would never believe that he had not been lying when he said that he
had nothing to do with Sergius Petrofsky. Even Jim Haskins would no
longer believe him. Then he forgot his own troubles in wondering how
this unexpected meeting would affect his newer friend, Sergius.

"Move farther back from those rifles," commanded Holloway. "That's
right. And just remember that I don't love either of you one little bit.
The only pity is that my dear little vegetable garden didn't succeed in
getting both of you for its luncheon. It's a lucky thing for you that you
didn't try conclusions with one of the really big fellows. That one was a
mere child—poor innocent thing!" He shifted his rifle to the hollow of
his arm and came toward them.

Sergius, his face white and strained with anger, still stood with his
arms half way in the coat. "May I—have I your very kind permission,
Mr. Holloway, to finish putting on my coat? I give you my word that we
are neither of us armed, except for the rifles."

"In just a minute, prince. Sorry about your word, but if you did
happen to get careless about it, where would I be? Rolly, I've got you
covered. Just go over and turn your friend's pockets inside out for me,
will you? And now your own? That's right. No, I wronged your serene
highness. You can put your coat on, though you must be a cold-blooded
fish to want it in this sun."

"We were just about to ascend," said the Russian stiffly.

"Oh, I see. Well, you're just about not to ascend now, so you won't need it. We saw you fluttering gaily about over the valley, and saw you drop into this place. Paul (he really seems to retain a regard for you, for some reason), your brother, asked me to come out and pick up the remains, if there were any, which I doubted myself, knowing what sort of place you had landed in. He asked me to extend to you his apologies for not coming himself. He sprained his ankle in the caves, but Miss Weston is looking after him so well that really it can't be much hardship."

Sergius' eyes narrowed, and Jones remembered that Jim Haskins had told him both brothers were seeking the girl's favor.

Holloway picked up the two rifles from the ground and tucked them under his other arm. "So nice of you," he murmured. "We're rather short on arms and ammunition. But I know you're anxious to be welcomed in camp. Turn to the right, please, and straight ahead. Don't be frightened of the little cabbages. I won't feed you to them this time."

Jones was beginning to detest the young American as much as he had formerly been inclined to like him. His mocking banter in this place that smelt like the tomb and was the home of detestable death, seemed as out of place as the tinkle of a pianola in Purgatory.

However, the man must know a safe way out, or he could not have appeared there himself, so the two prisoners turned their faces in the direction indicated and started off, with Holloway close behind.

They crossed the glade obliquely and came into view of a broad road, or trail, which had apparently been trampled over and through the fungi and several of the young and comparatively small death plants which lay crushed and broken. Two of them, each well above ten feet from root to crest, had been actually torn up by the roots and tossed to some distance from the place where they had been growing.

What power or agency had been strong enough to perform such a feat with such victims?

As they involuntarily paused, staring, Holloway's mocking voice answered the unspoken question:

"That's the work of another of my lovely island's children. Don't get scared. He doesn't prowl around much by daylight, but when he does take a walk, and things get in his way or annoy him, he just pushes them gently to one side—as you see. He's a foul brute, but not foul enough to feed upon such carrion plants as these. He was probably hunting something."

The nihilist was too proud, and Jones too overcome, to question Holloway in regard to the mysterious "brute" to which he referred, and after a moment of hesitation they marched on through the sickening mess of broken fungi and wilted, blood-sucking tentacles. But first, at Holloway's own suggestion, they all three again bound handkerchiefs over mouth and nose as a partial protection against the thrice-vile fumes rising from beneath their feet.

At last, however, a breath of purer air reached their nostrils, and raising his head, Jones's watering eyes beheld a scene of weird and unearthly beauty. Behind them lay the field of death cabbages, in all its foul ugliness. Before them was a forest—but such a forest! The trees were mere slender, graceful stems, shooting up to an unbelievable height, where they branched out into a feathery tuft of graceful leaves, resembling palms.

But these slender stems were all wound and garlanded with gorgeous blossoms, like glorious floral butterflies swaying and fluttering to every breath of air.

Here and there huge balloonlike growths had forced their way upward between the palms, bending them aside and so making their own path to the sunlight. These, however, unlike the cabbages, had nothing horrible or loathsome in their appearance, but were of the most delicate shades of pink, shading into lemon yellow at the summits. They, too, were overgrown in the riotous embrace of a thousand blossoming vines.

Underfoot the ground was thickly carpeted with moss in wide patches, like rich rugs of velvet green, starred all over with little points of brilliant blue and scarlet, which were also flowers. Between the butterflylike blossoms of the vines innumerable real butterflies were flitting. Their colors were so similar to the flowers that it was impossible to tell if a blossom one's eyes rested upon were really such or a butterfly, unless it suddenly spread its wings and flickered away through the slanting sunlight.

Moving forward slowly, like men in a dream of fairyland, they came at last entirely out of the zone of vile odors; and the more delightful by contrast, their nostrils were filled by the divine fragrance of this unlegended Garden of the Hesperides.

Again Holloway had his comment to make.

"You like this all right, now—but I just invite you to take the trip by moonlight!"

"By moonlight," said the Russian softly, forgetting for the moment his animosity toward the speaker. "I should think by moonlight this place would be—ah, celestial!

"H—m! Well, I've been here, and take it from me it was more like the other place."

"Impossible!

"In the bright lexicon of Joker Island, there ain't no such word, dear child. Your imagination needs exercise—or you wouldn't have come here, so I'll just permit you to exercise it on this. But I'll give you one tip: You've seen the flora, but you haven't seen the fauna—yet. Straight ahead, now, through that little lane between the vegetable balloons. No, not that way. Halt! Good Lord, man, if you'd gone down there you'd have wished you was safe inside one of those mild-tempered little cabbages back yonder!"

Sergius, absorbed in gazing at the wonders about them, had started to go to the left of the balloon in question instead of the right. The ground sloped sharply downward there, and as he drew back his foot in surprise at Holloway's evident agitation, there was a sudden rattle and slide off falling gravel.

Both he and his fellow-captive looked keenly down the incline, but could see nothing out of the way. A tangle of gray, leafless vines formed a veil across the bottom of the slope, through which they could see nothing.

Then, the perspiration sprang out on Sergius' forehead, and for the first time since Jones had met him the prince looked really frightened. For over that tangle of vines something was moving. It was a leg, and it had come out from between the vines. It was jointed in two places, the space between the upper joints being about three feet long, and at the end of it was a single, great, curved claw, black and gleaming like polished ebony.

Another similar leg followed it into visibility. Then two eyes came into view, round, black, and fastened upon the ends of stalks like those of a lobster.

"Good God!" breathed the Russian.

"What is the thing, Holloway?"

"Just a. little spider," responded their captor cheerfully. "But plenty big enough to make three mouthfuls of you. That's its web it's sitting in, wondering why you don't come on down to dinner. I'd shoot the old devil, but what's the use? He's only one. Shall we go on now?"

With cold shivers running up and down their spinal columns, Mr. Jones and his companion stepped carefully back from the entrance to the giant spider's den, and entered a little path or trail which led windingly away through the lovely, treacherous forest. Jones, for one, heartily wished that their guardian would march in front instead of the rear. The death cabbages had been bad enough, but they had seemed such vast, unnatural prodigies that already his memory reproduced them dreamily.

That spider was another matter. He had, heard of spiders as large as dinner plates, and shuddered at the thought of them. This spider had been as large as well, judging from its forelegs it could better be compared with an extra large dining-table.

And Holloway had spoken of it as "only one." How many more such fiends lay hidden, waiting for the false tread of a foot, or the careless speed of some hunted jungle thing? He began to be careful indeed to look where he trod, and suspicious of even the supposedly harmless flowers and butterflies. Beauty becomes more horrible than frank ugliness when one has learned that death lurks behind it.

Fortunately, however, for their peace of mind they saw no more of the "fauna" of which Holloway had hinted, although once in skirting a dark morass they heard distant crashing sounds, as if some large beast were threshing about somewhere in the depths.

"This place is like a Broadway cafe," Holloway informed them. "Nothing much doing in the daytime—but—oh you midnight suppers. Eat and be eaten, that's our motto after sunset."

"You seem to know a whole lot about the place," Jones ventured.

"Yes, indeed. Regular old homestead to little Willy. You see, I lived here for two years, and got real well acquainted with the inhabitants. Maybe we'll let you and your dear friend Prince Sergius try it, when it comes time for us to leave. You'd learn a whole lot you never knew before, believe me. That is, if you survived the first week or two."

Mr. Jones looked at him hopelessly. Was the man in earnest?

But Sergius laughed scornfully. "I should not particularly mind," he said, "so long as we were relieved of your company, Mr. Holloway."

"You don't say! How very rude and unkind you are, prince. But never mind. I'd be sore, too, if I were in your place, so I forgive you like a true Christian. And here we are—home at last all safe and sound."

For the path, turning sharply, passed out of the jungle and into the full light of day. Half a mile away, across a broad expanse of green meadow, the rim of the crater raised its black height, hidden from them until now by the forest. To the right, in the distance, some unidentifiable animals were grazing, and ahead, close to the wall, a pillar of smoke was rising, almost white against its dead blackness.

"There's our camp. Keep right on going. Don't worry, they're expecting us."

That they were expected was presently evidenced, for the figure of a man appeared coming toward them across the meadow. In a few minutes Jones was able to identify him, for it was Jim, Paul's cowboy retainer. He met then, with a grin, which suddenly faded as he recognized Mr. Jones. He looked from him to Sergius and then back again.

"Well, of all the—snakes!" he exclaimed, and his hand dropped suggestively to his hip-pocket. "So that yarn of yours was just a string of whoppers, was it? By jiminy, I've a notion to drill you right now, you—you low-down horsethief! Lettin' me get the notion that you was layin' smashed back there in the cave, and me mad as thunder because they wouldn't let me hike back to look for you. An' all the time you pikin' around with this here nihilanarchist bunch. Say, what kind of a low-down, lyin' cattle-rustler are you, anyhow?"

"Shut up, Jimmy," interrupted Holloway at last, although he had listened to the arraignment with a grin of pure enjoyment. "Rolly's nerves are all upset as it is. How is Prince Petrofsky?"

Jim's face relaxed again into a grin.

"Doin' fine," he answered. "I know now why he brought that female woman along. Gee! I wouldn't mind sprainin' a leg or so to get nursed that luxurious."

"He'll get well for pure joy when he sees who's here. Forward the army. We'll be right behind you, gentlemen. Sorry the hotel bus wasn't running, so as to save your walking all this way, but you know what these summer resorts are."

His cheerful nonsense bored Jones wretchedly, as they went on toward the camp. What sort of a greeting were he and Sergius likely to get? Not a very pleasant one, judging from the sample offered by Haskins. He heartily wised that Sergius had stuck to his original intention of "a mere reconnaissance." They would have been back with the nihilists by this time, and at that moment the nihilist camp actually seemed like home to Mr. Jones.

What could there possibly be in the crater valley of sufficient value to make all these people so very anxious to reach it? Unless the were seeking the rather morbid pleasure of being killed and eaten, he could conceive of nothing liable to be there which would repay the extreme trouble and risk attendant upon obtaining it.

A gold mine? How could anybody work a gold mine in a place like this? Diamonds, perhaps? He himself would have cheerfully forfeited a full ownership in Tiffany's just to escape from the place.

He had never had any opportunity to question Sergius Petrofsky, and as that gentleman stalked along moodily by his side now he did not look in a good humor to answer such interrogations. Both men had long since removed their heavy coats and were carrying them, but even so their clothing was saturated with perspiration.

Hot, weary, and disgusted, they neither of them looked as they came into camp, as if they had been upon any pleasurable expedition.

A fire was snapping and crackling cheerfully in the cliff shadow, and about it lay scattered various paraphernalia, but no one was in sight.

"All in the cave," said Jim, in an explanatory tone. "Some cliff-dwellers, our bunch, ain't we, Holloway?"

"First-class apartments," corrected the other. "Dry, airy, cool, but dogs and children barred. Hey, there! Anybody home?"

At Holloway's hail a woman appeared in the entrance to one of a large number of the dark openings which perforated the crater wall. It was of course Margaret Weston.

"Oh, did you find them, Mr. Holloway? Who is that with the prince? Isn't that the man we lost in the caverns?"

"It sure is, ma'am," grinned the cowboy, not giving Holloway a chance to reply. "He ain't crushed none, not so you could notice it. I take off my hat to you, ma'am. You was dead right about the snake, but I was too plumb pigheaded to know it."

"That is all right, James," said the girl, smiling sweetly. "A woman's intuition is sometimes correct after all, is it not? Prince Sergius," with a sudden severe formality, "your brother would like to see you as soon as it is convenient."

The nihilist bowed with a dignity equal to her own. His face was sternly set, but Jones, watching curiously, saw a look flash up into his eyes as they rested on the girl which confirmed the cowboy's statement in regard to his feeling toward her. He could hardly be blamed, either. Miss Weston looked a good deal more than attractive, standing there with one white, shapely arm extended to support herself on the precarious foothold of rocks at the cavern door. She looked very young, girlish and utterly out of place in that nightmare valley. Her smooth cheeks were slightly flushed, her scarlet lips were set just sufficiently to bring out their exquisite lines, and her big blue eyes were shining with some emotion, but one hardly favorable to Sergius, if Mr. Jones were any judge.

In fact, Miss Weston was angry, and Jones felt vaguely sorry for Sergius Petrofsky. He wondered again at the girl's ardent dislike for his friend.

"I am grateful to my brother," said Sergius slowly, "for sending such a charming messenger!"

"Thank you. But kindly reserve your compliments for some one who will better deserve and—appreciate them. Mr. Holloway, will you kindly accompany these gentlemen? The sailors are in the other cave, and I hardly think it safe for Prince Paul to receive them alone—"

Sergius flushed deeply. The thrust evidently went home.

"Certainly, Miss Weston," assented Holloway, with a smile of amusement. "But I was just going to start cooking supper."

"I am not myself such a bad cook as you seem to think," laughed the girl. "What use is a woman in camp if she can't do the nursing and cooking?"

"You're dead right, ma'am," commented Jim, but in a most respectful voice. Jones reflected sadly that even this woman-hater appeared to have been converted to admiration for the girl. Probably he regarded her diagnosis of his, Jones's, character as a symptom of most unusual wisdom.

"Go right in, gentlemen," commanded Holloway. "Here, Jim, will you take these rifles? And lend me your little popgun? Thanks. A rifle is no good at close quarters."

With a disdainful shrug Sergius turned his back on the voluble American and entered the cave, Mr. Jones close at his heels.

VIII

On one of the dark but cool chambers in the rock a rude couch of blankets had been laid. Beside it, upon a flattopped stone, stood an electric lantern of the type which, using large batteries, will burn for eighty or ninety hours, and which illuminated the place quite brightly. Beside it a bottle of arnica and some carefully folded bandages were arranged.

Upon the couch lay Paul Petrofsky, the lower part of one leg swathed in more and beautifully adjusted bandages. As the two captives entered, however, he sat up and gave utterance to an exclamation of joy as he recognized his brother.

For the first time, seeing them together, Jones realized the strong resemblance between the two men. There were the same broad, intelligent brow, the same high-bridged, symmetrical nose, the same thin-lipped, sensitive mouth, and pleasant, dark eyes. The only real difference between the two faces lay in the expression and in that slight inclination of Paul's chin to recede.

Sergius' eyes were keen as well as pleasant, his mouth was set in firmer lines, and his chin was of a squarish and very determined shape. Also, at time, his face wore a haughty and somewhat domineering look—a look which Paul's countenance never assumed.

If, knowing neither of them, Jones had been asked to choose, he would have unhesitatingly named Sergius as the supporter of aristocratic government, and Paul as the man to be easily led, particularly into any scheme, however wild, for the betterment of his fellow Russians.

"Sergius!" exclaimed the man on the couch. There was pure relief in his voice. "Then you are safe. I was afraid—"

"That some of your friend Holloway's pets had made a meal an your dear brother? I should not have thought that would have appeared to you as a great trouble, Paul."

His brother shook his head impatiently, with a slight frown.

"That is absurd, as you very well know. Because you have been misled by these murderous, bomb-throwing companions of yours is no reason for me to forget that you are my brother."

Sergius flushed and straightened himself.

"My companions are not bomb-throwers, and you very well know the difference between nihilism and the madness of anarchy, although you choose to pretend that there is none. You are in a position to say what you please to me, Paul, but you know my feelings on that subject and it seems hardly generous—"

"It is not a question of generosity, but of common sense," the other broke out. "Someday you will thank me for standing out against your fanatical views. Russia will never be saved by such mad dreamers as your so-called friends. It is I who truly serve Russia in her hour of need. How long, think you, will the war which is slaughtering our people continue after I turn over to the government the—that which we have come to seek?"

"Long enough, I hope, to destroy every member of the cruel beaurocracy which holds her in its bloody grip. Yes, it is your friends who are bloody, Paul, not mine."

"There is tyranny in every fixed government. Moreover, it is not the rulers of Russia who suffer most. It is the very peasantry which you profess to love so much. Turn your face from the mirage you are pursuing, my brother, and cast in your lot with us!"

"I will not desert my brothers," replied Sergius briefly, but with evident sincerity.

"Then," said Prince Paul with some firmness, "you will not be allowed to return to them either. Dick Holloway, I had hoped that after all I might persuade my brother—I have no brothers—to ally himself with us. Since he is not yet ready to do so, I must ask that you and James Haskins see to it that he remains in this camp. As for his companion, the spy, it would be no more than right if we should shoot him outright."

Jones started slightly, This amiablelooking Russian seemed to be even more arbitrary than his nihilist brother.

"Oh, I wouldn't go that far," counseled Holloway, with an amused grin. "I'll be responsible for it that—he doesn't leave us so easily as he did before. By the way, prince, I left the aeroplane where they landed. Do you want the thing brought into camp?"

"No, I think not," said Paul, after a moment's hesitation. "I fail to see how it could be of any use to us. If you or Jim chance to go that way again you might see to it that it is rendered useless for any one, however." He gave a significant glance in the direction of the plane's rightful owner.

Then he dropped back upon his couch with a little grimace of pain. "Sergius, will you remain here with me? I should very much like to hear of what befell when you descended into the valley. That is, if you don't mind telling me. Dick Holloway, please take this man Jones out with you and set him to work about the camp. We may as well make him useful since you are set on keeping him."

Holloway looked doubtfully at the two brothers. Sergius saw the look and laughed bitterly.

"You had better assure your friend, Paul, that I am unlikely to murder you in his absence. Also you are mistaken in regard to Mr. Jones's relations with me. I never met the gentleman until night before last, and we parted then because he managed to cut a hole in the side of his prison tent and escape. I will admit that I do now regard him as a friend, but that is because of his very excellent qualities. We are friends, however, and any treatment which you accord him I must beg you to offer me also."

He looked very haughty and dignified as he uttered these sentiments, and Mr. Jones's heart went out to him more than ever. The man had not only saved his life, but now he was defending him from undeserved oppression. Somehow, he determined, he would endeavor to repay Prince Sergius.

Paul shrugged his shoulders and smiled rather dubiously at his brother. "Of course, if you say he did not come to our camp as a spy I shall have to take your word. You are in a position to know if any one is. Holloway, we will have to treat the gentleman courteously, since my brother is determined to share his fate." He laughed. "I really don't care to make you wash dishes Sergius."

Holloway and Mr. Jones went back to the camp fire, leaving the two brothers alone together. There was no exit to the cavern chamber, save that by which they had entered, and even Holloway did not really believe that the nihilist would harm his brother for mere revenge.

Jones longed to ask some questions in regard to this mysterious war which had been again hinted at, but he still suffered from a deep-seated dread of what the answer might reveal, and also of being regarded by these strangers as hopelessly feeble-minded.

"Let it wait. If I'm really crazy I'm bound to find it out soon enough," he thought bitterly.

In a short time supper was prepared, consisting of canned goods and the fresh meat of some animal, probably one of those creatures which still grazed quietly in the distant meadow. Jones, for one, was ravenously hungry. He had eaten nothing save the bowl of stew brought him by Doherty for thirty-six hours or more, and did full justice to

Miss Weston's cooking, which was excellent. She explained this by saying that she had taken a course in domestic science to supplement a brief hospital training, preparatory to her work as a Red Cross nurse in the European battlefields.

The European battlefields! How much of Europe then was involved in this mad, chimerical war of theirs? Whoever the fighters might be, he felt that they had missed a very beautiful and determined young nurse when Miss Weston was sidetracked into this equally mad island affair. Mr. Jones was feeling more and more as if, having slept a single night, he had awakened into a new and entirely unfamiliar world.

Paul had managed to hobble out of his cavern retreat, supporting himself on the shoulder of his brother, and the whole party, including the two sailors, ate together without regard to caste or rank. Paul was glad to sit down at once, but Sergius first wandered about for a few moments, apparently inspecting the arrangements. Jones wondered if his reckless companion had designs on the rifles, three of which lay together close by; but if this were so he resigned them as impracticable, for presently he came and seated himself between Holloway and his brother.

As he did so he leaned across, behind Holloway's back, and whispered something to Jones, who had taken his place just beyond. Jones, however, did not catch the words, and he thought best not to attract the attention of the company by asking for a repetition.

The upper rim of the sun was just disappearing below the western wall as they finished, and only a few minutes later the sudden tropic night was upon them, with its wonderful stars and refreshing, fragrant breath of coolness.

It brought something more than coolness in its wake, it brought a rising wave of sound from the jungle beyond the open meadow. The valley of the day was no more, and the valley of night had swung wide its doors for all the creatures which crouched, awaiting the liberating touch of darkness.

The first intimation of this other valley, which none of the party save Holloway really knew, was a deep-throated roar from the jungle immediately opposite. This was followed by a sort of wild, bubbling shriek, as of a creature slivering from nightmare. The sound ended so abruptly that one could only judge the shrieker to have been swallowed by the roarer. Next there was a great snarling and yowling and crashing of branches, as if two enormous tom-cats were engaged in a combat to the death. The noise of battle was soon drowned out, however, by the full rising chorus of night life, the separate notes of which, all blended as into one mighty, discordant cry, rising harshly toward the white, indifferent stars.

Only Holloway remained entirely unaffected by the uproar. Miss Weston, the intrepid, actually trembled and shrank toward the protecting of her Russian lover—that is, of the Russian lover she favored.

The two sailors sprang to their feet and looked longingly in the direction of the caverns. Arizona Jim reached casually over and drew his rifle up beside him. Sergius also gazed desirefully in the direction of the rifles, forbidden to him and Jones, while the latter, shuddering inwardly, remembered that they had actually walked through the midst of all that only a couple of hours ago.

"Some opera, isn't it?" remarked Holloway, with an amused glance about the little circle of white faces. "When I first came here I used to lie all night and shiver and shake and try to make up sleep in the daytime. I had a gun, but only a little ammunition, you know. I found that a good-sized fire would keep all but the really big fellows away, though, so I got in the habit of building one in front of a small cave and sleeping behind it. If a little fellow came along, he was afraid of the fire. A big one couldn't get in the cave. Great Scott! For a while after I got taken off the island I couldn't sleep at all. Missed the noise, you see."

"Great Heaven! What was that?"

The whole party, except Holloway, sprang to their feet and stared wildly into the air. Something huge, black, monstrous had flapped out of the darkness and into it again, passing so close that the wind of its flight scattered burning brands right and left from the fire.

"Guess we'd better be going to bed," said Holloway, rising but with no undue haste. "I don't know exactly what those things are, because I've never caught a glimpse of the brutes by daylight, but the fire really seems to attract them instead of keeping them away. Once one of 'em made a grab at me in passing. Made a nasty gash on my cheek. I just dodged into my little boudoir in time."

"It looked like a—like a great, impossible bat," cried Margaret Weston, and there was a hysterical note in her voice. "Oh, why was I brought to this frightful place? Why did we not retire into the caverns before sunset, as we did last night?"

"Poor little girl," said Paul Petrofsky gently. "I never would have brought you here, if there had been any other way. Come. You shall sleep tonight on that nice, soft couch you prepared for me, Miss Margaret, and Dick Holloway and I will sleep in the cave entrance. Nothing shall come near you that can harm."

"There's really no need for you to be frightened," interrupted Holloway in a more serious and considerate tone than one usually heard from his lips. "There are five men of us, at least, who are wellarmed, and any one of us would die before we would let harm come to the only girl in Joker Island."

Sergius bit his lip, but said nothing. By his "five men" the American had carefully left him and Mr. Jones out of the number of Miss Weston's protectors.

"You and Rolly," continued Holloway, addressing the nihilist, "can sleep in Room 5, Suite A. Here it is, and here's a torch. Be sparing with it, for we haven't many more batteries."

He pointed out the cave which he humorously dignified with the title of Room 5. "Jimmy boy will be right at your door in case you want anything in the night," he added significantly.

The prisoners entered, Sergius leading the way with the torch. They found it to be a small but dry cavern, and as they spread down their heavy coats to sleep on, it seemed as decent a bedroom as could be expected. It also formed a very efficient jail, since, like the other where Paul had lain, it had but the one exit, and that way led past the presumably wakeful Jim Haskins.

At least he had enough to keep him awake in listening to the wild night chorus of Joker Island and keeping his little fire going at the entrance.

For a time the two companions in misfortune lay silent, listening to the uproar which was somewhat muffled by the rocky walls about them. It was Jones who spoke first, voicing a question which had been all along in his mind.

"Prince Sergius," he said, "what on earth are you and the rest of them after in this place? I mean, why did Holloway want to come back, and why did he persuade your brother to fit out a yacht and come after him, and why did you—" He paused suddenly, wondering just how sensitive the prince was on that subject.

But his companion laughed softly in the darkness.

"That American—that Jim—he did not tell you everything, eh?"

"I think he told me all he knew. But of course, if you don't want to trust me, just say so. I'm only curious, that's all."

"But I do trust you." Sergius reached over, caught Jones's hand, gripped it hard, and then dropped it as suddenly. "Really—do not laugh—you are the only friend I have within two thousand miles at least. Those men of mine? They are of the rough peasant type whom I pity but cannot love. My Captain Ivanovitch? He is—well, to be frank, I do not like him. He has not the least refinement. My brother? Ah, yes, I love him, but we are not friends—not now. He is my elder, the head of my house since our father died.

"Paul was educated in America, and our father sent me to Oxford, for he was a man of broad, splendid ideas. He thought thus we two should share the education of two continents, but instead it was so we grew apart. At Oxford I met other Russians, thinking men, one of whom—alas, he is now in Siberia—changed the whole course of my life. But I cannot now tell you of all that. Paul, in your free America, clung still to the old, I call them the cruel and tyrannous, ideals.

"But you I liked, even when I thought you were that beast, Richard Holloway. It is true that I threatened you, but then I was angry, because I wished you to do something reasonable and you would not. But when we met again and I asked you to come with me into this place of hell, you did not even hesitate. You came like an old friend—a comrade."

"But you saved my life afterward, prince," said Jones, amazed at this tribute and the evidently sincere feeling which lay behind it. "I am in your debt for that and for standing up for me to your brother."

"And why not? Comrades must not desert one another. And I do not like to be named prince. Such titles stand for all I most abhor, Call me Sergius and I will call you Roland, as friends should. Tell me, would you go yet further and accompany me upon a greater adventure than any of these dogs that hold us dare attempt?"

"What do you mean?" asked Mr. Jones, somewhat startled.

"I mean," the other replied, lowering his voice to a whisper, "that tomorrow they will destroy our only means of escape—the aeroplane. Tonight it still stands there, safe unless some night-devil has trampled it. In half an hour we could be on board the Monterey. Is it not worth some risk to attain that? And we could return, but next time we would not be trapped so easily. We would be upon our guard."

"Good Lord," groaned Mr. Jones. "What you propose is impossible, prince—I mean, Sergius. We should be killed before we had gone fifty yards into that nightmare out there."

"You hesitate? But I have not yet answered your question. Listen. In this island—this island which contains so many strange and unaccountable surprises—in its soil is a substance more valuable a thousand times than gold."

"Radium?" hazarded Mr. Jones.

"Radium—bah! No, it is a strange, secret substance, which for ages has been sought by science until it has been termed a vision of fools and madmen." He lowered his voice yet more. "It is that which was once named the Philosopher's Stone—and it will change the nature of what have been called the elements. My friend, this substance will transmute common lead to gold!"

"Oh, is that all?" sighed Mr. Jones. "I thought it was probably something about gold, but believe me, it isn't worth it, prince—it really isn't."

Sergius sat up, and Jones knew that he was staring at him in amazement.

"You are a very strange man, my friend. Has gold no temptation for you?"

"Not a bit—not that sort of gold, anyway. Do you realize that if this mythical stuff of Holloway's proves what he has claimed to you people, it will upset the financial systems of the entire world, and become itself of no more value than—than mud?"

"Not at all. Do you think we would be so mad as to flood the world with gold? No, we will give out that we have discovered a very valuable mine and we will only release it in such quantities as may prove judicious. For myself, I desire it only for the cause. Russia shall be freed from herself and become a blazing lamp of liberty to enlighten the whole world. Paul, he desires only to help the government in overcoming the Germans. I desire to make the Germans my brothers."

So, it was really Germany that Russia was fighting! It all seemed very strange. If it had been England, now—

"As for this Holloway," continued Sergius, "who discovered it, he thinks only of himself. He says he wants to be a captain of industry."

"But why didn't he bring some of the stuff away with him in the first place?"

"He could carry only a little, and that was used up in demonstrating to us its value. But there is a great deal more here—the whole soil is impregnated with it, and he discovered it by the chance of a leaden bullet falling into the fire. The heat melted the bullet and it sank to the earth beneath. And in the morning, when he swept away the ashes from before his cave, there lay a splash of gold upon the ground. He is a bright man, this Richard Holloway, and after thought he experimented with another bullet."

"Yes, he would," sighed Mr. Jones in spite of Sergius' assurance, the effect on himself and all his friends, if this improbable tale proved true, was staggering to contemplate. "Now I know why I dislike the man so much. Isn't the air in here frightfully stuffy? I can hardly keep my eyes open."

"A little smoke from the fire at the entrance, perhaps. Or—my friend, do not tell me that you ignored the warning I gave you!"

"Warning? What warning?" Jones felt himself growing drowsier and drowsier. He wished Sergius would shut up and let him sleep.

He realized that some one was shaking him vigorously. "The soup—the tomato soup! Tell me, surely you did not eat of it?"

"Yes—sure. Good soup. Mighty nice soup—nice girl—too—"

His voice dwindled away. He was drifting comfortably off upon a sea of the softest down. Then something hard, unpleasant, was thrusting itself against his teeth. His mouth filled with fire-liquid fire. Coughing, strangling, he sat up and recovered sufficiently to push his companion's hand away from his mouth.

"Wha'—wha' you tryin' to do?" he asked hoarsely. His throat and lips felt stiff and numb.

"Trying to revive you, my friend. Here, drink some more of this."

"No. 'S horrid stuff. Take—away."

"Drink. You must."

Again something was forced against his teeth in the dark, and his mouth was flooded with the fiery liquid.

It was "horrid stuff," but it was effective. Jones felt the numbness going out of his vocal organs, and his brain cleared.

"What's the matter with me?" he gasped. "Have I been poisoned?"

"No, no, just a harmless drug, but it would have been disastrous had you succumbed to it, though I pray Heaven the rest have done so. I warned you not to touch that soup. Why did you do it?"

"Was that what you whispered to me? I didn't understand. But do you mean to tell me that you have—that you have—"

"I've put them all to sleep, that's all. The stuff is a perfectly harmless soporific, but it tastes a little, and that is why I put it in the highly seasoned soup, which all would be most likely to eat. But it is fortunate

I had with me also the antidote, or my plan would have surely reacted upon myself, for I would not leave you here to meet their anger."

Jones staggered to his feet.

"I can't say I like the idea, my friend, but I suppose from your point of view you were justified. What are we to do now?"

"Get back to the aeroplane. It is useless for us to attempt the cavern without a guide, and even if I could awaken Holloway, I doubt if he could be induced to help us."

"You would leave them here—in a drugged sleep—defenceless? Why man what are you thinking of? It would be worse than murder! And the girl, too. Why, the idea is criminal!"

"For what sort of devil do you mistake me, Roland Jones? No, I have thought of everything. We will place them all in the cavern chamber where Miss Weston now lies. Then we will block, up the entrance with large stones, build before it a great fire, and they will certainly be as safe until morning as anyone can be in this perilous place."

"I see. Well, perhaps it could be done. But first, hadn't we better find out if every one is really asleep?"

IX

Having first lighted the electric torch, the two men crept stealthily through the narrow passage. In the doorway the fire had burned low, and beside it lay sprawled the figure of Jim Haskins. The nihilist stooped over him and felt cautiously of his heart. Then he straightened himself. "All right," he murmured, and they passed on out. At each of the two other inhabited caves they made a similar examination, and in every case Sergius' little dose had done its work. Every one of their captors lay helpless.

"Let us begin with Paul," said Sergius, in his natural voice, since no need of caution seemed to now exist. But he received an unexpected reply. There was a sudden rustling, a sound of footsteps, and there behind Paul's outstretched form appeared a slender figure.

"You here!" exclaimed Miss Weston. "What have you done to Paul? Have you killed him? Oh, you—you anarchist!"

She dropped on her knees and felt anxiously for Paul's heart.

"My dear Miss Weston, certainly I have not killed my brother." Sergius' voice showed not the slightest agitation at this discovery by the girl he so much admired. "He is only asleep. They are all asleep. We grew tired of seeing so many people asleep, and we are therefore about to leave."

She sprang up and faced him with flushed cheeks and blazing eyes. "You have drugged them all! How did you accomplish this dastardly thing?"

"The tomato soup, Miss Weston. You did not eat of it?"

"Of course not. I detest canned tomato soup. Well, I—I hope you are proud of yourself. I hope—I hope something will eat you! So, you were going away, leaving your brother and all of us to be killed, were you?"

"By no means. We were just about to provide against that little contingency. But your being awake alters matters."

"Oh, does it? Perhaps you are ashamed of your work, now that a woman has seen you at it?"

"Not at all. But on the other hand, I cannot leave you here, awake, to be terrorized all night. Asleep, it would not have mattered. When you awoke it would have been daylight and the others would have also awakened with you. Mr. Jones, the aeroplane will easily carry three passengers, We will have to take Miss Weston with us."

"Oh, I say," protested Jones, "do you think that is really necessary?"

"But yes. She will be far safer on the Monterey than here, under any circumstances. You need not fear me, Miss Weston. I am a gentleman and Paul's brother, when we have settled our brotherly differences, you may return to his side, if that is your choice."

He looked at her a trifle appealingly, but she flung back her head defiantly.

"You dare!" she stormed. "I will not go a step and leave my friends to be devoured."

Sergius took one stride across the body of his brother and seized the young lady in his arms, holding her firmly, but as gently as he could. She did not scream, but she fought desperately, and with an amazing strength.

Jones's gorge rose at the sight. This was going much too far. He sprang forward and seized his companion by the shoulder.

"Here, this won't do," he exclaimed. "You can't force the young lady in that way, Sergius."

The Russian turned a disgusted face to him and said over his shoulder, "Do you prefer to leave her here to be frightened into insanity? Is that your idea of chivalry?"

"Let me go—let me go!" cried Miss Weston, beating fiercely at him with her hands.

And just at that moment something black, monstrous, hideous shot down upon them out of the blackness beyond the fires. There was a harsh, grating scream, and the shoulder of a giant wing struck Jones, knocking him down, and grazed the rock wall. He was involved in a swirl of beating, struggling pinions, there were two more screams, one human, the other quite the opposite, and the thing, whatever it was, was gone.

Jones picked himself up, bruised and trembling from head to foot. The girl lay limp in Sergius' arms, her face white, arms and head hanging. Sergius himself was pale as a ghost, but he had not moved from his position.

"I don't know what it was, Roland Jones," he said with a rather stiff-lipped smile, "but do you still think we ought to leave her here?"

"Great Heavens, how can we take her? How can we go ourselves? Sergius Petrofsky, I believe that you have gone mad!"

"Not quite," said the prince patiently. "We have the rifles and the electric torches, and I really believe we can make the trip safely. I have myself passed through an African jungle in the same way, and never received a scratch. We will carry Miss Weston as far as the outer edge of the meadow, then we will revive her and go on. Later we will open negotiations with my brother—he will not then have so much advantage—and Miss Weston, for whom I have great reverence and respect, will be far safer on the Monterey. Come! In the midst of so many perils, the boldest course is best. You say that I saved your life. It was a very ordinary deed, but for this one night let me claim your gratitude!"

Jones was in a quandary. His innate chivalry revolted at the idea of forcing a woman into accompanying them, yet the arguments of Sergius seemed very plausible. And he loved this daring, fanatical, imperious new friend of his as he had never loved any man in his life before.

"All right. I'll do it. But afterward Miss Weston is to be free to return here if she chooses."

"Very well, if you wish it. I give my word."

With no more talk they hastily dragged the insensible members of the party into the selected cavern, and with considerable labor blocked up the entrance. In the morning the imprisoned ones could easily pull it down from within. Then they gathered all the fuel together and made one enormous bonfire, that blazed and roared skyward. Some of the logs were of very satisfactory size, and they felt sure the fire would burn for some hours. It was then nearly midnight and dawn would break shortly after three.

While they worked Jones found himself casting many apprehensive glances upward, but the flying monster did not return and they completed their task unmolested. Miss Weston, fortunately or otherwise, had not awakened from her swoon.

Their own two rifles and ammunition belts, together with an automatic pistol and cartridge clips belonging to Prince Paul, and a heavy, old-fashioned revolver looted from Jim Haskins, they had kept outside the cavern, together with two of the most powerful electric torches.

With one last anxious glance skyward, Mr. Jones picked up the two rifles, both torches and their heavy coats, which he was to carry until they reached the place where Sergius' remarkable scheme involved reviving the fainting lady. Sergius himself carefully raised his scornful idol in two muscular arms, and so burdened they started out across the meadow.

How they were to find their way along that thread-like trail, between the hidden dens of impossibly large spiders and past the other roaring, screaming, bellowing natives of Joker Island, remained to be shown.

X

They had reached the first of the scattered outer sentinels of the forest of slender palms. Dimly beyond it, by grace of the tropic star brilliance, they could see the looming mass which they must penetrate to reach the aeroplane.

So far they had met with nothing alarming. Everywhere, in and out, giant fireflies danced in a mystic saraband, very beautiful to behold, but also quite confusing to the eye. They had not yet used their torches, fearing to attract more of the terrible flying monsters, of which they had already seen quite enough to satisfy any morbid curiosity they might have felt.

"Here," whispered the prince, although he could almost have shouted without fear of being overheard above the general uproar, "we must awaken Miss Weston."

Jones saw his dark form bending over at the foot of the slender tree, and knew that he had laid his burden down.

"Shall I light up?" inquired Jones in an equally low tone, and speaking close to his companion's ear.

"On no account. Not yet, that is. Will you hold up her head, please? That is right. Now—this liquor would well-nigh rouse life in the dusty veins of an Egyptian mummy."

"If it's the same you gave me, you're right. Look out—there's something behind you—look out, I say!"

Over Sergius' shoulder he had caught a glimpse of two green eyes glaring, balls of fire set in the black velvet of night. Sergius, with the swiftness of a prestidigitateur, replaced the stopper in the small flask he had been holding to Miss Weston's lips, reached with unerring grasp for one of the rifles laid across Jones' lap, rose from knees to feet in the same motion and laughed softly and lowered the weapon. Stooping, he picked up a small stone and flung it straight at the glaring eyes. There was a startled snarl, a fiendish yell, and the eyes vanished, accompanied by a scuffling and crashing in the underbrush.

"A hyena," commented Sergius, resuming his interrupted task with unruffled composure. "No use wasting a shot on that sort of vermin."

"Good Heavens, man, have you the eyes of a cat? How could you tell what it was?"

"Oh, I can see better than most in the dark, I will admit. I should never have suggested this venture if it were not so. Now—ah, she is awakening."

There was a cough, a little, strangled gasp, and Miss Weston sat up very suddenly. Unlike more ordinary people, she did not exclaim "Where am I?" although the query would certainly have been excusable, but seemed to spring instantly to full consciousness and knowledge of the situation.

Without a moment's hesitation she reached up in the darkness and delivered a slap in Sergius' general direction which would have been splendidly effective had he not sprung back with the same speed he had shown in dealing with the hyena. A second later she was on her feet, panting and sobbing, but not, Jones feared, with panic.

"Oh, you did it—you did it! You cowards! You left them there and carried me away when I was helpless. Oh—if I live till morning you shall be punished for this. You shall, I say!"

Gently, but with irresistible strength, Sergius took her small hands in one of his, and placed the other over her mouth.

"Be silent," he said softly and sternly. "You must not endanger your own life because of your anger against me. Paul and the rest are, a thousand times more secure at this moment than we, unless you control yourself and use your splendid vigor and determination to a better purpose than recrimination. If I release my hold, will you come with us quietly and softly?"

A miracle occurred, for Miss Weston yielded—on that one point, at least. She must have nodded her head, although Jones could not see the motion in the darkness, for Sergius released her and stepped back.

"Do not imagine that you have greater concern for my brother than I, Miss Weston. We placed them all in safety, barricaded the entrance, and built a fire which will burn until morning. And now, you will please keep between Mr. Jones and myself. If we run, you must run also; and if we should crouch suddenly down, you must do likewise. Do you understand?"

"I understand," came the answer in a tone of suppressed rebellion.

"Very well. Will you give me one of those torches, Roland? You have your rifle ready and cocked?"

"Yes—but I'm a darned bad shot."

The nihilist sighed. "One cannot expect everything," he said. "If I tell you to shoot, aim between the eyes—you are likely to see them; at any rate. And now, forward!"

Two long, white beams sprang into being, and by the shifting rays Mr. Jones saw the narrow, trodden trail from which they had emerged in the afternoon. More than ever he marveled at Sergius' almost supernatural abilities. How had he managed to strike that one single place where they had a bare chance of entering the jungle successfully?

The Russian led the way, followed by Miss Weston, and Jones brought up the rear. And now they had entered the very center of pandemonium itself. Roars, shrieks, grunts, bellows rent the air upon every side.

"Don't be frightened!" Sergius called back over his shoulder. "These torches will keep most of the brutes off—but, good God, not this one!"

Jones caught, a glimpse of a mighty bulk rearing itself high over the head of their leader; there were three sharp, rapid reports; then the thing, whatever it was, with a terrific snarl of rage, had lurched forward and downward upon the unfortunate nihilist. Miss Weston, with remarkable presence of mind, had turned, run back to Jones's side, and then turned again to face this midnight terror, without a scream or act which could have impeded her sole remaining guardian.

He, staring with horror down his little, wavering beam of light, saw only a monstrous black head with snarling, savage jaws and two red eyes that glared like coals of fire.

"Shoot him—shoot him!" It was Miss Weston's voice, and she was shaking his arm viciously. "Shoot him—or give me that rifle!"

"Between the eyes!" gasped Jones.

"You're likely to see them!"

He had no idea of what he was saying, or that he had spoken. Then, as he stood there, shaking in every limb, he suddenly reached the extremity of terror, and passed beyond it into that unnatural coolness and calm which is so efficient and, sometimes, so hard to reach. The trembling palsy passed, and every nerve and muscle tautened to abnormal firmness. From numbed quiescence his brain leaped to lightning action.

He knew what he, "a darned bad shot," must do if he would save the friend who lay invisible somewhere under that dreadful head.

With a sure swiftness of which none of his acquaintances would have deemed Jones capable, he handed the electric torch to the girl, darted forward to within ten feet of the monster, raised his rifle and fired, aiming at the center of the forehead, and pumping one cartridge after another into place as fast as he could work the lever.

Undoubtedly the fact that the brute had paused at all in its attack was due to the dazzling effect of the electric torch, and if it had not been for an unusual piece of luck Jones would probably never have lived to marvel at his own feat. For at the first report the light-blinded brute snarled again, started to lift itself, failed, drooped, and sank slowly down upon the path. Jones, however, emptied his magazine before he realized that he had actually killed the creature with that first fortunate bullet.

Then he called back to the girl: "Come quick, Miss Weston; we've got to pull it off from Sergius!"

She ran up, still bearing the light, and the two looked down in consternation at the mighty bulk which lay like a monstrous black tombstone over the body of Sergius Petrofsky. It was a great, hairless mountain of flesh, The dropped head looked like the face of some gargoyle carven in unpolished ebony. Its fore legs were invisible, doubled under the body. Move it? They might as well have tried to move an elephant.

Nevertheless, catching hold of the upstanding, rounded ears, they tugged and heaved with all their might, but could only succeed in shifting the head a little to one side.

"Sergius! Sergius!" cried Miss Weston, dropping suddenly in a little heap of pathos beside that mountain of brute flesh.

She was answered by a moan. To their amazement, it did not come from beneath the monster, but from some little distance to one side of the path. Yet it was certainly a human moan, for it was followed by a voice: "Over here. I'm—I'm coming."

Miss Weston sprang to her feet and accompanied Jones in a wild rush toward the voice. There, sprawled out among the flowering, tangled vines, they found the nihilist himself; and as the circle of light struck his face, he sat and stared back at them with an amazement equal to their own.

"What—what hit me?" he gasped.

Jones laughed aloud in his relief. "It did. How in the name of all the saints did you get here?"

Sergius passed a bewildered hand over his head. "I—I begin to remember. Something seemed to come right up out of the ground. I—I fired at it—and then—and then—"

"It must have struck you with its paw and knocked you clear away from the path," interrupted Miss Weston in a calm, indifferent voice.

Jones glanced at her in astonishment. Was this the girl who had been sobbing out the name of Sergius a few minutes before? "If you are hurt, you had better get up and go on with us—although I would suggest that you let Mr. Jones take the lead, as he seems much the better shot."

Jones helped his friend to rise, and as he did so Sergius laughed without a trace of annoyance. "If you actually killed that brute, my friend, Miss Weston is right. Did you kill it?"

"I must have, because it's certainly dead, although I can hardly believe it myself. What on earth is the thing, Sergius?"

They had recovered the narrow path and stood beside the black hulk which blocked it entirely, overlapping on both sides into the underbrush.

Sergius examined the huge head with interest. "I never saw anything exactly like it before. Where did you hit it?"

"Between the eyes. You remember you told me to fire between the eyes, so I did. I fired about ten cartridges into it, but I think it died at the first shot."

The nihilist looked up at him with a curious expression. "It did? That's rather odd. The beast has a frontal bone as thick as a rhinoceros', if I am any judge. No; here are three bullets embedded in the bone, but not a sign of a hole. Ah, that was it, eh? My friend, by very well-deserved good luck your first bullet did not strike the forehead at all, but penetrated this left eye and went straight into the brain."

"Great Scot!" exclaimed the American. "And I was about ten feet away! It's a good thing the brute has a head as big as a barn-door, or I'd have missed it entirely."

Sergius smiled. "Nevertheless, you deserve great congratulations. If your first bullet had not gone a few inches astray, we should perhaps none of us be alive at this moment. But what a strange brute it is! I should say it was a monstrous bear, from the shape of the head, if it were not so hairless. I wonder, now, if this is the creature that pulled up the death cabbages there by the plane?"

"Prince Sergius," again interrupted Miss Weston, with a slightly impatient note in her voice, "would it not be better to come back in daylight to continue your zoological researches? If this creature has a mate, and it should come this way, Mr. Jones might not be able to kill the second one."

"And you are quite sure, after what has happened, that as a protector I am an entire failure, eh? Well, perhaps you are justified, but still I had better continue to lead the way. What do you think, Roland Jones?"

"Don't be absurd. I'm a rank, bungling amateur, and you both know it. Shall we climb over this thing, or go around it?"

"The underbrush is thick here—and there might be snakes, though we have seen none. I think we had better use your victim as a causeway."

The two men helped Miss Weston up to the gigantic shoulders, and they walked the length of the huge creature, more and more amazed at its bulk. From nose to hind quarters it must have measured a full fifteen feet, and in his heart Jones wished that he might have transported the head to his rooms in New York. How he could have gloated over the surprise of a friend of his who was a big game-hunter and very proud of certain rhino-heads and lion-skins, trophies of African expeditions.

He reloaded his rifle carefully and resumed his position as rear-guard with a new confidence in its powers which took no heed to the fact that only by a lucky accident had his shot struck a vulnerable spot.

Many times as they marched silently ahead, the underbrush by the wayside swayed and bent, crackling, to the passage of animals of which they caught not even a glimpse. Once a lynxlike beast as big as a large panther dropped silently into the middle of the path ahead of them, glared for a second into the bull's-eye of Sergius, and with another spring was gone before he could fire at it.

This incident, however, encouraged the three, for it seemed as if most of the jungle inhabitants shunned the blinding electric lights as they would have shunned a campfires.

And at length there came to their nostrils a whiff of noxious odor which told the two men that they had successfully passed the first barriers to their escape. Vile smell though it was, it came welcome enough just then, for it was the odor of the fungi that grew about the roots of the death cabbages.

Jones realized with pleasure that they had passed the great spider's trap without even being aware of it. He had subconsciously dreaded more than anything also going past that dark incline, at the foot of which waited the thing of long, black, shining legs and protuberant eyes.

But as the full force of the stench enveloped them, Miss Weston stopped dead, so that Jones almost collided with her in the narrow path.

"Stop—I can't go on into this—this horrible vapor!" she called after Sergius. He heard, for he turned back immediately and returned to where they stood.

"What is the matter?" he asked a trifle impatiently.

"This dreadful smell. I can't—"

"Miss Weston, a smell won't kill anybody. At least, this one will not. Mr. Jones and myself were in the midst of it for nearly an hour, and we were not harmed."

"But—"

"Do you wish to be left here, then?"

The question was brutal, but it served its purpose. A moment the girl was silent; then she threw back her shoulders and smiled contemptuously. "I presume you would not hesitate to do that, either. No, I will not oblige you by relieving you of my hampering company. I can certainly face anything that you can."

Sergius looked at her with plain admiration on his face.

"Believe me, Miss Weston, this charnel odor is no worse than that of the battle-fields to which you were going. I have been there, also. Will you take my arm now? For we must walk through a very disagreeable place."

"No, thank you!" she—well, she snapped, although it isn't a nice thing to say of a heroine. "I am sure Mr. Jones will offer all the help I may need."

"Very well." The prince shrugged, and without more ado they passed from the forest of slender palms into the safe way, broken, perhaps, by the very creature which they had encountered and ungratefully slain that night.

XI

As the three staggered out, one after another, from the acid-fumed fungi onto the wiry grass of the central space, their ears were rent by a sound of hideous and continued screaming which drowned out all other noise entirely. Startled and shuddering, both Sergius and Jones directed the rays of their lanterns toward the sound, and a most extraordinary picture leaped into view.

The scene of the tragedy was one of the larger death-cabbages. Its seventyfive-foot leaves were spread almost flat, and all the inner tentacles were writhing and squirming upward, so that at first glance it looked as if this vegetable flesh-eater were all on fire with slim, scarlet flames. Then, as they moved their search-lights upward, they saw what it was that screamed.

Clinging with huge claws to the upper stalk, just below the tuft, was a dark, winged thing, and all about its body and head the tentacles were wound and fastened. So wide were its frantically beating wings that even where they stood, a hundred yards away, the wind of them struck their faces in heavy gusts. The stalk swayed and bent under the strain, but the tentacles had firm hold, and continually new scarlet cords shot upward to aid in the binding of the captive, until its body was no more than a bundle of flaming red.

The screaming grew weaker; the wings fluttered spasmodically for a few moments longer, then drooped down helpless. The tentacles took hold upon them, also. Into the field of light a pointed, serrated thing rose slowly, followed by others upon all sides. The death cabbage was closing its doors to feast in sacred privacy.

A moment later the vision of trapped prey was shut from their eyes.

With a long, shuddering sigh, Sergius turned his own light slowly about the grim ranks encircling the glade. Everywhere it fell upon spread leaves and living, ready tentacles Only one or two other of the cabbages were closed. Doubtless their dinner had come to them earlier in the evening.

"What are they? What is this place you have brought me to?"

It was Miss Weston. Both men turned to her with a guilty start, realizing that in their fascinated absorption they had for the time forgotten her.

"I am so sorry," apologized Sergius, as if he and Jones had invented the vegetable horrors, as her tone implied.

"It is like—it is like a circle from Dante's Inferno!" exclaimed Jones, laying his hand pityingly on the girl's arm, and wishing with all his heart that he had never acceded to Sergius' wishes; that they had left the girl at the caves, or stayed there themselves. What might not the effect of having witnessed such a scene be upon the mind of a delicate, high-strung woman?

But she drew slightly away, and spoke again to the Russian, From first to last she gave Mr. Jones no more attention than one grants to a supernumerary—a necessary adjunct to the play, but scarcely of more human interest than the furniture.

"You are sorry!" she repeated scornfully. "Your sorrow is rather late, it appears. Where is the aeroplane?"

The nihilist bowed gallantly to her contemptuous tone.

"As usual, Miss Weston, you speak directly to the point. The aeroplane is—why, where in the name of Heaven is it?"

For his light, flashing up the glade, encountered only empty space. The aeroplane, which they had left not far from where they now stood, had disappeared.

Jones felt his heart begin a slow, systematic descent toward his toes. If the machine were actually gone, what would they do? Then he gave a joyful cry as his own light, dancing spritelike over the grass, flashed upon something broadwinged and motionless over near the wilted death-cabbage which had so nearly made a meal of him and Sergius.

"There it is! It's all right! It's there!"

"Thank God!" breathed Miss Weston, frightened momentarily out of her attitude of disdainful indifference.

"But how did it get there?" frowned Sergius. "Miss Weston, you must not go so near as that to the cabbagges. Will you wait here with Mr. Jones, while I go after the plane?"

"I will not," she replied instantly. "We will either all go, or none of us will go, whichever you please. Oh, I'm not troubled for your safety, Prince Sergius. Don't imagine that. But if you should be killed or injured, who is to pilot the plane?

"I am overwhelmed by your solicitude for me," murmured Sergius, bowing again. "If you must go, keep behind us. Here, take this light and one of the rifles. Yes, please, I want my hands free. Come on, then."

He set off at a swinging stride, followed by Jones and Miss Weston, who looked pale by the reflected light of her lantern, but very determined indeed.

The plane, they found, was fairly in the midst of the many-colored fungi. But worse, and more important, it was quite near to a thirty-foot vegetable which they had just had good testimony, would make no more than a good meal on all three of them. In fact, as they approached, it seemed to sense them, and stretched out a dozen hungry tentacles in their direction. Two or three of these, feeling blindly, encountered a rear strut of the aeroplane and curled about it. Then the tentacles contracted suddenly, and the aeroplane rolled backward an inch or so.

"That won't do," cried the nihilist, and seizing a forward strut he braced himself and pulled, but with no apparent effect. More tentacles reached toward him as he stood there, but he was partly shielded from them by the plane itself.

To his credit be it said that Mr. Jones, without an instant's hesitation, dropped his rifle, handed his torch to Miss Weston, and springing to Sergius' side flung his weight also into the tug-of-war. But it was evident that the strength of the vegetable was greater than their combined efforts. The utmost they could, do was to hold the machine where it was.

After several muscle and nerve-straining minutes, the nihilist said to Jones in a low voice, not to be overheard by the girl, "My friend, there is only one thing to be done and that is creep back there, over the tail, and cut some of those tentacles."

"Impossible! Why, the others would get you in a second."

"I don't care if they do. I will cut them also. They are strong, but a knife goes through them easily. Do you not remember yesterday afternoon? Miss Weston, will you keep both lights trained on the rear of the plane for a few moments, please? I am going to try something."

"I won't let you do it—" began Jones, but with a spring Sergius had mounted upon the plane and was working his way toward the rear.

The withdrawal of his strength was accompanied by a surge of the aeroplane backward, and Jones had to use all his muscle and attention to keep it in place. Sergius was now out of his sight, but by a sudden swaying and jolting and a scream from Margaret Weston, he knew that his too-daring companion must have been found by one or more of the questing tentacles.

The machine swayed again violently, then he heard Sergius' voice.

"Hold those lights steady, Miss Weston. Ah! two at once. Roland, we needn't have been so worried—one might as well be afraid of a stick of celery. You devil! Would you?"

There was a strangled, gasping sound, another scream from the girl, then the Russian's voice again, somewhat hoarser but still cheerful. "He almost got me that time—but not twice! That is right. Send me a few more feelers! Pull! Pull, Jones, with all your force!"

Jones obeyed with the strength of desperation, as a sudden lightening in the weight and a renewed swaying told him that Sergius had jumped to the ground, Slowly at first, then with gathering ease and speed the plane moved. In a minute it was out of the fungi and rolling clear upon the turf.

The second that he dared, Jones let go and ran around to the rear. To his great relief there was his nihilist friend, leaning against, a strut and wiping his forehead. Miss Weston joined them with the lights, and they all stared at one another in silence.

Then Sergius dropped his handkerchief, and brought his hand down upon his thigh with a resounding slap.

"What a fool I am!" he exclaimed. "What an utter fool! All I had to do was to climb into the pilot's seat and start the propeller. Even that brute could hardly have outpulled the engine. And my neck would have been saved a very unpleasant experience." He felt of it tenderly, then laughed.

"Well, it is over now. Some inquisitive beast must have come by here and given the plane a push, so that it rolled down that little incline."

He began a careful examination of wires, struts, taut varnished canvas, propeller blades and last, and most important, the engine itself and its tank. In a few minutes now their very lives might depend upon the thoroughness of that examination.

"I can find nothing wrong," he said at last, and his announcement was greeted with an involuntary sigh of relief from both his companions.

"Miss Weston," he continued, "I think you and Mr. Jones can manage to occupy that seat together. At any rate, in a few minutes we will be out of this intolerable odor. Here, Miss Weston, put on my coat, since you will find it cold in the upper air, if you will be so kind as to cover your face with your hands when we get up, you will not need goggles. Are we all ready?"

"I shall certainly not take your coat," said the girl indignantly, waving the garment away. "Not that your comfort is so important, but I know a little about flying, and if you became numbed by the cold, what would happen to us?"

Sergius laughed. "There is no danger of my becoming numbed in the few minutes that we will be in the air. Your dress is a great deal thinner than my tunic. I am sorry, but you will have to take it or we cannot start."

"Let her take mine," interposed Jones. "I have nothing to do but sit still, and it really doesn't matter whether I get numb or not.

"You are very kind, Mr. Jones." Miss Weston smiled sweetly upon him. "Yes, since you insist, I shall be glad to borrow your coat."

And suiting the action to the words she took it from him and slipped into it. Sergius frowned and looked as if he were about to say something, then checked himself and turned away, putting on his own coat without any further protest. But Mr. Jones caught what looked like an expression of amused triumph on Margaret Weston's beautiful face. It was the first time that she had really succeeded in annoying Sergius Petrofsky.

A few minutes later, having pushed the machine to the extreme end of the glade, turned so as to face the open run, they all took their places and strapped themselves in. The rear seat was a tight fit indeed for both Jones and Miss Weston, but it was only to be for a few minutes, and the girl murmured that at least she was glad she did not have to sit so close to Sergius.

Mr. Jones might have felt more flattered if she had not put in the "at least."

The Russian started his engine, the propeller began to revolve, and a second later the plane rolled forward across the uneven grass. They did not gather speed very quickly, however, and it looked as if the machine would refuse to rise in the limited course. Twice Sergius raised the elevator, and twice the plane continued on its rough and bouncing course up the glade, refusing to leave the earth.

They were now perilously close to the further end and the plane was running at a speed of about sixty miles an hour. To stop was impossible, and for a time it seemed as if their career was to end in the maw of a particularly wide-spread and hungry-looking death-cabbage, when just at the last minute he again raised the elevator, the plane tilted slightly and took the air beneath its taut canvas wings.

They barely cleared the crest of the deadly vegetable, and with their hearts still in their throats found themselves shooting onward and upward, away from thevalley of death.

Yet even as they drew in their first full breaths of relief and clean, cool air, Death itself, though in another form, rose after them.

The first consciousness that they were the object of attack came as Sergius banked his wings and swung in a wide circle, preparatory to straightening out on the seaward course. As the machine tilted against the light breeze, a large, dark thing shot by its nose, just missing the plane by a foot or so, and causing even the iron-nerved Russian momentarily to lose control.

The plane dipped and shot downward at a dangerous angle. They had risen scarcely four hundred feet, and there was not much room for evolutions. He just saved them from destruction, and rose again, casting anxious glances about in the darkness, for they had extinguished the electric torches before rising.

The girl was not aware that anything had happened, for she had covered her face with her hands to shield it from the sharp wind of their flight. Jones stared about as anxiously as their pilot, but could see nothing. Sergius' eyes must have been, as he had said, of an unusual kind, for presently he shouted and pointed into the darkness.

A second later something huge came up from below, actually grazed the left wing, and was gone again.

Jones knew that the dark thing must be one of the flying monsters, of which this was the third they had encountered, and he earnestly hoped that its interference was purely accidental. He said nothing, fearing to frighten Miss Weston, but on a sudden impulse he loosened the strap that held bah of them, with a vague idea that if they should be flung to the earth they might have some chance of jumping clear.

That Sergius was fully aware of the danger was made evident, for he began to climb in a swift, steep spiral. Birds of the night hardly ever fly high, and if they could reach the upper levels of the air, so easily accessible to them, they would be safe.

But the evil genius of Joker Island had no idea of permitting them to escape so simply. Again, with a wild beating of vast pinions, the winged peril was upon them. This time it struck downward from above and even the skill of the nihilist could not save them.

Of what happened next Mr. Jones was never able to give a coherent account. Probably the weight and impact of the creature partially stunned him. At any rate, his next conscious memory was of finding himself swinging and dangling over empty space, his arms and hands firmly buried in something that felt like warm fur, and that he was being carried along in great swoops and lunges, so that it required his utmost strength to keep from being jerked off.

XII

Wide, frantic wings were beating on either side of him, and even in that desperate moment he realized that he must have grasped the flying monster at the instant it struck the aeroplane. Doubtless much against its will, it was now carrying him along as an equally unwilling passenger.

As a matter of fact, he was clinging to its fur and the skin of its breast, which was fortunately very loose, affording an excellent handhold. But Mr. Jones was no acrobat, although he was certainly playing the part of one. Already his hands were numb and aching. He wondered if he could manage to climb around and up to the creature's back, but gave it up as a feat too great for his weakening muscles.

Suddenly he found himself laughing wildly. He had remembered the story of Sindbad and the Roc, which had carried him into the Valley of Diamonds. But the Roc bore the sailor in its claws, and this creature was not half so obliging.

Looking downward, Jones was sure that they were far higher than when the beast had struck them. He should, even swinging so dizzily through the air, have caught a glimpse of light where the fire must still be blazing by the cliff, or perhaps, if they were very high, the lights of the other encampment outside the wall. But all beneath was a black void, under what seemed a swirling, dancing firmament of stars.

Then, sick and giddy, the moment came when Jones knew he must shortly let go his grip upon skin and fur and whirl down, breathless, helpless, into the waiting arms of death. Suddenly he began to kick violently, and swing his body from side to side. If he went he was determined that his involuntary captor should go with him.

Came a harsh scream from above, a few mad circles, and then, though the wings still beat, he knew that they were dropping with dangerous speed through the empty blackness of space.

The fall, however, ended a great deal sooner than Jones anticipated, and not upon the earth but in the sea. There was one terrific splash, as beast and man struck the water.

Mr. Jones, being of course underneath, had decidedly the worst of the dive. In the first place he had expected to be hurled into the maw of a death-cabbage, perhaps, or to be dashed to pieces upon the earth, or, if he were lucky, that they might break their fall upon the crest of one of the tall, slender palms. The one thing which he did not anticipate was to be plunged into a cold bath. His mouth was open, and his lungs nearly empty of air when it happened, and the consequence was that he nearly drowned before recovered sufficient sense to let go of the fur to which he was still clinging with the tenacity of the dying.

Even then it was more by good luck than presence of mind that he reached the surface, for all the water was in a whirl with the flapping struggles of the creature which had brought him there. Fortunately, although evidently it could not swim, its convulsive efforts pushed it along, so that Jones came up at last a few feet clear of the worst of the turmoil.

The sea was running in long, smooth, oily swells, nearly as kind as quiet water to the gasping swimmer. He cleared his lungs, then turned on his back and floated, drawing in the air in huge draughts.

As his blood became reoxygenated, he began to feel a certain curiosity. What had become of the enemy? Turning again he swam slowly and quietly, reserving his strength, and looking anxiously about from the top of each swell as it came under him.

The sea, which was free that night from the phosphorescence that often characterizes those waters, reflected very little light, from the stars. He could see nothing—no land, no monster—nothing but the stars above and beneath—blackness. He felt as if he had been dropped into a sea of India ink, a sea where no man or beast had ever come or sun shone upon.

Then he remembered the possibility of sharks and hoped devoutly that no company of that sort would arrive.

His clothes dragged him down, and he determined to be rid of them, at least. He kicked off his shoes and at last, by working carefully, got rid of his khaki tunic. The puttees were hardest to deal with, but he finally got them off, followed them with his breeches, and even shed the thin, loosefitting silk underwear, as a last slight impediment to what he intended to be a fight to the finish for life and the chance to get back and finish his voluntary job of helping Sergius, or find and bury his remains. The latter contingency seemed the more likely one.

The water was warm, the slow, even swells friendly, and Mr. Jones felt sure that he could keep afloat till dawn, which could not now be far off. What he would do then depended upon circumstances, but he did not really believe the flying monster could have carried him far out to sea, and he hoped that when day broke he would see Joker Island within easy swimming distance. Until then it would be dangerous to strike out, perhaps in the wrong direction, so he floated a great deal, only swimming enough to keep his blood in circulation.

In one of the periods when he was on his back, his ears in consequence being under water, there reached them a peculiar, vibratory, explosive sound. He had heard it before, while floating in the quiet reaches of Long Island Sound, and with a great rush of hope Jones turned over and trod water raising himself as far as he could above the surface and staring from right to left through the blind veil of night.

Nothing.

He turned himself slowly, waiting for the rise of each successive swell to look long. Then he gave a wild shout and letting himself drop back struck out with frantic strokes.

Very small, very far away, he had seen two lights which were not stars, for one was red and one was green.

Had his mood of exultation lasted long he must have perished even on the threshold of salvation, for such a pace as he had set himself would have exhausted the most expert swimmer. Fortunately common sense returned in time, and he realized that since he saw both the red and the green it must mean but one thing. The vessel, whatever it was, was approaching him, probably at a far greater speed than he could possibly attain even if he could have kept it up.

He "loafed" again, rising on each swell with the deadly fear that this time one of the lights would have disappeared, sinking again into the trough with the blissful assurance that both lights still shone.

There is nothing much harder than to estimate distance at night across water. Knowing this from his own yachting experience, Jones floated several times, listening for the engine beat which the sea carried so much farther than the wind. And each time he fancied that it was louder, more distinct.

At last he raised himself again upon the crest of a swell and sent a long, anxious hail across the waste. To his inexpressible joy it was immediately answered.

Ten minutes later Mr. Roland C. Jones was picked up out of the watery vastness of the Pacific Ocean by his own power cruiser, the Bandersnatch, which had for three days been cross-quartering those waters in the vain, despairing hope of picking up some trace of him or his body.

XIII

Although the fact was not included in the extensive notices which later appeared in the New York papers in regard to the loss and rescue of the well-known millionaire yachtsman (his own friends told nothing, but one of the sailors talked), there occurred a peculiar psychological phenomenon as Mr. Jones came over the rail of the Bandersnatch.

It was as if a dark veil, which he had scarcely known existed, had been suddenly swept away from his mental vision. It had torn a trifle when he recognized one of the men in the dingey which rescued him as his old friend, Henry Martindale. He had sat in a silent, stupid-seeming daze as they were rowed back to the yacht by the sailor who accompanied Martindale, and listened to his friends' exclamations of joy, amazement and congratulation.

But as he stepped, barefooted and naked, upon the white deck of his own, familiar, beloved Bandersnatch, that veil split asunder from top to bottom and vanished forever from his brain.

In plain words, Mr. Jones remembered. He remembered how for two years, since the moment when a small, heavy clock, carelessly placed upon a shelf in his stateroom on the Lusitania, had fallen at a lurch of the vessel and struck him upon the temple, he had been the victim of that queer mental disease, amnesia. Cared for by the best doctors in London and New York, they had not been able to restore the delicate equilibrium of his brain.

The loss of his memory had been accompanied by physical deterioration, and this winter the physicians had ordered a long cruise through Southern seas in the hope of improving, if not curing, his condition.

They had, exactly as he had informed Jim Haskins, come around into the Pacific by way of the Panama Canal, and were bound for the Philippines when one night Mr. Jones actually did get up out of bed, dress himself, not in yachting clothes but in a grey morning suit, walk out on deck, straight across it, and over the rail, before the men on watch could stop him. In the sea that was running they had been unable to find him, but, although they had from almost the first, given him up as drowned, still his good friends Martindale and Charles Laroux could not bear to leave the spot of the disaster, but cruised up and down, back and forth, for three whole days and nights, ever on the lookout, ever hoping against hope that they might at least bear his body back to New York for burial.

Upon falling overboard the shock of his sudden immersion in the sea had, by one of those little jokes which Nature sometimes perpetrates, started his mental machinery going again at exactly the place where, figuratively, it left the rails. The equal shock of finding his rescuers to be his friends, and the rescuing vessel the Bandersnatch, completed the good work, and that deep abyss of two forgotten years, wherein had been lost the great war and many other memories less vast, was filled.

Once again he could spread out before him the pages of his past life and find not one leaf missing.

Curiously enough, his first thought, after the sweeping realization of it all came over him, was of his cousin, the Hon. Percy Merridale, whom he had been going to visit on that unlucky voyage across the Atlantic.

"Poor old Percy," he said, paying no heed to the flood of questions which were pouring from the lips of both his friends, "why, he was killed along with half his regiment at the very beginning of the war. And here I have been wondering what he would think because I did not arrive in London on time!"

"You have, eh?" asked Laroux, looking at him keenly. "Then you remember that you did start for London?"

"Oh, yes. I remember everything now. Lord, what chums you fellows have been, putting up with the crazy whims of a man with only half a mind. But by Jove, I'm cold. If you'll have the steward get me something hot to drink, and let me get dry and into some clothes, I'll be glad to tell you all about it."

With bitter self-reproaches at their own neglectfulness, Laroux and Martindale fairly hustled him below and to bed. They would hear nothing of his dressing, but on one thing he held out. He was perfectly willing to go to sleep—he had never felt so utterly tired out in his life—but they must promise to hold the Bandersnatch where she was, or at least near to it, until he awakened.

To this his friends agreed, and Jones slept the sleep of exhausted but perfect health for eleven straight hours.

It was three o'clock in the afternoon when he appeared on deck, and he immediately sought his two friends. They greeted him eagerly, for they were more than anxious to know how he could possibly have kept afloat for nearly three days, and settling comfortably down beneath the awnings on the breezy afterdeck, they all lighted their excellent cigars and the story began.

Before he had progressed very far their interest became other than that of curiosity, and as he went on, two of the three cigars were allowed to languish and die unheeded. From curiosity they passed to amazement, and from amazement to carefully suppressed incredulity.

This, however, caused Jones no uneasiness, for it was about what he had expected. Finishing the incident of the flying monster with the utmost complacence and indifference to their more than dubious glances, he called for Captain Janiver.

"Captain," he said, "I want you to locate for me an island which I know to be in this immediate vicinity, although beyond the horizon in some direction. What land is there hereabouts?"

The captain shook his head. "The only island I know of within a hundred miles is hardly worthy of the name, Mr. Jones. It is nothing but a high, barren chunk of rock sticking up out of the sea. As far as I know it has never even been named."

"Oh, yes, it has," smiled Jones. "That island is Joker Island, and I want you to put the old Bandersnatch's nose about and take us there just as fast as she'll slouch through the water."

"Very well, sir, but—"

"Why, Jones, old man, we were at that place ourselves, and there isn't anything there!" This from Laroux.

"You were there?"

"Of course. Janiver remembered the place and we went, on the slim possibility that you might have been washed ashore. We cruised all around it, and even landed wherever there was a beach. We found some footprints and a few old, tin cans, but there was certainly nothing else."

Jones grew suddenly very white. He had a sensation of sickness in the pit of his stomach, and an overwhelming consciousness of some dreadful disaster impending, he himself scarcely knew what.

"Captain Janiver," he said between his teeth, "put this boat about and do as I directed."

The captain touched his cap and obeyed, not without a curious glance over his shoulder. He was familiar with the idiosyncrasies of his owner—all developed, however, within the past twenty-four months, and he sighed as he gave the necessary directions.

"Too bad," he murmured, shaking his gray head sadly, "too bad. Such a goodnatured, quiet young fellow as he is, too."

As for Jones himself, he resolutely declined to speak another word on the subject until he had himself visited the scene of his recent adventures. Clinging passionately to the belief that they had actually occurred, he forced his mind to dwell upon the question of what might have happened to Sergius and Miss Weston after he left the aeroplane in such an unexpected manner.

He was possessed by a really loving concern upon this matter, although the love was not for the Boston girl but for Sergius Petrofsky, who had in the short space of three days won a place in his heart never before occupied by any man, even his faithful friends Harry Martindale and Charlie Laroux.

The two latter let him alone, when they perceived that he no longer wished to talk. Like the captain, they, were accustomed to some rather strange moods in their friend, although they had hoped for better things with the recovery of his memory.

About five o'clock the rapid little Bandersnatch raised a blur upon the southern horizon, which soon developed into a dark blot, then gradually took shape as the familiar black outline of the crater-wall of Joker Island.

With the sight all Jones's courage returned. He could not sit still, but paced back and forth across the deck, and when at last they came to; anchor in the very bay where the Monterey had lain, he fairly tumbled into the small launch which was lowered to accommodate Jones, his two friends and a couple of sailors.

Of course the Monterey was gone, but there was the place where the nihilists had been encamped, though now no tents raised their brown canvas against the cliff, Springing from the launch Jones rushed up the beach and examined the place where they had been. There were, as Laroux had said, a few tin cans scattered about, a good many footprints, and the ashes of a fire, but these might have been there for any length of time.

He ran down the beach, hoping to discover the marks left by the aeroplane's launching, but this had been upon the smooth, hard sand near the water, and the tides had obliterated them, if they had really ever been there. If they had been there! But they had been—it had happened! It was all so indelibly imprinted upon the tablets of his brain that it was clearer than any other event in his whole life.

The caves, then. Beckoning to Laroux and Martindale to follow him, he pressed on to the rocky promontory hiding the cleft, or ravine. Well, that was there anyway. And there were caves, too, hundreds of them. Into which of them had he crawled, following Prince Paul and Miss Weston, followed by Jim Haskins and the two sailors? This one surely, or—no, it might have been this, or any one of a dozen others.

He felt the touch of a hand upon his shoulder.

"Look here, old man," said Martindale with a gentle indulgence which seemed to Jones well-nigh intolerable by reason of its implications, "you must not take this so hard. Now listen. Charlie and I know you are absolutely all right now—absolutely all right. Don't let there be any question in your mind of that. Your memory has returned, and you can go on to the Philippines, or back to New York and take up your life exactly where you were before it—that accident on the liner—happened.

"But just now you are suffering from the memory of a particularly vivid hallucination. If we didn't think you were all O.K. we wouldn't tell you that, you know. We'd humor you, and say we thought it was all real. But you wouldn't want us to do that now, would you? You'll believe, won't you, that while you were here on the beach, thrown-up by the storm you—well, dreamed a whole lot of things that couldn't possibly have happened? Then, still dreaming, you started to swim out to sea again, thinking you were pursued by these impossible monsters, and so we picked you up, by about one chance in a million. The currents are very strong about here, Janiver says, and they carried you a long way—clear out of sight of the island. Can't you believe all this, which is the truth, and let the rest go along with the last two years?"

He spoke earnestly, with a deep and loving tenderness, which made Jones extremely uncomfortable. How could he convince these men that those things had really happened? That there, within the island, was at least one other friend of his, possibly in dire need of help, if he yet lived? Then Holloway, Prince Paul, Haskins, the beautiful, sharp-tongued girl—

Suddenly the mental defenses which he had raised gave way and went down before the flood of damning, almost unendurable conviction.

"Harry," he said hoarsely, staggering a little where be stood, "will you and Laroux get me back to New York? Just put up with me till—till we get back to New York, won't you?"

"Don't be a fool, Rolly," cried Laroux, springing forward and actually shaking him, but with a roughness that was all friendship. "You aren't crazy—you never have been crazy—you've been in a sort of delirium, like you have when you're down with fever. You're right as Harry or me. If you weren't you wouldn't be ready to believe the truth. It was nothing but plain, ordinary delirium, I tell you."

"Well, maybe it was," conceded Jones, with a somewhat sickly smile, "but whatever it was, I know I want to get away from this place and back to New York. I want to see brick buildings, and ride on every-day street-cars, and eat dinner in a Broadway cafe. You boys have been the best, most patient friends a man ever had. Will you promise me something?"

"Of course," broke in Laroux, "but look here, Rolly, just to satisfy you entirely suppose we stop in at Frisco and find out if such a yacht as the Monterey was chartered recently by a bunch of Russians, and—"

Jones held up his hand. "No," he said. "A man who's been off his nut for two years, and knows it, doesn't have to go around hunting up evidence to support the facts. I want to get back to New York just as fast as the old tub will travel. What I want you to promise is this. Don't ever mention any of this—this crazy dream of mine to me again. I know you won't tell it to anybody else. But—I just don't want ever to hear anything about it—again."

XIV

Three months had elapsed, and Mr. Roland C. Jones remained, to all appearances, a well and mentally sound man. Back in New York he quietly resumed the peaceful pursuits of his easy-going, pleasant, bachelor life. Laroux and Martindale adhered strictly and honorably to their promise and never mentioned to any one the singular delusion which had marked the termination of their friend's illness. Indeed, they themselves had practically forgotten it, thinking of it only as the overheard ravings of a sick man, not to be regarded as indicating mental unbalance since the man had regained his health.

Mr. Jones's first act on reaching New York had been to consult an eminent specialist in diseases of the brain, and have himself examined for insanity. The report was reassuring. Whatever he might have been in the past, this worthy physician declared him, to be now free from any taint of the disorder he so feared.

Jones went to the theater, danced, golfed and made brief cruises in the early spring, but an invitation to a flying meet was instantly and firmly declined. He never wished to see another aeroplane in his life. In fact, he did all that a man could to banish from his memory that dream which he had dreamed while cast upon the barren beach of an unnamed—absolutely an unnamed—rock in the Pacific.

If in visions of the night man-eating vegetables writhed their flaming tentacles, or strange yet familiar faces smiled or frowned upon him, he at least never spoke of the matter to any one.

So the three months had drifted by, and it was the latter end of March. One morning Jones slept later than usual—he never was an early riser—and when he sat up in bed, yawning, his window was a gray expanse against which sleet drove with a continual desolate rattling.

"Darn!" exclaimed Mr. Jones, at the end of his stretch. "Another day of 'indoor sports,' I see. How I hate a sleet storm! Philip!" he called.

Instantly his English man servant, an elderly but intensely efficient individual, appeared bearing coffee, newspapers, and the mail.

"You can get my bath ready. Now, let's see. Who's going to be married, and who desires the extreme boredom of my company—hello, I wonder what this can be—"

"This" was a small flat package, wrapped in white paper and addressed to himself in a small, perfect hand. Unlike a woman, he did not pause to contemplate its exterior, but untied the string immediately. Within the paper was a white pasteboard box, and inside that another box of Morocco leather, unquestionably a jewel case of some sort. He pressed the catch and it snapped open. What-in-the-world—

The whole room seemed to reel and sway about him dizzily. It vanished, and before him stretched a little glade all dark save where two white beams of light flashed and danced. Sergius—Miss Weston— the aeroplane—the flying monster! Was this some cruel joke that his friends had perpetrated against him.

For within the box, upon a bed of white velvet, rested an exquisite affair of gold, encrusted with blue-white diamonds. It was a tiny aeroplane, and enmeshed with it, its wings and the plane's interlocked, was a golden bat, with two tiny rubies for eyes.

Who had sent him this thing? Who had been so cruel as to taunt him with such a reminder of his time of madness? He raised box and jewel in his hand and was about to hurl it across the room when his eyes fell upon one of the letters scattered before him on the counterpane. The writing upon it was in that same small, yet distinctive hand that had appeared on the box-wrapping.

Dropping the leather case Jones hastily seized the letter and ripped it open. He, read:

My Dear Friend Roland

"Two weeks ago I read in an old newspaper of your rescue and of your return to your native city. Until that moment I— we all—believed you to have been drowned in the sea, as was the enormous bat which carried you thither. We found its body washed up upon the shore, and believe me, my friend, I wept over it for sorrow at your loss and for such an end to such an heroic deed as yours.

"I know, however, that you must have been far more overcome by your terrible experience than the newspaper account indicated. You will not need to explain to me that otherwise you would have taken your yacht back to Joker Island and, if necessary, risked death in the cavern labyrinth seeking to return to aid me, if I needed aid. There are some friendships which spring into being without the need of years to build them up, and though few words were spoken, I know that ours was such a one."

"Well, the old son-of-a-gun," murmured Jones, "and he means it, too." The eyes he raised to Philip, coming to announce the readiness of the bath, were perceptibly wet, to that worthy Briton's great, though unrevealed, astonishment.

"Get out, Philip," was Jones's only reply. "I'll bath after a while."

Alone once more he eagerly resumed his reading:

"But enough of that. I am coming to New York soon—this is written from Tokio, where I have caused to be made a small remembrance which I am also mailing you—and then we can talk together.

"After you had so courageously and with incredible presence of mind flung yourself upon the great bat—"

Jones grinned, remembering the actual state of his feelings in that moment.

"—and been snatched away into the air, I managed to right the plane and we went on across the wall. I did not even know that you were gone. Miss Weston tried to tell me, but you know how great is the noise in flight. We came down upon the beach and I was overcome with dismay and self-reproach when I discovered that you were missing. I could perhaps have pursued the bat and rescued you from the sea, but then it was too late.

"Well, the yacht—the Monterey—was gone. I afterward learned that the traitorous and rascally Ivanovitch, believing that I had been killed or captured in the valley, and wishing to make off with the yacht which he afterward successfully sold, had deserted me early in the afternoon of the day you and I took flight.

"And, of course, Laroux and Martindale had to wait until the Monterey was gone before they looked up the island," muttered Jones.

"There was nothing else to be done, so I took Miss Weston back into the valley. We arrived there a little after sunrise and found things at the cave just as we had left them. I pulled away the rocks and we applied my restorative to my brother and the rest. They were considerably annoyed at my little strategy, but Paul was, I am sorry to say, so rejoiced over the desertion of my companions that he forgave me and persuaded the rest to do so.

"After making one flight in vain, I crossed the course of a tramp steamer and succeeded in dropping upon her deck a letter wrapped about a stone. It was fortunate that I succeeded, for there was barely sufficient petrol left to take me to land. The captain of the tramp, more I fear for the reward which the letter offered than for humanity, turned his vessel to the island and took us all off, together with our possessions.

"I have little more to tell you, save that in the month we spent in the valley Holloway, Haskins and I (Paul never cared for hunting) killed off most of the more dangerous animals. They are a peculiar collection. Over on the eastern side we discovered a cavern, or grotto, much bigger than any which Holloway had before explored. In it—it was, of course, daytime—we found scores of those enormous bats hanging, asleep.

"They are nothing but bats, although they are so big. They are fruit-eaters, subsisting upon the fruit of the palm-trees, something similar to a large date. I do not believe that it is their custom to attack other creatures, but, that they were simply actuated by curiosity. Still we thought it best to kill them, and their skins are really wonderful pieces of fur.

"Two of the best are for you and also the hide and head of the bear-creature you killed. We bagged two more of them, and I think they were the last of their kind.

"After we killed off the bats the death cabbages began to wither and decay, and now they, too, are all dead. It is evident that they lived almost entirely upon the bats, which they attracted by their palmlike crests. I do not think the bats could have had any sense of smell, though, do you?

"And now, I come to my conclusion to a very long letter. Mr. Holloway was mistaken in regard to the quantity of the substance, of which I told you, to be found in Joker Island. We were able to obtain altogether only about a pound of it, enough to make perhaps a million rubles' worth of what I told you it would make.

"This is not sufficient for the purpose of which I spoke, so, as both Paul and myself are fairly wealthy, we agreed to divide it among our companions. The largest share was received, of course, by Holloway. We gave him our portion as a wedding present. Did I tell you that Holloway and Miss Weston were married two weeks ago here in Tokio?"

For the love of Pete! Jones thought. First I thought it was Paul, and then I thought it was Sergius, only she didn't want him to know it, and all the while it was Holloway! I'll bet Miss Weston had Jim Haskins wondering if he wasn't the lucky one, too. Guess I was the only one not in the running. Well—

"They have, of course, my very kindest wishes for their happiness, but Paul—perhaps you knew of his hopes—he felt very badly. He has returned to Russia and is now fighting at the front, having, I fear purposely, obtained his transference to a very dangerous position. And why am I not at his side? Because, although those men with me proved traitors, such a thing would hardly turn me against the cause. And it is upon a mission for the cause that I am now about to engage, after visiting you in New York."

"Hurray!" exclaimed the reader. "Just wait until I introduce you to Messrs. Cocksure Martindale and Laroux! Oh, when will I forgive you two for the last three months?"

"It is a mission of some danger, perhaps, but also I think that it might interest a man of your adventurous disposition. I will tell you more of it later. Until that moment, my friend, believe me ever and always your friend and comrade of the past, perhaps—who knows?—of the future."

Sergius Alexius Petrofsky

It was a long letter, but Mr. Jones read it through twice. Then he laid it down carefully, picked up the little box and stared at the golden bat and aeroplane with shining eyes and exultant face.

The sleet still beat upon the window, but it didn't bother Mr. Jones, for he was far away, on a little rock-walled island in the Pacific Ocean, which did have a name after all, and a most appropriate one—Joker Island!

FRANCIS STEVENS

THE CURIOUS EXPERIENCE
OF THOMAS DUNBAR

The man who was run down by an automobile, and the manner in which he afterward amazed those who picked him up.

I came back into conscious existence with a sighing in my ears like the deep breathing of a great monster; it was everywhere, pervading space, filling my mind to the exclusion of thought.

Just a sound—regular, even soothing in its nature—but it seemed to bear some weird significance to my clouded brain. That was thought trying to force its way in.

The waves and waves of whispering that washed all thought away—till I grasped again at some confused and wandering idea.

It was the definite sensation of a cool, firm hand laid on my brow that lifted me up at last through that surging ocean of sighs. As a driver from the depths I came up—up—and emerged suddenly, it seemed, into the world.

I opened my eyes wide and looked straight up into the face of a man. A man—but everything was swimming before my eyes, and at first his face seemed no more than part of a lingering dream.

And fantastic visions of the Orient! What a face! It was wrinkled as finely as the palm of a woman's hand, and in as many directions.

It was yellow in hue, and round like a baby's. And the eyes were narrow, and black, and they slanted, shining like a squirrel's.

I thought that of them at first; but sometimes when you just happened to look at him, they seemed to have widened and to be possessed of strange depths and hues.

In height he was not more than four feet five, and, of all contrasts, this little, weazened curiosity with the countenance of a Chinese god was clad in the very careful and appropriate afternoon attire of a very careful and appropriate American gentleman!

The long sighing was still in my ears, but no longer at war with thought. I lay in a neat white bedstead in a plainly furnished room. I lifted my hand (it took an astonishing effort to do it,) rubbed my eyes, and stared at the man who sat beside me.

His expression was kind, and in spite of its ugliness there was something in the strange face which encouraged me to friendliness.

"What—what's the matter with me," I asked, and I was surprised to note the question was a mere whisper.

"Nothing now, except that you are very weak."

His voice was full, strong, and of a peculiar resonant quality. He spoke perfect English, with a kind of clear-cut clip to the words.

"You had an accident—and automobile went over you—but you're all right now, and don't need to think about it."

"What is it—that whispering noise? Are we near the sea?"

He smiled and shook his head. His smile merely accentuated the wrinkles—it could not multiply them.

"You are very near my laboratory—that is all. Here drink this, and then you must rest."

I obeyed him meekly, like a child, weak of mind and body.

I wondered a little why I was with him instead of at a hospital or with him instead of at a hospital or with friends, but I soon dropped off. I was really quite weak just then.

Yet before I slept I did ask one more question.

"Would you tell me—if you don't mind—your name?"

"Lawrence."

"Lawrence what?" I whispered.

"Just—?"

"Yes," he smiled (and his face ran into a very tempest of wrinkles) "Just Lawrence. No more."

Then I slept.

And I did little but sleep, and wake, and eat, and sleep again, for some five days. And during this time I learned marvelously little of my host and his manners of life.

Most questions he evaded cleverly, but he told me that it was his auto which had nearly ruined my earthly tenement; Lawrence had himself taken me from the scene of the accident without waiting for an ambulance, telling the police and bystanders that I was an acquaintance. He had carried me to his own house, because, he said, he felt somewhat responsible for my injuries and wanted to give me a better chance for my life than the doctors would allow me.

He seemed to be possessed of a great scorn for all doctors. I knew long after that he had studied the profession very thoroughly, and in many countries, and truly held the right to the title he contemptuously denied himself.

At the time I considered only that he had cured me up in wonderfully short order, considering the extent of the injuries I had received, and that I had suffered not at all. Therefore I was grateful.

Also he told me, on I forget what occasion, that his mother was a Japanese woman of very ancient descent, his father a scholarly and rather wealthy American. And for some eccentric reason of his own, his dwarfed son had chosen to eschew his family patronym and use merely his Christian name.

During the time I lay in bed I saw no servants; Lawrence did all things necessary. And never, day or night, did the humming and sighing of the machines cease.

Lawrence spoke vaguely of great dynamos, but on this subject, as on most others, he was very reticent. Frequently I saw him in the dress of mechanic, for he would come in to see me at all hours of the day, and I imagine must have inconvenienced himself considerably for my welfare.

I had no particular friends to worry about my whereabouts, and so I lay quiet and at peace with the world for those five days in inert contentment.

Then an hour came—it was in the morning, and Lawrence had left me to go to his laboratory—when I became suddenly savagely impatient of the dull round. Weak though I was, I determined to dress and get out into the open air—out into the world.

Mind you, during those five days I had seen no face save that of my dwarfed host, heard no voice but his. And so my impatience overcame my good judgement and his counsels, and I declared to myself that I was well enough to join once more in the rush of life.

Slowly, and with trembling limbs that belied that assertion, I got into my clothes. Very slowly—though in foolish terror lest Lawrence should catch me putting aside his mandates—I hurried my toilet as best I could.

At last I stood, clothed and in my right mind, as I told myself, though I had already begun to regret my sudden resolve.

I opened the door and looked into the bare, narrow hall. No one in sight, up or down.

I made my way, supporting myself, truth to tell, by the wall, toward a door at the far end, which stood slightly ajar.

I had almost reached it when I heard a terrible screaming. It was harsh, rough, tense with some awful agony, and to my startled sense preeminently human.

I stopped, shaking from head to foot with the shock. Then I flung myself on the door, from behind which the noise seemed to issue. It was not locked, and I plunged almost headlong into a great room, shadowy with whirring machinery under great arc lights.

Before a long table, loaded with retorts and the paraphernalia of the laboratory, stood Lawrence. His back was toward me, but he had turned his head angrily at my sudden entrance, and his queer, narrow eyes were blazing with annoyance.

In the room were two or three other men, evidently common mechanics and none save Lawrence had more than glanced round. The screaming had ceased.

"Well?" his vice was little better than a snarl.

"That—that noise!" I gasped, already wondering if I had not made a fool of myself, "What was it?"

"Eh? Oh, that was nothing—the machinery—why are you—"

He was interrupted by a crash and splash from the far end of the place, followed by an exclamation of terror and horror, and a nice collection of French and English oaths from the men.

Lawrence had been holding in his hand while he spoke to me what looked like a peculiar piece of metal. It was cylindrical in shape, and little shades of color played over its surface continually.

Now he thrust this into my hands with a muttered injunction to be careful of it, and rushed off to the scene of the catastrophe. I follow him, at my best pace, with the thing in my hand.

At the end of the room were two immense vats of enameled iron, their edges flush with the floor, half filled with some livid, seething acid mixture, through which little currents writhed and wriggled.

The father side of the largest vat sloped up at an angle of about thirty degrees, a smooth, slimy slide of zinc about ten feet from top to bottom and extending the full length of the vat.

The surface of this slide was covered to about half an inch in thickness with some kind of yellowish paste, whose ultimate destination was the mixture of the vat.

Above towered an engine of many wheels and pistons, and this operated two great pestles or stamps, slant-faced to fit the slide; these, running from one end of the zinc to the other, worked the paste with a grinding motion, as an artist mixes his paints with a palette knife.

The grinding motion was quite swift, but the lateral movement was comparatively slow. I should say that it must have taken about four minutes for the two stamps to pass from one end of the fifteen-foot vat to the other.

In the vat floated a plank. On the surface of the slide, almost in the middle, sprawled a man, his arm spread out on either side, not daring to move an inch on the slippery paste, for the slightest motion meant a slip downward into the hissing acid.

Worst of all, there seemed to be no means of getting across to him. The great engine occupied one side entirely to the wall—on the other the second vat barred passage.

Beyond the vats the room extended some little distance, and there was a door there, open, through which one could see a fenced yard piled high with ashes and cinders.

And the great stamps, twenty cubic feet of solid metal in each, were making their inevitable way toward the man. When they reached him—well, their smooth surface would afford him no finger hold, even if their rapid movement allowed him to clutch them. They must push him down—they might stun him first, but most certainly they would push him down.

I need hardly say that I did not take in the full significance of all this at the time—it was only afterward that I fully understood the details.

Even as Lawrence ran he shouted:

"Stop that engine! Quick, men!"

I saw two stalwart workmen spring at the levers of the stamp machine—saw them twisting at a wheel—heard another crash, and a deep groan from all! The guiding mechanism had slipped a cog, or broken a rod, or something.

In my excitement, shaking so from weakness that I could hardly stand, I had half fallen against a piece of machinery that seemed to be at a standstill. Unconsciously my fingers grasped at a sort of handle.

I heard a whirring noise, felt something like a tremendous shock, and a burning pain. I let go the handle in a hurry, just as Lawrence wheeled on me with the cry, "For God's sake, you fool—"

But I could give no heed either to what I had done or to him. My eyes were still fixed on the unfortunate man on the slide.

The stamps were not more than five feet from his body now, and their low rattle and swish sounded in my ears loud as the tread of an army.

"A rope!" cried Lawrence in despair.

And then, in my horror, and in the sheer impossibility of standing by quiescent and seeing a fellow-being done to death in this manner, I did a mad thing.

Wild with resentment, as if it were a living thing I could have fought, I flung myself on the great, swiftly revolving fly-wheel of the engine, seized its rim in my fingers, and braced back with all the force in my arms and shoulders.

By all precedent and reason my hands should have been crushed to a jelly in the maze of machinery, but to my intense astonishment the wheel stopped under my grasp with no very great effort on my part.

For a moment I held it (it seemed to me to pull with no more force than is in the arms of a child,) and then there was a loud report somewhere within the intestines of the monster, I saw a guiding rod as thick as my wrist double up and twist like a wire cable, things generally went to smash inside the engine, and the stamps stopped—not three inches from the man's head!

And even as they ceased to grind, men came running in at the door on the father side of the vats—they had had to go clean round the workshop to reach it—and were at the top of the slide with a rope which they let down.

In a moment the fellow was drawn to safely out of the reach of as horrible a death as a man can die—death in a bath consisting largely of sulphuric acid!

I stood as one in a stupor, still grasping the eccentric, dazed by the suddentness of it all—hardly able to believe that the danger was over.

A touch on my shoulder roused me, and I turned to look down into the narrow eyes of Lawrence. He was gazing at me with something very like awe in his expression.

"Well," I said, smiling shakily, "I'm afraid I've spoiled your engine."

"Spoiled the engine!" he said slowly, but emphatically, "What kind of man are you, Mr. Dunbar? Do you know that that is a three hundred horse power Danbury stamp? That the force required to stop that wheel in the way you did would run a locomotive—pick up the whole mass of the engine itself as easily as I would a pound weight?"

"It stopped very easily," I muttered.

For some ridiculous reason I felt a little ashamed—as if such an exhibition of strength were really a trifle indecent. And I couldn't understand.

Of course, I thought, he exaggerated the power used, but though I am naturally quite strong, still I could, before my accident, boast of nothing abnormal—and was I not just up from a sick bed, only a moment ago barely able to stand or walk without support?

I found that I was nervously clenching and unclenching my hand, and became suddenly conscious that they felt as if they had been burned—the minute I began to think about it the pain became really excruciating.

I glanced at them. They were in a terrible condition—especially my right. They looked as if they had been clasped about a piece of red-hot iron.

"What is it?" asked Lawrence quickly. He bent over hands, peering at them with his little black eyes.

Then he looked up quickly, and I saw the dawning of a curious expression in his wrinkled face—a strange excitement, a pale flash of triumph, I could have sworn.

Then, "Where is it?" he cried imperatively, his voice sharp and strenuous. "What have you don't with it?"

He dropped my hands and fell quickly to his knees on the floor, his head bent, and began searching—feeling about in the shadows of the engines.

"Here—you there!" he cried to one of the men. "A light here! God! If it should be lost now—after all these years—all these years!"

"What" said I stupidly.

"The new element," he cried impatiently. "Stellarite, I call it. Oh—" glancing up quickly—"of course you don't know. The little piece of metal I gave you to hold—the iridescent cylinder—don't you remember?"

He spoke irritably, as if it was almost impossible for him to restrain himself to civil language.

"Oh, yes—that." I looked around vaguely. "Why, yes, I had it in my hand of course. I must have dropped it when I grabbed the fly-wheel. It's on the floor somewhere probably; but if you don't mind, could I have something for my hands? They hurt pretty badly."

Indeed, the air was full of black, swimming dots before my eyes, and iridescent cylinders had very little interest for me just then.

He almost snapped at me.

"Wait! If it's lost—but it couldn't be! Ah, the light at last. Now we can see something."

Still he was hunting, and now the men were helping him. I looked on dully.

Then an unreasonable anger seized me at their neglect—their indifference to my very real agony. I leaned forward, and, in spite of the added pain of raw flesh of my hand gave me, I took hold of Lawrence's collar and started to shake him.

He felt curiously light—rather like a piece of cork, in fact. I picked him up from the ground as you would a kitten and held him at a rm's length.

Then suddenly I realized that what I was doing was somewhat unusual, and let go of his collar. He lit on his feet like a cat.

I expected anger, but he only said impatiently, "Don't do that—help me hunt, can't you?" quite as if it were an ordinary incident.

The queerness of it all came over me in full force; I felt as if I were in a dream.

I stooped down and helped him search. But it was no use. The little cylinder of stellarite seemed to have disappeared.

Suddenly Lawrence rose to his feet, his face, whose multitudinous wrinkles had a moment before been twitching with mingled triumph and despair, wiped clean of emotion, like a blank slate from which all significance has been erased.

"Come, Mr. Dunbar," he said quietly, "it was quite time those hands of yours were seen to. You, John, Duquirke, go on hunting. But I'm afraid it's no use, boys. That vat of acid is too near."

"You think—"

"I'm afraid it rolled in," he said.

I was silent, dimly conscious that I stood, as it were, just inside the ring of some great catastrophe whose influence, barely reaching me, had this little wrinkled man in the grip of its vortex.

I followed him to a small office, opening off the laboratory; fitted up much like a doctor's, it was, with its cabinet of shining instruments. He explained its convenience while he bound up my hands with all the skilled gentleness of an experienced surgeon.

"Accidents are always on view in such a place as mine out there," he observed, with a nod of his head toward the laboratory.

"I wish you'd tell me what I've done," I said at last when the thing was over.

I felt no weakness, nor any desire for rest, which was odd, seeing the excitement I had been through and my recent illness.

"Two things, then, to be brief," he replied, smiling rather sadly, I thought. "You've accidently stumbled on a magnificent fact, and you've at the same time destroyed, I fear, all results that might have flowed from that fact."

I stared at him, puzzled.

"you lifted me just now like a feather," he said abruptly. "You think, possibly, that I don't weigh much—I'm not a giant. Duquirke," he called, "come here a minute, will you, please?"

Duquirke appeared, a very mountain of a man, all muscle, too. I am up to the six-foot mark myself, and fairly broad in the shoulders, but this fellow could better me by three good inches in any direction.

"You can't use your hands, of course," said Lawrence, "but just stoop down and stretch out your arm, will you?" Now, Duquirke, just seat yourself on his arm. That's it. Oh, don't be afraid—he can hold you all right. Ah, I thought so!"

We had both obeyed him, I in some doubt, the Canadian with stolid indifference. But what was my amazement to find that this great big man weighed really comparatively nothing.

I rose, still with my arm outstretched, with perfect ease, and there the fellow sat, perched precariously, his mouth open, his eyes fixed on his master in almost a dog-like appeal.

"What are you all made of?" I gasped. "Cork?"

I let me arm drop, really expecting to see the man fall light as a feather—instead of which he tumbled with a crash that shook the house, and law for a minute, swearing violently.

Then he got to his feet in a hurry and backed out of the door, his eyes on me to the last, his tongue, really unconsciously I believe, letting go a string of such language as would have done credit to a canal-boat driver.

"What is the matter with you all," I cried, "or"—my voice sank with the thought—"with me?"

"Sit down," said Lawrence. "Don't lose your head."

His eyes had widened, and the strange colors I had sometimes caught a glimpse of were blazing in their depths. His wrinkled face was almost beautiful in its animation—lighted as by a fire within.

"There's nothing at all astonishing or miraculous about any of it—it's the simple working of the law. Now listen. When we heard La Due fall (the fool had tried to walk across a plank laid over that death trap to save going round the shop—he was well repaid by the fright,) I handed you the cylinder of stellarite. I did not lay it on my worktable, because that is made of aluminum, and this cylinder must not come into contact with any other metal, for the simple reason that stellarite has such an affiliation for all other metals that for it to touch one of them means absorption into it. All its separate molecules interpenetrate, or assimilate, molecules, and—stellarite ceases to have it's 'individual being.' So I gave it to you, because I wanted my hands free, and ran down to the vats with you at my heels. I confess I would never have been so careless if I had not allowed myself to become unduly excited by the mere matter of life and death."

He paused regretfully.

"However, to continue, you for some reason seized hold of the lever of a dynamo of very great voltage and started the armatage revolving, at the same time stepping on to the plate of its base. Now, in the ordinary course of things you would probably be at this moment lying on that couch over there—dead!"

I looked at the couch with sudden interest.

"But you are not."

I murmured that such indeed the case.

"No—indeed of that thunderbolt burning the life out of you, like that—" he snapped his fingers melodramatically—"it passed directly through your body into the cylinder of stellarite, which, completing the circuit, sent the current back through your chest, but possessed a new quality."

"And that quality?"

"Ah, there you have me! What that quality was I fear it is now too late for the world ever to know. Well, you dropped the level, and, I think, the cylinder, too, when I shouted. A moment after you seized the fly wheel of the stamp machine, stopped it as if it had been the balance of a watch—and, well incidentally you saved La Due's life."

He ceased, the light faded out of his wrinkled face, his eyes darkened and narrowed. His head sank forward on to his chest.

"But to think of it—years—years—of effort thrown away just at the moment of conquest."

"I don't understand," I said, seeming to catch little glimpses of his full meaning, as through a torn veil. "Do you intend to say—"

"I intend to say," he snapped, with a sudden return of irritability, "that in the minute when you held the stellarite and the lever of the dynamo you absorbed enough of the life principle to vivify a herd of elephants. Why, what is strength, man? Is a muscle strong in itself? Can a mere muscle lift so much as a pin? It's the life principle, I tell you—and I had it under my hand!"

"But this is stellarite," I protested. "you can make more, surely?"

"Make!" he scoffed. "It's an element, I say! And it was, so far as I know, all there was in the world!"

"Maybe it will be found yet," I argued. "Or—if it went into the acid vat, would it have been absorbed by the metal—or what?"

"No—at the touch of that bath it would evaporate into thin air—an odorless, colorless gas. I have but one hope—that it rolled against some of the iron machinery and was absorbed. In that case I may be able to place it by the increased bulk of the assimilating metal. Well, I can but go to work again, test every particle of machinery in the vicinity of the vats—and work—and work. If I had but known before that it was electricity and animal magnetism that were needed to complete the combination—but now, it means years of patience at best."

He shook his head dismally.

"And I?" I mused, rather to myself than to him.

"Oh—you!" he smiled, and his face ran into that tempest of wrinkles. "You can pose as Samson, if you like! Your strength is really almost limitless!"

The End

A Note About the Author

Francis Stevens was the pseudonym of Gertrude Barrows Bennett (1884–1948), an American writer of science fiction and fantasy novels. Born in Minneapolis, Stevens wrote her first story at 17, finding publication in popular pulp magazine *Argosy*. Believed to be one of the first American women to publish a work of science fiction, Bennett gained a nationwide reputation as a leading short story writer with such tales as "The Nightmare" (1917), "Friend Island" (1918), and "Serapion" (1920). Additionally, Bennett published several novels throughout her career, including *The Citadel of Fear* (1918), *The Heads of Cerberus* (1919), and *Claimed!* (1920). To supplement her writing, Stevens—who was widowed in 1910 when her husband Stewart Bennett died at sea—worked as a stenographer to support herself, her daughter, and her invalid mother. Credited with influencing H. P. Lovecraft and A. Merritt, Bennett is recognized as a pioneering figure in the history of science fiction.

A Note from the Publisher

Spanning many genres, from non-fiction essays to literature classics to children's books and lyric poetry, Mint Edition books showcase the master works of our time in a modern new package. The text is freshly typeset, is clean and easy to read, and features a new note about the author in each volume. Many books also include exclusive new introductory material. Every book boasts a striking new cover, which makes it as appropriate for collecting as it is for gift giving. Mint Edition books are only printed when a reader orders them, so natural resources are not wasted. We're proud that our books are never manufactured in excess and exist only in the exact quantity they need to be read and enjoyed. To learn more and view our library, go to minteditionbooks.com

bookfinity & ◧ MINT EDITIONS

Enjoy more of your favorite classics with Bookfinity,
a new search and discovery experience for readers.
With Bookfinity, you can discover more vintage
literature for your collection, find your Reader Type,
track books you've read or want to read,
and add reviews to your favorite books.
Visit www.bookfinity.com, and click on
Take the Quiz to get started.

Don't forget to follow us
@bookfinityofficial and @mint_editions